ENCHANTED VENTURES

BELLES OF BROAD STREET BOOK 4

AK LANDOW

Enchanted Ventures: Belles of Broad Street Book 4

Published by Author AK Landow, LLC

ISBN: 978-1-962575-07-2

Edited and Proofread By: Chrisandra's Corrections

Cover Design By: K.B. Designs

Photo By: Wander Aguiar

Cover Models: Evan Keys & Griffin Forsyth

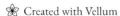 Created with Vellum

DEDICATION

For Brittany Mckeel. You're everything I write about in my books. You're smart, creative, selfless, empowering, dynamic, unapologetically you, and support other women just because it's the right thing to do. I'm lucky to call you my friend. Thank you for being uniquely you.

J is lucky to have you. Stay the course as the B in BJ.

"She believed in dreams alright, but she also believed in doing something about them. Prince Charming didn't come along, she went to the palace and got him."
-Walt Disney

DISCLAIMER

WARNING FROM AK:

Beckett Windsor is unlike any man I've ever written. He's no ordinary Prince Charming. He's got flaws.

He's going to put you through a rollercoaster of emotions. You'll love him, then swoon for him, then REALLY swoon for him, then be like WTF, then think he's an asshole, then slam your book shut, then think maybe he's not such an asshole, then fall back in love with him, and eventually you'll just want him for yourself.

You've been warned.

Knight & Lawrence
FAMILY TREE

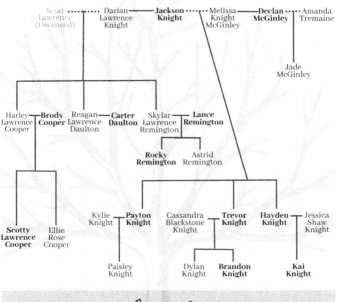

Scott Lawrence (Deceased) ···· Darian Lawrence Knight — **Jackson Knight** ···· Melissa Knight McGinley — **Declan McGinley** ···· Amanda Tremaine

Jade McGinley

Harley Lawrence Cooper — **Brody Cooper**   Reagan Lawrence Daulton — **Carter Daulton**   Skylar Lawrence Remington — **Lance Remington**

Rocky Remington   Astrid Remington

Kylie Knight — **Payton Knight**   Cassandra Blackstone Knight — **Trevor Knight**   **Hayden Knight** — Jessica Shaw Knight

Scotty Lawrence Cooper   Ellie Rose Cooper

Paisley Knight

Dylan Knight   **Brandon Knight**

Kai Knight

PROLOGUE

FOUR YEARS AGO

REAGAN'S TWENTY-EIGHTH BIRTHDAY PARTY

AMANDA

Deep breaths. Just take deep breaths. I inhale and exhale a few times in hopes of calming myself.

You're setting a good example for your daughter, Amanda. You set a bad example for so many years and it's clearly damaged her. Time to hold it together for her sake.

I get out of the Uber and look down at myself. I spent a pretty penny on this tight designer, strapless, pink cocktail dress. More than I've ever spent on a dress. These people are definitely not my normal salt-of-the-earth crowd. They're high society. I'm way out of my league attending this party, but Reagan called me and told me she's getting a birthday cake for Jade and singing to her. I haven't even met Reagan yet. It was nice of her to think of me and incredibly kind of her to think of Jade despite it being Reagan's special night. I couldn't say no.

I walk into the lobby of one of the oldest, most historic Philadelphia hotels and look up. Wow, that chandelier is something special. It must be fifty feet in diameter. As an artist, I would love to know the story behind the design. It's exquisite. I've never seen anything like it.

I can hear the beat of music coming from the ballroom down the hall. I'm late. The party is already in full swing. It took me a while to get myself together enough to attend. Alone.

As I reach the hallway, I see two couples walking in, hand in hand. I feel the tears welling in my eyes. Shit. I need a few more moments to compose myself.

I open a door to what looks like a private room, but before I can step in, I hear a woman yelling, "Yes, Jackson, like that!"

Whoops. I quickly close it. I then try two more doors, but they're both locked and there's moaning coming from them. What the hell? Is everyone having great sex except me?

I try a fourth door, and it mercifully opens into what appears to be a dressing room. I walk in and close the door, leaning back against it and taking a deep breath.

Now that I'm alone, I allow the tears to fall. What have I done? I think I made the biggest mistake of my life. And I've made *a lot* of mistakes, but this really might be the biggest of them all.

I let out an audible sob and then immediately hear a deep voice. "Are you okay?"

I suck in a breath and clutch my chest in surprise. Looking around, I see a man sitting on the couch, holding a drink.

He raises his unoccupied hand. "I'm sorry, I didn't mean to scare you."

I wipe my eyes. "I should be apologizing. I interrupted you. I'll leave."

He waves his hand around the room. "I'm alone. You're not interrupting me. Have a seat. Keep me company. We can cry together." He gives me a small, crooked smile. He's obviously just trying to make me feel better.

"Are you sure?"

He nods. "If you can't unload on a stranger, who can you unload on?"

I let out a small laugh as I walk toward the sofa and sit. I can see him better now. He's a broad, handsome man with dirty-blond hair, likely a little older than my forty years. He's in an expensive blue suit with the tie loosened and is holding a glass of what looks like some type of whiskey or scotch. His facial hair suggests he hasn't shaved in a few days.

It's not a large sofa, so I'm sitting less than a foot from him. He's wearing a cologne that I can't quite make out. It must be expensive. Everything about him oozes high society, from his clearly custom suit to his expensive watch.

We're silent for a few moments as he takes me in. "What's your name?"

"Amanda. What's yours?"

He gives me a bemused look before saying, "Beckett." I internally laugh. What a pretentious name. Everyone at this party probably has a name like his. I bet all the women are named Buffy or Bunny, and the men are named Ignatius or Prescott, with each of them being the third generation of men in their family with the same name.

"It's nice to meet you, Beckett. Just give me a second to get myself together and then I'll get out of your hair."

"No rush." He looks down at his nearly empty glass. "I need another scotch. Why don't I grab both of us a drink and then you can tell me why you're crying at a birthday party?"

I doubt I'll be explaining my life to this stranger, but I wouldn't mind a drink before walking in. "I'll have a piña colada. Extra cherries."

He lets out a laugh. "I didn't realize adults drank those unless on a beach vacation."

I shrug. "It's what I like. I know it's not *classy*, but a Cosmo isn't really my style. You don't have to get it if it threatens your sensitive male ego," I challenge.

He smirks. It's lopsided and cute. I can see his blue eyes now. They're a light shade and sparkle when he smiles.

"My ego can handle it, but I appreciate your concern. I'll be back in a few minutes with the most delicious piña colada you've ever had and *oodles* of cherries."

"Thank you."

When he leaves the room, I do my best to wipe my eyes clean of the tears. He doesn't need to see me cry. Again.

I wish I was one of those women who carried compact mirrors in their purses. I think the only things in my purse are lipstick, one two-year-old tissue, an equally old tampon, and loose mints. I use the crinkled tissue as best as I can.

He returns a few moments later with my drink along with another glass full of cherries. There must be twenty of them in there. I can't help but giggle. "Thanks for indulging me."

He winks as he hands me my drink and sits back in the same spot with a refreshed drink for himself. "You have a beautiful smile. I like it when you laugh more than I like when you cry, *Amanda*."

Before I take a sip of my cool, refreshing drink, I respond, "Me too, *Beckett*."

He rubs his finger over his lower lip. "Tell me what's wrong. Why does a beautiful woman like you look so sad?"

I'm silent.

He nods toward my ring finger, which has an engagement ring and wedding band. "Marital problems?"

"What makes you ask that?"

"You're crying and you're here without your spouse."

I nod toward his gold-band-covered ring finger. "The same could be said for you. You're at a party, drinking alone, without your spouse."

He looks down. When his eyes find mine again, I see them filled with tears. "Mine died about a year ago."

My face drops. "Oh, Beckett, I'm so sorry. Was she sick?"

He shakes his head. "Childbirth complications. She died giving birth to our daughter."

I move closer to him and take his hand in mine. He freezes for a brief moment before he allows me to hold it. "I'm truly sorry for your loss." I can't imagine that type of pain. It makes my problems seem mighty small.

He takes a deep breath. "Thank you. This is my first night out socializing since she left us. I haven't quite made it into the party." He holds up his glass. "I need a little liquid courage before I walk in and see hundreds of happy couples. Do you think that makes me an asshole?"

I shake my head. "No. I more than understand. I feel the exact same way." I bite my lip. "How's your daughter? Did...did she make it?"

He smiles. It's genuine and full of love. I know she made it. Phew. "She's the best thing that's ever happened to me. She's my reason for living."

I nod. "I get it. I have a daughter too. She's much older than yours, but she's the center of my universe. My reason for everything I do." *Everything*.

"How old is she?"

"She just turned eighteen."

His eyes widen. "Eighteen? You don't look old enough to have a daughter who's eighteen."

"I get that a lot. I was a baby myself when I had her at twenty-two."

"Wow. Is she in college?"

"No, not for another year. She's a senior in high school." I point toward the door. "She's here tonight. She came with her father and his wife. My daughter looks like she's twenty-five. I have no doubt she's at the bar ordering a drink and hitting on older men."

He lets out a laugh. "Oh god. I'm not prepared for that."

"Neither am I, but ready or not, quicker than the blink of an eye, life happens. Make sure you have a support system. I mostly raised her alone. It's hard."

"Her father..."

"Wasn't in the picture until she was seven." I swallow. "We were both addicts when we met. I cleaned up the minute I found out I was pregnant. It took him another eight years to do the same."

He nods. "Good for you for doing what was necessary for your daughter. You're obviously a good mom."

"I've had my good and bad moments as a parent, but I'm trying to be good for her now. Better than I've been in the past."

"What does that mean?"

I'm silent for a moment. I'm not sure what it is about this guy that I'm considering confessing to him something I haven't admitted to another soul, not even my best friends. Maybe it's because we're both unavailable. Maybe it's because we're both vulnerable.

"Let's just say that I didn't set a very good example for her with the type of men I dated throughout the years. They consisted of a long string of losers. I recently got married for the first time to the only truly decent man she's ever seen me date. If I'm being honest, that's the problem. He's too decent. There's nothing exciting about him. I think she's a little messed up when it comes to relationships because of me. I wanted to show her stability, but I think I made a mistake. I love him, but I'm not *in love* with him. Does that make sense?"

He's silent for a moment. I appreciate that he doesn't immediately try to make me feel better. "It does. I struggled in relationships for a long time. I didn't get married until I was in my forties. I'm sorry for what you're experiencing."

"Me too, Beckett. Me too."

He looks down at our hands, which I'm realizing are still linked. Neither of us seems to be in a rush to unlink them.

He turns my hand over, examining it more closely. "Do you paint?" He undoubtedly noticed the colorful array of paints in and around my nails that I couldn't manage to scrub off in the shower tonight.

"I do. I'm an artist."

His whole face lights up. "Really? I'm a collector. What's your last name, Amanda? Maybe I know your work."

"I doubt it. I'm not very successful. My last name is Tremaine, though I don't paint under my real name. I use a pseudonym."

"Tremaine? Did you know that was Cinderella's last name?"

I smile. "I do, but most people don't know that. I've always thought that's why I believe in fairytales. My daughter likes to make fun of me for it. She's a realist. I'm a dreamer." I look down and mumble to myself, "Though I don't think I ever found my Prince Charming."

He touches my chin and lifts it so our eyes meet. "Do you know my last name, Amanda Tremaine?" He raises one eyebrow like he assumes I know it.

"No, why would I?"

He smirks at me as though me not knowing his name is amusing. "Windsor."

"Like the royal family?"

He continues smirking. "Yes. *Lots* of princes in that family."

I look at his cocky smile. "Are you flirting with me, Beckett Windsor?"

He scoffs. "I wouldn't even know what that looks like anymore. I haven't dated since my wife, nor am I anywhere near ready to date again. But if I were, it wouldn't be with a married woman, happily or not." He brings my hand to his lips and kisses it. "Though if and when the time comes, I hope she looks just like you. You're stunning."

I'm honestly still not sure if he's flirting with me or not, but it doesn't matter. I am, in fact, a married woman. I hate myself for being attracted to him. Maybe it's because I can't have him. *Or maybe it's because he's ridiculously handsome and kind.*

Knowing that I might be treading in dangerous territory, I quickly finish the rest of my drink and stand. "I think it's time for me to go, *Beckett Windsor*."

He nods as he stands too. "It was truly a pleasure to

meet you, *Amanda Tremaine*."

He leans over to kiss my cheek and lingers afterward, his face close to mine. My heart begins to beat faster. I hear his breathing pick up. I can smell the scotch on his breath and his intoxicating, expensive cologne. It's a sexy combination.

Neither of us moves. We simply stand there, taking each other in. I need to step back, but I can't seem to find the will. I place my hand on his hard, muscular chest. His heart is beating as fast as mine.

He eventually plants a soft kiss on the spot where my shoulder meets my neck. My body immediately ignites. His kiss on my neck does more for me than anything I've done with my husband. Ever. We've only been married a few weeks, but we've been together for years. Never have I reacted to his touch as I am to Beckett's right now. I can feel the desire pooling between my legs.

My eyes move up and down his big, warm, sexy body until they return to the hand I placed on his chest. My wedding band catches my eye and I immediately step back. The tears return. "I...I...I can't do this. I need to go." Without another word, I turn and run out of the room. I hear him call my name, but I keep running.

I make it into the ballroom just in time to see a woman I assume is Reagan on the microphone welcoming everyone. Jade was right. Reagan is practically her twin, being another tall, gorgeous blonde. If Jade wants to know what she'll look like in ten years, she needs to look no further.

I take in my surroundings. There must be over three hundred people here. The décor in this room oozes wealth. A huge dance floor, club vibes, and at least three bars that I can see. Wow.

Reagan mentions something about her recent marriage

before practically dry humping her husband, Carter, in front of everyone. Jade mentioned that the family is extremely outwardly affectionate. I don't think I've been with a man like that since my college boyfriend.

Carter is a giant of a man. He's highly attractive, with a beard, and is clearly not afraid to publicly love his wife.

After Reagan pulls away and fans herself, she says, "While we're celebrating, I want to mention that it was my cousin Jade's birthday last week. Where are you, gorgeous?"

Reagan looks around the room. I haven't seen Jade either. She's a six-foot blonde. She's kind of hard to miss, unlike me who's a short brunette. Jade is all her father, Declan McGinley.

I finally see Jade make her way to the front of the room. She's grinning from ear to ear. I'm so happy for her that she's connected with this side of the family. It only happened a few months ago. She never knew they existed until recently, but she's always craved family, something I was unfortunately never able to give her. Jade's childhood may not have been a dream, but it was a hell of a lot better than my nightmare.

Reagan throws her arm around Jade. "Happy birthday, beautiful. She's eighteen now, gentleman, so take a number. The line is going to be long."

I roll my eyes at her comment. Jade has certainly never lacked for male attention. She revels in it, bouncing from man to man. And I mean men, not boys. She gravitates toward older men. It's been a bone of contention between her and me for ages. I think she fake dated a boy closer to her age, thinking she was appeasing me, but I know my daughter. She was never into him.

Declan and his new wife, Melissa, approach me. He kisses my cheek. "I didn't know you would be here."

"Reagan called and invited me just this week, knowing she was going to celebrate Jade's birthday too. It was extremely thoughtful of her."

Melissa kisses my cheek as well. "I love your dress. You look gorgeous."

I smile. "So do you." Melissa is the opposite of me in every single way. Like Jade, she's very tall and blonde. She's the epitome of wealth and class, while I'm usually found in ripped jeans and an old concert T-shirt. As always, she's dressed in a designer outfit, looking stunning. She's been nothing but kind to me and, more importantly, kind to Jade. As far as I'm concerned, she's the best thing that ever happened to an often-volatile Declan. I'm thankful she's in their lives.

Melissa looks around curiously. "Is Rick with you?"

I shake my head. "No, he had a few work commitments in New York." And I may not have told him about this party because I needed a minute to myself.

She nods in understanding. Rick works in New York City. I split my time between there and Philadelphia. Jade, who has always exclusively lived with me, now lives with Declan and Melissa three days a week when I'm up in New York, though I kept my home here. I love my little house in Philly. It's where I come to paint and spend time with my daughter as she finishes her final year of high school.

Declan smiles. "We're going to the bar. Can I get you a piña colada?"

"I can't believe you remember what I drink. No, I already had one. I'm going to head out soon. I just came to see Jade for a few minutes. Reagan mentioned celebrating her, so I didn't want to miss it, and I'd love to finally meet her new family. I'm going to go find her. You two have a great evening."

Declan and Melissa make their way to the bar while I make my way toward Jade. She smiles as soon as she sees me and runs to give me a big hug. "Hi, Mom. Thanks for coming."

I look my gorgeous daughter, who is wearing a seemingly expensive red gown, up and down. "You're so beautiful."

She runs her hands along the material. "I *love* this dress. It's the nicest thing I've ever owned. Melissa got it for me."

"I figured. You look like you're thirty years old. Stop growing up."

She laughs and then winks. "It works with the older guys."

I scowl at her. "Date boys your own age."

She gives me her mischievous smile. "Never." She looks around. "I found a hottie earlier. I was with him before Reagan called me up front. I don't know where he went though."

"How old, Jade?"

She mumbles. "I don't know. Probably in his thirties."

I shake my head. "That's way too old for you. What do you think a man that age is going to expect from you?"

"Great sex, I hope."

I blow out a long breath. "I'm thrilled that you feel so comfortable talking to me openly about sex, but I'm telling you as someone with more experience, you're not emotionally mature enough to be with a man that old. I can handle college-aged, that's it. Your beauty isn't a weapon. Stop using it that way."

I know my words are falling on deaf ears. My daughter is as stubborn as they come. Her interest in older men is the bane of my existence.

A familiar attractive couple, a bit older than me, walks

over to us. He's tall, with dark hair and green eyes. She's about my size, with dark hair, green eyes, and a killer body. She smiles as she wraps her arm around Jade in a loving, familiar way. "Jade, is this your mom? I've been dying to meet her."

Jade nods. "Yes. Aunt Darian, meet my mom, Amanda Tremaine. Mom, this is Aunt Darian and her husband, Jackson Knight." Jackson? Oh my. It must have been these two in the closet earlier. That's why they're familiar. I internally laugh. Good for them for still getting it on in public at their age. They must be at least ten years older than me.

I shake Jackson's hand and he smiles at me. Holy hell, he's hot. Between him, Declan, and Beckett, this place is crawling with attractive men.

I then offer Darian my hand, but she pulls me into a hug. "I'm so happy to finally meet you. We're thrilled to have Jade in our lives. You have no idea how much it means to me."

"Thank you for being so welcoming of her. She raves about all of you. And it was so nice of your daughter to give Jade a job." Reagan is the CEO of a huge company and offered Jade a paid internship during her senior year of high school. Jade is over the moon about it.

"I have no doubt she'll be wonderful. Please know that you're always welcome in our home. Jade's family, and so are you. We have weekly Sunday night dinners as a big family. Consider it an open invitation."

I'm flooded with warmth for Jade that she has this. It was just she and I for so many years. A big family will be good for her.

"That's very kind of you. I live part-time in New York, but perhaps sometime in the future."

She nods. "Wonderful. And Jade tells us that you're a talented artist. We're always in the market. I'd love to see your work sometime."

"Wow. I'd love that. Thank you."

"We'll set it up." Turning to Jade, she says, "Reagan wants to introduce you to a few new coworkers. Do you have a minute?"

"Of course." Jade looks down at me. "Mom, you'll be okay?"

I wave my hand dismissively. "Absolutely. Have fun."

She walks away and I decide I need one more drink. I turn toward the bar and crash straight into a chest. Looking up, I see Beckett steadying the drinks he's holding. His drink in one hand and a piña colada with at least five cherries in the other. He holds it out for me. "A peace offering."

I take the drink. "Thank you, but we're not at war. No need for a peace offering."

"I shouldn't have kissed your neck like that. I'm sorry. I've been so down for so many months. I think I was just relieved that I'm capable of being physically attracted to someone. It gives me hope where I thought there was none."

"I understand. It's not like I jumped away as quickly as I should have. How about we declare a formal treaty?"

He gives me that crooked smile of his and holds up his glass. "Friends?"

I clink my glass with his. "Friends."

"Good. Now you can fill me in on your art, friend. I want to know more about it."

"Honestly, I'm not very successful. I paint, but I don't sell many pieces. I created and sold a lot of jewelry when my daughter was younger to make ends meet, but I don't enjoy that like I do painting."

"You should do what you enjoy." He's clueless. Some people in this world need to do what's necessary to get by. He asks, "Are you classically trained?"

"I started down that path but ended up dropping out of school. That's a sad story for another day."

He nods in understanding. "What name do you paint under? You said you don't use your real name."

"Enchanted. Just the single word."

He smiles. "You really do fancy your fairytales, don't you?"

He's staring at my lips as I smile in agreement. He looks like he wants to kiss me. What's worse is that I want him to.

He glances over my shoulder and breathes, "Oh shit."

I start to turn around, but he stops me and whispers, "Please go with what I'm about to do. I beg you. I'll make it worth your while. Anything. I promise."

He pulls me and takes my left arm, placing it behind his back, out of sight. A slim, attractive redhead approaches us. "Beckett Windsor? How lovely to see you out and about."

Beckett pulls me close to his side. Our sides are touching, which admittedly turns my body into an inferno. *Stop it, Amanda.*

Without breaking his hold on me, he kisses the woman's cheek and gives a clearly fake smile. "Bunny. How great to see you."

The woman stares at our close proximity. "And who is this...person?"

"This is my girlfriend, Amanda Tremaine."

I stiffen but he continues to hold me close to him.

Bunny's face drops in obvious disappointment.

"Girlfriend? I thought you said you weren't ready to start dating."

He shrugs. "I thought I wasn't, but when the right person comes along, you can't help it." He kisses the side of my head. "This beautiful woman burst through the door and smacked some sense into me. I'm a lucky man."

Bunny looks me up and down, her eyes finding my ankle tattoos. "And how did someone...like *you* meet *my* Beckett?"

Ugh. I've been dealing with snobby bitches like her my whole life. I'm suddenly all for Beckett's fake-girlfriend scenario.

I smile. "*My* Beckett, being the avid art collector he is, came to purchase one of my paintings and left with my phone number." I run my right hand up and down his broad, shockingly muscular chest. "He can be quite charming." I look up at him. "Honey, we *do* need to finalize the purchase."

He has a huge, sideways grin on his handsome face. "You're right, baby. We do." He slowly looks my body up and down. "I can't wait to get your piece into my home."

We smile at each other as we stare into one another's eyes, and something sexually charged, yet playful, passes between us.

Bunny interrupts us. "You're adding it to your private collection? It must be quite extraordinary. You rarely add pieces to that."

Without breaking eye contact with me, he says, "That's my Amanda. Extraordinary."

He bends and takes me by surprise by meeting his lips with mine. I'd like to say I stopped him. I'd like to say I slapped him across the face for kissing a married woman. I'd like to say that I ran away as fast as I could. I'd like to say that kissing another man repulsed me. But I can't say any of that, because when his tongue enters my mouth, I completely lose myself in him.

My tongue pushes into his mouth too. He tastes like the scotch he's been drinking all night. Scotch and mint. It's delicious.

Our bodies are pressed together. I can feel him harden against my stomach. I want it lower, against the spot that's now throbbing and has been deeply unsatisfied for years.

I can't help but moan into his mouth as his fingers tightly grip my hips and my fingers run through his hair.

I have no idea how long we kiss, but when we break apart, I turn, and Bunny is nowhere to be found.

I look back up at Beckett. He licks all around his lips and slowly rubs the back of his fingers down my face. "I'll never be able to taste cherries again without thinking of you and that kiss."

I touch my now kiss-swollen lips and jump back. I quickly scan the room. Please, God, don't let Jade have seen me being the adulterating whore that I am.

I don't see her. I pray she didn't see me.

When he realizes that I'm freaked out, his eyes widen. "Amanda, I'm so sorry. I needed to get rid of her. I took it too far. It's my fault."

What have I done? I've only been married for a few weeks, and I just kissed another man. Well, he kissed me, but I didn't stop it. And worse, I loved it.

I need to get away from him and get the hell out of here, back to my husband. I turn to leave, mumbling, "Bye, Beckett. Have a good life."

I run straight out of the hotel and jump into the first cab I can find.

CHAPTER ONE

FOUR YEARS LATER

AMANDA

> Reggie: Pauly Shore just walked into
> your building.

Despite the horrible circumstances, I can't help but laugh at her calling him Pauly Shore, one of the most unlikable actors ever to walk the planet.

> Me: Okay. Thanks, Shia LaBeouf.

An equally disliked actor.

> Reggie: Ha! Good pull. That guy sucks.

> Me: Sadly, Mel Gibson now also falls into
> this category.

Reggie: Ugh. Truth. Are you sure you don't want me to come up to the apartment?

Me: STAY IN YOUR CAR! For once in your life, listen.

Reggie: Five minutes. If you're not down here in five minutes, I'm coming up.

Me: Fifteen. I hear his key in the door. See you in fifteen.

Reggie: Good luck. Love you. xoxo

The door to our apartment opens and Rick walks in. He smiles at me. He's handsome, in a nerdy way, with dark hair, glasses, and a kind smile. "Hey, sweetheart. What's for din—" Just then he looks around and notices my packed bags by the front door. He pinches his eyebrows in confusion. "What's going on? Where are you going? You just got home from Philly last night."

I'm already seated in our living room. I motion to the chair I've brought close to me. "Rick, come sit with me for a minute. We need to talk."

He curiously walks over to me and sits. "What's up?"

I lean forward and take his hand in mine. "I want to start off by telling you that you've been an amazing partner and husband all these years. You came into my life at a time when I needed stability, and you gave it to me in spades." I let out a breath. "But something is missing from our marriage. It always has been. You and I both know it. We're good friends who got married. We're not in love. If I'm being honest, I know we never were."

He winces, looking like I punched him in the gut. "Maybe you weren't, but I was."

I shake my head. "No, Rick, you weren't. We've lived in parallel for years with neither of us saying anything about it. We're both happy when I go down to stay at my place in Philly. I couldn't even tell you the last time we had sex. We're not right for each other. We both deserve someone who's a better match. We both deserve our happily ever afters."

He rolls his eyes. "You and your damn fairytales. Life isn't a fairytale, Amanda. That's your problem. You expect fucking Prince Charming all the time. Someone that looks at you with hearts in his eyes. That's not reality."

"Maybe, but part of me will always believe it can and should be." Tears begin softly spilling out of my eyes. "I want that for both of us. I want you to find your soulmate just like I want to find mine. Neither of us should waste any more time."

He visibly swallows. "I'm sorry that you look at our marriage as a waste of time."

"I don't." I squeeze his hand, a hand that has comforted me countless times in the past several years. "You gave me so much at a time in my life where I needed it. But now it's time for us to go our separate ways. We're friends, Rick. I want to stay friends. I care about you. I'm doing this as much for you as for me. You're such a wonderful man. I want you to find a woman who looks at you with hearts in her eyes. A woman full of love for you."

"But *you* don't love me."

"I do love you, but not the way a wife should love her husband. Even if you don't admit it right now, I know you feel the exact same way about me."

He's quiet for a moment before he looks at my bags. "What are you taking with you?"

"Just my clothes and a few personal items. I left everything else for you."

"Have you contacted a lawyer?"

"Just to file paperwork. I don't want anything from you."

"Alimony?"

I shake my head. "No. I make enough to get by. I'm used to doing it alone. I did it for nearly forty years. I'll be fine. I'm not interested in your hard-earned money. This isn't about that."

He slowly nods. "I assume you're moving back to Philly?"

"I am. Reggie is downstairs waiting for me."

"Have you told Jade yet?"

I shake my head. "No, not yet. I asked her to come by in the morning. I'll talk to her then."

"Is it okay if I check in on her from time to time?"

Now my tears spill freely. "Of course. Thank you for always caring about her. I know she cares about you too."

He stands, walks over to my bags, and picks up a few of them. "I'll help you."

The fact that he so easily accepted this tells me that I'm doing the right thing. If he truly felt this was wrong, he would tell me. He would fight for us. I desperately want a man who would fight anything and anyone for me. On some level, Rick knows I'm right, even if he can't admit it out loud just yet.

We walk down to Reggie's car in silence. She gets out when she sees us approaching. I mouth, "Keep your mouth shut."

She rolls her eyes but listens. She simply helps get the bags into her trunk.

I hug Rick goodbye and tell him I'll be in touch. As I

get into the car, Reggie takes my hand. "You did the right thing, Mandy. He was never right for you."

I nod. "I agree, but he's still a good man and I hated hurting him. He was never anything but kind to me."

"I know, but you're both better off. Now we can spend our energy finding you the right guy. Victoria has a long list of men for you. Speaking of which, I said we'd text her right away."

Victoria is our other close friend. She's a little older than us. I met her when Jade was a toddler. She has a daughter, Pandora, the same age as Jade. The girls became fast friends, as did we. She was a single mother at the time too, so we helped one another. She's since remarried and had more children.

Reggie quickly types on her phone. A few seconds later, my text tone pings a notification from our group chat with Victoria.

> Reggie: Patty Hearst finally saw the light. The juice is loose!

I let out a laugh at her insanity.

> Victoria: Finally! Sorry I'm not there. Love you both. Have a safe ride home. Don't stop at any strip clubs without me.

We smile at each other. Reggie presses her lips together. "Hmm, I hadn't thought of that. Maybe a pitstop at Thunder from Down Under is just what you need."

I roll my eyes. "I might need some thunder in my down under, but we've got a long trip and I'm not up for it. Let's get going."

"I guess we can't go without her. She was upset she

couldn't be here for you tonight. She called me five times today."

"It's a lot to ask of both of you. You have families and kids that need you. Thank you for helping me." I reach over and hug her. "It means so much that you drove all this way to be here for me."

She pulls back and winks. "Always, babe. Ride or die since we were thirteen."

Reggie and I have been best friends since junior high. We've been through everything together—and I mean everything. She was there for me when my father couldn't hold it together anymore. I was there for her family in their time of need. We went to the same college. We did *a lot* of drugs. When I found out I was pregnant with Jade, she held me and told me I could do it. She was the only person there for Jade's delivery and helped me as much as she could during those first few years with Jade. She was the one person I could rely on, even while still an irresponsible college student herself. I couldn't have gotten through it without her.

She starts up the car and we pull out onto the busy New York City street. "Let me just call Sam. I told him we'd call when we left. He'll pretend otherwise, but he's got his hands full tonight."

Reggie and her husband, Sam, have five kids, ranging in age from eight to eighteen. They've been happily married for nearly twenty years now.

She pushes the buttons on her dashboard and the phone starts ringing through the car. Sam answers, "Hey, sexy."

Reggie smiles. "Ooh, someone wants to get laid tonight."

"Always. How's Mandy?"

I chime in, "I'm fine, thanks, Sam."

"Glad to hear it. When will you guys be home?"

Reggie looks at the navigation screen. "We'll be at Mandy's in ninety minutes. I need to help her with her bags, so I'll be home in a little over two hours."

"Okay. The kids are fine. SJ's girlfriend is over. They're downstairs, supposedly watching a movie. The lights in the basement are off though. Should I turn them on?"

"Meh. He's eighteen. Let him be. Let Rose's mother worry about that. You and I were both doing worse at his age."

Sam sighs. "I guess you're right, as always. See you soon. Love you."

"Love you too."

She ends the call and I look at her while clutching my heart. "You two are so sweet together. You give me hope."

She smiles. "For some reason, he still loves my ever-expanding, fat ass."

"Don't say that. Your body is perfect." She's always been self-deprecating about her curvier figure. I hate it.

"No, *your* body is perfect. Insanely perfect. Disgustingly perfect. Unfathomably perfect. Belongs-in-a-magazine perfect. Defies-science perfect. I'm at least forty pounds overweight."

"Reg, you've had five kids and work insane hours at the hospital. Give yourself a break. I only had one baby, when I was still a child myself. It's a lot easier to bounce back from that."

"I also drink, smoke weed, eat too much, and am allergic to exercise." She grabs her stomach and squeezes it. "Thank god Sam says he loves my vagomic."

I pinch my eyebrows together. "What's a vagomic?"

"People like me who are so big that you don't know

where their stomach ends and their vagina begins." She points down. "Hence, vagomic."

I burst out laughing. "Holy shit. I've never heard that term. That's hysterical and wrong all at once. You're a nut."

She shrugs. "Whatever. I am what I am. I'll never be a crazy gym rat with a magazine-worthy body. Sam says it gives him something to grab me by."

"I love the way he loves you. You two are a real-life fairytale."

"No relationship is perfect, but I know I got one of the good ones. It helps that I don't need a damaged man with a boatload of issues."

My face falls as I cross my arms. "I don't need a damaged man with a boatload of issues."

She raises her eyebrow. "Sure."

"What does that mean?"

"It means I knew Rick was wrong for you because he's too fucking sweet and perfect. *All* the time. There's nothing wrong with him. He practically sings *Zip-A-Dee-Doo-Dah* out of his asshole. You've never been attracted to men like Rick. Besides a certain sexy Latino man, every man you've dated was damaged with issues. Look at your baby daddy. He's the grumpiest, edgiest, most damaged motherfucker I've ever met."

"Jade's twenty-two. Do we really still call Declan my baby daddy? I was coked out of my mind when we were together. So was he. I barely remember our time together. I doubt he does either."

"But you got Jade out of it, so all is good."

I tilt my head back and blow out a breath. "She's my everything. Thank god for her. At this point, I guess she's the only child I'll ever have. I just hope I haven't fucked her up because of how terrible I am at relationships with men."

"Pft. She's fine. She's one of the most sensational women I've ever met. You should be proud of the type of woman she's become. Look at all she's already accomplished. She has a great job and makes good money, owns a luxury condo, is the funniest human being I know, and does it all while looking like a fucking supermodel."

"Of course I'm proud of all that. I just worry about her relationships with men. She won't let anyone get close. She sleeps around without allowing for even the remote possibility of any emotional attachment. It's all my fault. She watched me engage in dysfunctional relationship after dysfunctional relationship. It's all she knows."

"She's young and hot. Let her get her kicks. When the right guy comes along, she's smart enough to know when to change her ways."

"Like me? I'm forty-four and still haven't found the right guy."

"I...no, forget it."

"What? Say it."

She pauses for a moment as if choosing her words carefully. "You've always been so focused on getting your happily ever after. You've tried to make the wrong men into something they weren't. The right situation should happen naturally. You can't force it. Let fate take its course. You haven't met the right guy yet, but I have faith you will."

"How will I know?"

"You'll feel something you've never felt before. It will be out of your control. You've always tried to control love. That's not how it works."

I blow out a long breath. "Maybe you're right. For now, I'm just going to focus on painting. I haven't done much of that lately."

"You're okay financially, right?"

"I'm fine. My paintings have nearly sold out for the past four years. Norma at the gallery has been begging me to paint more. She said there have been inquiries as to when more paintings will become available."

Reggie smiles. "That's awesome. I'm so proud of you. Your talent has finally been recognized."

"I wish I knew what started the frenzy for my work four years ago, but whatever it was, I'm thankful."

CHAPTER TWO

SIX MONTHS LATER

BECKETT

"Mom, Andie will be downstairs any minute now. Let me run."

I attempt to end the FaceTime call, but she continues talking. "Beckett, I want you to consider some of the women I mentioned. You need a woman. Andie needs a mother."

I clench my teeth. As if I'd ever let another woman in. "She has a mother. Jenny is her mother. It's not her fault she's not here to watch Andie grow up."

Her face turns softer. "I know, my love, but Andie needs a woman in her life."

"She has you."

"I don't live near you. I wish I did. Please consider Candy. She's always adored you. She's recently divorced and looking."

I sigh. I'm so sick of this same conversation, so I lie. "Mom, I'm seeing someone."

Her face lights up. "You are? Who?"

"No one you know. It's relatively new." As in fictitious.

She claps her hands in glee. "I'm so happy to hear it. My flight arrives on Friday night. I'll be in for the whole month. I can't wait to meet her."

Every six months, Mom flies up from Florida to stay for a month to help with Andie and give her those motherly things that I just can't give her as her father.

"We'll see. Like I said, it's new. Obviously Andie hasn't met her, so not a word."

I look toward the noise from the staircase and smile. "There's my baby girl. Are you all ready for your first day of kindergarten?"

Well, second attempt at a first day. We tried at the beginning of the school year, and it did not go well. It was more of an epic fail. The school's child psychologist suggested trying again in a few months and that's what we're doing now.

Andie is pouting. Her head is down with her thick, dark curls falling forward. "I don't want to go. Why can't I stay home with you?"

My mother gives me an *I-told-you-so* look. I should have put Andie in preschool, but I wanted her with me. When Jenny died, I sold my business and vowed to be both mom and dad to Andie. I couldn't bear to part with her. Now it's time for her to go to school and she's freaked out about it. I have only myself to blame.

Mom says, "Turn the camera so I can talk to her."

I do.

Andie gives a small smile and mumbles, "Hi, Gigi."

Mom lights up. "Hello, my beautiful angel. You look so pretty for your first day of school. Be a good girl for Daddy. No tears this time. Gigi is promising you a special girls' trip to New York City to see a Broadway show if you're a good girl."

Andie's face slightly brightens. She loves the theater. She and I go all the time. "I'll try, Gigi. What if no one likes me? What if I don't make any friends? When are you coming to visit?"

"You'll make plenty of friends. I promise. I'll be in at the end of the week, and I'm staying for an entire month. So you be a good girl and go to big-girl school all week and then I'll come for a long visit. Next week, I'll pick you up from school every day and we'll do something special."

Andie's face is now a full-blown smile. "Yay!" I love her relationship with my mother. They're so close.

Mom looks back at me. "Are you going to make a few calls about going back to work? I think it will be good for you now that Andie is in school."

I roll my eyes. "Yes, Mother. I somehow built and sold the biggest company in the world without you managing it. Imagine that."

"Hmm."

"I'm starting at Daulton Holdings next week. They held the job for me. One of the vice presidents had to take a long-term, emergency family leave, so I'll slot right in."

I had interviewed and secured a job at Daulton Holdings months ago when I thought Andie would be in school. When I decided to pull her, I had to let the opportunity go. I was upset about it. It's one of the biggest companies in the world. But the CEO, Reagan Lawrence-Daulton, told me to call her when I was ready, and when I reached out last week to tell her that Andie was going to school, she was more than thrilled to have me.

My job will be to find small businesses that need big company backing to take things to the next level of expansion. Being a venture capitalist at heart, it's perfect for me. I love helping the small guys become big ones. It's very rewarding.

"I can't believe you're going to work for someone else. I never thought I'd see the day. You haven't done that since you were sixteen."

"Owning a business is nonstop. I want to be done at the end of the day and be present for Andie."

The fact is, I never have to work another day in my life. I made hundreds of millions of dollars and then sold my company for billions after Jenny died. But with Andie going to school, I want to be challenged again. I just can't manage the hassles of owning a company when I'm the only parent my daughter has. I want to be there for her in the morning for breakfast, and in the evenings for dinner, baths, and bedtime.

"Good luck. Maybe you'll meet a nice woman at your new job."

She's testing me. "Mom, I told you I'm taken. We'll discuss this another time." I motion my head toward Andie. Mom gives me a nod of understanding.

We end the call and Karen, my chef, sets out our breakfast. Cherry crepes for Andie, and a healthy shake of unknown origins for me.

I take a sip. "This is good, Karen, what's in it?"

She smiles. "As always, it's best you don't know."

She rubs my shoulder in the motherly way she always has. "You know your mom is only trying to help, right?"

I sigh. "I suppose."

Knowing I was full of shit, she adds, "I, too, look forward to meeting your new *friend*."

I raise my eyebrow at her. "You're lucky I like your food, Karen."

She laughs as she turns her attention to Andie. "How are the crepes, little lady?"

"So yummy. Thanks, Karen."

They do look good. I give Andie my best puppy dog eyes. "Can I have a bite? Just a small one."

Andie narrows her eyes at me. "It's never just one."

Karen plops a plate with a crepe in front of me. "Don't worry, Andie. I know he can't resist anything with cherries. They're his weakness. I made an extra."

Andie gives Karen a little fist bump before turning to me. "Daddy, tell me my morning joke. Make it a good one today."

"They're *all* good." Somehow, I've cornered myself into a daily tradition of corny dad jokes. I did it a few mornings in a row once, and now Andie begs to hear them every day. I spend hours researching them to make sure I always have a few on hand.

"Why did the coach have to kick Cinderella off the softball team?"

"Hmm. I don't know. Why?"

"She kept running away from the ball."

Andie giggles uncontrollably while Karen moans at the corniness. Whatever it takes to make my baby smile.

My BODYGUARD, Nico, opens the car door for Andie and me. Andie smiles. "Good morning, Uncle Nico."

Nico flips one of her curls. "Good morning, Curly Sue."

Andie giggles, like she does every time he calls her that. She adores my two-hundred-and-fifty-pound Italian bodyguard who has about fifteen years on me. I think she sees him as a bit of a grandfather at times, calling him uncle even though he isn't. He equally adores her.

Nico has been with me since I hit it big over twenty years ago. The paparazzi's interest in my life skyrocketed along with my business. I was a bit of a playboy before I met Jenny and, for some reason, they loved to follow and photograph me. When it became intrusive and unsafe, I hired Nico to run my security team.

While interest in me has simmered down since Jenny died and I sold my business, I keep Nico around for safety and because I can't bear to let him go. He's practically a member of the family at this point. I have a lot of money, which always makes me a potential target. Andie too. I need to keep her safe.

I haven't dated since Jenny passed, but if and when the time comes, I'm fearful that the paparazzi will be back in my life. It's probably one of the reasons why I've avoided dating. One of the many reasons. Relative anonymity for the past few years has been nice. That, and I can't have the only woman who has piqued my interest.

Nico drives us to The Primary Academy, Andie's

school. The school psychologist said to make my goodbye as quick as possible, so that's what I did. Andie was hysterically crying. It was heartbreaking to leave, but I did it. I know it's time. Of course, I called the school ten minutes later. They told me she was fine and already playing with a new friend. Let's hope it sticks.

We make our way to Daulton Holdings. Nico looks at me in the rearview mirror. "Your mother is coming at the end of the week, right?"

I narrow my eyes at him. I swear he and my mother flirt constantly when she's in town, though I think it's harmless. I hope it's harmless. "She is. Perhaps it's a good time for you to take a vacation."

He smiles at me. "No, I'm good. You never know what kind of trouble your mom and Andie will cause."

I roll my eyes and shake my head. I catch a glimpse of him laughing to himself in the rearview mirror.

We arrive at Daulton, and I make my way up to the office. I stop by the desk of Reagan's assistant, Sheila. She's a little older than me and wears colorful glasses.

She looks confused. "Mr. Windsor? I don't think she's expecting you until next week."

"I know. I thought I'd come by and get some of the administrative items out of the way so I can hit the ground running on Monday. Is she available?"

Oddly enough, Sheila doesn't pick up the telephone and buzz into her office. She simply stands and puts her ear to Reagan's door.

After a few seconds, she says, "Have a seat. It will be about ten minutes. Maybe fifteen."

That was extremely bizarre. I ask, "Is Skylar available?"

She sits back at her desk and buzzes Skylar who agrees to see me. I immediately head down to her office and knock on the door.

"Come in."

I walk in and smile. "Wow, you look wonderful."

She rubs her severely pregnant belly. "I don't feel wonderful, but I'm not nearly as big as Reagan, so it could be worse."

Skylar is Reagan's younger sister. They look alike, both good-looking, tall blondes in their early thirties, but unlike Reagan who has blue eyes, Skylar has big green eyes. They're both extremely attractive and extremely taken, and both are at least eight months pregnant.

Skylar is the Vice President of Strategy and Operations, focusing on both property development and building new businesses from the ground up. She has a very good reputation in the industry. Though I'll be focusing on existing businesses, I'll still work closely with her.

"I haven't seen her yet. Frankly, it was odd. Sheila listened at her door and then told me to wait ten minutes."

Skylar lets out a laugh. "Someone should give you fair warning. Reagan and Carter get intimate in the office at some point every day. *Every* day. Sheila is the gatekeeper. She'll keep you out of the line of fire."

"I...I...I have no words for that." I barely remember what sex feels like.

She waves her hand dismissively. "Honestly,

everyone is used to it. You will be soon enough. You're starting on Monday, right?"

"Yes. I came in to set up a few things so I can be ready next week. I know you, in particular, have been stretched thin."

"I have. I'm thankful that you're coming onboard. It's perfect timing with Reagan and I about to give birth and Dominic on indefinite leave."

Dominic Mazzello is also a VP at Daulton Holdings. I met with him six months ago when I interviewed here. He and I hit it off immediately. I was looking forward to working with him.

"Do you know why he left?"

She shakes her head. "I don't know much. It was very sudden. I know he relocated to Cuba for the time being. Some sort of family issue. His girlfriend is heartbroken. She's inconsolable right now."

I scrunch my face. "Sorry to hear it. Well, if there's anything you think we can get out of the way now, I'm all ears. I have some time today."

Skylar and I sit for about thirty minutes as she updates me on Dominic's files. It sounds like she's truly been doing both jobs since he left. I'm happy that I'll be able to relieve some of the burden for her.

When we're done, I head back toward Reagan's office. Sheila looks up at me. "They'll see you now."

I walk and see Reagan and Carter sitting on a small couch in her office. He's rubbing her feet and doesn't bother to stop when I walk in.

Reagan smiles at me. "Beckett, we weren't expecting you. I'm thrilled you're here. Did Skylar update you on things? Sheila said you were in her office."

I nod. "She did. I should be good to hit the ground running next week."

"Great. IT is setting everything up for you. You can head down there when you leave here, and they'll get you your laptop, email address, security pass, and other necessary items."

Carter adds, "We've been working on a sport apparel company out of Italy. I think things are going to come to a head right around the time Reagan gives birth. We want to get you up to speed on it so you can take the reins if we're not around."

"Is that Veloce?"

Carter smiles, seemingly impressed that I know. "Yes, it is."

"I've heard they're growing at a rapid speed over there." I may no longer be in the game, but I always keep my ear to the ground.

"They are. Too fast. They need help with expansion. Their office is in Rome and busting at the seams. Americans are clamoring for their product, and they need our help."

"That's right in my wheelhouse."

Reagan nods. "I know it is, and I'm so happy to have someone with your experience and expertise here. I'm sorry we're going to throw you to the wolves, but between our pregnancies and Dominic's sudden departure, the timing necessitates it."

"It's fine. My mother will be in town for my first month here. That will free up things for me with regards to my daughter. I can dig in right away. It's been a long time for me. I'm genuinely looking forward to getting the wheels in my head spinning again."

"Great. Jade and Thorunn in the design department will be around to help you with the creative aspect. Veloce has none of that now, and they need it for the US expansion plans. Thorunn has been here forever, and my cousin, Jade, is a bit of a savant. They're both intimately familiar with the inner workings around here. I think Jade is on vacation in a week or two, but she'll be available otherwise."

I met Jade when I interviewed here months ago. I didn't know it until just after the interview, but she's the daughter of Amanda Tremaine, the woman I met at Reagan's birthday party four and a half years ago. The only woman I've been attracted to since Jenny passed. Too bad Amanda is married. I haven't gotten her out of my mind though. I've laid awake many nights wondering about her, remembering a special kiss cut short.

CHAPTER THREE

AMANDA

I clink ice cream spoons with Reggie and Victoria. Reggie announces, "To moving on and getting you some vitamin D. Big, hard, orgasm-inducing vitamin D."

I enthusiastically nod in agreement. "Ooh, that all sounds very nice."

Victoria shakes her head in disbelief. "That might be the quickest divorce in history."

I shrug. "When there are no assets to divide, no children to consider, and no real animosity, it can be done in six months."

My divorce became finalized today. Rick had one or two meltdowns along the way, but it's otherwise been fairly painless. I'm hopeful that we're parting as friends. That's what we've been the whole time anyway.

I'm sitting in my kitchen with my two best friends, each of us with a pint of our respective favorite ice creams. There's a pint of Rocky Road waiting for Jade. That's her favorite flavor. She's coming by in a bit.

Reggie nods toward Jade's ice cream. "Is she working late?"

"I'm not sure. She's been *very* busy lately. I think she's seeing someone but won't admit it when I ask."

Victoria seems to agree. "Pandora said Jade hasn't been going out with the girls at all. She thinks there's a secret boyfriend too, but said Jade is tight-lipped about it."

Just then we hear the front door open and close. Jade walks into the kitchen looking completely disheveled, which is very unlike her. She's become the epitome of well-put-together style over the past four years.

The three of us look at Jade, and then at each other, and start laughing hysterically.

As she takes her ice cream and spoon, she says, "What are you three nutjobs laughing at?"

Reggie looks her up and down. "Your buttons are uneven, your pants are unzipped, your hair is a mess, your face is flushed, and your lips are puffy. You just had sex."

Jade's grin widens as her mischievous eyes sparkle. "Maybe I did. Are you three jealous?"

We all giggle. I raise my hand. "I am. Anyone special?"

Her face turns serious. "I don't do special."

I know my daughter. Her words are hollow. I think there *is* someone special in her life right now. I hope I'm right. It's about time she had something resembling a healthy relationship with a man. At least I hope it's healthy.

Reggie shakes her head. "If I looked like you and had your body, I'd whore myself all over town to every hot guy walking by. As of now, Sam practically has to slap my thigh and ride the wave in."

Jade holds her stomach in hysterical laughter. "Oh shit, that's a good one, Aunt Reggie."

I lightly smack Jade's hand. "Don't encourage her. I

hate when she says stuff like that about herself." I turn to Reggie. "Cut it out."

She simply smiles and winks at me.

Victoria asks Jade, "Do you know if Pandora is seeing anyone?"

Jade shrugs. "I think she was a few months ago but not now. She's dickpressed like my mom."

Victoria looks at her in confusion. "What's dickpressed?"

"When you're sad or upset about the lack of dick in your life."

The three of us start giggling. She's not wrong. "I think you're right about me. I'm completely dickpressed."

After Reggie and Victoria leave, Jade and I sit on my couch. She takes my hand. "Are you *really* okay? I know you wanted this, but I'm sure it's not easy. Breakups were never easy for you." She spent half her childhood scraping me off the floor as I bounced from bad breakup to bad breakup.

"I'm fine. It was a hard decision, but I know in my heart it was the right one. I want a man I can't live without who feels the same for me. Maybe I'm still a fool for love, but I want something truly extraordinary. Someone that gives me something I've never had before."

I see her deep in thought, as if contemplating my words. I squeeze her hand. "I know you're seeing someone, and I suspect it's special. Tell me about him."

She turns her head away. This is how I've damaged her. I dated so many losers who disappointed us while she was growing up. They treated me poorly, often stealing from us on the way out the door. And we didn't have much. She's afraid of giving in to a relationship because of me. She assumes all men will let her down because that's what they've done to me. I wish I'd set a better example for her.

"I don't know if I'm ready to discuss it, Mom. It's casual."

"It's been months. I know it has. You've been different. It's okay if your feelings for him are more than casual."

Tears well in her eyes and I pull her close. She whispers, "I don't want to get hurt."

I hate myself for making her assume all men will hurt her.

"Not all men are bad. Just the ones I choose. Despite my less-than-ideal experiences, I believe that."

"Rick wasn't a bad guy."

I nod. "I agree. He wasn't. Just a little...boring."

She giggles. "There's no way he was rocking your world. No way he made your toes curl."

"No, he didn't do any of that. Is that what's happening? Your world is being rocked? Are your toes curling?"

She's silent. I know I've hit the nail on the head. "Mom, I'm just not ready to talk about it. I have to admit certain feelings to myself before I can admit them to you. Maybe when I get back from my trip."

"Just tell me this, is the age gap reasonable?" She's always been attracted to older men. I imagine it has something to do with Declan and how he wasn't in her life until she was seven. And then she tortured him for a long time. So much so, that I had her seeing a therapist, Dr. Pearl, since she was eight years old. She still sees Dr. Pearl sporadically to this day.

What Jade doesn't know is that I've also been seeing Dr. Pearl for the past four-plus years. Staying in my marriage has been a struggle for me. More so than I ever let on.

As for Jade, it took time, but she eventually accepted Declan into her life and has a good relationship with him and her stepmom now. It wasn't until her mid- to late-teen years that she found peace with him, but at least she eventually found it.

Jade sighs. "What do you want me to say, Mom? You know I'm only attracted to older men. I can't help it. I have no interest in guys my age. I never have."

I blow out a breath. "Can I ask a few questions?"

"You can ask. It doesn't mean I'll answer."

"Is he married?"

"No."

"Has he ever been married?"

"No."

"Does he have kids?"

"No."

This is all promising. I'm now hopeful that he's under forty. I can live with that.

"Does he collect social security?"

She laughs. "Not that I'm aware of. He's younger than you."

"I suppose I'll take it as a win and leave you alone for now. You know you can tell me anything, right? I love you no matter what."

"I know, Mom. I love you too."

"Are you excited for Mexico?" She's going to Cancun next week on vacation. We barely did any traveling when she was growing up, not having the money for it. I'm happy she's doing it now.

Her face lights up. "So freakin' excited. I'll send you some photos of the outfits Melissa and I picked out."

"I can't wait to see them. Are you really going with work friends or are you going with your mystery man?"

Her face drops. "I don't want to lie to you."

Wow. Her going away with a man is a big deal, but I need to let her talk to me when she's ready. "Okay. Hopefully we can have a real conversation when you get back."

"Maybe. Tell me what's going on with you." She looks around at the mess in my house. "It certainly looks like you've been painting a lot."

"I have been. I'm thrilled they're selling. I have an appointment at the gallery in the morning. Norma said there's a real demand for my work."

"That's so awesome. I'm proud of you."

"Thank you. I'm proud of me too. How's your dad?"

"He's fine. He and Melissa just got back from another trip. With Reagan and Skylar about to give birth, I know they wanted to be home."

Declan and Melissa travel a lot. He's a professional photographer and is often sent on weekslong assignments all over the world. Melissa loves traveling with him. She's fluent in several languages, and I know she immerses herself in the culture of wherever they travel.

"How are Skylar and Reagan holding up?"

"They're fine. Reagan is huge. Way bigger than Skylar. They bicker about it at the office constantly. It's hysterical."

"They're lucky their kids will be so close in age."

"For sure. She might claim otherwise, but I think Reagan is secretly happy that Skylar is having a baby too. She can help Reagan, and the babies can grow up together." This is Reagan's first child but Skylar's third.

"Aunt Darian must be over the moon."

"Hell yes. She's like a lunatic with excitement. Grandkids nine and ten come in the next month or so."

I shake my head. "Wow. That's incredible. She's so blessed. I can't imagine."

"She said she's going to have to buy another dining room table."

I laugh, knowing it's a running joke that Darian keeps buying new tables as the family grows. She's on her third or fourth in the past ten years.

———

LATER THAT NIGHT I turn on my computer and click on the Zoom link. Dr. Pearl's face appears. She's in her uniform cardigan sweater, with perfectly brushed, short, dark hair that's a little grayer than it used to be. I have no doubt that my daughter is at least partially responsible for it. She's probably ten years older than me.

She smiles. "Good evening. Did everything go through today?"

I nod. "Yes. I'm officially a divorcé."

"How do you feel about it?"

"Is it wrong to say I'm both happy and sad? Happy to finally put an end to this chapter, but sad that I hurt a nice man. I'm also sad that I wasted so many years with him, but then I feel guilty about feeling that way. He did nothing wrong."

"You're entitled to your feelings, Amanda. Did you do anything special tonight? I hope you weren't alone. Even though you wanted it, I have no doubt you're feeling emotional. Divorce is a big deal."

"My two best friends and Jade were here. We had an ice cream party."

"Good. I'm glad you weren't alone."

"Speaking of not being alone, I know Jade is seeing

someone. Likely an older man. She won't tell me anything, but I'm pretty sure she's going away with him."

"You know I can't and won't say anything."

I smile. "It never stops me from trying."

She returns my smile. "No, it doesn't. You're relentless."

"I know. I just worry about her; about the negative influence I've been in her life. I stay up at night fearing she'll become me."

"A loving, caring, selfless, kind person?" She sarcastically adds, "Yes, that would be truly horrific."

Tears form in my eyes. "I just don't want her to be alone like I've always been, making mistake after mistake. I don't want her to face the struggles I've faced in my life."

"She won't. Jade is fine, and you're not a negative influence. Just the opposite. You're a good mother. A great mother. Just because you personally struggled at times doesn't make you a bad mother. Her needs always came first for you. That's the very definition of a good mother. But she's an adult now. It's finally time to put your needs first. We've discussed this."

I'm silent. I know she's right. We've been building toward this for over four years.

"Amanda, you dated Rick because you thought a stable man was best for Jade. You were never truly attracted to him. You then took it a step further and entered into your marriage because you thought it was best for Jade. You knew it wasn't best for you, yet you did it anyway. Jade is a self-sufficient adult. It's okay to think about yourself now. You're entitled. Find what you want. *Who* you want. It's time. Have you gone on any dates?"

I shake my head. "I told you, out of respect to Rick, I wanted to wait until the divorce was finalized."

"Well, it's finalized. Get back on the horse. You're more

than emotionally ready to meet another man. You have been for a long time."

"It's not like I can snap my fingers and make a man appear."

"Have you looked in a mirror? You probably could."

I let out a laugh. "You're full of compliments tonight, Dr. Pearl."

She smiles. "You're an attractive, compassionate, intelligent woman. You just need to put yourself out there. You can't stay hidden in your house painting and expect to find someone. I can't imagine you'll have much trouble drawing attention."

"I plan to. I'm not sure how, it's been a while, but I'll try."

"Have you thought about contacting *him*?"

"Who?"

"You know who.

"Beckett Windsor?"

My kiss with Beckett was the impetus for originally contacting Dr. Pearl for myself. I was conflicted over both my kissing him and how I felt about it.

"Yes. Beckett."

"You don't just call a man like Beckett Windsor." After our encounter, I looked him up and realized who he was. I had no clue at the time that he was the wealthiest man in America.

"You never know unless you try."

I sigh. "He's probably dating someone anyway. A man like him doesn't stay single for long." From what I saw online, before he met his wife, he didn't lack in the dating department. There are thousands of pictures of him with drop dead gorgeous models.

I'd be lying if I said I didn't have a Google alert set to

him. Though I've never seen anything of his dating life since that night. There's plenty from before he got married, but nothing since his wife passed.

"You shared an intimate moment that deeply impacted you. It might be worth finding out."

"It impacted me because it was adulterous. I cheated on my husband." And it was the best kiss of my life.

"You told Rick right away and he moved on from it very quickly. He forgave you. You need to forgive yourself."

"It's not exactly how fairytales begin. *I met a sexy man while I was married to another man and was so weak that I kissed him.* I don't think Disney has done that story yet."

She straightens her already stiff shoulders just a bit more. "Do you really want to get into a conversation about Disney fairytales? Belle fell in love with an animal before she knew he was human. An *animal*. That's actually against the law in most states. Oh, and he was her abductor, holding her against her will. Cinderella's prince couldn't *possibly* recognize her when she went from a fancy dress into more drab clothing. He had to check her shoe size to confirm her identity. What a narcissistic moron. Sleeping Beauty was told one simple thing *not* to do her entire life and yet she still managed to be stupid enough to do it. *And* the prince, a complete stranger, kissed her while she was asleep. That's a consent issue. It's a violation. A felony."

Dr. Pearl crosses her arms and continues her rant. "Snow White lived alone with seven strange men as their housekeeper and cook, with no pay, and then ate poisonous fruit she received from a strange witch. How dumb do you have to be? Ariel couldn't even engage in conversation with her prince, yet he supposedly fell in love with her. For what? Her body? That's nothing but superficial. Oh, and she was a fish."

I let out a laugh. "Wow. That's a really fucking depressing way to look at fairytales. Thanks for ruining my childhood for me, Dr. Pearl."

She smiles. "It's the truth, so don't talk to me about perfect fairytale journeys. They're *all* imperfect. Every single one of them are fucked up in their own way. But in the end, they all get their happily ever afters. Isn't that what you're really seeking?"

"I never looked at it that way."

"Every love story has its own unique journey. No couple has an idealistically perfect road, void of bumps. Not even the couples in fairytales."

"You're kind of blowing up my world, Dr. Pearl."

"Just saying it how it is."

I let out a breath. "I hear you. My friends want to fix me up. Let me get back in the saddle. I haven't gone on a first date in nearly a decade. Give me a minute before I jump into the deep end."

CHAPTER FOUR

AMANDA

I'm up early Saturday morning, putting the finishing touches on my latest painting. I have a meeting later this morning at the gallery that has been selling my paintings. I want to bring this one with me. I could use the cash.

After getting it finished and dried, I seem to have no time to shower or change my clothes, so I head straight there in my paint-covered jeans and T-shirt. I walk in with my covered painting. Norma, my contact at the gallery, notices me right away. She runs over to me with her assistant, Clara, following a few feet behind her.

Norma screeches, "Amanda! I'm so happy you're here. I can't wait to see your latest masterpiece."

"Thanks, Norma. Hey, Clara."

Clara gives a small wave. "Hi."

"I think it came out well. Hopefully someone will be interested in it."

Norma gives me a knowing smile that I can't quite read. "I'm confident it will sell quickly."

"You haven't even seen it."

She rubs her hands together in excitement. "Then let's have a look."

I remove the cover and she gasps. "Oh, Amanda, it's exquisite. He'll love it."

"Who will love it? You already have someone in mind?"

Clara pinches her eyebrows together. "Of course. Beckett Windsor. He's purchased nearly all your paintings for the past five years. He asks to be notified as soon as something becomes available."

Norma snaps, "Clara! Keep your mouth shut."

Clara's eyes widen before she hangs her head in disgrace.

I look at Norma in shock. "What do you mean? They haven't been selling to random customers? *All* have gone to him?"

Norma is silent, practically shooting daggers at Clara.

I'm getting mad. "Norma, answer me."

She mumbles, "Not all. Maybe ninety percent."

My chin practically falls to the floor. "You mean to tell me that Beckett Windsor has purchased roughly fifty paintings of mine?"

She scrunches her nose. "Well...yes. Frankly, you should be honored. He's one of the top collectors in the country. The fact that he's so enamored with your work speaks volumes."

I'm seething. "Give me his address. I need to have a chat with him."

She shakes her head. "I'm not permitted to do that. We have confidentiality issues."

I grit out, "Well, you can give me his address, or I will start using a different gallery to sell my work. I imagine Mr. Windsor will then gladly take his business elsewhere."

She thinks for a moment before quickly scurrying away to look it up, and then she scribbles it on a piece of paper and hands it to me.

I run out to my car. I can't believe he's been buying nearly all my paintings. I'm angry. *Really* angry. How dare he. I thought I was finally seeing success. It turns out, I'm his pity project.

BECKETT

It's late Saturday morning and I'm on my iPad, catching up on the news. I'm drinking my juice while I hear Mom and Andie laughing in her playroom. There's nothing better than the sound of your child's laughter.

I love her relationship with my mother. They're incredibly close. Mom is so patient with Andie, which is why I'm patient with my mother. I know she's always well-intended, despite her unending desire to intrude into my personal life.

I look up at Karen. "This juice is delicious. What's in it?"

She sighs. "You don't want to know. It's good for you. That's all you need to know."

I chuckle. "Thanks, Karen."

I can't remember the last time I was able to sit on Saturday morning and simply read the news and enjoy my juice. Probably when my mother last visited.

At some point, Mom walks into the kitchen without Andie. "She's grown so much since I was last here. She's so articulate. Her mind is always working on overdrive, asking a million questions."

"She's amazing, Mom. So smart. I'm blown away by her every single day."

Mom rubs my head like I'm a child. "You're a good man, Beckett. You're such a good father. I'm not sure how that's possible, given the one you had, but I'm so proud of you. Speaking of which, have you seen your biological father and the child he's dating?"

I let out a laugh. "His *wife* is my age. And I don't see them outside of our monthly dinner, despite only living fifteen minutes away." We have dinner together and then Andie sleeps over there. It's the only time each month my father sees her. He never remotely considers seeing her in between visits. It strikes me as odd, but I won't beg him to spend more time with her. He was a hands-off father and is mostly a hands-off grandfather.

I see a small smile creep up on her lips. My parents have been divorced since I was a preteen. I don't know why they ever got married. My mother is warm and loving. My father is anything but.

He wanted me to follow in his footsteps and go to law school. His head just about exploded when I dropped out of college to start my company. Even though I am incredibly successful, it somehow still bothers him that I'm not a lawyer like him. The fact that I've been a stay-at-home dad for five years has put a strain on our relationship. He doesn't understand it. He considers me less of a man for it.

Mom looks over at Karen, who's chopping and preparing our lunch. "Oh, Karen, that looks delicious. It smells good too."

Karen smiles. "It will be ready soon, Mrs. Windsor."

"Karen, you've been here for a decade. As I've told you before, call me Glinda."

"Yes, ma'am."

Mom shakes her head and sits at the table. "Beckett, darling, tell me about the woman you're dating."

Crap. I was hoping she'd forgotten that fabricated story. I see Karen subtly moving closer so she can listen. I lift my eyebrow at her, and she silently giggles before moving back to her food prep.

I look at Mom. "What do you want to know?"

"What's her name?"

I blurt out the first name that comes to my mind. The one that's often on my mind. "Amanda."

"Amanda who?"

Once again, I blurt the first name that comes to me. "Amanda Tremaine."

"Another French girl. Tell me about her."

"She's a talented artist."

"How long have you been dating?"

"A few months." I'm going to hell for this.

"Tell me more. I want details. I don't know why you haven't mentioned her until just the other day."

Mercifully, my cell phone rings, and I see that it's Nico. He's hanging outside at the front gate of my property today with my security personnel. A delivery person must be here and he's asking if he should send them down to the house.

I accept the call and put it on speaker phone. "Hey, Nico. What's up?"

Mom whispers, "Tell Nico to come down to the house to have lunch with us."

I shoo her away.

"Sorry, what were you saying."

I hear Nico chuckle. He heard my mother. "There's a woman at the front gate demanding to see you." He mumbles, "She seems kind of pissed."

"Really? What's her name?"

"Amanda Tremaine."

Mom's eyes light up. She leans forward and speaks into the phone. "Send her right down, Nico."

You have to be kidding me. What are the chances of this happening?

Mom claps her hands together. "I didn't know she was coming."

"Neither did I. She shouldn't be here."

"Why not? She's your girlfriend."

"Umm...she hasn't met Andie."

"It's been a few months. It sounds like it's time. I'm so excited." She's practically jumping up and down.

"Mom, wait here. Let me go outside and greet her."

"Of course."

There's zero chance of her listening to me.

I practically sprint out the front door as a car pulls up my large, circular driveway. It stops and Amanda steps out.

It's the first time I've seen her since the night we met years ago. I swear I feel my heart beat harder and faster. She's in tight, torn jeans and a paint-covered T-shirt, her hair is in a messy bun, and she doesn't have on an ounce of makeup. She may be the most beautiful woman I've ever seen in my life.

But this beautiful woman looks mad. Really. Fucking. Mad.

I walk right up to her and quietly say, "Amanda Tremaine. To what do I owe the pleasure of your company?"

Her eyes narrow and she points her finger at me. She's so adorable. "I just found out you've been buying my paintings. You've got a lot of nerve. I don't want or need your money. I'm not a charity case."

Shit. I was supposed to remain anonymous. Damn gallery.

Naturally, at that moment, Mom decides to come outside. I whisper to Amanda, "Please go with what I'm about to do. I beg you. I'll make it worth your while. Anything. I promise."

She places her hands on her hips. "Are you for real right now? I've definitely heard you utter those words before."

"And I meant them back then. I bought your paintings. I did, in fact, make it worth your while."

"You motherfu—"

I silence her by grabbing her face and kissing her lips. It's not deep since my mother is standing thirty feet away, but it's enough to stop her mouth from moving. And she doesn't fight it, so that's good. In fact, I think I hear her moan into my mouth, but it's hard to hear anything over my mother's squeals of joy.

Amanda's lips are soft. She still somehow smells and tastes like cherries. Since the night we met, I'm obsessed with all things cherry.

I pull away and whisper, "Just go with it. Pretend

like we've been dating for a while. I swear I'll do whatever you want."

She blinks a few times before tilting her gorgeous head to the side. "Anything?"

"Anything."

I grab her left hand. I don't need Mom seeing her wedding rings, though I don't seem to feel any. She must not wear them when she paints. Judging by her appearance, she was definitely painting today.

We walk toward my mother, and I plaster a smile on my face. "Mom, meet my girlfriend, Amanda Tremaine."

Amanda's eyes widen, but before she can protest, Mom practically tackles her in a hug. "I'm so thrilled to meet you, Amanda. Beckett was just telling me about you and here you are. Let me look at you."

Still holding Amanda's shocked arms, Mom pulls back and examines her. "You are the prettiest little thing. No wonder he's so enamored with you."

"Mom. Enough. Leave her alone. She just got here. I'm sure she just stopped by to say hello. She needs to get back to her studio to paint."

Mom waves her hand dismissively at me. "Nonsense. Don't be rude. Amanda just arrived. She'll stay for lunch. She needs to eat." Turning to Amanda, she says, "You'll stay for lunch, right?"

Amanda gives me a mischievous smile. "I would love that, Mrs. Windsor."

"Please, call me Glinda."

"Like the good witch in *The Wizard of Oz*?"

Mom laughs and threads her arm through Amanda's. "I'm usually good, sweetie, but sometimes I can be bad."

Amanda starts laughing as they walk into the house, arm in arm.

I can only shake my head.

I look up. I swear, if I get through this unscathed, I promise to never tell a lie again.

CHAPTER FIVE

AMANDA

I don't know what I'm walking into, but for some reason, I can't stop myself. I'm wildly amused watching a powerful man like Beckett Windsor squirm in front of his mother. It's my chance for a little payback.

Glinda's arm is still looped through mine as we walk into the house. She's much taller than me. I can see where Beckett got his height. She's attractive, with his same darker blond hair and blue eyes. Her hair is shoulder-length and styled perfectly.

She smiles down at me. "Do you have any children, Amanda?"

"Yes, I have a daughter."

"How wonderful. Is she around Andie's age?"

I remember Andie was nearly one when Beckett and I met, so she must be about five now. "No. My daughter is much older. She's twenty-two."

Glinda stops short. "How old are you? How is it

possible that you have a child that old? I had you pegged at around thirty-five."

I squeeze her arm. "Flattery will get you everywhere, Glinda. I'm forty-four."

"I see. Have you been married before?"

"Yes, once, for a short time, but it didn't work out. We got divorced." I hear Beckett clear his throat behind us, but Glinda doesn't pay him any attention.

"How did you and Beckett meet?"

I don't want to lie to her. "We met nearly five years ago at a party for my daughter's cousin. We only got reacquainted recently." Like three minutes ago.

"How wonderful. What does your daughter do? Is she in college?"

"She graduated early. She's very high up in the design department at Daulton Holdings. Reagan Daulton is her cousin on her father's side."

Glinda's eyes light up. "You must be thrilled that she and Beckett will be working together."

What?

Beckett interrupts. "Mom, I need to talk to Amanda for a minute." He takes my hand and pulls me toward the stairs. "We'll be down in a bit for lunch."

Glinda has a huge grin. "Yes, you two go upstairs. Take your time." She winks at me. "Have fun." I can't help but let out a laugh. I think I love Glinda.

Beckett practically pulls my arm out of my socket as we make our way up the biggest staircase I've ever seen in my life. I think Jade and I once had an apartment smaller than this staircase. This whole house is insane. I can't even call it a house. It's a mansion. More like if a mansion swallowed a mansion.

We walk down a long hallway until we reach a bedroom

I assume is his. He closes the door and lets out a huge breath while he runs his fingers through his dirty-blond hair. He breathes, "Holy shit. What a mess."

I look around. I *know* I've lived in houses smaller than this bedroom. It's more of a suite, with multiple rooms within a room. I've never seen anything like it. There's a sitting room, a study, and two giant walk-in closets. I can't see the bathroom, but there are double doors leading to it. Who the hell has a bathroom with double doors? Why is that even necessary?

"Amanda, I'm so sorry about this. I don't know what to say."

"Are you a grown man who's afraid of his mother?"

He smiles. It's adorably crooked and takes me right back to the night we met. "Will you judge me if I admit that I am?"

"Yes."

"Judge away. Listen, my daughter doesn't have a mother. The past five years haven't been easy. My mother loves her and gives herself wholeheartedly to Andie. I don't have it in me to be an asshole to her. She's well-intentioned. Aside from a small handful of short visits here and there, she stays with us two months of the year. That time is everything for Andie. I try to placate my mother when I can. It's my way of thanking her."

"I can understand that, but why did you lie to her about who you're dating?"

"She's completely obsessed with me finding a woman. She talks about it constantly. I'm talking about daily calls regarding specific insipid women she wants me to date. She pushes and pushes. None of the women interest me. So I told her a few days ago that I was dating someone just to get her off my back. She asked me this morning for a name, and

I randomly answered Amanda." He puts his head down and mumbles, "Amanda Tremaine."

"Why me?"

"I...umm...was looking at one of your paintings when she asked. It was the first name that popped into my mind. And then, by some crazy twist of fate, you showed up at my house minutes later. I had no way of knowing that would happen."

"What is it you want me to do, Beckett? This is nuts."

"She's here for a month. She lives in Florida but, like I said, visits two months of the year. I need her off my back. I'll do whatever you ask if you continue the charade. I'll do anything to not have to consider the women she suggests or hear about it every time we're talk. Maybe a weekly dinner with us or something. That's not too bad, right?"

This is insane. I came here to give him a piece of my mind, not enter into this shitshow. "Beckett, putting this silliness aside, I'm really upset that you bought all my paintings."

"I told you at the party that I'd make it worth your while."

"That's not what I meant, and you know it. I'm not a charity case. I would have been fine with you buying one painting. The success I thought I was having all these years was a facade. It's humiliating."

His shoulders fall. "That's not how I intended it. I genuinely like your work. Look around."

I just then notice two of my paintings in his bedroom. For some reason, it makes me feel better that he has them hanging. On the way here, I was imagining a warehouse where he leaves my paintings, never to be seen or enjoyed by anyone.

I sit down in one of his chairs to think. "I don't want

you to buy any more of my paintings. Promise me you won't."

He shrugs. "If that's what you want."

"It will take time, but I want to buy back the paintings you bought."

He shakes his head. "No. Absolutely not. I love them. I want to keep them."

"Beckett..."

"Let's come to an understanding. What can I do to make it right with you with regard to the paintings I've bought, and how can I get you to pretend to be my girlfriend for a month?"

"I have no idea, but I know for sure that I don't want you basically paying me to date you. I'm not comfortable with the optics of that scenario. It's basically prostitution. I'm not for sale."

He lets out a laugh. "I know you're not. You're very talented. I genuinely feel like your paintings are an investment." He visibly swallows. "They've been very soothing to me during a difficult time in my life."

"You're just saying that because you need me right now."

"I mean it. I swear." He paces for a few minutes, rubbing his big lips in thought.

I find myself mesmerized by it. He's incredibly handsome. My memory didn't do him justice, nor do the photos online. I know in this moment that I didn't imagine the extreme attraction I had to him all those years ago. It's as strong now as it was then. Maybe stronger now that I'm single.

At some point, he stops and turns to me. "I have an idea. What if I agree to introduce you to a few wealthy, well-known art collectors?" Before I can protest, he holds up his hands. "I'm only agreeing to make the introductions. It's up to you and your work as to whether you complete the sales. They all know art very well. If they value your work, they'll buy it. If not, they won't. I promise not to attempt to sway them one way or the other. No charity. I'm simply getting them to the table for you to then take the lead. Our deal has nothing to do with them purchasing or not purchasing your work." He smiles. "No prostitution-like scenarios here."

Hmm. That does sound more reasonable. I think I can live with that. No one is being forced to buy anything. He's just introducing me to the right people. An opportunity any artist in my position would give their right arm to have.

"What's expected of me on the fake dating end of things?"

He blows out a long breath. "Honestly, I don't know. It's not like I planned this. I didn't expect you to show up. I planned to use my daughter as an excuse for you not being around all month. Now my mother has invited you to lunch with her."

"Your daughter is here?"

"Yes."

"Oh, Beckett. We can't do this. Not when an innocent child is involved."

He slowly nods. "You're right. Have lunch with us. I'll make up some excuse after you leave. I'm sorry I asked. I'm a bit of a mess right now."

"Okay. Lunch I can do. After I leave, let your mom down easy."

We walk back downstairs, and I can hear Glinda talking with a child in the kitchen. We walk in and I see Andie for the first time. She's adorable. Besides her blue eyes, she looks nothing like Beckett. She's got a darker complexion and much darker, curly hair.

As soon as she hears us, she turns our way, narrowing her eyes at me. "Who the hell are you?"

Beckett steps forward. "Mind your manners, Andie, and watch your mouth. This is my friend, Amanda. She's joining us for lunch."

Andie looks me up and down with pure venom. I can't help but smile. That's exactly how Jade spoke to and treated new people in our life when she was a little girl.

"It's nice to meet you, Andie. I can't wait to hear all about you."

She crosses her arms. "When are you leaving?"

Glinda snaps her head at Andie. "Andrea Windsor! Do not speak to people like that!"

Andie cowers at her grandmother's chastising and lowers her head. I walk over and crouch down, so we're eye to eye. "It's okay, Andie. My daughter didn't like new people when she was your age either. She was protective of me like you are of your dad. I think it's very sweet."

Her face softens. "You have a daughter?"

I nod.

"How old is she?"

"Twenty-two."

"What's her name?"

"Jade"

"Is she pretty like you?"

I smile. "Thank you for saying I'm pretty. I think you're pretty too." I play with a strand of her hair. "I love your curls. And yes, she's very pretty. Do you want to see a picture of her?"

She nods. "Okay."

I take out my phone and pull up a picture of Jade. Andie's eyes widen. "She looks like a Barbie doll."

I let out a laugh. "You're right. She does. People have been telling her that her whole life."

"She doesn't look like you at all."

"You're right again. She looks like her dad. You can't tell in the photo, but she's super tall. Even taller than your grandmother."

"Gigi says I'm going to be tall. I'm the tallest girl in my class."

"Gigi?"

"That's what I call my grandma."

I look over at Glinda and she smiles lovingly at her nickname.

Our truce talk is interrupted by a large, bald man entering the kitchen. The same man I saw at the front gate when I came in.

Glinda's face lights up. "Nico. I'm so glad you can join us for lunch."

Beckett narrows his eyes at Glinda, but she waves him off.

Nico nods. "Thanks for inviting me, Glinda. I'm happy you're back in town."

I think something is going on with them. I look at Beckett and he sighs in frustration. He has no control of his household. This is wildly amusing.

We all sit down to a huge spread of food. I'm introduced to their chef, Karen, who seems as excited to see me as Glinda. She's an older woman with gray hair and kind eyes. It's clear she has affection for Beckett. For some reason, I like that his security guard is eating lunch with us, and his chef looks at him like a mother looks at their child. At least he treats his staff well.

I learn that Nico is Beckett's longtime bodyguard, and that Andie calls him Uncle Nico. He's enormous. Beckett is a big man, but Nico is even bigger. I'd guess he's in between Beckett and Glinda's ages.

He and Glinda shamelessly flirt. It's adorable.

Glinda bats her eyelashes at him as she touches his arm. "Nico, I think you've gotten even stronger since my last visit."

He's in a suit. It's not like you can see his muscles. She just wanted to touch him. Beckett rolls his eyes at it.

He smiles at her. "Thanks, Glinda. Beckett has been working out a lot. I join him in the gym sometimes."

Now that he says it, I realize he's right. Beckett is much more muscular than the last time I saw him. The T-shirt he's currently wearing is stretched across his broad chest. His biceps are bulging. I only saw him in a suit last time, but he's definitely bigger. He's sexy as hell.

He smirks at me when he catches me ogling him. I quickly turn my eyes away.

At some point, Glinda shifts her attention from Nico to me. "Amanda, I believe I heard Beckett mention that you paint. Are you an artist?"

"I am."

"Tell us about your work."

"I paint a lot of different things. Landscapes, portraits, still life. Some realistic, some more abstract. You name it, I paint it. I gravitate toward whatever inspires me in the moment." I point toward a painting hanging on the wall in the kitchen. "That one right there is one of my paintings."

She stands and walks over to it, examines it, and then turns back to us looking confused. "Your name isn't on it."

"I don't sign my real name on my work. I made that

decision years ago when I had Jade. I thought if I ever hit it big, I'd want some anonymity."

She smiles as she sits back at the table. "It's signed *Enchanted*."

"Yes, that's how I sign everything."

She turns to Beckett and gives him a coy smile. Something passes between them. Almost like she just realized something about him. He stares back at her in challenge.

Andie breaks the tension, "What does enchanted mean?"

I answer, "It can mean to be charmed, but it can also mean to be placed under a magic spell."

"Like in fairytales?"

"Exactly."

Beckett nods. "We have a lot of her paintings in the house. Andie, the beach painting in your bedroom is one of Amanda's. I know that's your favorite."

Andie's eyes widen. "The one next to my poster of Arizona Abbott?"

"Yes. That's the one."

"Wow. I love that painting. It looks so real. Can you show me how to paint like that, Amanda?"

I turn to Beckett, and he shrugs. How did we manage to corner ourselves into this?

I look back at Andie. "Who's Arizona Abbott?"

Andie stares at me in shock. "Only the greatest, most awesome, most beautiful softball player ever."

Beckett smiles on with pride. "Andie and I catch a lot of women's college and professional softball games on television. She loves it. Admittedly, I do too."

Andie nods enthusiastically. "I wish Philly had a pro women's team so we could watch Arizona in person.

Maybe I could paint her one day. You never answered me, Amanda, will you show me how to paint? Can she, Dad?"

Before either of us can respond, Glinda says, "Of course she can. She'll be staying here with us all month so I can get to know her properly during my visit."

Beckett grits, "Mom! Stop it."

They start bickering but my head is spinning. I'm realizing that I'm not sure I can make ends meet if I don't sell paintings. I obviously didn't realize that my success the past few years was solely due to Beckett buying my work, and I won't take another dime from him. The fact is, I need him to make these introductions. I meant what I said, I don't want his charity, but I'll take the opportunity to introduce my work to legitimate art collectors.

I know Glinda is manipulating things, but as long as we have ground rules, staying here won't be so bad. I'll meet the collectors, spend some time with Beckett, and I can teach Andie to paint. I used to teach young kids to paint when Jade was younger and we needed the money. I think I'd enjoy doing it again.

BECKETT

When lunch is over, Amanda pulls me aside. "If you introduce me to four legitimate collectors, I'll do this. One month. I'll stay here. You can placate your mother and I'll teach Andie how to paint. She seems to genuinely want to learn."

I'm shocked. "You'll stay here? With me? With us?"

"Yes, but nothing physical can go on between us. I told you, my body isn't for sale."

I can't help but look her up and down. It's a fucking good body.

"Let me get this straight. You're going to stay here the whole month my mother is visiting, pretending to be my girlfriend, sleeping in my room, hanging with my family? All in exchange for *two* introductions."

She playfully narrows her eyes at me. "I said *four* introductions."

I put my face in hers. "Let's compromise and do three."

She nods and holds out her hand. "Deal, Mr. Windsor." The way she says that makes my dick twitch.

I take her hand, pull her close to me, and whisper in her ear, "I would have agreed to four."

She giggles and whispers back, "I would have stayed for two."

We both smile at the *Pretty-Woman*-like movie dialogue.

I need to wrap my mind around the fact that I'm going to be sleeping next to and pretend dating a woman I'm wildly attracted to but am not allowed to touch.

This isn't going to end well, but I'm in too deep to put a stop to it now.

CHAPTER SIX

THIRTY YEARS AGO

AMANDA

"Dad, did you hear me?" I look at him passed out on the sofa of our trailer. He must have gotten trashed again last night. I didn't hear him come home. It seems to be happening more and more often lately. It used to be one or two nights a week, now it's five or six. At least he comes home though. My mother split when I was three. I haven't seen or heard from her since.

I get no response, so I shake his arm again, this time much harder. "Dad!"

His eyes and mouth open. I have to turn my head in disgust. He smells like death. He grumbles, "What?"

"I told you all summer. I need the extra money for the advanced painting class after school. I earned enough money babysitting to pay for half. You said you'd pay for the other half. Today is the deadline."

He reaches in his jeans pocket and pulls out three crinkled one-dollar bills. "This is all I have to my name."

"What? Haven't you been working at the gas station?"

"I got fired two months ago."

"What do you do all day?"

"A few odd jobs here and there."

"Where does that money go?"

He starts laughing. "Joe's Tavern, I guess."

Oh my god, he's still drunk.

"What about the painting class? I need five hundred more dollars."

His face turns sad. "Sorry kiddo. Maybe next year."

It's my first year of high school. It wasn't easy to get into this program. If I don't start now, they likely won't take me next year. It was such a big deal for me to get in.

I run out of the trailer in tears and cry for a brief moment until I see a bunch of eyes on me.

I do my daily dodging of drunk, creepy old men as I make my way to the main road to begin my two-mile walk to school.

At some point, I hear a car horn honk and turn around. It's Reggie and her older brother. Oh thank god. She lowers the passenger window and shouts, "Need a ride, sexy?"

As soon as she sees my tear-soaked face, her eyes widen and she jumps out of the car. She takes me in her arms. "What's wrong?"

Through my sniffles, I say, "He doesn't have the money. I can't take the painting class."

"What? He promised you months ago he would make it happen."

"I know. He lost his job and any money he's made he's been spending on alcohol. He's drunk all the time now."

"He's such an asshole."

"He is, but at least he's here. That's more than I can say for my mother."

She nods like she understands, but I know she doesn't. She has two stable, loving parents and an actual house. She has a brother who looks out for her. She doesn't have to worry about where her next meal is coming from or whether some old, drunk guy is going to try to touch her as she comes and goes from her home. I would give anything to have her life.

"I'll get in the back with you. I've got something that will help."

We both slide into the back of the car. I look at her brother, Jared, in the front seat. "Hey, J. Thanks for the ride. I hate walking."

"No problem, Mandy. We're always happy to give you rides. Just call."

I don't have it in me to tell him that our phone got turned off last month. "Thanks. I appreciate it."

Reggie pulls out a joint. Jared rolls his eyes. "Smoke it quickly before we get to school. I don't want to get into trouble."

Reggie has been smoking more and more lately. I rarely join her because I can't afford it, and I know there are addiction issues in my family. I used to think it was only my mom, but now I'm starting to think it's my dad too. I certainly don't want to end up like either of them.

She takes a long puff and then hands it to me. "Just take one hit. It will take the edge off."

I suppose I deserve a little edge-reducing therapy, so I take a hit. I feel it right away. It numbs my body. Oh, this is nice.

"Do you want to come over after school and have dinner?"

I sigh. "I can't come over every night. I'm sure your parents think it's crazy that I'm always there for meals. I was at your house almost every night this summer."

She shrugs like it's not a big deal. "They love having you. You're practically their third child."

I can't help but hug her. "You're the best friend I've ever had. I hope I can be a good friend to you one day."

She wiggles her eyebrows up and down. "You're a hot guy magnet. You bring all the boys to our table at lunch. That sounds like a good friend to me."

In the front Jared yells, "La la la. I didn't hear that. My sister doesn't like boys yet. She braids hair at night."

Reggie and I giggle. What he doesn't seem to know is that Reggie *really* likes boys. That, or he's purposely ignoring it. She's kissed way more boys than me. And she's done more than kissing. I haven't. I'm trying to stay focused on making a better life for myself. Boys are a distraction.

JARED DRIVES us to their house after school. Before we walk inside, he says, "I'll drive you home tonight. I don't think you should walk after dark."

"You don't have to if you're busy. I'm used to long walks."

"It's fine. I'm happy to."

"Thanks, J."

Reggie and I do our homework until her mom calls us down for dinner. I look at the beautifully set table with real plates and silverware. There are steaks, potatoes, and green beans. They're so lucky they get to eat this way. I'm lucky they include me.

We sit down and everyone talks about their days. It's

so...normal. At some point, Reggie's parents look my way. Her mom clears her throat. "Mandy, Darren and I have discussed it, and we'd like to help you pay for the painting class."

I widen my eyes and look at Reggie. She puts her head down, refusing to make eye contact with me.

I turn back to her mom. "That's really nice of you, but I can't accept it. I think you guys do enough for me."

She nods. "We thought you might say that, so we have a proposition for you. We will lend you the money to cover your painting class, and when you sell your first painting, you'll reimburse us."

Tears sting my eyes. "You think I'll sell paintings one day?"

Her face lights up. "We have no doubt. You're incredibly talented."

"Thank you for believing in me." Is this what supportive parenting feels like? I'm going to be the most supportive parent ever one day.

She looks at me in question. "Well? Is it a deal?"

I think for a moment. This might be my only chance. "If I accept your loan, I want to pay interest."

She smiles. "If that's what you'd like."

"Yes, fifty dollars in interest. And I'd like you to make a contract so that I'm legally obligated to pay you back."

Her dad laughs. He's a lawyer. "I can accommodate your request. I'll draft the paperwork after dinner and then we'll sign it and write you the check."

Tears spill over my face. "Thank you. Thank you so much. Thank you for believing in me. I won't let you down, no matter what. I promise."

We finish our meal and Darren does as he mentioned. He prepares a contract for the loan. I carefully read it and then sign it, feeling like an adult for the first time in my life.

I walk out of their house with a huge smile and a check in my pocket for the entire class tuition. They said I should use the money I earned this summer for extra supplies, if needed. That was the only way they'd agree to the interest being added.

Reggie still has more homework to do, so Jared drives me home without her. I look at him, with his dark hair flopping over his forehead. "Your parents are amazing."

He nods. "Yep, they're pretty great."

"I'm so lucky to have Reggie and your family in my life. Thank you. I hope I can be as good of a friend one day to her and all of you."

"You know, she wasn't wrong in what she mentioned earlier about how you attract the guys at school. I think it helps her a lot that she's best friends with the prettiest girl in the whole school."

I can feel my cheeks burn. "You think I'm pretty?"

"I meant what I said. You're the prettiest girl in our school." He mumbles, "The prettiest girl I've ever seen in my life."

We pull up to my trailer park and he shifts the car into park. Turning to me, he licks his lips. "Can I...can I kiss you?"

What? Jared is two years older than us. He's cute, very cute, but I've never looked at him that way. I just see him as Reggie's brother.

He notices my hesitation. "You don't have to. I would beat myself up about it all night if I didn't at least ask. This is the first time we've ever been alone without Reggie."

I bite my lip. "It's fine. I've only kissed two boys. I don't know if I'll be any good at it."

He smiles. "I'll bet a million bucks you are. Just do what I do."

I nod as he moves closer to me. I lick my lips and swallow in anticipation.

He softly grabs my face and tilts it to the side. He tilts his to the other side and slowly brings his lips to mine.

The kiss is nice, but before I know it, his tongue is in my mouth. I think of what he said, so I do the same and slide my tongue into his mouth.

He moans when my tongue moves around his mouth. I think that's a good thing.

After a few minutes of the best kiss I could ever imagine, he pulls away. "You owe me a million bucks."

I smile. "Just add it to my running tab with your family."

He laughs as he gets out of the car and opens my door. Taking my hand, he walks me to my front door.

I'm on cloud nine right now, but it doesn't last long. When we reach the door to my trailer, I open it. My father is standing there in the same dirty clothes he was in this morning, which are the same clothes he wore yesterday. Possibly the day before too.

He's got rage on his face. "Where the hell have you been?" Oh god, he's drunk.

"I was at Reggie's for dinner."

He looks at Jared. "Is that so? Funny, that guy doesn't look like Reggie. Don't turn into a whore like your mother."

I turn to Jared with my head down. "You should go."

"I'm not leaving you with him in his state. Pack a bag. You're coming home with me."

Out of nowhere, my father punches Jared square in the face. I scream. "Dad, what are you doing?"

Jared wipes the blood from his lip and then grabs my father's shirt. My father may outweigh him, but Jared is young, strong, and sober, giving him the edge. He pushes my father until he's seated on the couch and points at him. "She's not fucking staying here with you ever again." He turns to me. "Pack as much as you can. No arguments."

I'm torn on what to do. My father needs me. But I nod my head and make my way back to the bedroom. The truth is, I'd rather stay with Reggie and Jared's family. I hate being here. I'm always afraid here. I feel safe there.

We only have two bags. I place as many clothes as I can in one, and as many of my books and art supplies as I can in the other.

When I walk back out, Jared looks at me. "Are you ready?"

"Yes."

My father practically growls at me. "If you walk out that door, don't ever think about coming back."

Before I can answer, Jared takes my bags and says, "No problem."

He and I leave to make our way back to his house. He holds my hand the whole ride. "Don't worry. We'll take care of you."

"Why are you doing this?"

"Because we care about you." He squeezes my hand. "*All* of us."

I can't help but sob throughout the short trip back. Why is my life so fucked up? Why did I get such crappy parents?

When we both walk in the house, Reggie's mom looks at us in question. Then she takes in my tears, Jared's split lip, and my two packed bags. She seems to understand what went down without either of us saying a thing.

"Mandy, the guest room dresser is empty. I'll clean out the closet over the weekend."

"I can stay with Reggie."

"No, you should have your own room. We don't get many guests anymore. The bed is empty way more nights than it's not."

With my head down, I whisper, "Thank you."

CHAPTER SEVEN

PRESENT

AMANDA

I had promised Jade that I would go to Darian and Jackson's house for their weekly Sunday night dinner tonight. I think it's her way of checking up on me before she leaves for Mexico.

As always, Darian is extremely warm to me when I arrive. She hugs me when she opens the door. "Amanda, it's so great to have you here. I understand you're permanently back in Philly now. I hope we'll see you more often."

I smile. "I'd like that. Thank you. Is Jade here?"

"Not yet. I'm sure they'll be here any minute."

This house is big and beautiful. Extremely modern. It was the biggest I had ever seen until I stepped foot in Beckett's house. That house could swallow this one whole.

I walk into a giant sea of warm welcomes. Darian's three daughters, Harley, Reagan, and Skylar, are there with their respective husbands, Brody, Carter, and Lance. Harley and Skylar each have one son and one daughter. Jackson's three sons, Payton, Trevor, and Hayden, are here with their spouses, Kylie, Cassandra, and Jess. Payton has a daughter, Hayden has a son, and Trevor has twins, one of each.

Reagan, heavily pregnant at this point, pulls me aside. "Do you know anything about Jade's love life?"

Of all her cousins, Jade is closest with Reagan. Besides looking alike, they have very similar personalities and obviously work together every day. They both lack a filter, love to stir the pot, and speak sexual innuendo as second language.

"Why do you ask?"

"Because I think she has a secret boyfriend."

I nod in agreement. "I think so too. She basically admitted it to me but wouldn't give me any details."

"This is a big deal for her."

"I couldn't agree more."

"I hope he's not living in a retirement home. I don't want to see her get hurt."

"She said he's younger than me, so that's promising." I squeeze Reagan's hand. "Thank you for caring so much about her. I can't tell you how incredible you all have been for her, especially you. Giving her that job when you did changed her life for the better."

She shrugs like it's no big deal. "I gave her the opportunity. It was up to her what she did with it."

I can't help but feel a similarity to what I'm doing with Beckett. He's giving me the opportunity. It's up to me what I do with it.

She continues. "She's the one that worked her ass off and hit it out of the park. I hope you realize how good she is at what she does. She might have Declan's temper, but she clearly has your creativity."

I let out a laugh. "She definitely has his temper." Declan has a terrible temper and Jade is no better. "Did your dad have that temper?" Reagan's father and Declan were brothers. He passed unexpectedly about ten years ago. I never met him, but he's most definitely revered in this family.

"He didn't take anyone's shit and got into a few fights here and there, but he didn't outwardly growl as much as Declan. He was like a significantly more evolved version of Declan."

We both laugh at that.

Speak of the devil, Declan walks in with Melissa and Jade behind him. Jade lives near them in the city. I suppose it's easier for her to travel out to the suburbs in their car.

She immediately makes her way to me when she sees me. "Are you okay?"

"Yes, I'm fine. Stop worrying. I'm the mother. I'm supposed to worry about you. Not the other way around."

"Are you sure?"

I was a mess every time a man left me while Jade was little. She took care of me countless nights while I cried myself to sleep. She probably thinks I'm doing the same now, but I'm not. Unlike the other breakups, this one was my doing.

"I swear. I'm great. I'm happy to be home, I'm painting consistently again, and I have a few meetings in the pipeline with art collectors."

"That's great. How did that happen?"

"A purchaser from the gallery is setting them up." I suppose that's the truth.

Reagan grimaces and then grabs Jade's hand and places it on her stomach. "Can you feel it?"

Jade feels for a moment before saying, "Holy shit. It's like the movie *Alien*. That baby is really moving."

Reagan looks at me. "Do you want to feel it too?"

"Do you mind?"

"Not at all."

I place my hand on her stomach and can feel the baby kicking right away. Tears fill my eyes.

Jade notices right away. "Mom, you can still have another baby. You're young enough. Women have babies at your age all the time."

I shake my head. "I think grandkids are about it for me."

She scoffs. "I hope you have a secret child somewhere cause I'm never having kids."

"Oh stop it. You'll change your tune." I hope.

I look around as the adults attempt to corral all the kids into the giant playroom Darian and Jackson have in their house. There are so many kids. It's nice.

Darian encourages us all to sit. I look around and don't see Beth. I turn to Cassandra. She is much older than Trevor. She's Darian's longtime best friend. I know there was a whole lot of drama when they first got together, but it seems to be in the past. I only know because Jade mentioned it once.

"Where's your sister, Cassandra? Isn't she normally here?"

She's been here every time I've come, and I was even at her house a few months ago when she hosted a family dinner.

Cassandra practically winces. "She's nursing a broken heart. I have Luke with us. He's in the playroom. She wasn't up for getting out of bed. Hopefully she'll snap out of it soon."

"I'm sorry to hear it." I didn't realize she was dating anyone.

Reagan looks at Jade. "That reminds me, Beckett Windsor is finally starting tomorrow."

Jade smiles. "Oh good. We're replacing one hottie with another." She turns to me. "Beth's boyfriend worked at Daulton before he skipped town in the middle of the night."

I nod in understanding.

"Mom, you know Beckett, right?"

"I met him at Reagan's party years ago. We talked about art. He's a collector."

Reagan nods. "He is. I think he's known to be one of the biggest and best collectors in the country."

I know he's a big collector, but I didn't realize the extent of it. I hope he meant what he said when he praised my work.

Jade shrugs. "I feel like such an underachiever. All I collect are cheesy pickup lines. I swear, men are getting much more creative and much dirtier with their lines. I had a guy last week tell me he wanted to put his one-eyed genie in my pink panini."

The table erupts in laughter. Except Declan. He looks murderous. "Who said that to you? Give me a name."

She rolls her eyes at him.

Reagan shakes her head. "That sounds like something Collin would say." I think Collin is a childhood friend of Carter's. I'm fairly certain I met him once or twice throughout the years.

No one else notices, but Jade flushes. That's interesting. I wonder if it's Collin she's seeing. I assume he's

Carter's age, which is about five or six years younger than me.

Carter nods. "True. He would say that. He's full of cheesy pickup lines." He throws his arm around Reagan. "You must have heard a lot before we got together. What's the cheesiest one you received?"

She thinks for a moment. "Hmm. Oh, I remember a good one. *Got a little Irish in you? Want a little Irish in you?*" She smiles. "Come to think of it. That might have been Collin too."

We're all laughing. Skylar chimes in. "I had a guy once say to me, *if you want a facial, all you have to do is tell me.*"

I forgot that no topic is off limits for this family. It's probably why Jade fits in so well and loves her time with them.

She continues, "Oh wait, that was Collin too."

This Collin guy sounds like a character.

Harley smiles. "A guy once licked his hand and then wiped it on me and said, *let's get you out of these wet clothes.*"

Jess, who's a nurse, giggles. "At the hospital this week, I had a guy say to me, *do you feel sick? Because I think you're suffering from a lack of vitamin me.*"

I laugh at that one, though her husband, Hayden, doesn't look as amused.

Jade turns to me. "What about you, Mom? You picked a few winners in the day. What was the cheesiest line you've ever heard?"

"Oh god, there were a lot back when I used to date. One that always made me laugh was, *do you want to sit on my lap and talk about the first thing that pops up?*"

She lets out a loud laugh. "That's hysterical." She turns. "What about you, Melissa?"

"Your father uses horrific lines on me each and every

day of my life. Worse than anything I endured while dating. Yesterday was a new low for him."

Jade perks up. "Spill it."

Melissa looks at Declan and he scowls. She loves ruffling his feathers as much as Jade does. She turns to her three sons. "Boys, cover your ears." She smiles. "He said, *why don't you come over here and I'll put something in your ass so you have an excuse to be a brat.*"

All three of her boys make gagging faces, but everyone else is in a fit of hysterics. I can't help but smile as I shake my head. That sounds exactly like Declan.

When dinner is over, Declan pulls me aside. "How are you managing?"

I rub his arm. "Honestly, I'm fine. I appreciate you asking, but I'm more than okay." Have I always been such a mess with breakups that both Jade and Declan feel the need to hover? I suppose I know the answer to that.

"He didn't mistreat you, did he? I'm happy to take a ride up to New York and have a little chat with him. Man to man."

Declan beat the crap out of at least two of my ex-boyfriends that I know of. They stole from us, and he went to retrieve our items in a violent way.

"Your days of beating up the men who mistreat me are behind us. The divorce was all me, not Rick. You know he's a good guy." I smile. "Besides, aren't you getting a little old to get into fistfights?"

He puffs out his chest and crosses his arms as Melissa joins us. She smiles at me. "Did you see some of the outfits Jade and I picked out for her trip to Mexico?"

"Yes. She sent me pictures. They look amazing. You have such a great eye for fashion. I'm so happy she has you for that. I'm clueless."

"You have an eye for art. I have an eye for fashion. We all have our strengths. I always wanted to study art, but life happened. You know how it is."

Like me, Melissa became pregnant very young. I think she was only nineteen when she and Jackson found out they were having Payton. She dropped out of school and supported them while Jackson got his degree. Once his business was up and running, she went back for hers. They have an extremely amicable relationship. Melissa and Darian are very close, and Melissa has never been anything but incredibly kind and inclusive of me.

AFTER DINNER, I pack a few bags at my house and head over to Beckett's. He had given me a key and told me to come whenever I was done.

I slowly walk in, feeling awkward about it. It seems quiet, though I see a light on in one of the rooms. I walk into what looks like a family room, but it's completely different from the rest of the house. At least the parts I've been in. Everywhere I've seen is modern and minimalistic. This room is like a log cabin, with wood floors, darker tones, big leather sofas and chairs, and lots of blankets. It's cozy. I love it.

I see Glinda cuddled up with a book in a big chair by the fireplace. It's large and made of stone with a rough wooden mantel. She looks up when she sees me and smiles. "Amanda. I'm so happy you're back."

"I didn't mean to disturb you."

"It's fine. I'm just catching up on some reading. I don't get much done while I visit, chasing after Andie all day."

"I'm a reader too. What do you read?"

"Will you judge me if I say romance?"

I smile. "That's what I read too. I'm a sucker for a good happily ever after."

She stares at me for a moment. "You're a dreamer, aren't you?"

I nod. "To a fault."

"Any particular reason?"

"I didn't have an ideal childhood. When I was very young, dreaming of a better life was my form of escapism. Books too. I immersed myself in them. I could have let it drag me down, but I suppose I always chose to believe in a better life instead. It kept me sane when things got *really* bad."

"I'm sorry you endured so much pain. I had a similar upbringing. It's why I'm so intrusive in Beckett's life. I know I annoy him, but he's my only child. My pride and joy. His happiness, and Andie's happiness, mean everything to me."

"I understand. I feel the same about my daughter."

"You two are close?"

"Very. We basically grew up together. I'm just afraid some of my baggage has become hers."

"I doubt that. What children need is to feel loved. I didn't. I've known you for one day and I know, without a doubt, that your daughter always felt loved by you. You exude warmth. Look at how quickly Andie went from dubious to in awe of you. You have a way about you. That special innate quality. Something every child wants in a parent."

"Thank you for saying that." I shuffle a bit nervously. "Is Beckett upstairs?"

"He and Nico are in the gym. They've been in there for

quite a while. They should be done soon if you want to head down there."

I look around, clearly having no clue where it is. This house is like a maze.

She looks at me skeptically. I'm sure she finds it odd that I don't know where it is. If I were really Beckett's girlfriend, I would probably know.

"Down the blue hallway. When it forks, stay to the right."

"Thank you. Have a good night."

"You too."

As I start to exit the room, she says, "Amanda?"

I turn my head. "Yes."

"Safeguard his heart. He might seem hard on the outside, but I assure you, on the inside he's quite fragile. He may not always react as you'd like, but he's an extraordinary man underneath a lifetime of baggage."

That last part feels loaded, but I say nothing in return. I nod wordlessly as I leave the room. I know Beckett has been through a lot, losing his wife and raising his daughter on his own.

I think I pass over ten rooms along the way to the gym. As I get closer, I hear grunting, though I'm not prepared for what I see when I walk in.

The gym is bigger and nicer than most commercial gym spaces. What really stands out is that there's a full boxing ring in the middle. Beckett and Nico are in it. Beckett is wearing gloves while Nico holds up pads for him to punch over and over again.

Beckett is wearing gray sweatpants and a tight T-shirt, showing all his bulging muscles. I noticed he was bigger than when we met, but now I see he is completely ripped. Sweat is pouring off his body. It's like seeing a fantasy come to life. Or the beginning of some sexy porn.

I watch for a few minutes as he moves with what appears to be expert precision. I wonder why he knows how to fight so well. It seems odd for someone in his position. He and Nico dance around with Beckett going on full attack mode. Nico occasionally throws a swing at Beckett, but he quickly ducks out of the way each time.

At some point, he notices me standing, ogling, in the doorway. He stops, completely out of breath. "Sorry, I didn't hear you come in."

"I just got here."

"We're all done." He grabs a towel and wipes his face. "I'll show you around."

With a towel around his neck and gray sweatpants I won't soon forget, he gives me a quick tour of the house. I think I'll need a map to remember where everything is. But there's one room I won't forget. We walk into it, and my chin nearly drops to the floor.

It's a painting studio. And I don't mean a few canvases, brushes, and paints. It's a professional studio with everything you can imagine. Countless supplies. Thousands and thousands of dollars of supplies.

I look at him in question.

He shrugs. "I had a few items sent over this afternoon. If you're going to be here and we're going to introduce you to collectors, you need to be painting. Is it okay for you? If there's anything missing, just let me know."

My mouth moves a few times before words come out. "You...you did all this for me?"

"Well, not *only* you." He nods toward a child-sized easel next to the regular one. "Andie's been talking about it all day since you left."

He points to the windows in the room, which must number at least twenty. "I know you can't tell right now, but during the day, there's a ton of natural light in here. And you have an amazing view of the grounds. Hopefully it will inspire you."

"I don't know what to say. Thank you for all of this."

He smiles. It's so genuine and boyish. "Selfishly, I'm excited to watch your process. I love art, but I've never watched it come to life."

Why is this man so damn dreamy? Did I mention that he's wearing gray sweatpants and that they're damp around the waistband?

As we make our way to his bedroom, he looks around nervously. "Do you want me to sleep on the couch?"

"For a month? That sounds painful. It's not necessary. We're not spring chickens. We can manage this."

"Okay. Make yourself at home. The entire second closet is empty. Use it as you please."

"Was it your wife's?" I feel like I'm intruding on her space.

He shakes his head. "No, we never lived here. We designed and built it. It was supposed to be ready by the time Andie was born, but they were a little behind. We moved in a few weeks after the funeral."

"That's a shame."

He makes a face. It's pain but not sorrow. I don't know what to make of it.

He takes a quick shower and then walks out in a robe. "It's all yours."

I nod and head into the bathroom to get ready for bed. This bathroom is insane. There are two completely different sections, his and hers, that meet in the middle for a shower big enough to fit my car. It's not just separate vanities and sinks, but separate toilets too. I've never seen a bathroom in a house with two toilets.

I put on my usual sleepwear: an old, cropped T-shirt with shorts. When I walk back out, I see him in athletic shorts and a T-shirt. He stares at me, moving his eyes up and down my body. Saying nothing, he turns and walks into his closet. A few seconds later he emerges with one of his big T-shirts and hands it to me. "I don't know if I'll be able to manage myself sleeping next to you in that. Can you wear this over it?"

I giggle. "Sure." Admittedly, if he were in boxer briefs instead of looser shorts, I'd feel the same. I was already getting antsy at the notion of him not wearing a shirt. I'm glad he is.

We both lay in bed, staring at the ceiling in a dark room. This feels so awkward.

At some point he turns to me. "Can I ask you the question I was afraid to ask earlier?"

I turn toward him. "Sure."

"Are you really divorced, or did you just say that to my mother to keep up the ruse?"

"Do you honestly think I'd be here in your bed if I weren't? Real or fake, I wouldn't do that."

"You may be in my bed, but you're not *in* my bed. Not yet." He reaches over and rubs my lower lip with his thumb. "When the time comes, believe me, you'll see the difference."

I gulp, at a complete loss for words.

He leans forward and kisses my forehead. "Goodnight, Amanda. Sweet dreams."

At that, he turns and faces the other way. What have I gotten myself into?

I'M AWAKENED in the middle of the night by Beckett laying on top of me, sucking my nipple from the outside of my shirt.

"Beckett, what are you doing?"

He doesn't respond or stop. He's so heavy on top of me. I can't move. I look down and his eyes are closed.

I say his name a few more times, but I get no response. Not even a remote sign of acknowledgment. Is he awake? I don't think he is.

His hands move to my breasts. He sleepily mumbles, "I love these," as he kneads them over and over.

I feel his erection on my leg through his shorts.

I shake him but he doesn't break stride. I give him one more hard shake and his eyes blink open and closed a few times.

He looks up at me and removes his mouth and hands from my breasts. He pinches his eyebrows together. "What's going on?"

"I think it should be me who's asking you that. I was pretty clear on my rules, Beckett." Though, if I'm being honest, I don't mind him on top of me, touching me.

He rolls off me and blows out a breath. "I'm so sorry. I haven't done that in years."

"Done what?"

"I...umm...used to get a little frisky in my sleep."

"You weren't awake?"

He shakes his head. "No. It's kind of like sleepwalking."

"So...you don't sleepwalk, you sleepfuck?"

He lets out a laugh. "I've never called it that, but yes, I suppose I do."

"That may have been information you should have

shared with me before I agreed to this," I say more playfully than seriously.

"It's been over six years since it's happened. I didn't even think about it." He runs his fingers through his hair. "Honestly, it only happens when I go to bed impossibly turned on."

Wait, what?

He turns to me. "You know I'm attracted to you. I have been since we met. Honestly, I've thought of you so many times throughout the years but had you in this untouchable place in my mind because of your marriage. Then you showed up at my house, you're in my bed, you look the way you do, you smell the way you do, and then you told me that you're divorced. I guess my libido got the best of me. I apologize. I'll try to contain it."

My head is a jumbled mess. Do I even want him to contain it? I feel the exact same way about him. The physical draw to him is overwhelming. There's clearly something between us.

He takes my hand and kisses it. "I want to respect the boundaries you've set for our arrangement. You're doing me a huge favor, and I appreciate it. But when our thirty days are up and we no longer have a business arrangement, will you consider dating me? For real?"

I rub his sexy, scruffy face with my fingers. "I think I'd like that too. But not until then. It doesn't sit right with me if we start up before then."

He nods as we both attempt to fall back asleep, both a little too restless and worked up to do so.

CHAPTER EIGHT

BECKETT

After tossing and turning for another hour, I finally fell back asleep. I wake up in the morning and Amanda isn't in the bed. I have a moment of panic, thinking I scared her away and she left, but I look around and her stuff is still here. I inhale the scent on her pillow. It smells like cherries.

Phew. I look down at the bulge in my shorts and squeeze it to try and get some relief. I'm going to have a boner for thirty straight days. My right arm is about to get the workout of a lifetime.

After giving myself a moment of relief in the shower, I get dressed and go looking for her. I walk around for a bit until I hear voices coming from the new studio. I know that studio was severe overkill, but I want her to spend time here. I don't want her to rush home to paint every day. I need her in my space.

I quietly peek into the room. My heart just about explodes at what I see. Amanda and Andie are both painting. Amanda is teaching her how to blend colors on the canvas and explaining how it gives things depth. Andie is hanging onto every word she says.

I have no idea how long I stand there watching. I think I could watch this forever.

At some point, I feel a hand on my back. I turn my head and see Mom looking at the same thing. She whispers, "Amanda is wonderful."

I sigh. "I know."

"How come she's never been here before?"

I nod toward Andie.

"It's clear how smitten you are. It seems like it was time. I'm happy I suggested it."

Andie and Amanda both turn around. "Good morning, Daddy. Come see what I painted. Amanda is showing me how to paint the ocean. She said not to use all one blue color. Look how good it is."

I walk over and kiss her head. "It's beautiful. When you're done, we can frame it and hang it near Amanda's painting in your room."

Her face lights up. "Really?"

I nod as I turn to Amanda. I feel like it would be normal to greet her in some way, so I kiss her head. "Good morning."

She turns her head and inhales me. "Hmm, you smell good."

Her eyes then widen in shock at her own words, but I simply smile at her. "And you smell like cherries, as always." She smelled and tasted like cherries the first night we met. For nearly five years I haven't been able to see, touch, or smell cherries without thinking of her. I now always keep them in the house. She must use some sort of cherry-scented lotion because I was smelling it all night. It's probably what caused my *sleepfucking*. I love her new term for it.

Mom interrupts my thoughts. "Andie, you know what I smell? Karen making waffles. Should we go help her put on the final touches?"

"After Daddy tells me his morning joke of the day."

Amanda questions, "Joke of the day?"

Mom rolls her eyes. "Andie and Beckett have a tradition. He tells her a new joke every morning. It's truly amazing how many corny dad jokes he has in that big head of his."

I smile. "I've got a good one for you today, Andie. Very thematic. What's blue and smells like red paint?"

I see Andie deep in thought for a few moments before admitting, "I don't know. What?"

"Blue paint."

Amanda gags. "Oh my god. That's terrible."

Mom just shakes her head. "They're all terrible, but it never stops him."

I wink at Andie. "You like them, don't you?"

She giggles. "I love them. I write them in my journal every day, so I never forget them."

"I didn't know that." It makes me happy.

"Yep. Every single day."

Mom holds out her hand. "Let's go, Andie. We need to get you fed."

Andie looks down at the paint-covered brushes and then back up at Amanda. Amanda takes them. "I'll clean them. Go help Gigi and Karen. We'll be down in a few minutes to eat with you."

Andie hugs Amanda's legs. "Thanks for teaching

me. Can we work on it more when I get home from school?"

"Of course. Just leave your smock here so you don't get paint anywhere else in the house."

I turn to Mom and see tears in her eyes before Andie joins her and they leave the room.

I hold up the *smock* Andie handed to me on her way out. "I see you made use of my T-shirt."

"She came in and asked to start painting. I didn't want her getting paint on her school clothes, so I took it off and gave it to her."

But it's left her back in that tight, cropped, midriff-baring shirt that sends my cock into orbit.

I grab her by the waist and turn her so she's flush to my body. She gasps at the surprise move.

With my other hand, I pull her hair so her eyes are forced to meet mine. "Once again, I can't have you walking around in this shirt. I'm telling you right now, if I see you in this top again, I won't be held responsible for my actions." I rub my erection on her for added effect.

Her face flushes and her breathing picks up. She stares at me with those big, honey-brown eyes and slowly nods.

"Good. I'm glad you understand. Now throw on a different shirt and meet me in the kitchen for breakfast."

Again, she simply nods.

I make my way down to the kitchen and Karen hands me my juice. "Thanks, Karen. What's in it today?"

She rolls her eyes at me like she does every time I ask. "As I always tell you, it's best if you don't know."

I laugh. Amanda then enters the kitchen in an oversized sweatshirt. I subtly nod at her in approval.

She looks around the room. "Karen, these waffles smell amazing. Are there enough? I don't want to take away from anyone else."

"Of course, sweetie. Beckett doesn't eat them. He's all into healthy living."

Amanda turns to me with a look of disgust. "How boring. Do you indulge in anything?"

Before I can answer, Mom does. "Well, he puts cherries on everything. And not fresh cherries. It's always Maraschino cherries. And he does love Cherry Coke and cherry ice cream. Hmm, it's interesting. He wasn't into cherries while growing up. It wasn't until about five years ago that he became so enamored with them. Amanda, remind me when you two met for the first time."

Amanda bites her lip and giggles. "About five years ago."

"And what is the scent of your lotion?"

"Cherry."

Karen's eyes flash with amusement, as do my mother's.

I scowl at all of them. "I'm so happy I amuse all of you. I need to get to my first official day of work. Andie, Gigi will take you to school. Be a good girl."

After the tears the first day, she was completely fine. I probably should have done this months ago. I panicked at the beginning of the year when she was so upset. Rookie mistake.

"I will. Gigi wants to come in and meet my new best friend."

I didn't know she had a new best friend. "Who is that?"

"Dylan Knight."

Dylan? I don't want her first best friend to be a boy. "I think your best friend should be a girl." I might need to vet this person. Perhaps I should call my private investigator to look into this five-year-old thug.

At the same time, both Andie and Amanda say, "Dylan is a girl."

I look at Amanda in question. How does she know?

"She's Jackson Knight's granddaughter. Cassandra and Trevor Knight are her parents. They're a hoot. Dylan has a twin brother, Brandon."

Andie has a dreamy look when she says, "He's *really* cute. He's in my class too. He has the greenest eyes I've ever seen."

I'm about to rain holy hell when Mom grabs my arm. "Go to work, dear. We'll see you tonight."

She and Amanda exchange amused looks as I head out to my first day of work in six years.

NICO and I drive to the office. I walk in and see Jade immediately. She smiles. I've never seen someone whose smile always seems full of mischief like Jade. "Welcome, Beckett. It's good to have you here."

"Thank you. I'm excited to get started."

"It's perfect timing with Dominic leaving. Poor Skylar has been working herself silly to cover his work and hers for a while now."

"I'm happy to help."

"When I interviewed you months ago, you didn't mention that you met my mother. She told me about it recently."

"I didn't know she was your mother at the time."

I'm going to assume Amanda hasn't told her about our arrangement. Unless Jade indicates that she knows, I'll keep my mouth shut.

"Oh, right. I guess I didn't let on when you noticed her paintings in my office. I think I was surprised you knew her real name. She usually safeguards it."

"I was introduced to her work when I met her at Reagan's birthday party. She told me about her pseudonym. I now have a bunch of her pieces. I love them. She's very talented."

"She is. Have you maintained any contact with her?"

Jade's fishing for information. She's a sneaky one.

"I haven't reached out. I work directly with a gallery for her pieces."

She nods. I just then notice the can from which she's drinking. I've never seen it before. What is it? I squint to read the words. No, it can't be. "What are you drinking?"

"Pussy Juice."

The drink is legitimately named *Pussy Juice*.

"There's a beverage called *Pussy Juice*?"

"Yes, it's like Red Bull but better. It has natural energy and natural ingredients. See?" She points to the subheading on the can. It actually reads *natural energy* and *natural ingredients* on the can. She winks.

"You should try it. Nothing beats a little Pussy Juice in the morning."

I think when I interviewed here six months ago, I remember Dominic telling me that Jade likes to push buttons. I'm not biting on this one. Time for a topic change.

"I'm good on both energy and my morning juice. Thanks though. I have no clue where they're putting me. Do you know which office is mine?"

"I assume Dominic's office."

I wince. "Isn't he only on leave?"

"No one knows. It's pretty fucking weird. I don't think he's coming back anytime soon. I believe you're using his assistant too. His name is Avery. He's a hoot. You met LeRond, Carter's assistant, right?"

"I did. I got a kick out of him." I met LeRond when I interviewed here months ago. He's been Carter's assistant for fifteen years. He's eccentric and hilarious.

"Avery is his husband. Avery only started recently when he was out of work. The two of them together are a comedy show. Enjoy the fireworks. I have a meeting, but we're happy to have you. I assume I'll be working with you. Reach out when you need me. I'm away next week in Mexico, but I'll be around otherwise."

"I will, thank you."

I head down to Dominic's office. Considering the fact I interviewed with him months ago, I know where it is. There's no one at the assistant's desk, so I walk in.

He must have emptied it out. The only evidence of

him is the good whiskey and Cuban cigars sitting in the corner. Though, if I remember correctly, he had very few personal effects when I was here. He mentioned keeping a low profile in the office. There's definitely something suspicious about Dominic Mazzello.

The only items I brought were photos of Andie and my mother. My mother is young-looking. People will probably think it's my former wife, but I don't care.

I open up the laptop I retrieved last week and see I have a bunch of emails. I start reading through them. A few minutes later, a man walks in.

"Mr. Windsor?"

I stand and hold out my hand. "Are you Avery?"

He smiles as he shakes it. He's got shoulder-length, dark hair that's slicked back. He's tall and skinny and must be about ten years younger than me, so in his upper thirties. "Yes, sorry I missed you when you walked in. I was battling the coffee machine. If you tell me how you like your coffee, I can grab you some."

"I don't drink coffee but thank you."

He gasps in shock. "I've never met a grown man who doesn't drink coffee. Are you a robot?"

I let out a laugh. "No. I just try to engage in clean living. If I need an afternoon caffeine hit, I like a good Cherry Coke. That's my one indulgence."

"Duly noted. I'll make sure we have plenty on hand. I'll put it right next to the Pussy Juice Jade likes. *I* certainly prefer Cherry Coke to Pussy Juice." He winks at me.

"I think I'll refrain from commenting."

He lets out a laugh. "I've updated your calendar. You have a meeting in forty-five minutes with Mrs.

Lawrence-Daulton, Mr. Daulton, and Mrs. Lawrence-Remington."

"Cheez. Their names are a handful."

"*They're* a handful, especially our fearless leaders." He looks around like he's making sure we're alone, and whispers, "Just so you know, the Daultons engage in office *fun* once a day. Sometimes more."

I chuckle. "So I've heard. I know to check in with Sheila before I enter her office."

"And LeRond before you enter Carter's."

"Duly noted. Thank you."

"My pleasure. Let me know if you need anything."

At the appointed time, I head down to Reagan's office. Sheila gives me a warm welcome. I see Reagan's door is open, so I know I'm in the clear.

I walk in and see Carter and Reagan sitting together, while Skylar is sitting with a tall, blond man. Their close proximity and the fact that he's stroking her arm suggests that it's her husband. That, or this office is a brothel. I'm not sure I'd be surprised if it was at this point.

They all stand when they see me. Reagan and Carter shake my hand. Skylar does the same before introducing me to the man with her. "Beckett, this is my husband, Lance Remington. Lance, this is Beckett Windsor."

Lance smiles and shakes my hand. "It's an honor to meet you, sir. We studied you in business school."

He's got a bit of country twang to his voice. He clearly didn't grow up in Philadelphia. "Nice to meet you as well, Lance. I suppose a few schools discuss my business model." I wink. "I got lucky and it worked." I nod toward Skylar's stomach. "Congratulations to you."

"Thank you. We're excited. We have to leave for a doctor's visit in a few minutes. That's why I'm here." He looks at Reagan. "Do you want me to wait outside?"

"No, it's fine." She turns back to me. "He works for my stepfather."

I smile. "You're learning from the finest, Lance. Jackson Knight is the best developer I've ever worked with."

"Yes, sir, he is. I love working for him."

We chat for a bit about files that Skylar will transfer to me. It's so nice to be back in the business world. I've missed it. My mind was on overdrive for twenty-five years and it came to an abrupt halt the day Jenny died and Andie was born. I need to get some healthy balance back into my life.

CHAPTER NINE

FIVE AND A HALF YEARS AGO

BECKETT

I look around. At least the house was half packed before we left for the hospital. Most of her clothes were already in boxes, anticipating the move shortly after Andie was born.

My mother walks into my study. "I gave Andie a bottle. She should be out for at least three hours."

I blow out a breath. I know my eyes are red from both crying and sleep deprivation through my first week of fatherhood and widowerhood. "Thanks, Mom. I definitely couldn't get through this without you. When do you have to go home?"

"I was already planning to stay for two weeks. Why don't I tack on a few more and get you through the move? Let's get you into a routine with Andie."

"It might not be for another month or so."

"That's fine. I'm here for you. Always."

"I know. Thank you."

"How are you holding up?"

"I'm plugging along as best I can. This wasn't exactly part of my plan."

She nods in understanding. "I saw all her clothes in boxes by the front door. Are you sure you're ready to part with them so quickly?"

"What's the point in holding on? She's not coming back. Her parents don't seem to want them. I'd rather donate it all. I can't have it around here anymore."

She gives me a sympathetic look. That's all I seem to get from people lately. This should be the happiest time in my life; instead, the birth of my daughter is marred by deep tragedy.

"I understand. I think it will be nice to get a fresh start in a new space she never lived in. You and Andie can make the home yours."

"Except Jenny decorated the whole house. Her touches are everywhere."

"Not the whole house."

"Aside from the casual family room and the gym. Everything else was all Jenny."

"What about work? What's going on with your company? You've got a lot to juggle."

"I've spoken to a few of the top companies in the world about buying me out."

"You're not going to work anymore?"

"I need to be both mother and father to my daughter. I can't do that and run one of the biggest companies in the world."

"Just take a step back. Hire another CEO."

I shake my head. "I'll never be able to let go of

control. I know myself. It's best if I sell out. It's not like I need the money."

"I know, but you need to keep your wheels turning. At some point, you'll need a life outside of Andie."

"She *is* my life now."

"Beckett, you're young. I know you can't imagine it now, but one day happiness will find you again."

I look at her accusatorily. "Did it for you?"

"I never had it in the first place. Maybe one day my prince will come. I haven't lost all faith."

I sigh. "It took me over forty years to find Jenny. I'm not overly optimistic, but I can't think of this right now."

"You're right. I'm sorry. I'm going to get some sleep. It's been over forty-four years since I've done this. Do you want the first shift or the second tonight?"

"I'll do both. I'm not sleeping anyway. You get a good night's rest."

"Are you sure?"

"Absolutely."

"Okay. I'll see you in the morning. Karen is doing some grocery shopping. If you want anything specific, text her."

I smile. "She knows everything I like."

"I know she does. Good night. I love you."

"Love you too. And Mom, thank you for being here."

She nods and heads upstairs to her room. She's my angel. I'll never take her for granted again. I'll never complain about her meddling in my life. I could never have survived this week without her.

I look down at my pinkie. Jenny's wedding band and engagement ring have been there since they handed them to me at the hospital. I can't seem to gather the courage to take them off.

I look up. "Why did you leave me, Jen? I need you. Andie needs you. It took me so long to find you."

I was a bachelor for forty years. I made my first million by the age of twenty-one, and by twenty-five, I was listed among the wealthiest men in America. Every single day since, I've been unsure of people's motives for getting close to me. Women were hanging all over me, but it was never about me, Beckett. It was about Beckett Windsor, the wealthy entrepreneur.

That's until my sweet Jenny came along. Something felt different with her. I think I knew right away she was the one.

I rub my thumbs over the pads of my fingers. I can still feel her curls in my hands. The way her silky smooth body felt under mine. The awe I felt at seeing Andie grow inside her belly.

I squeeze my eyes shut. Is there any chance this is just a nightmare? Please let me wake up and it be over.

I open my eyes, but my reality doesn't change. I'm a widower at forty-four with a newborn daughter. All the money in the world doesn't mean anything if you don't have someone to share it with. Someone to love.

I've got to stop this pity party. For my daughter's sake, I need to focus on her. She's going to get as much love from me as a child would normally get from both a mother and father. I will do *anything* to make her happy. To fill the tremendous void she'll feel growing up without a mother. I can't imagine it. My mother did everything for me.

She'll also now grow up without siblings. Just like me. I was dead set on giving my child a sibling. I always wanted one. I know my mom would have had more kids if she could have. Jenny and I talked about having another baby as soon as she was physically able. Having a stable, loving, big family was my dream. That dream is shattered too.

I decide to open Jenny's laptop. There must be some odds and ends for me to tie up for her. I see a few pictures of us as her screensaver and smile. There are a bunch from when we were dating, our wedding, our honeymoon, and then nine months ago in Fiji where Andie was conceived.

I can still feel my wife's soft body on my hard one as we made love on our private beach. Tears find my eyes again. I miss her.

I'm reading through a few new emails to see if there's anyone left that doesn't know what happened, when a message pops up on the screen.

Jaques: Est-ce que c'est sauf de parlait?

Jenny was French Canadian. She grew up in Quebec. Her parents still live there and barely speak any English. She came over to the States for college and then stayed. She always maintained a significant French accent. It was cute and sexy, and I loved it. I did my best to pick up the language throughout the past few years. I'm not fluent, but I'm pretty sure he wrote, *is it safe to talk?*

CHAPTER TEN

AMANDA

Beckett and I lay in bed on our second night together. I turn to him. "What's your dad like? Is he warm like your mom?"

He turns and looks into my eyes. "He's the opposite. He's cold. I'll never understand why they got married. It's so obvious that they're a mismatch. They got divorced when I was in elementary school. I have few memories of them together. I spent very little time with him. He's a big Philly lawyer. The only thing he ever cared about was me going to law school, and when I didn't, he barely spoke to me for years."

"What? You're one of the most successful people on the planet. How in the world could he think poorly of you?"

"He was a third-generation, male Windsor lawyer. It's like I fucked up the lineage by doing something else. And

112

the fact that I've stayed home with Andie for the past few years drives his male ego nuts."

"Does he see Andie?"

"He remarried about ten years ago to a woman my age. She hosts a ridiculously fancy dinner party once a month. Andie and I are invited. I kind of think it's about appearances. He looks like the doting grandfather. For the past year or two, Andie sleeps over that night. She hates it, but she muscles through it. He doesn't otherwise see her."

"What about Jenny's parents? Are they in the picture?"

"They live in Quebec and don't speak English. They come here one week a year and stay with us. That's it. I've told them the door is always open and I'll always pay for them to come, but that's all they do. Andie doesn't really remember them from visit to visit."

"That's sad. At least she has your mom. She's amazing."

"She's the best. I don't think I could have survived without her, especially at the beginning. I was a longtime bachelor and then single father to an infant. My mother stayed the first few months to teach me how to be a parent."

"She taught you well. You're a wonderful father. Andie adores you."

"I try my best. What about your family?"

I shake my head. "Jade has no grandparents. My mother split when I was a toddler. I have no memories of her. My father was an alcoholic who died shortly after I started college. Jade's father was estranged from his family due to his drug use. We were both junkies when we met. I got clean when I found out I was pregnant. It took him another eight years. By the time he got clean, his parents were gone. Jade didn't know her cousins until a few months before you and I met, when Declan started dating Melissa. Did you know Melissa when she was married to Jackson?"

"I did. Jackson is a few years older than me. We were both young and came up in the business world together. We've always had a kinship. He's a good guy. We ran in similar circles. She was always there on his arm."

"When she and Declan got serious, she brought him to meet her family. When they walked into Darian and Jackson's house to introduce him, it was the first time Declan had seen Darian in well over twenty years. Apparently, they had given him an ultimatum about choosing drugs or family, and he chose poorly. He never reconciled with his brother before he died. As I understand it, both Declan and Darian were shocked to see each other. But the good thing was that it was finally an opening for Jade to meet that side of the family. They have been incredible to her. Reagan gave her a job before she even graduated high school."

"They really respect Jade at Daulton. Despite her age, she has a crazy amount of responsibility. I was shocked when I first met her."

"I know. She's special. The whole thing worked out perfectly for her."

"I'll be working with her. I was with her today. I assumed she didn't know anything about us, so I said nothing."

"Of course she doesn't. I wouldn't even know how to explain this."

He nods. "It must have been hard for you, growing up without your mother and living with a sick father."

I sigh. "It was a nightmare. I grew up the worst way possible in a shitty, shady trailer park. When my dad lost his job, I was just entering high school. He spent his days at the local bar. My best friend, Reggie, who is still my best friend to this day, had this picture-perfect family. At least at that time they did. When things got unbearable with my father, they took me in. I lived with them throughout high school. I'm forever grateful to them."

"Wow, that's incredible."

"They paid for my first true painting class my freshman year in high school." I smile at the memory. "I forced them to sign a loan document that ensured they would be reimbursed, with interest, when I sold my first painting. One of my proudest days was when that happened. Jade was a baby. I didn't have any money to spare, but living up to my end of the bargain was more important to me than eating. I proudly gave them that check, even though it was every cent I had to my name that month."

He smiles as he tucks a loose strand of hair behind my ear. "You're adorable. Where does your sense of righteousness come from?"

"From wanting to be the opposite of my parents. From wanting to show my daughter the difference between right and wrong. I wasn't a perfect mother, and I think she has some baggage because of it, but I know she has a good value system."

"What makes you think you were imperfect? I think you're perfect."

"I have a natural, God-given ability to find the biggest losers on the planet and date them, thinking I can change them for the better. She witnessed the same routine over and over again. I think it's damaged her relationships with men. She won't get serious with anyone, and she has a thing for older men. I'm placing the latter part on Declan's shoulders. His vacancy at the beginning of her life undoubtedly caused that."

"Does she date?"

"You've seen my daughter."

He smiles.

"She garners a lot of attention from men. She always has."

He lets out a laugh. "I bet."

"She's looked like this since about fifteen and uses it as a weapon. She unapologetically moves from man to man, though I think she's secretly dating someone right now. I'm pretty sure she's going to Mexico with him next week."

"That's promising."

"Depends on who the man is, but I'm happy that she's possibly in a relationship. I think it will be good for her as long as he treats her well."

"Do you really think Jade would tolerate a man not treating her well?"

Now it's my turn to laugh. "Nope. She's much stronger than me in that sense."

He rubs my face. "Don't sell yourself short. You're a special woman. Despite always wanting me to date my entire life, I think you're the first woman my mother has genuinely liked. She's quite smitten with you."

"What about Jenny?"

He shakes his head. "She was happy that I was happy, but they weren't close. Jenny spoke with her mom for hours every day. She didn't make room for my mom in her life."

"It was her loss. Your mom is incredible."

"Agree."

"Does it still hurt? Losing her?"

"It hurts, but not for the reasons you think. I mostly just hurt for Andie having to grow up without a mother."

"What does that mean?"

He blows out a breath. "Nothing I care to discuss right now."

I decide not to pry, but I'm surprised by his answer. "Okay."

It's dark and quiet for a while, though it's clear neither of us are asleep.

Beckett whispers, "Are you still awake?"

"Yes."

"Can I ask you something and you promise to give me an honest answer?"

"Always."

"Did you really not know who I was the first night we met?"

"I honestly had no clue. I don't waste time on social media or gossip sites. I Googled you when I got home and was in complete and total shock."

"I love that."

"I wasn't in a good place, Beckett. I immediately told my husband that I kissed another man."

"You told him?"

"I couldn't live with that guilt. I was beside myself."

"I kissed you, not the other way around."

"I didn't stop you, and I kissed you back." I whisper, "And I liked it. A lot."

He reaches over and squeezes my hip. "So did I."

I WAKE in the morning to Beckett wrapped around me like a blanket. His hands are on my boobs on the outside of my shirt. What is it with him and my boobs?

I give myself two minutes to quietly enjoy it. It's not so bad having him hold me like this, enveloped in his yummy scent.

I don't want to embarrass him again, so I carefully

wiggle out of his hold without waking him. I brush my teeth, put on a bra, and head down to the kitchen.

I hear Glinda and Nico chatting. I'm dying to know if something is going on between them. They practically make googly eyes at each other every time I see them together.

I walk in and smile. "Good morning."

They both turn and return my smile. Glinda points to the coffee pot. "The coffee is fresh if you want a cup."

"I would love it. That's what I came for. Andie finished her painting last night before bed. I told her if it's dry, I'll wrap it and she can bring it to school for show and tell."

Glinda perks up. "I want to see the finished product."

"That's up to the artist." I look around. "Is Karen here?"

"She should be back from the market any minute. I told her to make cherry French toast today. Let's see how disciplined Beckett really is."

I giggle. "You're a bad, bad woman, Glinda Windsor."

"I'm not. I'm just starting to understand a few more things about my son and what drives him at times." She winks at me.

I smile as I leave and make my way to the studio. When I walk in, Andie is already in there. She gives me a guilty look. "I know you said not to touch it, but I wanted to see if it's dry."

"That's okay. Is it dry?"

She enthusiastically nods.

I give it a quick feel to make sure. It's dry. "I think—"

Before I can continue my thought, she's hugging my leg. "Thanks, Amanda. This is the best painting I've ever made. I can't wait to show it to everyone."

I crouch down so we're eye to eye. "It was all you." I tap her chest. "The talent is in here. I just helped guide it out."

"Really?"

"Really. I know a lot of adults who couldn't paint something this good. After school today, do you want to try painting people? It's a lot harder."

"Yes!" She hugs me again. "I can't wait."

"Good. Go get Gigi. She wanted to see your masterpiece before we pack it."

She leaves and I see Beckett in the doorway, dressed like a god in his suit. In his deep, gravelly voice, he says, "You're very good with her."

"I did raise a daughter."

"Thank you for the time you're spending with her. In just a few days, you've managed to *enchant* everyone in this house."

I smile. "I have a name to live up to."

When they return, Glinda gushes over Andie's painting. "This is your best painting ever."

Andie nods. "I know. I'm so excited." She turns to Beckett. "What do you have for me this morning?"

He scratches his sexy chin. "Let me think... If you're American when you go in the bathroom and American when you come out, what are you while you're in there?"

Andie shrugs. "I don't know."

"Euro-*pee*-in."

Glinda and I smile while Andie falls on the floor in a fit of laughter.

CHAPTER ELEVEN

AMANDA

The past three weeks have flown by. I've gotten so much painting done being in this space all day. And I'm enjoying having a full house in a way I've never experienced. I chat with Glinda in the mornings, I spend time with Andie after school, and then every night we're all together playing games or watching movies. It's the simple family life I never had but always wanted for Jade.

When Glinda and Andie go to bed, Beckett and I stay up and talk for hours. We know so much about each other now. It's like months and months of dating all compressed into a short period of time.

We've gradually gotten more and more comfortable around each other. Cuddling in bed has become our normal. Other than a few unconscious groping sessions, which I admittedly let go on longer than I should, he's remained respectful of my boundaries for the month.

I feel like this is a new level of intimacy for me. I've never simply gotten to know a man without anything physical happening between us. Our minds are connecting before our bodies. But it's not easy. I want the physical connection with him. I'm counting the minutes until this arrangement is over, and I can tell he feels the same. I feel it against my back every night.

Beckett set up the three meetings with collectors during this last week so that I had time to add to my collection. I feel ready to show them what I've got.

It's Sunday and we just met with a collector in town from Miami. Beckett arranged everything, but at my request, he remained silent and let me do the talking. He did recommend I significantly raise my prices. I was flipping out, as I've never sold anything at this rate, but I took his advice. The collector loved everything and severely overpaid for two paintings, asking to be informed of my future work.

He paid more than I normally make in a year. I'm floating in the clouds right now.

When we walk out, Beckett smirks at me. "I told you real collectors would appreciate your art."

I can't help but jump into his waiting arms. I sink my nose into his neck and take him in. "Thank you, Beckett. Thank you so much. This is the biggest sale of my career."

He squeezes me tight, and I can feel and hear him inhale me. It's getting harder and harder to resist him. Even his embrace is familiar and comforting to me now.

He releases me, and I slowly slide down the front of his big body. "The pleasure is all mine." His words are loaded, as our bodies are pressed together and we stare at each other.

It's not until Nico clears his throat by the car door that we eventually break apart.

We get into the black Suburban and he immediately takes my hand. He's always finding ways to touch me—my hand, my arm, my back. Him fondling me all night has become our normal. I can't say I mind it at all.

I turn to him. "What got you interested in collecting art in the first place?"

He looks down to where our hands are joined and rubs his thumb over mine. "It's my shared interest with my father. We aren't close and we never were. Our interests are polar opposites, but the one thing we've been able to talk about throughout the years is art. He has an extensive collection as well."

"It's nice that you have that."

"It's better than nothing. How did you get into painting?"

"I sketched a lot as a young kid. We couldn't afford painting supplies, so I started painting some of my sketches in art class at school. I had a teacher in junior high who used to give me access to the studio when she probably shouldn't have. She encouraged me to apply to an after-school painting program in high school. You know the rest of that story, including Reggie's family helping me."

He stares at me and nods as we pull through the front gates. He's still holding my hand, rubbing his thumb over mine. The sexual tension is getting thicker by the minute. I know it's about to reach a boiling point.

Glinda and Andie are at a play in Philly today and Karen is off, so the house is empty. We walk through the front door in silence and head up into our bedroom to change. Yep, I already think of it as our bedroom.

He's respectful though. He always goes into his closet to change in and out of clothes. I've never seen him in his underwear. I've never even seen him without a shirt. Like a creeper, I peek into the gym when he works out, hoping to get a glimpse, but he always has a shirt on. I'm dying to get a look at his body.

He walks straight into his closet and quickly emerges in athletic shorts and a T-shirt, his sneakers in hand.

"Are you going to work out?" I'm trying to mask my disappointment. I want to spend time with him.

"I'd much rather bend you over and fuck you senseless, but the gym will have to do. For now."

I think I'd like to be bent over and fucked senseless. I *know* I would. "One week. One week until our business arrangement is over."

"Yep. I've repeated that about a thousand times in my head today. Every day, for that matter."

Me too. The sexual energy between us already has my body temperature rising. I'm so damn attracted to him.

I bite my lip. "Would you maybe be interested in getting a little creative with our *non-physical* arrangement?"

His eyebrow arches. "What do you have in mind?"

I look down, unable to make eye contact during what I'm about to say. "I have to admit, I've been...*finger painting* a lot the past few weeks."

He grumbles, "I'm going to set a world record for *polishing the banister.*"

I look back up at him and smile that he's feeling the same way. "What if I were to...*finger paint* with you in the room, watching me, telling me what you want me to do?"

He takes a few deep breaths as the bulge in his shorts becomes more pronounced. "I'd say I'd like that very much."

I remove my shirt, leaving me in a white lace bra. You can definitely see my nipples through it. They're impossibly hard right now, practically poking through the fabric.

He stares at them, the bulge in his shorts now looking

like it might burst out of its confines. I'm dying to touch him.

I slowly slide my skirt down, revealing the matching panties. He grabs his cock on the outside of his shorts and breathes, "Holy shit. You're so fucking beautiful."

I seductively walk over to the bed, lay down on my back, and spread my legs open wide. "Tell me what you want me to do, Beckett."

His hand is inside his shorts now. "Rub yourself over your panties. Tell me what you feel."

I rub my panty-covered pussy. "It's warm and wet. I can feel the wetness seeping through my panties. My clit is throbbing, begging to be touched."

The hand not in his pants clenches as if he's trying to control himself. "Slide your fingers into your panties."

I do.

"What does it feel like?"

"Slippery. Warm. Needy. Swollen."

I see sweat now covering his brow. Seeing the effect I have on him is turning me on even more.

"Take your fingers out."

That surprises me, but I listen.

"Slide your fingers into your mouth."

I do, putting on a show of licking them clean.

"Tell me, do you like to taste yourself?"

I nod. "I do."

He licks his lips. "I bet you taste so good. Put them back into your panties."

I listen as my fingers move down my body until they return to my folds.

"How many fingers do you like to slip into your pussy, Amanda?"

"Two, sometimes three."

"You'll need at least three to prepare for my cock next week."

Oh god.

"Slide three in for now."

I do.

"Deeper. As deep as they can go."

I'm knuckle deep now.

"What does it feel like?"

I breathe, "Tight. Soft. Ready."

"Pump them in and out. You have no idea the things I'm going to do to that pussy next week."

I arch my back and moan his name. "Beckett. I want this to be you."

"Me too, beautiful girl. Now move your wet fingers to your clit."

I slide them up and convulse. Oh god, I'm so sensitive, so turned on by what we're doing.

"Touch your tits with your other hand."

I grab my left breast and squeeze it hard.

"Pull down your bra cup. Let me see your nipple."

I wasn't going to let him see anything, but I'm lost in the moment and don't hesitate to do as he asked.

"So perfect. Just like I dreamed. Is your nipple hard?"

"Yes."

"Does it need relief?"

"God yes."

"Squeeze it. Squeeze it hard while you rub your clit."

I do and I'm writhing all over the place.

"That's going to be my tongue next week. I'm going to devour every inch of your sweet body."

I breathe, "Yes."

I feel my orgasm quickly working its way to the surface. "Beckett, I'm about to come."

I look at his hand in his pants pumping his erection. I can tell he's almost there too, but I can't wait. The image of him like this is too much for me. I arch my back and yell out his name as I come harder than I've come in a really long time.

As soon as I stop my movements, he practically stomps over to me. He pulls my hand out of my panties and sucks those fingers into his mouth. My mouth widens at watching the deep pleasure he's taking in my taste. It sends him right over the edge as he grunts into his own orgasm, soaking his shorts.

He pulls his hand out but doesn't stop sucking my fingers, moving his tongue over them, savoring every last drop.

I grab his hand. His fingers are covered in his come. I suck them into my mouth and lick them clean, never breaking eye contact with him.

His eyes flutter as he pulls my fingers from his mouth. "One week. My mother leaves on Saturday. We're meeting with the last buyer on Saturday night. After that, you're mine."

I nod as we simply stare at each other. I can't wait.

BECKETT

It's taken every ounce of restraint I have not to rip her panties and bra off and sink some part of myself into her. I won't soon forget her taste. She's so fucking sexy. I'm struggling to manage myself. I'm trying to do this the right way though. I don't want to fuck it up.

We're both breathing heavily, staring at the other. We both just came, but neither is truly sated.

Her nipple is still out; my mouth is literally watering.

My fingers itch to touch her. The image of her sucking my come-soaked fingers into her mouth will have to sustain me for the week though she doesn't look like she wants to wait. Her face is flushed, and her lips are parted.

It feels like we're both about to crack, but it has to be her, not me.

Our sexually charged stare down is ended by her cell phone ringing. It's on the table next to the bed. She looks down at it and appears confused. She moves her eyes back to me before accepting the call. "It's Melissa. That's odd."

She accepts the call. "Melissa..."

"What...?"

"Slow down. What happened...?"

"A fistfight? Fucking Declan..."

"You have to be kidding me...."

"Is everyone okay...?"

"Do you know where she went...?"

"No, I'm not home. I'll head there now..."

"Yes, I'll let you know. I'll call if she shows up."

She ends the call and takes a huge breath as she stands and walks into her closet. I don't usually intrude on her space, but I want to know what's going on.

I stand there, waiting. She looks up at me while she gets dressed. "It's Jade. Declan found out about her boyfriend and, apparently, he got into a huge fistfight with the man. They literally crashed through a glass wall at Darian and Jackson's house. She said that the guy professed his love for Jade in front of the entire family, which of course she couldn't handle. She took off. No one knows where she went. She's probably headed to my house. I'm sorry. I need to go."

"Of course. If you're upset, I'll drive you."

"No thanks, I'm fine. I can drive myself."

She finishes throwing on sweatpants and a sweatshirt. "I don't know if I'll be back tonight. I'm really sorry. I hope your mom and Andie understand."

"Don't worry about us. Find Jade. Will you reach out later and let me know she's okay?"

She nods as she walks over and throws her arms around my waist. I hug her in return, taking in the scent of hair. I want to go with her and care for her. I'm so far gone for this woman.

I can feel her starting to sob. I kiss her head. "She'll be okay."

"She's like this because of me. I've fucked her up so badly. I make bad decision after bad decision."

I keep stroking and kissing her head. "Stop saying that. You're a wonderful mother. Don't forget it. Life is messy. Relationships are messy. Love is messy."

She nods her head into my chest as she starts to calm down. I lift her face and softly kiss her lips. "I'm here for you if you need me."

"Thank you. I have to go."

I walk her down and watch as she drives away. This will be our first night apart in three weeks. My heart fucking hurts.

B<small>Y THE TIME</small> I <small>SHOWER</small>, work out, and then shower again, Mom and Andie are home. Andie runs into the house and right past me without a word.

I clear my throat. "Hello, little lady."

She turns back. "Sorry, Daddy. Hello." She gives me a quick hug before she takes off for the studio. After a minute or two, she returns. "Where's Amanda?"

"She had to go be with her daughter."

Mom looks at me. "Is everything okay?"

"I'm not sure. Apparently her father got into it with her boyfriend."

"Oh no."

Andie looks up at me with worried eyes. "Is she coming back tonight? She said we could finish my latest painting."

"I'm not sure, baby. Her daughter needs her mom right now."

Andie's lower lip starts trembling. She's really come to rely on Amanda. I have mixed feelings on this.

I pick her up and kiss her cheek. "How about ice cream sundaes for dinner tonight? It is *Sunday*, after all."

Andie smiles and then scrunches her nose. "That was a terrible one, Daddy."

"I guess you don't want that for dinner. Karen left chicken and broccoli. We'll have that instead."

"No! Ice cream sundaes. Extra cherries."

I tickle her and she giggles. "Okay, deal."

We enjoy our sundaes, I give Andie a bath, and then she goes to bed.

Mom pours us two glasses of wine as we sit in the family room. "Have you heard from her?"

"No. She was really upset when she left. She blames herself for anything that goes remotely wrong in Jade's life. Jade's an adult. One that's mature beyond her years. Amanda can't do this to herself."

"You really care about her, don't you?"

"I do."

"Then explain why you've been faking this relationship the whole time."

I look at her in shock. She knows.

"I'm not stupid, Beckett."

"I know you're not. I'm sorry. I was just sick of you being on my case all the time about dating. It's hard for me, Mom."

"I know you loved Jenny—"

"It's not about Jenny. It's about me. Dating isn't simple for a man like me. No one ever wants the real Beckett. They want Beckett Windsor, the billionaire."

"Tell me what's true about your relationship with her."

"We did meet five years ago. We did have a connection. She had no clue who I was, and I loved that so much. Unfortunately, she was married. Unhappily, but still married. We shared a kiss. A magical kiss. She freaked out and left abruptly, but I was never able to get her or the kiss out of my mind. I didn't see her again until the first time you saw her."

"What about all her art in this house?"

"After we met, I looked into it. I was planning to buy a piece or two, to help her out, but for some reason, I was just drawn to her work. I can't explain it. It's like, if I couldn't have her, I wanted the next best thing."

"How did she end up here that day?"

"She had just found out about me buying all her art. She was pissed as hell. The timing was nothing more than a coincidence."

"Or perhaps it was fate."

I smile at the thought. "Maybe you're right."

"Why did she agree to this ruse? What's in it for her?"

"She wanted to pay me back for the pieces I bought, which of course I wouldn't accept. I told her if she stayed for the month, I would introduce her to three collectors. No guarantees, just the introductions. I'm presenting her with the opportunities. It's up to her what she makes of them."

"And what about your obvious attraction and chemistry? It's mutual, I can tell."

"We both feel it, but one of her conditions was nothing physical between us while we have this business arrangement. She said it would make her feel like a prostitute. I've tried to respect that. We've discussed it. In a week, when this is over, we want to give it a go and date for real."

"Andie is already attached to her."

I blow out a breath. "I know. I'm concerned about that if this goes south."

She stands and kisses my head. "Well, see that it doesn't. She's wonderful. I don't think a kinder, more genuine woman exists. I adore her."

She starts to walk out of the room, but I stop her. "Mom?"

"Yes."

"Why didn't you like Jenny?"

She pauses, as if choosing her words carefully. "Honestly, I never thought her intentions with you were true and honorable. I can't place my finger on anything specific. It was just my gut instinct. Perhaps I simply never connected with her. Amanda and I are cut from the same cloth. That's why I understand her. You'll never get anything but truth and honor out of her. She values that over anything materialistic. She's lived without *things* before. Like me, there was a time where all she had was her moral compass. Hers points dead north. Of that, I'm sure."

I nod in understanding and agreement. "You won't tell her you know, right? I don't want her to leave."

"I don't want her to leave either, but you might want to think about what's going to happen come next weekend."

"I will."

CHAPTER TWELVE

AMANDA

I've run every red light on the way to my house, but when I arrive, there are no signs of Jade. Shit. Where would she go? My poor baby.

I walk in and turn on all the lights. Looking around, I can't believe how empty it feels here now. I've only been at Beckett's for three weeks and I'm already used to a house full of people and laughter.

My phone rings and I see that it's Declan. I answer. "She's not here."

"Fuck. I screwed up."

"No shit. She's twenty-two. You can't beat up her boyfriends."

"He had his hands all over her body."

"You impregnated me when I was her age. It was more than your hands on me. She's an adult. She has sex, Declan. Accept it."

"I will do no such thing. He's a lowlife. I know guys like him. I *was* him."

"Is it Collin? Carter's friend?"

"Yes. How did you know?"

"I suspected."

"She's a fool for falling for his bullshit lines."

"Jade is a lot of things, but a fool isn't one of them. Because of us, she's never let a man in before. Now she finally has, and you throw the poor kid through a glass wall. Are you insane?"

"He's no kid. He's nearly forty. He's more age appropriate for you than her."

I see headlights shine in my driveway. It's Jade's car. "She's pulling in now."

"I'm on my way."

"No. Don't even think about it. She'll want to sleep here with me tonight. Come by in the morning after she's calmed down and had time to think. Don't come tonight, Declan. I mean it."

"But—"

I hear Melissa in the background. "Listen to Amanda. She's her mother. She knows what's best. We'll go by first thing in the morning."

She's so level-headed. I don't know how she puts up with him.

He sighs. "Fine. If anything changes, call me."

"I will."

I end the call just as Jade walks in the door. I hold my arms open for her. She collapses into me. "You heard?"

"Yes, Melissa called me. She figured you were on your way here."

She stands back to her full height. "Are you two besties now?"

"No, but we both love you and care about you. It sounds like we're not the only ones."

Her face drops. "She told you about that?"

"Yes. Why didn't you tell me?"

"We were supposed to be casual."

"Well, him professing his love for you in front of everyone doesn't sound very casual to me. Why did you leave?"

She hangs her head. "It was too intense."

I cross my arms. For a smart woman, she's not very smart about certain things. "He told you he loves you and you walked away?"

She shouts, "Yes, I'm fucked up. You know this about me. That's why you've had me in therapy since I was eight."

She doesn't get it. "I had you in therapy to deal with the anger you had for your father. You wouldn't talk to me, so I hoped you'd talk to her. Jade, you could have stopped at any point. Certainly, once you became an adult. Whether you admit it or not, you want to get past whatever ails you. Whatever has held you back from being in a real relationship all these years. Do you love him?"

She's silent for a bit before she croaks out, "I might. But what if he leaves me?"

This is my fault. She fears all men will leave because that's all she saw from me.

"What if he doesn't?"

She starts to cry. I can count on one hand how many times in my life I've seen my daughter cry. She prides herself on being so tough. He must really mean a lot to her. She's in love. I can see it written all over her gorgeous face. My baby is in love.

I gently touch her arm. "Tell me what you love about him. Articulate it."

Her defenses pop right back up. "He's hot as fuck."

Oh, Jade. I roll my eyes. "I'm aware. What else?"

She sits on the couch and exhales slowly before finally giving me a genuine answer. "I don't know, Mom. He likes me for me. *Loves* me for me. He likes my humor. He likes my wiseass comments and gives them right back to me in return. He makes me laugh. I can be myself with him, and that's what he wants. Me. Just as I am, complete with all the fucked-up parts. And the sex. Ahh. Holy shit."

I giggle. "Toe curling?"

She smiles. "*Everything* curling. He just...he makes me feel good. He makes me feel safe. He makes me feel cherished. He makes me feel wanted. He makes me feel good enough. I know it sounds weird. Does that make sense?"

We're so much alike. We crave all the same things, things we both missed in different ways growing up. I'm feeling so much the same right now with Beckett. She has no idea how much I can identify with her.

I caress her hair. "It makes perfect sense. You're the most wonderful woman I know. Of course he loves you. Why don't you call him? Tell him what you just told me."

She gives me her mischievous smile. "That he's good in bed? He knows."

I can only shake my head. "You know what I mean."

"I don't know if I'm ready. I don't know if I deserve him."

"Deserve him? Jade, you deserve the love of a good man."

She won't look me in the eyes.

"Look at me." She does. "You deserve to be happy. If he makes you happy, then I don't know what in the hell you're doing here. You need to eventually let yourself trust a man with your heart. It's always a risk. Sometimes the risk is worth the reward. Do you trust him?"

She's silent. She does trust him. I can see it. Wow.

Eventually, she nods. "Yes, I trust him. But what if it backfires?"

"There aren't any guarantees, but it sounds like you're in love with him as much as he's in love with you."

"Can we not talk about this right now? I can't deal with what happened today. Dad lost his shit. He broke a fucking glass wall. He's psycho."

"I knew you'd want to avoid it. Dad wanted to come here. I told him to come in the morning. Your old room is made up for you. You can shelve this for the night and then you need to be an adult and deal with them. Both Collin and your father."

"You're kind of bossy."

"At least you got one thing from me."

She laughs.

We get her favorite ice cream and watch one of her favorite childhood movies. We giggle and eat too much, just as we did when she was younger.

Admittedly, it's hard for me to focus on the movie at times. Maybe I should heed my own advice. I need to trust in what I'm feeling for Beckett, the way he makes me feel about myself.

I pull out my phone to text him.

Me: Sorry I left so abruptly. She's with me.

He responds immediately.

Beckett: Is she okay?

Me: I think so. We're doing a girls' night. We've got some stuff to work through in the morning. I'll let you know when I'll be back.

Beckett: Whatever you need.

Me: I miss you.

Beckett: My bed is so empty without you in it. I keep smelling your pillow.

Me: I guess no sleepfucking for you tonight.

Beckett: I may have faked it the past two times. I just wanted an excuse to touch you.

Me: I know. I didn't mind.

Beckett: One more week, cherry pie.

Me: Cherry pie?

Beckett: When I finally got a little sampling of you today, that's what you tasted like. Cherry pie.

I quickly look over at Jade to see if she notices my cheeks flushing. She doesn't.

Me: One more week. Good night.

Beckett: Sweet dreams, cherry pie.

When the movie is over, Jade starts toward her old bedroom but stops and looks around. "This house doesn't look very lived in right now. I'm thinking that maybe I'm not the only one whose toes have been curling."

I start toward my room without breaking stride. "Let's deal with your love life and then we'll get to mine."

She lets out a laugh. "I'm just happy to hear you have one."

Not yet, but maybe soon.

DECLAN AND MELISSA arrive first thing in the morning. Melissa suggests she and I go for a walk to get coffee so that Declan and Jade can be alone. I happily agree.

Melissa, being nearly as tall as Jade, looks down at me. "How was she last night? Yesterday was intense."

"I think she's in love with him, but this is new territory for her. She's never let anyone in before."

"Just remember that it's new territory for Declan too. No one will ever be good enough for her in his eyes. Though misguided, it comes from a place of love."

"I know." I smile. "It's amazing. Even all these years later, his temper hasn't waned in the slightest. He's exactly as hotheaded as he was back in the day."

She laughs. "I have no doubt. What about you? Have you dipped your feet in the dating pool yet?"

I'm silent.

Her eyes widen. "You've met someone." It's not a question. It's a statement.

"I'm not sure what we are. I'm definitely not ready to talk about it. The situation is a little odd."

"Say no more. Whenever you're ready."

We enjoy our coffee. When we return, Declan says they found some common ground. Jade is in her room talking with Dr. Pearl. That reminds me, I'm overdue for a session. She has no idea what's been going on with me.

Declan and Melissa leave, and when Jade surfaces she says she isn't ready to go home. I'm obviously not leaving her. I text Beckett that I won't be back today but will return tomorrow.

CHAPTER THIRTEEN

AMANDA

At some point in the early evening, Jade changes her mind and decides to go home and sleep at her place. After a few hours alone, I realize that I don't really want to stay here by myself, so I drive back to Beckett's house.

When I walk in, Glinda is surprised to see me. "Hey, sweetie. I didn't think you were coming back tonight. How's Jade?"

I can't help but smile. "In love. It's so nice to see."

"How exciting. Do we like him?"

"I don't know him. He's friends with her cousins. I think I've seen him once or twice in passing at various events, but I've never met him. He definitely loves her though, and I'm simply thrilled about it."

"That's wonderful. Beckett didn't know you'd be returning. He's not here."

I can't mask my disappointment. "Oh. Where did he go?"

"I don't know. He and Nico said they had something to attend."

"All right. I'm turning in. It's been an emotional twenty-four hours."

"I'm glad you're back."

"Me too."

I'M AWAKENED in the middle of the night to the bedroom door flying open. Nico is holding a clearly drunk and seemingly battered Beckett. Nico mumbles, "Shit. I thought you weren't here tonight."

I pop right up and notice swelling and blood around Beckett's lips and eyes. "Oh my god. What happened to him?"

"He'll be fine. He drank a bottle of whiskey to numb the pain. He's had ice on the injuries. He doesn't bruise easily. He'll be good as new in the morning."

"Where did this happen?"

"It's not my business to discuss."

He carries Beckett to the bed and lays him down. He nods my way and just before he closes the door, he says, "I'll see you tomorrow."

I glance at the clock. It's after two in the morning. Where the hell was he?

Beckett is mumbling incoherently. I run into the bathroom and wet a washcloth. I sit next to him and start to clean the wounds on his face, but he immediately picks me up to straddle his body. My legs are on either side of his waist.

I continue to clean as he slides his hands up my shirt

and grabs hold of my bare breasts. I can only roll my eyes. He's truly obsessed with them.

"What happened?"

He starts squeezing my breasts and laughing.

"Beckett!"

He sighs. "Sometimes I like to feel the pain. I *need* it. Sometimes I like when people don't give a shit what my name is. Do you care about my name?"

"No. I care about you. And I don't like seeing you hurt."

His jaw ticks. "I've been hurting for as long as I can remember."

"Why? What happened to you?"

"No one cares about me. The real me." He moves his hands to the sides of my body and caresses me in a more delicate manner. "But I think you might."

I rub the unbattered parts of his face. "I do care about you."

He lifts one of his hands and rubs my face in return. "You're so perfect. I think I might be in love with you, but don't tell Amanda. I don't want to scare her away. I don't want her to leave me."

As he finishes the sentence, his face falls to the side and he passes out cold. I continue cleaning his wounds as carefully as I can.

When I'm done, I try to undress him, but he's like dead weight. I can't lift any part of him, so I simply lay a blanket over him and get into the bed.

I turn and look at him. Even in his sleep, he looks worried. Something is weighing on him. I wonder if I know him as well as I think I do.

BECKETT

I wake in the morning wrapped around Amanda's little body. My hands are under her shirt. She has the best tits. I'm dying to explore them fully.

I can't help but tweak her nipples a bit. She mumbles, "I know you're not sleepfucking."

I chuckle. "Damn, I never should have admitted that to you."

She giggles before turning around and facing me. I decide to leave my hands on her tits, but when she gives me an incredulous look, I reluctantly pull them away. I may also pout a little bit.

She touches the side of my face. "Does it hurt?"

Oh shit. I forgot about that. I look down. I'm still in my clothes from last night. "It's nothing."

"It doesn't look as bad as I thought it would. You must have superhuman healing powers."

"I'm kind of like Superman. Maybe Batman. Who's the sexiest superhero?"

"Stop joking. Tell me what happened."

I sit up. Ooh. My head hurts. "Nothing for you to worry about."

"You showed up in the middle of the night, wasted, looking like you went twelve rounds with Mike Tyson. Consider me officially worried."

"You've seen me train. I fight from time to time. It's not a big deal."

"I thought you sparred to keep in shape, not to actually fight people."

"Sometimes I like to fight."

"You're the dumbest smart person I know. Why do you like to fight?"

I lean my head back on the headboard. I close my eyes, hoping she'll forget her line of questioning.

"Beckett!"

Damn. She didn't forget.

"The men in the ring with me don't give a crap about my name or status. I'm just their enemy in that moment. It's refreshing."

"What about pain? Last night you said something about needing to feel pain."

I have a big mouth when I drink. Standing, I say, "I don't have time for this. I need to shower and get to work."

"I don't want you fighting."

I turn back to her. "Well, you have no fucking say in what I do. We're not married. We're not even dating."

Like a child, I storm off into the bathroom and take a long, hot shower, full of shame for the way I treated her.

When I'm dressed for the day, I find Amanda and Andie in the studio painting. They have such a seamless, easy relationship.

At some point, Andie notices me. "Hi, Daddy. You were wrong. Amanda came back. I told you she would."

"Happy to be wrong." I walk in and kiss Amanda's head, whispering, "I'm sorry."

She nods.

I turn to Andie. "You're not dressed. Don't you have school?"

"We're off today. Amanda and I are painting all day."

"Sweetie, Amanda has to finish a few paintings to

show some important people. She might need to be left alone."

Amanda waves me off. "It's fine. We work well together. You're my official assistant, right, Andie?"

Andie grins widely before turning to me. "Got one for us this morning?"

"Hmm. Since you don't have school, maybe it should be educational. How do you fit one hundred math teachers into a room that only fits ninety-nine people?"

Andie thinks for a moment. "I don't know. How?"

"You carry the one."

Amanda snort laughs.

Andie looks confused. "I don't get it."

"That might be first grade math. I'll tell it again next year."

"Then tell me another. Math that I can do."

"I'm not a corny dad joke machine."

Amanda nods as she smiles at Andie. "Yes, he is."

Andie giggles.

I think for a moment. "Do you know why we make soup with two-hundred and thirty-nine beans?"

"Why?"

"Cause one more would make it too-farty."

Both of my girls are in a fit of giggles now, just how I like them.

IT's the middle of the night when I hear a cell phone ringing in our room. I lift my head and see that it's Amanda's. She's out cold.

I'm once again holding her with my hands up her

shirt. She doesn't ever seem to mind though, often subtly wiggling into me, encouraging it.

I pull them out and squeeze her hip while whispering in her ear, "Amanda, your phone is ringing."

She stirs for a moment before reaching for it and accepting the call. She croaks out, "Hello..."

"Collin? What's wrong? Relax. Tell me what's going on..."

"Oh my god. Is she okay...?"

"Which hospital...?"

"I'll be there in twenty minutes. Calm down, sweetie. She'll be okay. I'm sure the whole labor scene grossed her out. I'll see you soon."

She ends the call and sits up. "Jade and Collin are at the hospital. Both Reagan and Skylar are in labor. Carter and Lance were out of town, so Collin and Jade were in the delivery room helping. Apparently Jade passed out. Collin sounds frantic. He said they won't tell him anything because he's not her husband. I need to head down there."

"I'll drive you."

"No, you go back to sleep. You need to be here for Andie when she wakes in the morning."

I sit up. "No, I want to be there for you. Mom is here with Andie. She'll be fine."

"How will I even explain your presence?"

"I don't really care, but I'll wait in the lobby if you prefer. I just want to be there for you. Let me."

"Okay. We need to hurry though."

We quickly get dressed and make our way to the hospital. When we walk in, a man I assume is Collin is waiting by the front door.

My first thought is that he's older than I would have imagined for Jade. He must be close to forty. He's got shoulder-length hair, is well built, and has worry written all over his face.

He introduces himself to Amanda, warmly hugging her, and then shakes my hand. "She's still out cold. They said we can go in when you arrive. Declan is causing a whole shit storm up there."

She sighs. "What else is new?" She turns to me. "You'll wait here?"

"If that's what you want." It's not what I want.

She nods and I sit. For nearly two hours, I sit and wait. I wish she'd let me be there for her. I'm going out of my mind.

She eventually walks back into the lobby looking completely dumbfounded.

I stand and quickly make my way to her. "Is everything okay?"

"I'm...umm...I'm going to be a grandmother. Jade and Collin are having a baby. She's pregnant. Everyone is in a bit of shock."

I smile and hug her. "Congratulations. How did Jade take it?"

"In typical Jade fashion. She cracked like six inappropriate jokes and then kicked me out of the room so she and Collin could take a shower together."

I can't help but laugh. "That sounds like Jade."

"She just wants to get to Reagan and Skylar when they're done, so I don't need to be here."

"Any word on them?"

"I don't know. I wasn't on the maternity floor."

As we make our way to the car, she's distant. I squeeze her hand. "Are you okay?"

"I'm just in shock. Even though I know my age, I don't think I ever officially closed the door on me having more kids until just now."

"You want more kids?"

"I've always wanted more. I just never met the person I wanted to have them with." She looks away. "I guess that ship has sailed now. I suppose it's time for my heart to catch up to Mother Nature."

She's a bit distant on the ride back to my place. The sun is just coming over the horizon as we pull in through the front gates.

When the car stops, she turns to me. "Thanks for coming with me."

"My pleasure. Why don't you run a bath for yourself, and I'll make your morning coffee and bring it to you."

She smiles. "Is this just an excuse so you can see me naked?"

I unashamedly reply, "Absolutely."

About fifteen minutes later, I make my way into our bathroom with her coffee in hand. She's in a bubble bath with her hair up. Her cheeks are flushed from the warm water. Her eyes are closed, and her head is leaning back. I can't stop staring at her. She's like a work of art. Perfection.

She must hear me because she opens her eyes and I hand her the coffee. She smiles. "Thank you."

She takes a few sips before placing it on the ledge. I move behind her and start massaging her shoulders. She moans in delight and my cock stands at immediate attention. I can't wait to hear those moans this weekend when I'm inside her.

"That feels so good."

Yep, sweetheart. You're going to be screaming that this weekend.

She aimlessly runs her fingertips over my working hands until she begins to pull them down toward her tits.

I grab them and tug on her nipples. I can't help myself as my lips find her neck. I love the way she tastes and smells. She's so soft and feminine.

I whisper in her ear, "I can't wait to be inside you this weekend. I'm going to make you come over and over again."

Her hands are over mine, encouraging the movements. She tilts her head back and spreads her legs wider. "I want you so badly. I'm physically throbbing for you. Touch me. I can't wait any longer."

I happily start to move my hand down her body, dying to touch her, when we hear, "Daddy? Amanda?"

Andie's voice coming from the hallway is like a bucket of ice water. I lift my hands and kiss her cheek. "This weekend. After our final meeting on Saturday night. Don't make any plans that involve walking for a few days."

She bites her lip and nods.

CHAPTER FOURTEEN

AMANDA

It's Friday morning and we're meeting with the second collector. It's an early morning meeting, so we're up and dressed before breakfast.

We're in the kitchen with Andie, Glinda, and Karen.

As she does every morning, Andie lights up when she sees Beckett. He does the same when he sees her. She jumps into his arms and lifts her eyebrows in wait.

"Hmm. I went to the beekeeper to get twelve bees. He gave me thirteen. I said, *sir, you gave me an extra*. He said, *it's a free bee*."

Andie giggles, like she does every morning. Glinda rolls her eyes, like *she* does every morning. I love their little tradition.

Beckett asks her, "Are you looking forward to seeing Grandy and Buffy?"

My jaw drops. "Your father's wife's name is Buffy?"

Glinda scoffs and mumbles, "Fricking pretentious names. Nothing is worse than his though."

I ask, "What's his name?"

"Ignatius Prescott Windsor the third."

I burst out laughing.

"Can you believe he wanted to name Beckett that? He'd be the fourth. Ugh. I refused. Beckett is still pretentious, but I like it."

Beckett clears his throat. "I happen to like my name."

I smile. "It suits you, but your mom is totally right. I couldn't agree more. It reminds me of that woman, Bunny, you introduced me to the night we met."

Glinda lets out a laugh. "Bunny Pendleton?"

Beckett nods.

"She's been after him since they were kids."

Beckett sighs. "Anyway, we're all going to dinner tonight, right?"

Glinda fake coughs twice in an over-exaggerated fashion. "I think I'm coming down with something. It's best I stay home."

I love her.

I nod in agreement. "I'll stay with Glinda."

Andie also nods. "I'll stay with Amanda and Gigi."

Beckett looks annoyed. "Mom did her time with him. She doesn't have to come. You two are coming, like it or not."

REGGIE AND VICTORIA hold up their piña coladas. Reggie proclaims, "Congrats to Amanda for being the superstar I always knew she'd become. I'm so fucking proud of you."

We clink our glasses and each take a huge gulp of our frozen drinks.

I had another incredibly successful meeting with a collector this morning. Beckett forced me to raise my prices again. He said it makes my work seem more in demand. He was right. I sold three more pieces. And this guy mentioned that he has friends he knows would love my work. I can't believe it. I've never been this financially stable in my life.

"Thank you. This is all a dream come true. It's all thanks to Beckett."

Reggie shakes her head. "Beckett made the introductions, but it's all thanks to *your* talent."

Victoria nods. "Agreed. You're brilliant and it's finally being recognized."

Reggie holds her glass back up. "And tomorrow night, may you have category-five orgasms."

I giggle and nod. "Amen to that."

Victoria pinches her eyebrows. "What's a category-five orgasm?"

Reggie and I smile at this decades long joke of ours. She motions for me to tell Victoria. "You know how hurricanes are categorized from one to five with five being the strongest?"

Victoria nods. "Yes."

"We rate orgasms similarly. Category fives are the type that you very rarely have, but when you do, you practically black out from the pleasure."

Her eyes widen. "Shit. I don't think I've ever had one of those. Maybe a category-four once or twice, but never near-blackout level."

Reggie shrugs. "You need to get Cliff on that."

Victoria turns to Reggie. "Do you have them?"

"Sometimes. I normally live in the three to four zone, but Sam will up his game and sprinkle in a five a few times a year."

She looks at me. "What about you?"

"I haven't had above a category-three in twenty years. The closest I came was when Beckett talked me through masturbating last week."

Reggie fans herself. "That was so fucking hot. I told Sam about it and that I want to do something similar."

I nod. "It was crazy hot. I think the forbidden aspect of it made it hotter."

Victoria rubs my arm. "Are you excited for tomorrow? Your arrangement is over and you're free to be together."

"I think I'm excited and scared."

She pinches her eyebrows together. "Why scared?"

"In the back of my mind, I always think about how different we are. You haven't seen his house, but it's so over-the-top ridiculous. If I had all the money in the world, I don't think I'd want a house that big. It's not comfortable to me. I love parts of it, but not all of it. I just wonder where our relationship could ever go. I don't see myself in that lifestyle, and the last thing I need is another broken heart. I've had more than my fair share in my lifetime."

Reggie shrugs and nonchalantly says, "Prince Charming lives in a palace."

I smile. "I suppose he does. Enough about me. What are you and Sam doing for your twentieth anniversary tomorrow night?"

Her face lights up. "I don't know. He's surprising me. He said to dress up and pack an overnight bag. I'm so excited."

I love that, after twenty years, my best friend is still so in love. "I bet it's going to be so romantic. Did you buy any special lingerie for your evening?"

Her face drops. "Do I appear to be the type of woman

who'd look good in lingerie? I took a bath yesterday, and I swear I saw the water in the toilet rise."

Victoria starts laughing but I smack her arm. "Cut it out. As far as I know, Reg, you're the only one of us who's kept a man happy for twenty years. And not just any man. A great man. A man who's attracted to you and madly in love with you. I've certainly never been able to do that."

I see a smile creep up on her lips. "I suppose you're right."

"I say we make a quick stop after lunch and buy you something special to wear to bed tomorrow night. My anniversary gift to you two."

Her smile grows bigger as she nods. "I think I'd like that."

WE'RE on our way to Beckett's father's house for dinner. I'm nervous. I'm in a white, knee-length, casual dress with a pink sweater and strappy sandals. Glinda told me to prepare for assholes, so I'm keeping my expectations low.

Andie is in a red polka dot dress and smiles goofily in the back as Beckett sings along to some child friendly music. I love that he willingly embarrasses himself just to make her smile.

Andie leans forward. "Dad, tell me a joke."

"I'm not a machine. That's a morning thing. It gives me time to research."

I've seen him Google corny dad jokes before bed at night to prepare himself. I love it so much.

Andie pleads, "How about a mind twister? I like those."

I raise my hand. "Can I tell one?"

Becketts smiles. "Please do."

I turn back to Andie. "What word becomes shorter when you add two letters to it?"

She takes a few minutes to think, clearly running through a list of words in her head. "Ugh. I don't know. What?"

"Short."

Beckett lets out a laugh. "That might be the corniest one of them all."

It takes Andie a minute, but she gets it and starts giggling. I don't think I'm as good at this as Beckett, but I'm trying.

We pull up to yet another mansion. It's not as impressive as Beckett's, but if I saw this house a month ago, it would've been the biggest I'd ever seen.

Beckett grabs Andie's bag from the trunk. She's staying over before Glinda picks her up in the morning for their promised trip to New York City. Nico is picking them up Sunday morning and dropping Glinda at the airport to go back to Florida, and then Andie will come home with him.

A valet takes Beckett's car, and we make our way inside. People I assume are Beckett's father and his wife greet us at the door. Beckett and his father shake hands like business associates. They don't hug like a father and son should.

Both his father and his father's wife give me a once over, both glancing for extended periods at the tattoos around my ankle and the added piercings in my ear. They don't care that the tattoos are a tribute to my daughter and a friend lost too soon. They're just judging me, disliking me immediately.

Beckett's father looks back to him and sternly says, "How's it going, Mr. Mom? What did you do today, get your nails done and have yourself a little bikini wax?"

Beckett simply rolls his eyes and throws his arm around me. "Dad, Buffy, this is my girlfriend, Amanda Tremaine."

They hold their hands out for me to shake, which I do. I try to smile. "It's nice to meet you both."

Without answering, they turn to hug Andie, but not as grandparents should. It's an arms-length hug. And they call her Andrea. When Beckett reminds them that she prefers Andie, they make a comment about it being a masculine name and not appropriate for a young lady.

They invite us inside. It seems there are about twenty other people already here. The large, exceedingly long dining room has an equally long fancy table set for everyone. They even assign seats. We're seated next to his father and Buffy.

I smile to myself as I think how different this is from dinners at Darian and Jackson's house, which often consist of Chinese takeout boxes and paper plates. Their house, despite exuding excessive wealth, is informal, warm, and all about precious family time. This house is formal, cold, and all about appearances. The money isn't different. Jackson and Darian have a lot of it. It's the people that are different.

His father looks at me. "What is it you do, Amanda?"

"I'm an artist."

Beckett's eyes light up with pride. "You should see her paintings, Dad. She's so talented. If you want to come by the house sometime, I have a lot of her work up. I think you'd really like it."

His father gives a smug look. "Ah, I see. I imagine you can open a lot of doors for her."

Beckett's jaw tightens, understanding the implication. "It's not like that."

"So you haven't introduced her to someone like Greg LeMaine?"

That's who we met with this morning.

"Well, yes, and he loved her work."

His father gives a self-satisfied smile. "I thought as much."

Dinner is horribly awkward. I have nothing in common with any of these people. Andie seems equally bored, so she and I make our own good time, chatting away. I learn that she's really becoming good friends with Dylan Knight. I bet the two of them are adorable together. I encourage Andie to invite Dylan over for a painting party. She's excited at the prospect.

At some point, Andie asks to use the restroom. Beckett starts to stand, but I grab his arm. "I'll take her."

"Are you sure?"

"Absolutely." Not only am I happy to take Andie, there's no way in hell I'm being left alone at the table with these people.

We make our way toward the bathroom, and I encourage her to take her time, in no rush to return. When we're done, I ask her if she's still hungry. She says no, so we find some fancy couch to sit on.

I intertwine my fingers with her little ones. "Andie, what's your favorite fairytale?"

"Hmm. Daddy doesn't like fairytales, so he never reads them with me."

She's right. He reads to her all the time, but never fairytales. And I've never seen any princess items around the house. Jade had a ton of that stuff as a kid.

"Why doesn't he like them?"

"He says he doesn't like the princesses in those stories. He said he wants me to be stronger than them. That they're not role models. I think he once called them *bimbos*. What's a bimbo?"

I can't help but smile. Beckett Windsor, the feminist. Dr. Pearl would love him and his thoughts on fairytales.

"I guess it's a woman who may be pretty but isn't very smart."

"Like Buffy?"

I let out a laugh. "*Exactly* like Buffy." I tickle her stomach and she giggles. "You, madam, are both beautiful *and* smart. I can't wait for you to meet Jade. She's beautiful and smart too."

"Can I meet her soon?"

"Maybe. We'll talk to your dad."

Our conversation is interrupted by Beckett's father. "There you are. Andrea, it's rude to leave the table for more than a few minutes. You should head back."

We start to stand, but he holds up his hand. "Actually, I'd like to have a word with Amanda. Andrea, you head along. We'll be there in a minute."

When Andie leaves the room, Beckett's father motions for me to sit, which I do. He closes the door to the room before turning back to me.

"Amanda, what's your endgame with my son?"

"What do you mean?"

"Where do you see this going?"

"I don't know. We're dating. We're getting to know each other."

"You can't possibly think that someone of Beckett's stature could end up with a woman like you, do you?"

"That's for Beckett and me to decide, not you."

"I saw the way my son looks at you. I don't like it. I don't like it at all."

He looks my body up and down in a lascivious manner and then adjusts himself. "Trust me, I understand the appeal. You're an incredibly attractive woman. The kind you enjoy a small handful of times at most." He licks his lips. "Maybe even on the side of a marriage. But you, young lady, are not marriage material for people in Beckett's world. He needs to present himself a certain way to society, and you're most definitely not it. You're too different. You must know that on some level. Run along before you get hurt. I'm only telling you this for your own good. I'm trying to spare you the eventual pain."

Tears sting my eyes as he articulates insecurities that have run through my head many times over the past month.

"And what about Andrea? She needs to be raised by a proper woman so she can become one. Not a woman who undoubtedly grew up in a trailer park. If you care about them, do what's best for both of them and leave now before anyone sinks deeper into this."

Now the tears stream down my face. He's right. I need to get out before we get any deeper. I'm falling for Beckett. I think he's falling for me too. But I don't belong in his world. We need to end this before someone gets hurt, especially Andie. She doesn't deserve it.

He pulls out a checkbook. "Now, I bet I know what you really want. What will it take for you to walk away? Better yet, what will it take for you to walk away from Beckett but then perhaps be available to me a night or two a week?"

I stand and gather myself, wiping away the tears. "I'm not for sale. You can shove your money up your pretentious asshole. Go to hell."

I open the door and walk out. Beckett is standing there. He undoubtedly notices my teary eyes and looks concerned. "Is everything okay?"

I swallow down the pain, not wanting to cause any kind of scene. "Yep. Fine."

He reluctantly nods. "People are leaving. We should get Andie settled and then head out."

I forgot she was staying here. "Let's take her with us."

"No, it's her one time with my father a month. It's important."

"Beckett, I don't want her staying in this place. It's not best for her."

He stiffens. "You'll have to remind me when Andie's parenting became a joint venture for us. You have no say in this matter. You're not her mother, you never will be. She's staying."

I think that hurts more than anything his asshole father just said to me. I hold back my tears as I wordlessly nod and make my way to Andie.

I crouch down and hug her. I know this is likely the last time I'll see her. I squeeze her tight. "I'll really miss you."

She hugs me back. "I'll miss you too, but I'll see you in two days, right?"

I can't lie to her, and I can't hold back the tears. I manage to croak out, "Have the best time with Gigi in New York. You're so lucky to have her."

She pulls back and wipes my tears from my face with her little fingers. "Don't cry, I'll be home soon. We can paint together when I get home, I promise."

I stand and Beckett says his goodbyes to her.

I take in her adorable face one last time before we head out the door.

CHAPTER FIFTEEN

BECKETT

Amanda was silent the entire ride home. Something has shifted between us, and not for the better.

We pull into the driveway of my house. I turn to apologize for snapping at her, but she doesn't listen and immediately gets out of the car and walks quickly toward the front door.

As soon as it opens, she practically sprints upstairs.

Mom walks out of the family room, her favorite spot in the house. "Where's Amanda?"

"She ran upstairs. Something is wrong. She was upset when she left a room she had been in with Dad. Then she basically demanded that Andie not sleep there."

Mom looks behind me, noticing no Andie. "What did you say to upset her after your father quite obviously was rude to her?"

I mumble, "Something about her not being Andie's mother and having no say."

"Oh, Beckett. You're a fool." She points toward the stairs. "Go up there and make this right. Don't ruin the best thing that's ever happened to you."

I nod. "You're right."

I run up the stairs, two at a time. When I enter the bedroom, she's frantically packing her bags.

"What are you doing?"

Her head is down in her bags. "I'm packing. Our deal is over tomorrow. Your mom is flying out and I'm meeting with the final buyer. I'm heading home after dinner."

"I don't want you to leave."

She turns her head and I see her tear-stained face. "It's time for me to go. I don't belong here."

"What about us?"

"There is no us. You're a fantasy for me, not reality. We come from two different worlds. Two worlds that can't mix."

"That's bullshit. What did my father say to you?"

"Nothing I didn't know deep inside."

She walks into the bathroom and closes the door, walking out a few minutes later in sweatpants and a sweatshirt. She's never worn that much clothing to bed before. It's always a T-shirt and small shorts. She's blocking me from her body.

Without another word, she climbs into bed and turns the other way.

I WAKE in the morning to an empty bed. I quietly walk downstairs, seeing Mom's bags by the door. Every time she leaves it's like a double-edged sword. I'll miss having her around, but it's nice to get a little privacy back.

I hear Amanda and my mother in the kitchen. Drinking coffee together and talking has become their early morning ritual.

I move closer so I can hear what they're saying.

Amanda says, "I'll really miss you, Glinda. No matter what happens, can we still be friends?"

"Of course, sweetie, but nothing is going to happen. Beckett wants and needs you in his life. So does Andie."

It's silent for a moment before I hear Mom say, "Don't cry. Everything will be okay."

Amanda sniffles. "We're too different, Glinda. I don't belong in this crazy house in this crazy world. I'm a jeans and T-shirt girl. I'm happy with a book and fireplace or family game night, not some fancy dinner party full of snotty assholes."

Mom lets out a laugh. "Now you know why I was *sick* last night."

"It made me sick to be there. Sorry, but your ex-husband is the biggest dickhead I've ever met. I'm not sure how you were married to him."

"I can't disagree with that. Did Ignatius say something to you? You shouldn't listen to a word that pompous ass says."

"It doesn't matter. He just opened my eyes to the truth I've always known was there."

I hear a chair screech as if one of them stood up. I

peek in. Amanda is walking over to Mom and hugs her. "Thank you for being so wonderful. I hope they know how lucky they are to have you."

I see Mom tearing. "They're lucky to have you too."

Amanda croaks, "Goodbye Glinda."

I hide as she makes her way out of the kitchen and quickly walks back upstairs.

Just then, Nico walks in. "Are you ready Glinda?"

She nods and motions toward her suitcases. Nico grabs them and heads out to the car. She pulls me into a hug and kisses my cheek. "Make things right with her."

"I will. I promise."

I watch her leave and then head upstairs. Amanda is in the studio. She's writing in a notepad.

"What are you doing?"

"I'm leaving some instructions for Andie for a few of the styles she wanted to learn. Please read them to her. Tell her to call me if she's having any problems."

"Why don't you stay and teach her?"

She steels her face. "No. Our deal was one month. I've lived up to my end of the bargain. I can't be in this house anymore, living this life. It's not me." She pauses for a brief moment. "I'm comfortable in two rooms in this house. The family room and this studio. Does it ever strike you as odd that I spend minimal time anywhere else? I can't be here anymore. I don't belong."

"But if you—"

"What time and where are we meeting with the last buyer?"

"Seven. We're going to a small club to see a band play with them. They're younger and more casual than the other two buyers."

She nods as she stands to close the door in my face. "Okay, I'll see you at seven."

DESPITE BEING in the same house, we didn't talk or see each other all day. I was in my home office, and she was in her studio.

It's just before seven and I walk in the bathroom to see Amanda putting the final touches on her makeup. "You look beautiful."

She's in a strapless, short, tight leather dress. The zipper runs diagonal across the front from top to bottom. Her hair is in a stylish ponytail, tight on the sides and looser up top. She's wearing a black choker that's making my dick twitch. I've never been more jealous of a piece of plastic jewelry in my life.

Our eyes meet in the mirror, and she forces a smile. "Thank you."

"You're very rock and roll tonight."

She lets out a small laugh. That's progress. "You said we're going to club to see a band play."

I can't help but smile. "It's a jazz club."

Her eyes widen as she looks herself up and down. "Oh, maybe I should change."

I grab her arm. "Don't you dare." I need this image to jerk off to later. "You're perfect just as you are. I think you'll like this place. It's a hole in the wall, off the beaten track. Jackson Knight introduced me to it years ago."

"Okay, and the buyer is meeting us there?"

"No, they'll be here any minute to pick us up. I thought they could take a look at some of your pieces in person. They've only seen pictures, being from Texas, and we can't exactly bring paintings into the club."

She nervously nods. She doesn't like the sales end of her business. It's a necessary evil, but she simply enjoys the creative aspect.

She pinches her eyebrows. "They? Two of them?"

"Yes, a husband and wife. They're good friends of mine." I look around as I notice that all of her belongings are gathered together. "Are you looking forward to getting back to your normal life?"

She smiles in a way that doesn't quite reach her eyes. "I am." She nods toward her packed bags. "I'll head out after our evening."

"You don't need to rush."

"I have no reason to stay here. Your mother is gone, and our deal will be over."

Before I can respond, the doorbell rings. "That must be them."

"Is Karen getting the door?"

I hold out my hand for her. "No, I gave her the rest of the weekend off. It's rare to get a quiet house to myself. Nico will go out with us, but then I'm dismissing him too."

I had given them all the weekend off, thinking Amanda and I would want privacy in the house.

I hold out my hand, and she places her soft hand in it as we make our way downstairs. I'm realizing it may be one of the last times I get to hold it. I'm going to savor the sensation.

I open the door and see my friends smiling. "Blaire, Axel, this is the very talented Amanda Tremaine. Amanda this is Blaire and Axel Broxton." Axel is a giant of man with dark, curly hair. Blaire is a petite, stunning redhead.

Amanda holds her hand out and smiles, clearly having no clue who they are. She's so adorably naïve sometimes. It's endearing.

"It's nice to meet you two. What brings you to the area?"

Blaire and Axel both smile, loving that she doesn't know them. Blaire answers, "Axel had a...work obligation in New York City." Yep, the NFL draft where he got to announce his team's draft pick. "Beckett said we absolutely had to stop by Philly to see your work. Our kids have never been, so we took them sightseeing today."

Amanda's face lights up. "How old are your kids?"

"Our daughter, Carrie, is eleven, our other daughter, Danica, is two, and we have triplet sons who are four and may very well be the spawn of Satan."

Amanda laughs. "Wow. You have your hands full."

Axel nods. "God yes." He pulls Blaire close. "My wife is superwoman." He nuzzles into her neck. "And she puts up with me."

Blaire smiles in agreement. "He's usually more difficult than the kids."

Amanda laughs again as she motions for them to come inside. "Please come in."

They take about thirty minutes to look at her artwork in the studio and around the house. It's clear that they like it. They're already asking her how many pieces are available. Amanda is beaming. It's wonderful to watch.

We head outside to their limo, with Nico joining the driver in the front, and begin our journey to the jazz club. Blaire's phone rings and she quickly grabs it. "It's my brother FaceTiming. Let me just make sure everything is okay with them." She looks down at the phone. "Hey, Beau."

"Hello, baby sister. Is everything good out there?"

"Yes, the kids loved Philly. They ran up the Rocky steps today. I'll send you some videos. We'll be home tomorrow."

"Great. What are you guys doing? It looks like you're dressed up in a limo."

Axel places his hand just under Blaire's dress and brings his face to the screen. "I have my hands up your sister's dress."

Beau growls and Blaire slaps his hand away.

Amanda and I look at each other and smile at their family's playfulness.

Axel grins. "I'm going to defile your sister in the limo. She's got to go. We'll see you guys when we get home. I need you to take our kids for a day or two so Blaire and I can spend it in bed, bringing the al dente noodle to the spaghetti house."

"You're an asshole, Broxton. Go back to the cave you crawled out of."

Axel laughs and Blaire ends the call, shaking her head in exasperation. "Why do you get him riled up?"

He kisses her nose. "Because it's so easy, Bear."

She simply rolls her eyes at him.

Amanda asks, "How often does he do that with your brother?"

Blaire deadpans, "Daily."

Axel and I chuckle. He's such a character.

Amanda says, "I love the sibling relationship." I know she wishes she gave Jade a sibling. I feel the same for Andie.

After chatting a bit in the limo, we arrive at the jazz club. I hit the limo intercom. "Nico, check for paps."

I may not garner attention from the paparazzi anymore, but Axel certainly does.

"Yes, sir."

A few moments later, there's a tap on the window and we hear Nico say, "The coast is clear."

We make our way inside where I see the longtime hostess, Sabrina. She smiles when she notices me. "Mr. Windsor, I didn't know you were coming in."

"Hello, Sabrina. I forgot to call ahead. Can you do me a favor and get us my regular table?" She's never failed me on that front.

She scrunches her nose. "Mr. and Mrs. Knight are sitting there now. It's his favorite table too."

"Is anyone with them?" It's a huge, circular booth big enough for all of us.

She has a concerned look on her face. "No, but they...umm...like their *privacy*."

I let out a laugh. "I bet they do. We'll go say hello and see how it goes."

The four of us walk over to the best table in the house. Jackson's face is buried in Darian's neck and her eyes are closed. I clear my throat. "Get a room, you two. And get out of my booth."

Jackson removes his head from her neck, looks up

at me, and laughs. "It's not your booth tonight, Windsor." He motions his hand. "Join us."

I look at Darian and she nods in agreement. Her eyes light up when they move to my hand, which is holding Amanda's. "Amanda? It's good to see you. Are you two an item?"

I can see Amanda struggling with how to answer. Being deceitful is against her grain. I shake my head. "We're just good friends."

Darian's eyes then find the Broxtons. "Holy shit. Axel Broxton?"

Amanda innocently asks, "Oh, do you know Axel and Blaire?"

Darian looks equally shocked and appalled. "Axel is the best tight end in professional football. He caught one hundred and ten passes last year for over fifteen hundred yards. He scored fourteen touchdowns. Of course I know Axel Broxton. Who wouldn't?"

Amanda looks at Axel and he simply shrugs at her. "It should have been fifteen touchdowns, but I got a bullshit call."

He then turns to Darian. "Tell me more about you thinking I'm the best tight end. Do you think I'm better than Travis Kelce?"

Darian nods. "Hell yes."

"Am I hotter?"

Darian smiles. "Now that I've seen you in person, absolutely."

He raises an eyebrow at Blaire. "I told you. People think I'm hotter." He turns back to the table. "My wife keeps telling me I'm the second hottest tight end in football."

We all laugh as we shuffle into the booth. Amanda is next to Darian. She whispers to Amanda, "You really didn't know who he was?"

Amanda shakes her head.

CHAPTER SIXTEEN

AMANDA

Apparently, I'm clueless. I had no idea that Axel was a famous football player. I suppose he looks like one, being so big and muscular. And Darian was right, he's insanely hot. His eyes are such a unique shade of blue. He and Blaire seem so funny and down-to-earth though. I would never have guessed that he's famous.

The waiter comes over and asks for our drink orders. Beckett orders a scotch for himself and a piña colada with extra cherries for me. I'm expecting a snotty comment about my drink choice, but Blaire just screeches that she hasn't had one of those in a long time and orders one too.

Our conversation flows easily through dinner. Even though Darian and Blaire are both professionals with advanced degrees, they never exclude me or make me feel uncomfortable. They both ask me a lot of questions about my art.

Jackson and Axel are both extremely affectionate with

their spouses. Beckett has his arm around the back of the booth, but that's it.

A bit of sadness rolls over me, realizing that this is my last night with him. I'm going to miss him. I can't help but keep my body pressed to his, taking in his scent, knowing it won't happen again.

After we eat, Jackson and Axel grab their wives' hands and take them to the dance floor where they proceed to dirty dance to the sultry music. I think Jackson's hand is legitimately up Darian's dress. Axel's might be up Blaire's too.

Once they're out of earshot, Beckett turns to me. "Are you having a good time?"

"I am. They're very sweet. I haven't really gotten to know Darian that well over the past five years since it's always such a big group. It was nice to get this time with her. When Blaire mentioned how much she likes my work, Darian asked about commissioning a piece. I don't think I would charge her though."

"Definitely charge her. She can more than afford it."

I take one of my cherries, pop it into my mouth, and chew it. "I know, but she's been so wonderful to Jade. This can be my way of thanking her."

He stares at my mouth. It's almost awkward how long he silently stares at me chewing the cherry. "Are you okay?"

"You know, I'll finally admit out loud that for nearly five years, the sight, smell, and especially the taste, of cherries has made me think of you. If I'm being honest, it always makes me think of our kiss."

Yep, I remember that kiss too. His big, juicy lips look particularly yummy tonight.

I swallow the cherry and he seems mesmerized by the process.

I don't know if it's the two drinks I've had, the excitement of selling so many paintings tonight, or the fact that it's our last night together, but I can't seem to help myself. I grab his face and bring my lips to his.

He doesn't hesitate for a moment, pulling my body as close as he can in the booth and pushing his tongue into my mouth. He tastes like scotch and mint, taking me right back to our first kiss all those years ago.

His tongue and lips expertly swipe across mine. My body fills with desire as it hastily exits its long-dormant, inactive state. Smelling him, tasting him, and feeling his hands move up and down my body is electrifying my every nerve ending.

I'm mildly aware of our surroundings, or I'd throw my leg over his and grind down onto him to relieve the fast-building ache between my legs.

I moan into his mouth as my fingers move through his silky hair. He has one hand on the back of my neck and the other moving up my inner thigh.

I'm not sure where this is headed, especially given our surroundings, but I know I want him. Badly. I need his hand to move up just a little higher.

All of a sudden, we hear a throat clear and reluctantly pull apart. We turn and look up at the Knights and Broxtons smiling at us.

Darian winks. "Just friends, huh?" She turns to Blaire. "Do you kiss your friends like that?"

Blaire smiles as she shakes her head. "Nope. Not that I recall."

I shrug. "I'm part French. That's how we treat our friends."

They both giggle, and I can't help but join them.

As we're leaving the club, Darian makes Axel and Blaire

promise to visit when Axel plays in Philly next season. She mentions inviting us as well, but I keep our answer vague. The sad fact is that, after tonight, Beckett and I have no reason to be together.

The limo first drops Axel and Blaire at their hotel. As soon as they exit, Beckett pulls me onto his lap and starts kissing me again. His hands find my breasts and his lips move down my neck as he mumbles, "I've wanted you for so long."

I pull away from him and he looks at me in confusion. "What's wrong?"

I take a deep breath. "I'm sorry if I misled you back there, but it was an error in judgment."

He shakes his head. "Our deal is over. There's nothing holding us back. I'm so attracted to you. You don't feel the same?"

I rub his gorgeous face with my hand. "It's not that. I *am* attracted to you. Very much. Beckett, I told you, we live in two different worlds. I've endured so much hurt in my life, most of which was caused by me making poor, impulsive decisions. I can't let this be another. I have a history of trying to make the wrong person fit into what I imagine for my life. I know I'm not the right person for you. You're way out of my league."

"I don't agree. Stop saying that. You're amazing. I'd be lucky to have you."

I shake my head. "I'm sorry. I can't."

I hate the look of hurt on his face. He turns his face, unable to maintain eye contact with me, mumbling, "Coward."

Maybe I am a coward, but a lifetime of bad decisions and disappointment does that to a person.

"Were you just using me this whole time? You're just

like everyone else in my life. You're right, it's best for you to go."

I know he's lashing out in pain. That seems to be his M.O. But there's no point in disputing it. It's time for me to leave. If him being angry with me makes it easier for him, then so be it.

We sit in silence for the last few minutes of the drive. It's filled with tension, and I hate that these are our final moments together.

We pull into his driveway and Nico opens the car door for us.

Beckett turns to him as we step out of the car. "You can go home, Nico. I don't need you for the rest of the night."

"Are you sure, Mr. Windsor?"

"Yes. The front gate security is enough. Please manage the transportation for my mother and Andie from New York in the morning."

"I was planning on it. Have a good night. You too, Ms. Tremaine."

I catch him by surprise when I hug him. "I'm heading out tonight, Nico. I won't be back. It's been a pleasure knowing you."

He squeezes me back and whispers in my ear, "He's a good man."

I whisper back, "I know."

"He cares about you."

I pull back and give a small nod as Nico leaves.

Beckett and I walk into the house, and I immediately head upstairs to grab my bags. When I return downstairs, he's still standing by the front door looking lost.

I place my bags on the ground, wrap my arms around his waist, and kiss his cheek, taking in his scent one last time. "Goodbye, Beckett."

He simply nods as he begins to open the door for me, but just as quickly as he opens it, he closes it. "Stay with me tonight. Not because of some stupid deal or any obligation. Stay with me because you want to be with me. The real me. Not Beckett Windsor, the billionaire. Not Beckett Windsor, the man who can open doors and introduce you to the right people. Just me. A man who wants you. The authentic you. Exactly as you are."

My eyes fill with tears. I want it too. I just know how this story ends, and it's not a fairytale. I look up at his blue eyes. "You're an amazing man and wonderful father. You'll find the right woman one day. The one who belongs in your world. Then you'll know that what I'm doing is right." I kiss his cheek one last time. "Goodbye, Beckett."

I open the door myself and walk out to my car, unable to look back, and pack my trunk like I've done so many times before. I get into the driver's seat and just sit for several long minutes. I'm questioning myself, but how can I trust my feelings when they've always been off target?

I'm tempted to call Reggie, but I know she and Sam had a big date tonight. I don't want to interrupt them.

Looking down at the keys in my hand, I notice that Beckett's house key is still on it. I carefully remove it. I should bring it back inside. I'll do so quietly. I'm sure he's already gone up to bed.

I slowly turn the key and open the door. As I step into the house, I suck in a breath and fall back against the door, closing it.

Beckett is walking down the last few steps. He's in gym shorts and no top, looking like he's about to go work out. I've never seen him shirtless. It's not what I expected. He's full of muscles, but that's not the part that's surprising. He's got a huge tattoo all over his stomach and chest with a smaller one next to it. In a million years, I would never have expected him to have tattoos.

"I...I...I forgot to leave my key." I hold it up as if needing to show proof.

He nods as he walks over to me. His chest is heaving. I'm realizing he's never let me see him without a shirt. He almost looks angry that I'm seeing him now. I don't know why.

He holds out his hand for me to drop the key. I do but then can't help but trace my fingertips over his gorgeous artwork. It's some kind of creature I've never seen before. It's a cross between a bird and lion. I wonder what it means. And there are big eyes. Big, open eyes. The artwork is so intricate.

I breathe, "Beckett, these are beautiful."

He doesn't flinch, but I can see the evidence of his cock hardening under his shorts at my touch. He's so close that I can smell the scotch and mint on his breath.

His fingers begin to twitch. I know he wants to touch me, but I also know I've pushed him away and the ball is in my court.

Without a single word, he stares at me, waiting to see if I'll make the first move. He looks like an animal stalking its prey.

My nipples harden at the intensity of his gaze. I'm growing slick between my legs as the ache is nearing an unbearable level, impatiently waiting for some relief.

Maybe just one night. One night to know what it would be like to indulge in Beckett Windsor completely. To give in to this intense attraction that's been building for a long time. My body is now begging for it. My brain is starting to lose the battle of wills.

I look down at his big hands, taunting me. I desperately want them all over my body.

I stare at the now *fully* impressive bulge he's unashamedly sporting in his shorts. He's not bothering to attempt to hide it. I need to feel it—feel him—between my legs. I don't think I've ever wanted anything more. The pull to him is officially out of my control.

Done fighting this, I reach for the zipper at the top of the dress and slowly pull it all the way down until the dress falls from my body to the floor, leaving me in a black, satin, strapless bra and matching thong.

His eyes slowly move up and down my body, taking in every inch. His hands are still twitching, but he doesn't touch me. What more does he want from me?

I reach behind my back, unclasp my bra, and let it fall to the ground. As my breasts fall free, he finally snaps, letting out a growl as his hand roughly grabs my ponytail and tilts my head back.

He licks up my neck and grazes his teeth over my chin. He then wraps his other hand around my throat and applies a little pressure. "We're going to do this my way. You have five seconds to stop it."

Despite the delicious pain in my scalp from him pulling my hair and the pressure around my neck, I reach down and rub his hard cock through his shorts, letting him know I'm not stopping it this time.

He pulls it just a little harder and roars, "You're mine now."

His hands roughly grab my breasts as he open-mouth kisses his way down my body until he's on his knees in front of me. He spends glorious time on each nipple, squeezing my breasts together and sucking them hard into his mouth.

His warm mouth and body are pressed against me, setting fire to every nerve ending.

He moves his hands down until they reach my black panties. He easily rips them from my body like an animal, and then sinks his nose into my pussy and inhales me deeply. "I've dreamed of this for so long. You smell like... like...you belong to me."

He spreads my legs and slowly licks through my slit once. I nearly collapse, having been so starved for his touch. "You taste like it too." After licking through me again, he looks up at me. "You're so wet. Why have you denied yourself what you clearly want?"

I can't think of a single reason right now.

He throws one of my legs over his shoulder and then the other, before he stands to his full height with me wrapped around his face and my back leaning on the top of the door.

I gasp at the unexpected move. A thrill races through me as I realize I'm at least eight feet above the ground, completely naked, wrapped around his head.

He rubs his face through my wetness before spearing my channel with his tongue. His hands roughly grab my ass as he uses them for leverage, sinking his tongue in and out of me. He's igniting my body as he physically breathes life back into it.

I run my fingers through his hair until I find my grip. My hips take on a life of their own, gyrating against his face, desperate for every ounce of pleasure he's giving my body.

His tongue slowly moves up to my clit as he slides his fingers deep into me. After a few pumps, when they're sufficiently coated in my oozing juices, he moves them around to my back entrance.

Admittedly, it's been a long while since I've engaged in

any ass play. Rick wasn't into it and, if I'm being honest, I've missed it. I swivel my hips, encouraging Beckett's movements.

He teases me back there for a moment. I breathe, "Beckett, please. Do it." I want it. I need it.

I can sense him smile into me as his fingers push deep into my tight hole. I think my eyes roll into the back of my head. I feel pins and needles running down the backs of my legs. I throw my head back and moan, "Fuck, yes."

Beckett more than knows his way around a woman's body. His tongue and fingers expertly push me to the edge in no time. But when his thumb pushes into my pussy, I practically lose consciousness at the trifecta of sensations.

My legs start to shake as my orgasm rises to the surface and then slams into me at full speed. I'm screaming his name and pulling his hair. "Ah, Beckett. Oh god. Oh god."

My quivering thighs squeeze his head as my world goes completely dark. I hope he's holding me tight because I have no sense of balance right now.

It's not until the orgasm begins to subside that I realize I may be suffocating him. I blink open my eyes and release the tight hold of my thighs around his face and head.

He pulls his fingers and thumb out of me, but keeps slowly licking through my pussy, taking every drop of what I'm giving him, guiding me through the last remaining tremors.

Eventually, he pulls his head back and slowly slides me down his big, hard body until my feet once again meet the floor. I look at his face covered in my juices. It's so fucking hot. I can't help but grab his face and stand on my tippy toes while licking over and around his lips before sucking his tongue into my mouth.

He pulls me flush to him, kissing me back. I mumble into his mouth. "Get inside of me."

He immediately pulls down his shorts and boxers in one go until they fall to the floor. I look down as his cock springs free.

Holy. Shit.

It's been a long while, a very long while, but I've been with big men before. My college boyfriend and Declan were both huge. What they didn't have were piercings running up their cocks.

Beckett's enormous dick has an eight-pronged Jacob's Ladder. Between the tattoos and this piercing, I couldn't possibly be more shocked. Maybe I misjudged him.

He notices me staring and gives himself a few pumps while he displays his famous, sexy Beckett smirk. "Have you ever been with a man that has a piercing?"

I shake my head.

His smirk grows. "I'm about to rock your world."

He grabs the backs of my legs and easily lifts me, wrapping them around him. I imagine we should have some sort of safe sex discussion, but we've shared a bathroom for a month. He knows I'm on the pill and we both know it's been a long while for the other.

He swivels his hips and runs his Jacob's Ladder through my wet, sensitive flesh. I dig my nails into his shoulders, trying to contain the crazy pleasure this is already bringing to my body. He's not even inside me yet and I can feel things building back up. If he keeps going, I'll be able to come from just this.

While flicking his tongue back and forth over my nipples, he walks us into the family room, my favorite room in the house, and then sits on the couch with me still straddling him, his cock continuing to rub through me.

He runs his hands up and down the sides of my body, causing goosebumps to spread everywhere. His hands are so big, his body is so powerful. The anticipation of what's to come is making my mind spin.

He lifts his head from my breast and runs his thumb over my lower lip. "You're the most beautiful woman I've ever seen."

I smile as my hands move all over his broad chest and meticulous artwork. "You're the sexiest man I've ever seen."

"I've waited so long for this."

I nod. I know the feeling.

His hands continue to move all over my body, studying me, as if he's having a hard time believing that this is finally happening. He admits, "It's been a while for me. A *long* while."

"I know. For me too." I smile. "Your skills seem pretty sharp so far."

He lets out a laugh before running his nose up my neck. "I love the way you smell." He then sticks his thumb, which was inside me, into his mouth and licks it. "And the way you taste is even better."

If my panties were still on, they'd probably melt off right now.

I lift up and place his tip at my entrance, unwilling to wait another second for this. Just before I sink down, he quietly whispers, "This is going to change everything."

And when I sink down, it does.

My breath catches at the overwhelming sensation. His giant cock with the piercings already has my whole body uncontrollably shaking.

He smiles. "It feels good, doesn't it?"

I can only nod as I lose the battle of control with my

own body. We haven't even moved yet and I'm at a loss for words. My toes are numb.

"I need you to talk to me. Tell me what you like, what you need." He tugs my ponytail. "Do you like getting your hair pulled? I think you do."

He then gently squeezes his hand around my neck. "Do you like being choked? Your pussy got so wet when I squeezed it earlier."

His hands move down to my breasts where he pinches my nipples hard. "Do you like pain with your pleasure?"

His hand moves around to my ass and he applies a little pressure. "We already know how much you like me to touch you back here."

He thrusts his hips up, pushing so completely deep inside me. I suck in a labored breath, feeling like I can't breathe.

"Tell me, cherry pie, and then we can get started."

Started? I'm about a minute away from finishing.

I have to force words out, barely able to speak. "All of it. I want all of it."

As I finally start to acclimate to him and catch my breath, I begin feeling a bit bold. I pull his hair. "Do you like getting your hair pulled?"

I move my hands to his neck. "Choked?"

I reach around and grip his balls. Hard. "Do you like a little pain?"

I then slide a hand around to his ass, applying a bit of pressure. Staring at him in the eyes, I say, "Any limits, Beckett Windsor?"

He gives me a smirk and echoes my words. "All of it. I want all of it."

That's what he gives me and what I give him. All of it.

Beckett proceeds to fuck the living daylights out of me.

I think we hit every position imaginable. I've lost track of the number of times he made me come.

When it's over, we both lay on our backs on the carpeted floor, covered in sweat, breathing heavily.

Through labored breaths, I manage, "Holy shit."

He rests his hand on my upper thigh and, in equally labored breaths, says, "That was incredible. You're amazing."

It's him who was amazing.

We're silent for a few minutes as we come down from our shared high. Eventually, he rolls toward me until he's resituated between my legs, rubbing his cock through my severely sensitive and swollen wetness.

Pinning my hands above my head, he rubs his nose on mine and says, "That was even better than my fantasies."

I smile. "You fantasize about me?"

"Oh, you have no idea the things I want to do to you."

"Is there anything left? I think we checked about a thousand boxes in the past hour."

He releases my hands and raises his eyebrow in challenge. "How about I show you?"

I trace his sexy scruff with my fingers. "Okay. Next time, show me." Yes, because I know without a doubt that one time with him won't be enough. I'm not sure a thousand times will be enough.

"How about now?"

"Now? We just finished." He wiggles his hips and I feel him harden on top of me. "You must be kidding me."

"I have a lot of pent-up desire for you. I'm not sure my thirst will ever be quenched." He kisses me hard but then abruptly stands and walks out of the room. I can't help but watch his muscular ass as he goes. His body is a dream. He's thick and sexy. I still can't get over his gorgeous artwork. I want to know more about it. And that piercing. Why doesn't every man have a piercing?

I stretch my arms over my head. Ouch. I'm sore. Every inch of me. I smile thinking of the reasons I'm sore. Everything we just did...The way he made me feel...

I hear him moving around the kitchen.

When he returns, his hands are behind his back, and he has a mischievous look on his face.

"What do you have back there?"

"Do you trust me?"

"I'm lying naked on your living room floor. I suppose I do."

"Close your eyes."

I indulge him.

"I'm placing something over your eyes so you can't peek."

I feel a soft material cover my eyes. I then feel something cold and slimy running down my body.

I screech but he holds me down. "Don't squirm."

The cold sliminess works its way down from my neck until it's circling my nipples. I can feel juices dripping down the sides of my body. Each time he moves it around my nipple, he sucks it into his mouth and moans in delight. I can't place what he's using.

"You have the best tits."

"You've both shown me and told me about a thousand times in your sleep over the past month."

He chuckles. "My sleepy self knows what he's talking about."

"Yep, that sleepfucker has all the moves."

I feel him laughing again.

He then moves the slimy object down my body until he

reaches my pussy. He slides it through me and then into my opening.

I gasp. "What did you just put inside me?"

"Nothing I won't personally remove with my mouth in a few minutes."

He then repeats the same process two more times with two objects that feel the same as the first.

I squirm at the sensation of having three foreign objects in me. "Beckett, what is it?"

I feel him move up my body. He gently slides another cold, slimy object over my lips. I immediately lick them. "Cherries?"

"Yes. Maraschino cherries. Five years. For five years I've had a physical reaction to the smell and taste of cherries. Eating them off you, from inside of you, is my ultimate fantasy."

"There are cherries inside me right now?"

"Not for long."

He continues running cherries over my lips, teasing me before he feeds each one to me. "Have you ever engaged in food play before?"

I shake my head. "No."

"Have you ever been blindfolded like this?"

"No."

"Being blindfolded heightens your other senses."

I lick my lips again. He's right. The texture and taste of the cherries seem tenfold.

I feel him lean over me and bring his mouth to mine. As he's kissing me, two more cherries drop into my mouth. We manage to both kiss and chew them together.

Cherry juice is running all over our faces, but neither of us cares. Why is this so hot? I've never remotely done or considered anything like it before. I'm loving it. It's messy and sexy at the same time.

He pulls away slightly, though his body still touches mine. He seems to reach for something.

"Open your mouth."

Still unable to see, I do.

I hear squirting and then the texture and taste of whipped cream hits my tongue. I hear the sound of the can and then feel the cold as he draws a line of whipped cream down the middle of my body. I feel it melting onto my skin. I shiver with anticipation of what's to come.

He slowly licks and nibbles his way down my body.

I smile. "This is a lot of calories for you."

"Don't worry, I plan to work them off." He continues his delicious path until his face is at my center. He spreads my legs wide and mumbles, "Time for my treasure hunt."

I feel his tongue enter me in search of the cherries. Feeling and hearing it, yet not seeing it, definitely has my senses on high alert.

He licks and sucks me ferociously. Somehow, I'm both laughing and feeling pleasure at the same time.

I can hear two cherries get sucked out and then him chewing them. "Yum. Even more delicious after being inside you."

Holy hell, that's hot.

When the third comes out, I don't hear any chewing. I keep listening, but I don't hear it.

He moves up my body until I feel a much warmer cherry on my lips. He moves it around and around. My tongue slides out to taste it. It's a mix of sweet and salty this time.

He eventually drops it in my mouth, and I swallow it down as his lips take mine in what might be the most delicious, sensual kiss I've ever experienced in my life. His sweet lips move over mine. Our cherry-flavored tongues explore each other's mouths.

I wrap my legs around him. After the marathon session we just had, I can't believe I'm ready for more, but I am.

He slowly slides back into me.

I breathe, "Oh god. Every man should be forced into cock piercings."

"Does it feel good, cherry pie?"

I moan, "Sooo good."

He spreads my legs wide and rocks in and out of me, completely blowing my mind. Again. He's hitting category-five level orgasms over and over again.

We go at it through most of the night until we collapse in a heap of our fluids, sweat, whipped cream, and sticky cherry juice.

CHAPTER SEVENTEEN

AMANDA

I'm awakened by the slam of a door. In my semi-conscious state, I hear Glinda say, "Andie, go into the kitchen and turn on the waffle maker. You know how to mix the batter. Start it for me. I'll be there in a minute."

I try to move, but Beckett is draped over me. His head is on my chest and his leg is tucked snugly between mine. Very snugly. We're under a big, furry blanket on the floor of the family room.

I hear the sound of footsteps running upstairs and then eventually back down. Before I can process anything, Glinda appears in front of us. She's holding my dress and has a huge grin on her face. She lets out a breath in relief. "It's about time, you two."

I rub Beckett's back. "Wake up."

He mumbles, "No. I'm staying here all day." He wiggles his hips. I can feel his erection on my leg. "Better yet, I'll get back inside you and stay there all day."

I quickly cover his mouth and whisper, "Your mom is here."

He turns his head and opens an eye. "Oh Christ. Tell me I'm having a nightmare. Tell me I'm not a middle-aged man whose mom just walked in on him naked with a woman."

I giggle and Glinda's grin couldn't possibly get any wider. I happily feel like a teenager getting busted by an adult.

We hear Andie's voice. "Gigi, where are the cherries and whipped cream? I can't find any."

Glinda looks at the empty can and bowl next to us and bites back her smile. She yells, "I think your daddy ate it all. He must have been *really* hungry. We'll pick up some more at the store today."

Beckett groans, and I giggle again before pinching my eyebrows together. "Glinda, what are you doing here? I thought you were flying out of New York."

"Beckett didn't tell you?"

I shake my head.

"Reagan needs him to go to Italy for a project this week. She told him yesterday afternoon after we had already left. He asked me to stay an extra week with Andie." She starts to turn. "I'll keep Andie in the kitchen so you two can clean up. I'm leaving your scattered clothes on the banister." She looks back and winks at me. "And your ripped panties."

She leaves the room, and he collapses his head back on my chest. "Sorry about that. Two months of the year. I have two months where my mother is in my business every day, but you know why I put up with it."

I run my fingers through his hair. "It doesn't bother me. I adore your mom. You're so lucky to have her. A parent that loves and cares about you isn't as common as you'd think."

He nods in understanding.

"You're going to Italy? Why didn't you tell me your mom was staying longer?"

I can feel him swallow. "Honestly, I wanted our stupid deal to be over so we could be together for real. I wanted you to stay for me, not for our deal or my mother." He looks up at me and scrunches his nose. "Does that make sense?"

I lean forward and softly kiss his lips. "It does."

"Will you come with me?"

"Come with you where? To Italy?"

I try to slide out from under him, but he maintains a tight hold. Sitting up, he moves me to straddle him. He's so damn strong. He can carry me and toss me around like I weigh nothing.

"Yes. Come with me."

"No, I can't."

"I want you to."

"I can't afford that and before you say anything, you're *not* paying for me."

He sighs. "Reagan is flying me out on the company jet. I'm staying at a friend's house the first night and then I have a boat we can stay on when we go to the coast. There are no expenses. I'll have painting supplies brought onboard. You can paint there."

He kisses up my neck and then licks along the same path. Nibbling on my ear and rubbing his hands all over my body, he whispers, "I want you to myself. I've been waiting so long for you. Rome is like nowhere else on the planet. It's like seeing pages of a history book come to life. The Amalfi Coast is more beautiful than any place you've ever been. Photos and movies don't do it justice. You need to experience it in person. Think of the beautiful landscapes you can create. I promise you that you've never seen anything more breathtaking."

He continues kissing and licking me. How am I supposed to deny him anything right now? And he does make a compelling argument. When will I ever have an opportunity like this? I'm already dreaming of all the paintings I could create.

He slides my hair behind my ear and holds my face so our eyes meet. "Please come. It would mean the world to me. I have one meeting I need to go to in Rome. You can sightsee. And then we can have some fun on the Amalfi Coast. I want to make love to you on my boat under the stars." He briefly closes his eyes. "I've dreamed of it so many times."

I bite my lip as I genuinely consider it. He pulls it out from my teeth. "It makes my cock stir every time you do that. All. Fucking. Month."

I defiantly bite it again, and I watch as he hardens in front of my eyes.

I nod down toward it. "Food and lip biting do it for you?"

In a deep voice, he says, "*You* do it for me."

I run my hands up his chest. "You can be very sweet when you want to be."

He wraps his arms around me, pulls my naked body flush to his, and rubs his lips across mine. "Full disclosure, my intentions for our time in Italy are less than sweet."

I smile into his mouth. I can't deny that it sounds good to me.

The voices of Andie and Glinda in the kitchen remind us of where we are and who is in the next room. He sighs.

"No distractions for five days. No interruptions. You and me, alone, making up for too much lost time."

"You, me, and Nico?"

"Nico knows how to be invisible." He kisses me as his thumb brushes across my nipple. He whispers, "Please say yes."

He bends his head and sucks my nipple into his mouth. This man wreaks havoc on my body and mind.

With my nipple still in his mouth, he looks up and gives me his best pleading eyes.

I take a deep breath in resignation and then nod.

His entire face lights up as he easily stands with me still wrapped around him. God I love how strong he is.

"Great. I'll set everything up."

THIRTY MINUTES and a pleasure-filled shower later, we enter the kitchen fully clothed. Andie runs into Beckett's waiting arms. "Daddy, I missed you."

He rubs his nose on hers. "I missed you too. Did you have fun with Gigi in New York?"

"Yes! The show was really good, and we went for pancakes at Flippers."

"Ooh, lucky girl. Those are the best pancakes in the world."

"They are, and they had lots of cherries and whipped cream. It's a good thing, because Gigi said you ate all of ours."

He nods as he looks at me. "I sure did. Best cherries I've ever had."

I see Glinda smile and I jokingly hip check her. I mumble, "You're nosey, old lady."

She giggles. "I'm just happy you've finally seen the light. It's about time you gave in to what we both know you wanted."

"You knew this whole time we weren't really together?"

"I may be getting old, but I'm not blind. I know my son. He's clearly been smitten, and you've kept him at arm's length for whatever reasons. I don't need to know, but I'm glad it's finally changed."

"I *do* care about him. I hope you know that."

She rubs my arm. "I know you do, sweetie. That's why I'm such a fan of your budding relationship."

"He invited me to go to Italy with him."

She looks giddy with excitement. "And?"

"I think I'm going to go."

She smiles and then hugs me. "I'm so happy to hear it. You'll have the best time. Have you ever been?"

I shake my head. "I've never left the country. I'm lucky Jade forced me to get a passport just in case."

"It's one of the most beautiful, romantic places on earth. You'll love it. You, more than most, will appreciate the beauty and history."

I fidget nervously. "He said that I can be casual except for our one night in Rome. I was going to ask Jade's father's wife to help me find a dress. She's very fashionable. Do you maybe want to come with us?"

Her face genuinely lights up as she hugs me again. "I would love nothing more."

Andie tugs on Beckett's arm. "Where's my morning joke, Daddy?"

His eyes sparkle. "I have a good one for you today. What does a duck say when he's at a bar and wants to buy everyone a round of drinks?"

She asks, "What?"

"Put it on my bill."

She starts belly laughing and I can't help but join. "That's a good one, Daddy."

DESPITE BECKETT'S PROTESTS, I'm on my way back to my house. We may have played happy couple for the past month, but in reality, we're on day two. I'm not staying there anymore. At least not for a while.

I'm not sure what I'm doing. I know I don't belong in Beckett's world, but after last night, I can't deny the attraction and chemistry we share. I don't want to stay away. I'm probably heading for heartbreak, but I've been there many times before. When it inevitably ends, I'll pick myself up and manage my way through it like I always have.

When I pull into my driveway, I notice Jade's car. I hope I didn't miss something. I don't think we had plans.

I walk in and she's sitting there with a big smile on her beautiful face. "Where have you been, young lady? Imagine my surprise when I came early this morning with your favorite coffee, only to discover that my dear, innocent mother clearly didn't sleep at home last night."

I try to contain my smile. "Umm, I got up early and went out."

She crosses her arms and shakes her head. "Nope. I don't believe you. Your bed wasn't slept in."

I giggle. "I slept at Reggie's."

"Nope. I called her. She wasn't even home last night. Something is going on. Look at your fucking smile. You're finally getting laid. You can't hide that from me."

I plop down next to her and grab the coffee she's holding. After I take a long, slow sip, I say, "Maybe I am."

"Spill the dirty details."

"No."

"Is it toe curling?"

"Yes. *Very* toe curling."

"Your dickpression is officially over."

I giggle. "It is, but..."

"But what?"

I scrunch my nose. "I know this might be awkward because we're mother and daughter, but we can discuss everything, right?"

"Of course, Mom. The dirtier, the better. You know that. What's on your mind?"

"It's just that I don't think I can discuss this with Reggie or Victoria. They...umm...can't identify like I think you can."

"Just spit it out."

"You've briefly mentioned a certain piercing that Collin has." I don't feel like I need to spell it out.

"The one on his dick?"

I guess she felt the need to spell it out.

I nod. "Yes."

"What about it?"

"Hypothetically speaking, let's say I was seeing someone with something similar."

Her eyes light up. "What are we working with? A stud, a Prince Albert, a Jacob's Ladder..."

I squirm at the last one and she smiles. "Damn. Very nice. Nice for you, that is. Have you ever been with anyone with a pierced cock before?"

I shake my head. "No. It's...it's..."

"Fucking amazing? Orgasms that blow your sensory control out of the roof?"

I let out a breath. "Yes. It's like perma-orgasm from start

to finish. It helps that he knows what he's doing and has a *very* generous build, but the piercing drives me nuts. I lose my mind."

"No shit. Now you see why I fell in love with Collin so easily. So what's the problem?"

"Are there any limitations? Can you do...everything?"

She looks confused. "What couldn't you do?"

I'm silent, preferring not to spell it out to my daughter, though I think we've officially shattered all appropriate boundaries.

She thinks for a moment before saying, "Oh, anal. Yes, it's fine. It feels amazing there too."

I close my eyes for a moment, letting out a long breath. "No, that's not what I was getting at. I was thinking more along the lines of blow jobs, but thanks for the *extreme* overshare."

She lets out a laugh. "Mom, we're talking about your boyfriend's pierced cock and how good the orgasms are. I don't think there's such a thing as oversharing between us anymore."

I smile. "True."

"Blow jobs are fine. Use your imagination and get a little creative with it. Who is this guy?"

"No one I'm ready to discuss. It's newish."

"Ish?"

"I'll tell you if and when I'm ready. Why don't we move on to something else? How are you feeling?"

"Fine. Collin is already driving me nuts over this pregnancy though."

"How so?"

"He's fucking taking care of everything for me. He won't even let me pump my own gas. He said the fumes might be bad for the baby."

"That's so sweet."

"Ugh. I don't like being coddled."

"You know what I had during my pregnancy with you?"

"What?"

"No one that gave a shit about me. Reggie did to some extent, but she was still a kid herself, dealing with school and her own drug issues. Pumping gas was the least of my worries. Paying for it was much bigger. Enjoy what you have, Jade. You're stable, successful, you have a home and a man who's madly in love with you. Don't take it for granted. Not everyone has that."

"Now I feel like an asshole. Alright, I'll ease up on him, but only because of his piercing. If he starts taking it easy on me in bed, he's going right back in the doghouse."

I can only shake my head at her antics.

"Mom, you never talk about that time in your life, before you got pregnant with me. What happened to you in college? Why did you drop out and spiral into addiction? Will you tell me what caused it?"

"It's not something I like to talk about or something I'm proud of."

"I want to understand what happened."

I sigh. "Fine, but please don't think less of me."

She grabs my hand. "Never. I owe everything to you. I wouldn't be where I am today without you. Nothing you tell me will change that."

I squeeze her hand in return. "I love you. Even though it was unplanned, having you was the best thing that ever happened to me, and worth everything I endured. You are my proudest accomplishment."

She nods. "Tell me."

"As you know, I was studying art. What I never told you

was that I was seeing an amazing man." I smile thinking about him. "We were in love. He's probably the only man that has ever truly loved me."

"Mom, Rick loved you in his own way."

"Maybe. It was different though. I know what all-encompassing love feels like. I never had that with Rick. I had it with my college boyfriend, but unfortunately, I ruined the best thing I ever had. I started doing drugs. He was an athlete, destined for professional baseball, so I kept the drug use away from him. At least I tried to. When I was high one night, he took the drugs away from me and tried to remove me from a bad situation. The police came and found my drugs on him. He was arrested and suspended from the team. I was in a shame spiral after that. His best friend came to me and told me that I was dragging my boyfriend down and was going to ruin his career if I didn't do something drastic. I realized he was right. I staged a whole fake bedroom scene with other men so he'd break up with me. But my boyfriend ended up getting into a fight with one of them, and he sustained a career-ending injury during the fight. I couldn't handle what I had done to him. I immediately dropped out of school and was in a bad place for nearly two years until the day I found out I was pregnant with you. I haven't touched any drugs since."

Jade has tears in her eyes. She hugs me. "Mom, you can't blame yourself for what happened. Your heart was in the right place."

Tears slowly trickle down my cheeks. "It's my fault though. He lost everything because of me."

"Whatever happened to him?"

"I have no idea. I never saw or spoke to him after he left for the hospital that day."

"You didn't look him up?"

I shake my head. "No, I can't. For my own sanity, I can't. It's not easy knowing you negatively impacted someone's life on a deep level. Someone who never showed you anything but love and adoration."

"Maybe you should reach out to him. It might help you move past it."

Before I can answer, our conversation comes to an end when we hear my front door open and then close. Collin shouts, "Honey, I'm home."

I wipe my tears and let out a laugh. "I love that he's already so comfortable with me."

He walks into the room and smiles at Jade like she hung all the stars in the sky and then kisses my cheek. "Good morning."

"Good morning to you."

He sits down next to Jade and pulls her close. She leans into him as if it's the most natural thing in the world. My heart practically bursts seeing her like this. I wasn't confident it would ever happen for her.

He looks down at her. "Are you still mad at me?"

"I'm not mad at you, but you can't do everything for me this entire pregnancy."

"I know. I'm sorry. I just want my baby mama to be safe."

She leans her head on his shoulder. "I know. Just keep the orgasms coming and we're square. I hear they're good for the baby."

He laughs. "Deal. You two want me to take you out to breakfast?"

I have so much to do if I'm leaving for Italy this week. "I already ate. You two go."

Jade nods. "Mom didn't sleep at home last night. I caught her doing a walk of shame this morning."

I wink at her. "There can only be a walk of shame if you actually feel shame. My conscience is clear."

Collin grins. "Good for you, Mom. Glad everything still works at your old age," he jokes.

I narrow my eyes at him. "I'm about a minute older than you, Collin. Relax with the mom thing."

He gives me his mischievous smile. "Okay, Mom."

He and Jade both laugh. She legitimately found her perfect match.

BECKETT

I look around my bedroom, empty of Amanda's belongings for the first time in a month. I wanted her all month. She was here, but I couldn't have her. Now I have her, and she's gone. I hate it.

Mom pokes her head into my room. "Andie is asleep. I think I'm going to go to bed early. She drained me of all my energy in New York. She's nonstop."

I nod. "Thanks, Mom. I really appreciate everything you do for her."

"I know you do." She looks around the room. "You miss her, don't you?"

"I do. I got used to having her around."

"Beckett, I'm sorry if I've been overbearing through the years. I just want you to be happy."

"I know, but you need to let me navigate my way through things in my own time. I'm not interested in just any warm body at this point in my life. Especially the type of women who pursue me. They're interested in my bank account, not me."

"Amanda isn't interested in your bank account. In fact, I think it works against you with her."

"It definitely works against me. She has this inferiority complex. She's damaged from the hard life she's led. Her independence and integrity are important to her."

"That's what makes her special."

"I know."

"You treat her like a princess, Beckett. She deserves nothing less."

I smile, thinking of everything we're going to do in Italy. "I plan to."

CHAPTER EIGHTEEN

AMANDA

I look at the computer screen. "Good morning, Dr. Pearl."

She smiles at me in her little cardigan and perfectly styled hair. "Good morning, Amanda. It's been a while."

"Yes, I know. I'm sorry."

"Catch me up on things with you."

I blow out a breath. "Well, you're not going to believe it."

I proceed to tell her about the events of the past month leading through our night together over the weekend.

"Wow. I'm nearly at a loss for words. That's quite a story."

"I know. It's been crazy."

"I'd like to go back to the night with Beckett's father."

"You always focus on the negative."

She smiles. "That's why you pay me the big bucks. Tell me why you let it get to you the way it did. It seems to me like you and Beckett were very much on the same page about wanting to explore a real relationship, and then a few comments from a stranger caused you to completely alter course."

I contemplate her thoughts for a few seconds. "I think he hit the nail on the head with regards to every insecurity I have about being with a man like Beckett Windsor. That I can't navigate his world. That I'm not good enough. You know I didn't grow up like him."

"And you think something completely out of your control makes you undeserving of him? Your upbringing is something you endured and through which you persevered. It doesn't define you as a person. Everything you've done since to create a different life, a different path for your daughter, that's what defines you."

"I know you're right. I can't help that it makes me uncomfortable. His money makes me uncomfortable."

"Does Beckett ever make you feel embarrassed about your different upbringings? About his wealth?"

I think for a moment and answer honestly. "Not once. He never makes me feel anything but good about myself. He's always complimenting me. Always making me feel good."

"Yet you let someone who doesn't know you at all get under your skin?"

"I suppose I did."

"Tell me more about your time with Beckett."

I can't help but smile. "He's incredible. He's sweet, generous, romantic, considerate, and so damn sexy."

"You've fallen for him."

I blow out a breath. "I have, and I'm scared shitless. I know what we did the past month is unconventional, and I'm sure you have a lot of opinions on it, but in some ways, it was special. We spent so much time talking and getting to know each other. I've never done that with a man before. Things always turn physical so quickly. Beckett and I achieved this intense level of intimacy before the physical came into play."

"It was like hundreds of dates all in a month."

"That's exactly what it was like."

"And you've established relationships with both his daughter and mother?"

I smile. "Yes. I adore them both. His daughter, Andie, is like a breath of fresh air. Watching him be a wonderful father to her warms my heart, but it's a little bittersweet. I see what it could be like having a devoted father, and then I ache for Jade that she didn't have it for so long."

"Jade's doing fine. Declan has been a good father to her for a long time. And Collin is unfathomably perfect for her."

"You've met him?"

She allows a small smile to creep through. "Yes, he likes to ruffle my feathers just like she does. Him doing a purposeful naked walk-by during her sessions has become the norm."

I burst out laughing. "She really did find the perfect man for her. You should see them together. They're completely in sync with each other. He loves her so much. And he's already incredibly warm and comfortable with me."

"Yes, I agree, so stop *aching* for her. Everyone faces some adversity in their lives. Some more than others. It impacts us all nonetheless. How you come out on the other side is what matters. Jade is there."

"You're right. I know you are."

"And Beckett's mother? Tell me about her."

"Oh god, I love her. She's the mother I always wished I

had. She stays with Beckett for a month every six months to help with Andie. Beckett says it's to help give Andie the things he feels he can't. She exudes warmth. She alluded to growing up like me, so I feel like she understands me. We have a camaraderie that's hard to explain."

"It sounds like she's a fan of your relationship."

"Very much so. I'm pretty sure she's constantly manipulating things to get us together."

"Does anyone make his mother feel less than worthy because of how she grew up?"

I sigh. "No, not even for a second."

"So let me get this straight. Beckett clearly wants you. He's not remotely hiding it or playing childish games. His mother, who's heavily involved in his life, adores you and wants you together. You seem to get along with his daughter, who you've spent a lot of time with. But then his father, whom you met less than an hour earlier, misjudged you, and you spiraled."

I'm quiet. She's right. I can't let people like that continue to get to me. His opinion of our relationship doesn't matter. It's Beckett, Glinda, and Andie that matter.

"I understand what you're saying. I think Beckett and I have moved past it. He's taking me to Italy this week. He has business there and begged me to come along."

"Well, you're full steam ahead now."

"I guess so. Do you think I should put on the brakes?"

"I think you're old enough to know what and who you need. Your path is yours to create. There are no rules."

I nod. "I want to go. I'm excited to both go to Italy and to spend that time with him."

"Good. And the physical? You're compatible?"

I let out a breath. "Best of my life."

She smiles. "I'm happy for you. This was a long time

coming. I want you to have a wonderful time on your trip. Let him treat you well. You're deserving."

I nod.

"Do you hear me, Amanda? You're deserving."

"I'm trying."

"I know."

CHAPTER NINETEEN

AMANDA

I called Melissa and she was thrilled to help me find something special to wear for our one fancy evening. She really does have impeccable taste. She's revamped Jade's wardrobe over the past five years into something truly spectacular. It's like seeing the pages of Vogue magazine come to life.

We head into the boutique she recommended. As we begin looking through dresses, she asks, "I love that you asked me to help you. Why didn't you ask Jade though? She has great taste."

"She has work today, and I'm not ready for her to know certain details about this man yet. You know how she is. She'll push and push."

Melissa lets out a laugh. "That's true. You don't have to tell me about him, but can you tell me about the party you're going to?"

"Can you keep a secret?"

"Of course."

"He's taking me to Italy."

Her eyes light up. "Oh, I love it there. It's so romantic. Where are you going?"

"He said Rome for a night. He has a work obligation there. That's where we have a fancy event. Then we're going to the Amalfi Coast for a few days before coming home. He said I can be casual there."

She nods. "Okay, that helps, but know that Italy casual and real-world casual are slightly different. They're pretty fancy over there."

"Oh. I didn't know that. We're staying on a boat, so maybe it won't be too bad."

"We'll find stuff. Don't worry." The front door of the boutique chimes and Melissa looks up and smiles. "Glinda Windsor? I haven't seen you in years. How is it that you don't age like the rest of us?"

I turn and see Glinda smile as she walks over and kisses Melissa's cheek. "You look well, Melissa. Happiness suits you."

"It does." Melissa points at me. "Glinda, this is my friend, Amanda Tremaine."

Glinda throws her arm around me. "I know Amanda. I'm here for her, to help her pick out a dress for the romantic getaway to Italy."

Melissa's eyes toggle between me and Glinda a few times before it clicks. "Beckett Windsor? Beckett is the man you're going to Italy with?"

"Yes."

She looks at Glinda and breaks into a huge smile. "I *love* this."

Glinda nods. "Me too. He's incredibly smitten with her."

"Of course he is. Amanda is fantastic."

"I agree."

I look at the two of them. "You guys know I'm standing right here, don't you?"

They both giggle.

I ask, "How do you two know each other?"

Melissa thinks for a moment before answering. "We've sat on many charitable boards together through the years, though I couldn't tell you when we first met. It's been decades."

Glinda nods in agreement. "I think it was when you were married to Jackson. At one of Beckett's famous holiday parties."

"Yes, you're right. That's exactly when we first met." She lets out a laugh. "Remember that year a certain senator drank too much and made a spectacle of himself?"

"Oh god. I nearly forgot about that debacle."

I feel so out of place. I slowly walk away and quietly begin browsing dresses while they catch up. At some point, I look up at the saleslady. "There are no prices on these dresses. How much are they?"

The woman looks at both Melissa and Glinda before turning back to me. "Mr. Windsor called ahead. He's already taken care of it."

A blow out a breath. "This was a mistake." I turn around and start heading for the door.

Glinda catches up to me and grabs me by the shoulders. "Let him do this one thing for you."

"I don't want his charity, Glinda."

"It's not charity. Sweetie, I don't know the men you've been with in the past, but I'm gathering you haven't always been treated very well. Let me ask you something. Would it give you genuine joy to do something nice and special for Beckett? Or for your daughter?"

I reluctantly nod, knowing where this is going.

"That's right. Don't rob him of his joy. He wants to do this for you. He's so excited for the trip. Honestly, I haven't seen him this excited for anything since...well, since before his world fell apart."

"I want him to be happy, but it makes me uncomfortable when he buys things for me. He knows this."

"How about after we leave here, you buy something special for him? It can be an *I-can't-wait-for-Italy* gift exchange."

"Will you at least tell me how much these dresses cost?"

"It's better that I don't."

I turn to Melissa. She shrugs. "I go through this with Jade all the time when I want to buy her clothes. I can't begin to express to you the joy it gives me to buy nice things for her. She wears them like a boss."

I smile at that. "She does."

She winks at me. "No doubt, with your body you'll wear whatever dress we choose like a boss too. Just this once, let him spoil you. You deserve it, Amanda. When was the last time you were spoiled?"

About twenty-five years ago. "Fine, but will you two promise to help me find something for him when we're done? I want to give him a nice gift too."

They both smile and nod.

The saleslady looks tickled pink as she pours us three glasses of champagne. I guess drinking alcohol and trying on clothes is how the other half rolls. Target and JCPenney don't offer these types of amenities, though maybe they should.

About eight dresses and three glasses in, we're all giggling and having the best time. Glinda looks between me and Melissa. "You mean to tell me that Melissa is married to the father of your daughter, and you two are here shopping together?"

We nod.

"So you two are friendly even though you've had sex with the same man? And Melissa is now married to him?"

Melissa and I smile at each other. Glinda is wasted.

She bursts out laughing. "I love these modern families." She looks at me. "It doesn't bother you that your daughter spends time with Melissa?'

"Of course not. Melissa loves Jade and treats her like her own. Why would that upset me? I wouldn't want her to have an evil stepmother. I love their relationship. And I haven't been with Declan in well over two decades."

Glinda sighs. "I don't even remember what sex feels like. I miss it. The men in my community in Florida all have more nose and ear hair than hair on their heads."

Melissa and I giggle. I can't help but ask, "What about Nico? I sense something between you two."

Glinda blushes. "Hmm. Can you imagine what it would be like to be with a man that big? I bet he's big *everywhere*."

Now it's mine and Melissa's turn to burst out laughing. We also look at each other in an unspoken acknowledgment that Declan is a *very* big boy. She doesn't know that Beckett is too.

Melissa asks, "Who's Nico?"

"Beckett's bodyguard. He's definitely sweet on Glinda. They flirt shamelessly."

Glinda playfully smacks my hand. "We do not...well, maybe a little. But he doesn't want to jeopardize his job. I understand that."

I shout from the dressing room as I make my way in to try on another dress, "Glinda, Beckett wants you to be happy. You do everything for him and Andie. You deserve some fun too."

I hear her breathe, "Maybe one day."

I put on the latest dress and walk back out. They both gasp.

Melissa claps her hands together. "That's the one."

I look down. "You think?"

It's a black and white snakeskin-looking dress with a deep plunging neckline. I've never owned or worn anything like this in my whole life.

They both nod. Glinda squeals in excitement. "Beckett won't be able to keep his hands off you."

Melissa and I giggle again.

We have one more glass each while they wrap my dress. I thank Melissa as she leaves. I drag Glinda to a store before getting into the Uber with her to make sure she gets home safely.

BECKETT

I'm working from home today and Andie is still at school. My mother and Amanda come stumbling into the house at two in the afternoon.

They're giggling and falling all over each other. I think Amanda is practically carrying Mom along with what looks like a small, wrapped painting and what I assume is her new dress in an opaque cover so I can't see it.

They're laughing uncontrollably. I love their

relationship. Though Mom looks a little unsteady. Amanda does too, to a lesser extent.

"Are you two drunk?"

Mom nods. "Amanda and Melissa gave me lots of champagne and it's made me horny. Is Nico around?"

Amanda silently laughs. I nearly fall over in shock at my mother speaking like this. I've never once heard her talk this way. I'm officially disgusted.

"Mom, why don't you lie down for a bit?"

"With Nico?"

"No. Alone."

She scrunches her face in disgust. "Ugh. I'm always alone. Fine. I've got BOB."

"Who's Bob?"

"My battery-operated boyfriend."

Amanda snort laughs while I shake my head in disgust. Ugh. Gross.

Mom starts to zigzag toward the stairs. I grab her waist to steady her. "Let me help you."

I practically carry her to her room. When she's laying on her bed, she touches my cheek. "She's a keeper, Beckett. She wants you for all the right reasons and none of the wrong ones."

"I know, Mom."

She mumbles, "Don't screw it up," as she drifts off to sleep.

I close her door and walk down the hallway. I find Amanda leaning on the door jamb to my bedroom. She crooks her finger, encouraging me to walk toward her. "Come here, big boy."

I raise an eyebrow. "Big boy?"

"You're a *very* big boy, and I have something I'm

dying to do to a *very* big part of your body." She looks down at my crotch and licks her lips.

"How much have you had to drink?"

"Not as much as your mother. Now pull your pants down and pull out that gorgeous cock of yours. I keep thinking about it. I can't get it out of my mind. I've been all wound up since I left you yesterday morning."

I smile as I make my way to her and pick her up. She immediately wraps her legs around me.

She runs her fingers through my hair. "Thank you for my gift."

"You're very welcome."

"I got one for you too."

"You're my gift."

I walk us into my bedroom and close the door. She pulls my face and aggressively kisses me, immediately pushing her tongue into my mouth.

"You taste so good." She grabs onto my hair and grinds her body over mine. "I want you so badly right now."

I run my hands under the back of her shirt. "I always want you."

I fall back onto the bed. She's straddled on top of me with fire in her eyes. She immediately removes her shirt and bra, which I had already conveniently unsnapped.

I run my hands up her stomach to her perfect, full tits, teasing her nipples with my thumbs.

Her hands are on top of mine, encouraging my movements while she circles her hips over my erection.

"Take your shirt off. I want to see your body. Your sexy artwork."

If I knew how into my tattoos she'd be, I might have revealed them earlier.

I sit up and she removes it for me, running her hands all over my chest. "You're so hot."

Her fingers move down to my belt where she makes quick work of pulling my pants down enough for my cock to spring free. As soon as it does, she starts giggling.

"Is there something funny about my dick?"

She shakes her head. "I'm laughing because I had to ask Jade if it's okay to suck pierced dicks. Collin has one."

"You told Jade about my piercing?"

"I didn't tell her who. She doesn't know about you. I don't want her to know anything about us."

I can't deny that it stings for her to say that, but I immediately forget about it when she kisses her way down my body and runs her tongue up my length.

"You rocked my world this weekend. Now it's my turn to rock yours." Her eyes meet mine. "I'm dying to suck you clean."

My cock practically explodes at her actions and words.

She licks her way down to my balls, running her mouth over them a few times. She moves on to my taint, flicking her tongue over me, covering it in her saliva. Ooh, she's dirty. I love it.

She moves back to my dick as her tongue works its way over and around my piercings. She's so fascinated with them.

When she eventually seals her lips around me, I watch myself slowly disappear into her mouth. Her lips move all the way down, taking as much of me as she can until I can hear her gagging. It's music to my ears.

I pull her hair, which I learned the other night she likes. "Open your throat, cherry pie. Take me deep."

She playfully smiles as she does. I maintain my grip on her hair, thrusting into her. She moans every time I go deep. I love that she's enjoying this.

"Look how good you take me. You look so perfect like this."

Her nipples harden to the point where I wonder if it's painful. She's enjoying my words of praise.

She establishes a perfect rhythm of in and out. One hand is on the base of my shaft while the other massages my balls.

I encourage her with my words through it all, which seems to add to her gratification.

At some point, her hand on my balls starts to travel back across my taint and to my back entrance. She feels around my anus, testing her limits.

Her eyes lock with mine, but I don't flinch. She slips two fingers in and immediately finds my prostate.

I growl, "Oh fuck," as the combination of pleasure is too much, and I shoot my load down her throat.

She takes it all down, licking every last bit until it's all gone.

Lifting her head, she gives me a sexy smile. "I didn't think you were going to let me do that."

I grab her face and kiss her lips. "I'm all for equal opportunity pleasure. Just remember that when I make your ass mine."

She gives me another sexy smile. "I can't wait."

"Me neither."

CHAPTER TWENTY

AMANDA

We're on the plane, on our way to Italy. I'm practically jumping up and down with excitement. This is a big deal for me.

Beckett said he needed to discuss logistics with Nico for a bit, so they've been chatting. I'm trying to research everything I can about Rome and the Amalfi Coast. As Beckett mentioned, it appears that Rome is more historical, while the coast is stunningly beautiful.

At some point, he makes his way back to me and flashes my favorite sexy smile. "Are you excited?"

I giggle. "Does it show?"

"You're physically bouncing in your seat. More than Andie when I let her have dessert for dinner."

He sits and I lean into him. "I'm just finding it hard to believe that I'm getting to do this. It's like a dream. I can't wait."

"I love that I get to be here for your first time." He lifts my chin. "The first of many. Italy is special. You're special. I want you to have the best experience possible. I need you to do something for me."

I look into his blue eyes. "Anything."

"Let me spoil you a little bit this week."

"You're already spoiling me by taking me and buying me that dress."

He gives me those puppy dog eyes of his. "Please. Let me show you everything the right way. The shopping is incredible. Let me buy you a few things."

"I don't need anything."

"The very definition of spoiling is getting things you don't *need*. I know you don't *need* them, but I want to *give* them to you, and I just can't battle with you over it at every turn. What's the point in having the money I do if I can't watch the people I care about enjoy it? You can't be buried with your money. Let me use it. Please."

"I don't know, Beckett. I just want you and your time."

"I know, and I adore you for that. Don't deprive me of the pleasure of showing you Italy the right way." He pinches his thumb and index finger close together. "Just a little bit."

I blow out a breath. "I feel like my definition of a little bit and yours are quite different."

He smiles as he takes my hand and kisses each of my knuckles slowly. "We can both be flexible, but we agree you won't battle me every time I want to treat my girl like the princess she is?"

How am I supposed to argue when he's so damn swoony?

I think of what Dr. Pearl said and respond. "Okay. Only a little bit. A few small things."

He winks. "Deal."

I'm confident that will not be the case.

WE ARRIVE first thing in the morning, Rome time. His meeting is at noon, so he wants to immediately show me around for a rapid tour. We hit the Colosseum, the Pantheon, the Spanish Steps, and the Trevi Fountain. At the Trevi Fountain, I learn that if you throw one coin over your shoulder into the water, you're guaranteed to return to the city. If you throw two, you're promised that you'll find love. If you throw three, you're guaranteed marriage. Naturally, Beckett makes me throw all three, and kisses me while I do it. It may be the most romantic moment of my life. There was even a crowd of women clapping for us, practically drooling over my man.

When we're finished, he takes my hand. "We need to drop our bags at my friend's place, and I need to change for my meeting."

"No problem. I'll just walk around all afternoon."

"I've already made arrangements for you."

"What are they?"

He winks. "You'll see. Trust me, you'll love it."

"I don't want to be stuck in shops all day when I'm surrounded by so much history and beauty."

He pulls me close and softly kisses my lips. "Trust. Me."

I nod as Nico picks us up and we make our way to his friend's house. I realize I never asked him about where we're staying. "What's your friend's name?"

"Sergio."

"What does he do?"

"He's a politician. He won't be there when we arrive, but he'll be at the party we're attending tonight. You'll meet him then."

"Do you have a key to get in?"

He smiles. "They know we're coming. Don't worry."

We pull up to a stunning building that spans several city blocks. I look at Beckett in question. "What's this?"

"His place."

It doesn't look like an apartment building. It looks like...no, it can't be. I read the sign out front. *Quirinal Palace*.

"We're staying at a palace? A freaking palace? Who's your friend?"

He mumbles, "The president of Italy."

I blink a few times as I let that register. "Your alleged *friend* is the president of the entire country?"

"Yes."

"And this is his palace? Like an actual palace?"

He laughs. "Yes, but he doesn't even live here. He only works here."

"He has a palace with what looks like over a thousand rooms, and he doesn't bother to live in it?"

"He doesn't like living in the city."

I have no more words for this insanity.

Nico carries our bags as the staff welcomes us. They were clearly awaiting our arrival and practically rolled out the red carpet.

I don't think I've uttered a word as I continue to process the fact that I'm sleeping in a fucking palace tonight. Kings and queens have probably slept here.

We're shown to our room and, well, it's in keeping with a palace. I'm still not able to form words.

Beckett rubs my back. "Relax. It has a bed and a bathroom like everywhere else."

I joke, "Where's the party tonight, The Vatican?"

He scrunches his face. "Will you be upset if I say yes?"

"Beckett, I..."

Before I can finish my thought, he kisses me. I mean *really* kisses me. His lips move over mine. His tongue is in my mouth. His taste is quickly becoming my favorite thing in the world.

I thread my fingers through his hair and moan into his mouth. His hands move up the back of my ripped Ramones concert T-shirt. I wonder if anyone has ever worn a Ramones T-shirt in this palace before. I'm guessing not.

He gives my ass one squeeze before finally breaking free, leaving me breathless. "Now that you're calm, we can move on. I need to get dressed for my meeting."

"I'm far from calm, Windsor."

He chuckles. "I like it when you call me by my last name. I feel like you're about to spank me or something."

"Is that what you'd like, *Windsor*?"

He smiles. "I wouldn't mind giving you a little spanking."

He slaps my ass before unpacking and changing into a business suit. I shamelessly watch him. Boy, does he wear a suit well.

He catches me ogling him and winks at me. "Like what you see?"

I nod. I might orgasm from watching him like this.

"Good. I can't wait to see you dressed up tonight. We need to leave with Nico. He's dropping me at my meeting and then he's taking you where I've planned."

We drop Beckett off at a more traditional, business-style building. As soon as he gets out, I ask Nico, "Where are we going?"

"I'm under strict orders not to tell you."

"He's not going to make me *shop* is he?" I can't help but say it like it's a dirty word.

Nico smiles. "I think you'll like the afternoon he planned for you. In fact, I know you will."

"Hey, Nico, what's going on with you and Glinda?"

I notice him stiffen. "Nothing. She's an incredible woman. We're friends."

"I know, but don't you want to be more than friends? You should ask her out."

"I don't think Mr. Windsor would like that."

"Why not? He loves his mom, and he adores you."

"I can't jeopardize my job, ma'am."

I think I need to talk to Beckett about this. I can't imagine he'd begrudge his mom and Nico their happiness.

I sit back and take in the gorgeous city as we drive through it. We eventually head up a big hill, pulling into what appears to be some kind of park. It's definitely not a shopping area, which makes me happy.

When the car stops, an adorable, warm, older man opens the door with a big smile. In heavily accented English, he asks, "Ms. Tremaine?"

"Yes."

He holds out his hand for me. "*Prego*. I'm Mario. Welcome to Savello Park."

I take his hand as he helps me out of the car. Nico opens the window. "Mario will take care of you. I'll be back for you in a few hours."

"Okay. Thanks, Nico."

Mario loops his arm through mine. "Do you know where we are?"

I motion toward the sign. "Other than the name, no."

"Savello Park is also known as *Giardino degil Aranci*, the Garden of Oranges. It's considered one of the most romantic, picturesque places in all of Rome." He points to the lining of trees. "Not only are the orange trees majestic, wait until you see the view of the city."

The small park is gorgeous with all the trees lining the edges. It's like they were placed there for purely aesthetic reasons and grown to absolute perfection. I feel as though I'm looking at a painting come to life.

We make our way to the edge of this small park, and I gasp. The views overlooking all of Rome are simply spectacular. You can see for miles.

I turn and notice an easel and several painting supplies. I smile. He understands me. He arranged for me to paint all afternoon. I think I fall just a little harder for Beckett Windsor in that moment.

I look around and realize we're alone. The park is empty. "This must be a public park. Where are all the people?"

He gives me a coy smile. "Mr. Windsor must know someone pretty high up because the park is closed to everyone except you this afternoon."

Yep, the freakin' president of Italy. That's who he knows.

Mario points to a table of fruit and refreshments. "Should you get hungry or thirsty. I've also left you several buckets of water for your paintbrushes. I'll be on the bench over there. Just call if you need me."

"Thank you, Mario."

I look around. I don't know what to paint first, this gorgeous park or the spectacular views.

I sit and get started as a few ideas start to take shape.

Before I know it, five hours have passed. I love my three small creations. I'm putting the final touches on the smallest one when I feel two familiar hands snake their way around my body and a sexy scent invades my senses.

I lean back into Beckett and whisper, "Thank you for this. I'll remember today for the rest of my life."

He kisses my neck. "I told you to trust me." Still holding me close, he examines the paintings. "You're so talented. These are beautiful. I knew they would be. You could sell them for a fortune."

"Not a chance. These two are for us to remember our time here." I point to the smaller one. "This one is for Mario." It's him on the bench, reading his newspaper, surrounded by the historic, picturesque orange trees.

I turn my head back to him. "How was your meeting?"

"Very good. In fact, Jade's designs for their new offices and stores in the US blew their minds. She's extremely talented."

I smile. "Thanks for telling me that."

"It's the truth." He takes my hand. "Let's give Mario his gift and then get dressed for this evening. We're already running late."

I've never seen a person as happy as Mario when I present him with his gift. He's adorable.

We then head back to the palace to get showered and dressed for dinner.

CHAPTER TWENTY-ONE

BECKETT

I'm straightening my bowtie when Amanda walks out of the bathroom. My chin drops. "How did I get so lucky? You're stunning."

She's in a black and white dress with a low neckline and a sinfully high slit up the side, showing a sliver of her toned legs. There's more than a hint of her perfect, full breasts showing down the middle. They seem to defy gravity. Her hair is up in a loose bun with pieces falling down. Her makeup is there, but minimal. She doesn't need any. She's so naturally beautiful.

She blushes before her eyes move up and down my body, and then she bites that lip of hers. "I've never been into the whole tuxedo thing, but you in a tux might change my mind."

I walk a full circle around her, examining every glorious inch. "Do you mind if I make two minor modifications?"

Her face drops. "Oh. Sure."

I stand behind her and remove the necklace with Jade's name on it that she always wears. "Don't freak out. This is just a loaner for the evening. I didn't do anything crazy like buy it for you." Well, not yet.

I hold a blue, velvet necklace box out in front of her. "Open it."

She does and gasps. "Oh my god." She gingerly touches it like it's going to burn her. "It's the most spectacular thing I've ever seen."

"It's a purple diamond. It's not exactly like a wine glass, but it's close. It's actually called a grapevine mood diamond. Legend says that when your heart is full, it appears more purple, as in your wine glass being full. When it's not full, it appears more like a traditional diamond color, meaning your glass is empty." In reality, it has to do with how certain light hits it, but the story I told her is the more romanticized version.

She continues gently touching it in awe. "It's very purple right now."

I kiss her neck. "I suppose that means your heart is full." I take it out of the box and hold it close to her neck. "May I?"

She nods and I clasp it around her neck. I turn us so we're standing in front of the mirror.

She touches it again. "It's beautiful."

"It's you who is beautiful."

"I'm afraid something will happen to it. Maybe I shouldn't wear it."

"It's insured. Don't worry, enjoy it. Jewelry is meant to be worn and enjoyed. You can't appreciate its beauty if it remains in the box."

"I'm afraid to ask what it's worth."

"You don't want to know."

"I suppose I don't. What's your other *modification*?"

I smile as I slide down to my knees. I slowly run my hands up her bare thighs until they meet her panties, pulling them down and off, and then placing them in my pocket.

I take advantage of the slit and sink my face into her pussy and give her a long, slow lick. When I'm done, I look up at her. "I want you bare for me tonight. I want to touch you and smell you all night until I can't take it another minute. And then we're going to come back here and I'm going to fuck you until the sun comes up."

Her cheeks flush and her breathing picks up. She swallows a few times. "My slit might be a little high for this party."

"Don't worry, I'll be glued to you all night. No one will see what's mine." I apply a little pressure to her pussy. "You'll enjoy tonight. I promise."

We walk outside and get into the limo. Nico is in the front with the driver, and the partition is up. I immediately run my hand under her dress and dip two fingers into her.

She grabs my wrist. "Beckett. What are you doing?"

"I told you. I want to touch you, taste you, smell you. All night."

She gradually releases my wrist, spreads her legs a bit, and leans her head back, giving in to the pleasure.

As I pump my fingers in and out a few times, her jaw slackens and she grips my shirt. I take it nice and slow. I want to keep her on the edge all night, never taking her over. She's going to be begging for it, dripping for it, by the time we get back.

I give just a few more pumps before I pull my fingers out and suck them into my mouth. She watches on with heavy eyelids. Her breathing is labored. "Please. Finish before we get there."

I take her hand and kiss it. "Not yet, cherry pie."

I give her a few moments for her breathing to even out before saying, "I should tell you that there may be cameras at the event tonight. I can't control that."

"Cameras?"

"Paparazzi. The Italian paparazzi, in particular, can be aggressive."

"Oh, well I can't imagine they'll care about me."

But they care about me. Perhaps I shouldn't share that.

We arrive at The Vatican and Nico opens the door for us. Amanda looks around in wonderment as we get out of the limo. Camera flashes go off in our faces immediately.

It's undoubtedly overwhelming for her.

I whisper, "It's easier to just smile for a few photos and then they'll move on. If you play hard to get, they want you more."

She nods in understanding as we both smile for a few photos with my arm around her.

I feel her stiffness as she takes in our grand surroundings, and we make our way to the front door. "Relax. It's just a party. We're going to drink, eat, and dance. By lunch tomorrow, you'll be in a bikini on a boat deck with the best piña coladas you've ever had and all the cherries you can eat. I've had three cases brought on board."

She giggles as I feel her begin to relax. "Are the cherries for me or you?"

I lick my lips. "Both. Amanda-dipped cherries are now at the top of my food pyramid."

She smiles and I swear my heart explodes. I'm so far gone for her.

"They won't have piña coladas tonight. They'll only have Italian wines. They're strict about that here. You don't have to drink it."

"It's not like I can't drink wine. I just prefer a good, cold, cherry-filled piña colada."

"I prefer a cherry-filled Amanda."

She stops us in our tracks and brings her body in front of mine. She wraps her arms around my neck and softly kisses my lips. "Thanks for today. It was one of the best days of my life."

I place my hands on her waist and pull her close, giving her another kiss. I mumble into her mouth, "The day isn't over yet. I promise it's going to get better for you."

Our tongues touch, and the kiss escalates. It's a bit much while in public, and potentially way too much for our current location, but I find that I simply don't care. I love that she doesn't either. But when I catch a few flashes going off, I break the kiss. I don't want her to regret it later.

We make our way inside and to our table, where everyone stands at our arrival. I hug my friend. "Sergio, it's so good to see you."

He slaps my back. "You as well. Is everything good at the house?"

"Yes, thank you. Let me introduce you to Amanda Tremaine."

He smiles. "Tremaine? You brought a French girl to my house? Tsk tsk."

I let out a laugh. "She's one hundred percent American, I assure you." I wink at Amanda. "As American as warm cherry pie."

He holds out his hand and Amanda takes it, looking like a deer in headlights. Sergio soothes her nerves as he kisses her hand. "It's a pleasure to meet you, Ms. Tremaine."

"Thank you for letting us stay in your..."

"House," Sergio finishes.

Amanda lets out a laugh. "Yes, thanks for letting us stay in your little ole house."

Sergio laughs. "I like her."

I grab her hand. "So do I."

I introduce Amanda to Sergio's wife and the other people at the table whom I assume she doesn't realize are among the highest-ranking Italian politicians.

She does a great job at making small talk, better than I had assumed. I think they're all as enamored with her genuineness as I am.

We're sitting as they begin serving dinner. I'm speaking with Sergio on my right. Amanda is to my left speaking with the woman on the other side of her. Under the table, I run my hand up and down the inside of her thigh.

I spend the entire meal teasing her. I run through her a few times, but I mostly just work around where she's now dripping for me.

She spreads her legs a bit in encouragement,

constantly shuffling her hips toward my roaming fingers.

As dessert arrives, I slowly slide two fingers into her. I hear her suck in a breath when I do, but she doesn't stop me.

Sergio asks her, "Did you enjoy your time in Savello Park today?"

Amanda bites her lip and tries to play it cool, as if my fingers aren't pushing deep inside her body. "It was wonderful. I assume I have you to thank for the hours of privacy?"

"When I heard that a talented artist wanted to paint there, I couldn't resist."

She closes her eyes briefly. "I hope I did the beauty justice."

"No doubt you did."

I look around. Everyone is eating and chatting. Amanda is gripping the sides of her chair, about to come.

I pull my fingers out and she whimpers. I run them through the cannoli placed in front of us. Without breaking eye contact with her, I slide them into my mouth and suck both her cream and the cannoli cream off them.

"This dessert is delicious."

Everyone at the table nods in agreement.

Amanda breathes, "Beckett, I need you."

I mouth, "Soon."

As we finish dessert, I take her hand while she's speaking to a woman at our table. "I've been dying to dance with my girl all night. Will you excuse us?"

The woman smiles and we leave for the dance

floor. As soon as we're there, I pull her into my arms. "Are you doing all right?"

"Everyone is very nice."

"I wouldn't have brought you otherwise."

She narrows her eyes. "You're the only one that's not being nice."

I laugh as I rub her face. "I will be in less than an hour. For what it's worth, I'll never eat a cannoli again without thinking of your sweet cherry-pie taste."

She runs her fingertips through my scruff. "I'm going to sit on this later and you're going to finish the job."

I smile. "Is that so?"

She nods. "You've got me all twisted up, and you're doing it on purpose."

"The payoff will be worth it." I squeeze her neck just a drop. "I'm going to fuck you while you wear nothing but that necklace."

Her eyes flutter. She's so on edge right now. Right where I want her.

I discreetly pull her panties from my pocket and sniff them. Now it's my eyes that flutter.

Her face flushes as she watches me. I hold them to her nose. "Smell."

She inhales.

"So good, right?"

She nods as she pulls her body as close to mine as she can.

Making sure we're out of view, she reaches down and rubs my cock a few times. She brushes her lips across mine. "Is it time to go yet? It feels like it is."

She looks up at me with fire in her eyes. Desire and

need are written all over them. I can't wait another minute. I think we're both finally about to snap.

I take her hand and practically growl, "Let's get out of here."

I hear her breathe, "Thank god," as we make our way back to the table.

We say a few quick goodbyes and thank-yous. I had texted Nico to have the limo out front, and it's there when we walk out.

Without bothering to say a word to him, we practically dive in. I hear Nico chuckle, but I don't give a crap.

As soon as the door closes, she's straddling me and her mouth crashes with mine. She's biting, sucking, and nibbling on my lips. Her hands are all over my body. I haven't seen her this ravenous, even after her shopping trip the other day. It's so fucking hot.

"Oh god, Beckett, get inside me."

I run my fingers into her and push them deep.

"I need more than fingers."

"Not yet."

She rides my fingers hard, but when I feel her orgasm cresting, I pull them out.

She begins to yell out in frustration, but while her mouth is open, I shove my fingers in. "Now suck your pussy cream like a good girl."

And she does. She sucks hard.

"Tell me how good it tastes."

She moans.

Mercifully, the car arrives at the palace. We don't bother to wait for Nico to open the door before rushing inside. I can hear him laughing again.

We burst into our room, and she looks like a bull

charging a red flag. She shoves me onto the bed. Well, I let her shove me because it's so damn sexy and I want to see what she'll do.

As soon as I'm down, she makes good on her promise and climbs over me, pulls up her dress, and sits right on my face. "I swear to god, Beckett, if you don't make me come right now, I'm flying home tonight."

I smile into her as I get right to work. I don't tease her anymore because I know I don't need to. She's already on the cusp. She's been there all night.

I pull her lips apart and suck on her already swollen, sensitive button. She's writhing over me, fully riding my face without a care in the world. Her juices are everywhere. They're flowing out of her. I'm bathing in her.

It takes all of thirty seconds for her to scream my name out in a loud orgasm. She's squeezing my face and pulling my hair, completely lost in the pleasure. My cock is aching for her.

As soon as it's over, she slides down my body. "Now. You need to get inside me now."

Like clumsy teenagers unable to control themselves, we remove my clothes together. She licks up my face. "I should tease you for hours as payback."

"Touching you, tasting you, and smelling you is a tease for me too. Now stand up so I can get you naked and take advantage of you."

She rises and turns so I can unzip her dress. It falls to the floor, and she stands there, naked except for the necklace, like I've been imagining all night.

I run my eyes all over her. She's perfection. She's built like a real woman, all softness and curves. I don't think I'll ever get enough of her body. My cock is leaking seeing her like this.

She turns back around and momentarily slows down as her hands run all over my tattoos. She's quickly become intrigued by them, but I suppose I knew she would. That's why I waited so long for her to see them. I know I'll have to answer her questions soon enough.

Our tender moment quickly ends as we simultaneously reach for each other.

"I can't wait another second to be inside you."

I easily lift her, and she wraps her legs around me. My tip finds her entrance and I push in.

Her head tilts back. "Oh god. I need this. I need you."

I walk until her back meets a wall and then push in deep, as far as I can. She gasps for air. "Yes. You're so deep. So damn good."

I give her a few seconds before pulling back and then slamming into her. She screams as she grabs onto my hair for dear life.

I do it over and over again. Her gorgeous tits are bouncing all over the place. She's so fucking hot. I'm consumed with need for her, and I love her need for me. To see her like this. To make her feel unending pleasure. It's spread all over her face and her body.

She's fluttering all around me, sucking in my cock, totally absorbed in her pending orgasm.

She tilts her hips, giving me the best possible angle each time I slam into her. She's scratching, pulling, and clawing at me.

I think the entire room is shaking as I pummel into her. We might take the old palace down, but she happily takes every ounce my big body gives her small one.

We're in a rhythm now. More like lovers who know each other's bodies well, not like a couple who has only been intimate a small handful of times. We're so perfect together. I hope she feels it too.

Her screams escalate. It's not long before another orgasm makes its way through her body. Her legs squeeze my body as she rides through it, and her fluids gush down onto my balls.

She's dazed. It's clear she can't see straight right now. I peel us off the wall and move us over to the desk. It's undoubtedly centuries old. Kings and queens have probably used it. I doubt they envisioned me bending her over it and fucking her senseless on top of it.

There's a window above the desk. I flick open the curtain to a beautiful view of the city.

I place her down and bend her over the desk. She's only just starting to regain her senses from her latest orgasm, leaning most of her weight over the desk.

I pull her hair until my mouth meets her ear. "Do you want my cock back inside you?"

She breathes, "Yes. Please."

I slide my fingers into her. "Is this where you need it?"

She nods.

"Do you realize how well your pussy takes my cock? It was made to take it."

She's getting wetter, if that's even possible. "Oh god, Beckett."

She likes the praise. I wonder if she's ever truly explored this side of herself.

I slide them out and to her back entrance, pushing two fingers inside. She lets out a long moan.

"What about here? Do you want me here? I've been thinking of this ass, this perfect ass. I wonder if it will take my cock as well as your pussy does."

"Yes. Everywhere. I want you everywhere."

Dropping to my knees, I lick the come dripping down her legs. "I'll never get enough of your taste, sweet girl. My cherry pie."

I look up and watch as she glistens further. Every word of praise pushes her that much more. Drives her closer to the edge.

I want to draw this out more than I already have, but the need to be back inside her is overwhelming.

I stand and slam back into her pussy. She yells out as she grips the end of the desk.

"Queens may have sat at this desk, cherry pie, but none hold a candle to you."

She uses her hold on the desk for leverage and she fucks me every bit as much as I fuck her. I'm not an inexperienced man, but this is unequivocally the best sex I've ever had in my life. My attraction and affection for her hit me hard. I know in this moment that I will do anything to keep her and protect her. I love her. She's mine.

CHAPTER TWENTY-TWO

AMANDA

I wake to Andie's sweet voice. She's giggling, as always. She's such a happy kid. Beckett has made sure of that.

I hear Beckett whisper, "Shh, baby. Amanda is sleeping."

I turn my head and see Beckett sitting up in the bed with his phone, smiling into the camera. I've never seen a man so devoted to his daughter.

He notices I'm awake and his smile widens. It's the lopsided smile that I get lost in. God, he's handsome.

He looks back into the camera. "You got lucky. She's awake. Do you want to say hello?"

Andie screeches, "Yes!"

He discreetly motions for me to cover up. I look down and realize the sheets are at my waist.

I cover my body and then sit up. He turns the camera and I wave. "Hi, Andie."

"Hi! Amanda, do you love Rome? Where did you go?

What's your favorite part? Did you look pretty at your party? Can I see pictures?"

I laugh at all the questions. Beckett says, "She looked like a princess last night."

I turn to him. He's so damn sweet. But then he whispers in my ear, "And then fucked me like a queen."

So much for sweet. I let out a laugh before turning to the camera. "It's so beautiful in Rome. Have you been here?"

"Yes, I think, once. We usually go on Daddy's boat, but we stopped in Rome one time." She turns to the side, "Right, Gigi?"

I hear Glinda's voice. "Once that you remember. You've been a few times."

"Oh." She looks back into the camera. "Daddy said you painted yesterday. I can't wait to see it."

"I'll send Gigi pictures and she can show them to you."

Andie looks more closely at the camera as though she's examining us. "Amanda, did you forget your pajamas?"

I hear Glinda cough-laugh before deflecting. "Andie, Daddy and Amanda have to get going to Daddy's boat. Why don't you say goodbye?"

"Wait! Daddy needs to tell me his morning joke."

Beckett turns the camera back to himself. "Want to hear a good pizza joke?"

Andie nods. "Yes, of course."

He scrunches his nose. "Never mind. It's too cheesy."

Andie giggles. I hear Glinda's voice. "Good lord, Beckett, do you Google terrible jokes every night before bed?"

He lets out a laugh. "Something like that."

"Bye, Daddy. Bye, Amanda. Have fun on our boat. I love it. I can't wait to go on it this summer."

We both say goodbye and he ends the call.

I look at him. "It sounds like Andie has been here a lot."

"We spend a few weeks each summer off the coast on the boat. It's our happy place."

"Oh, it's big enough to spend more than a few nights?"

He gives a sly smile. "Just barely."

"If she loves it here, why didn't we bring her?"

He pulls my legs down and slides his body between them, pinning my hands over my head. Kissing me softly, he says, "Because I'm selfish and I want you to myself."

AFTER ANOTHER ROUND of category-five-orgasm-inducing sex, we get packed and dressed. "How long is the drive to your boat?"

I see the corners of his mouth raise in amusement. "Well, normally about five hours, but I have something else in mind for us."

Fifteen minutes later, we're in a helicopter, leaving the roof of the palace, and heading toward his boat. I guess this is how the other half lives.

I squeeze his hand for the entire ride, admittedly a little scared, though loving the view.

He places his hand on the pilot's shoulder. "Give her a lap when we get there."

"Yes, sir."

In less than an hour, we're over the most turquoise-colored, majestic water I've ever imagined. It almost seems fake, like it was contrived on a movie set or created in a painting. But it's my current reality.

He leans over. "We'll ride around the island on my

smaller boat tomorrow, but I thought you'd like to see it from up here."

"You have two boats?"

"Yes. One for sleep and one for fun."

Yep, because it's totally normal to have two boats. In Italy.

As we finish the circle, I notice a sea of boats that look anchored about one hundred feet offshore. It's hard to tell the difference between them, but I ask, "Which one is yours?"

He winks as we get closer to a boat that looks like a swan. Oh, and it's the biggest boat here by tenfold. And it's not a boat. It's a floating mansion.

"That's your boat?"

He nods.

"Why does it look like a swan?"

He points to it. "Do you see the head of the swan?"

"Yes."

"That's the other boat. The smaller, sport boat. The neck of the swan lowers it to the water. You'll see tomorrow. Today I just want you to myself."

The pilot presses a button and says, "Whirlybird three to Enchanted. Are we clear for landing?"

A voice comes on our earphones. "Enchanted to Whirlybird three. You are clear."

I look at Beckett. "Your boat is named Enchanted?"

He nods.

"When did you buy it? When did you name it?"

Though he's normally so confident, he looks a bit like a teenager caught doing something naughty. He doesn't make eye contact with me for a few moments.

He eventually steels his shoulders and looks me in the

eyes. He takes my hand and kisses it. "A little less than five years ago. The day after I met you."

WE LAND as I continue to process what he said. Do things like this happen in real life?

As we step off the helicopter and onto the boat, I'm realizing that I have no concept of real life anymore.

"How big is this boat?"

"Four hundred and fifty feet long."

"How many rooms?"

"Thirty."

"It's just going to be us?"

"I have a crew, plus Nico. But don't worry, we'll have privacy."

"I wasn't worried. I just didn't appreciate what we were doing. I thought we were going to be rocking back and forth at sea for a few nights on a one-room houseboat."

His eyes sparkle with mischief. "I promise we'll be rocking the boat."

I laugh. "Even you can't make this boat rock."

"Wanna bet?"

I'm not sure how he can be so playful. Maybe I'm just in shock at our surroundings.

"Relax, Amanda. This is my happy place. I want it to be yours too. Let's get changed into our swimsuits and enjoy piña coladas and cherries by the pool."

Because, of course, there's a pool on the boat. It's totally normal to have a pool on a boat.

I make it a point to introduce myself and try to remember the names of everyone on the crew. They're all extremely warm and welcoming.

We head down to our room. It's not really a room. It's kind of like Beckett's bedroom at the house. It's a suite with several rooms.

Our luggage is delivered, and we get changed. I throw on a bikini with a cute pool dress, grab the latest Jade Dollston romance novel, and anxiously wait by the door.

Beckett walks out in his swimsuit. Man does he wear it well. I can't take my eyes off his body. "Will you tell me about your tattoos?"

"I will. Let me show you something first."

He takes my hand, and we head up a few flights of stairs. We emerge to a circular room surrounded by windows. The views are amazing.

I notice there's a painting area set up with nearly as many supplies as he had at the house. I turn to him. "Is that for me?"

He smiles as I wrap my arms around his neck.

I run my fingers through his hair. "You're so getting lucky tonight."

He lets out a laugh. "It's been a few hours, I'm more than ready."

He kisses up my neck. "Are you ready for some food, sun, and piña coladas?"

"I am. I've been hearing about these special piña coladas for days. I hope they meet my very high expectations. I'm kind of a piña colada snob."

He laughs again as he leads me to the pool area where lunch is waiting for us, along with two piña coladas, each with at least ten cherries.

The pool area is like a resort with two dozen lounge chairs, multiple tables, and a bar. Is this a private boat or a cruise ship?

We sit to eat, and I take in the majestic scenery. The

island in front of us is small yet beautiful. It's almost like a little mountain in the middle of the ocean. It looks like there's a small town by the docks. "Where are we?"

He points to the land. "The small, mountain-looking island right there is Capri, it's one of my favorites. We'll take a boat ride around it tomorrow and then dock for lunch and shop all the way at the top. There are a few special places I want to take you. Things you can't see anywhere else in the world."

"I can't wait." I look up and down his body. "Tell me about the tattoos. When did you get them?"

"After Jenny died."

I point to the bird-like creature that I've never seen before. It covers his entire chest and abdomen. "What's that?"

"It's a Griffin, which is a mythological creature, sort of like dragons and mermaids."

"I've never seen or heard of it before. It's so unique."

He nods. "It's a combination of a lion and an eagle. It was known to be the protector of treasure. It was my pledge to protect Andie at all costs. She's the treasure of my life. My everything. There's nothing I won't do to make sure she's happy and safe."

I can't help but smile at him feeling that way. "And what about the eyes? They're big and open."

He looks pained. "That's what they are. Big and open."

"Why?"

"Do we have to talk about this?"

"I want to understand you."

"What about you? What caused you to spiral into addiction? We've talked a lot about our lives, but I don't know that story."

"Is this your way of deflecting?" I notice he does that when he gets uncomfortable. He lashes out too.

"You want me to reveal something painful. Is it so much to ask for the same in return? You know more about me than I do you."

"I'm happy to answer your questions. I'm not a fan of secrets." I look off toward the water for a moment as memories flood me. Bad memories. "I ruined someone else's life. My actions were directly responsible for the man I loved losing his dream. It wrecked me. I dropped out of school and started using to the point where I needed it to get by. I was weak. It's a pathetic tale as old as time."

I tell him the whole story of my college boyfriend, the same one I recently shared with Jade. He has a similar reaction to hers, saying that my heart was in the right place, but I'll never see it that way. My actions were unforgivable.

"Was he the first man you were ever intimate with?"

I shake my head. "No."

"Who was?"

I bite back tears. "Reggie's brother. He passed away when we were teens."

"How?"

"A brain tumor. It was terrible. He was such a good, special guy. He protected me from my father. He was the reason I was living at Reggie's. He saw my father's alcohol abuse before others, before he truly became known as the town drunk. Jared saved me from the horrors likely awaiting me."

He listens but says nothing in return, looking pained.

"Jared gave me a ride home one night from dinner at their house. When he realized my father was drunk and being verbally abusive to me, Jared said that he wasn't leaving me with my father and that I needed to pack my bags. Fortunately, their parents were open to me staying with them, where I remained throughout all of high school. He and I fooled around a little for the first year I lived there. Nothing major. He was the first man to ever make me feel seen and cared for. Safe. When he got sick, their family struggled. I did my best to be there for all of them in their various moments of need. Just before he got really bad, he asked me if I would physically be with him. He didn't want to die without experiencing the ultimate act of intimacy. It was my gift to him for saving me."

"How do you feel about that? The reasoning I mean."

"Giving my virginity to a caring man in his moment of need, after he helped me in mine? I'm at peace with it. It was meaningful. He told me I was the reason he was dying happy."

He points to my ankle. "The tattoos?"

"One is obviously for Jade, the other is for Jared. I chose the name Jade because it's both a color and his first initial."

He's quiet for a few moments before practically blurting out, "Jenny never loved me."

I pinch my eyebrows together. "What do you mean?"

"After she passed, I found out that she was just like every other woman I had ever been with. She wanted my money. Not me."

"I'm sure that's not true. How could you possibly know that?"

"I was on her computer when her lover messaged her. He didn't know she had died in childbirth. I played the role for a bit so I could gather information. She loved him. Having my child was her way of financially securing their future. She was planning to leave me after Andie was born. She was going to take Andie to live in Quebec and use my child support and all the other leverage for the life she wanted. A life without me."

"Oh, Beckett." I have tears trickling down my face. I stand and sit in his lap, bringing him into an embrace. "I'm so sorry." I think I'm beginning to understand some of his issues a little more clearly.

He wraps me in his arms. "It's okay. I've had a long time to come to terms with it. I feel like a fool, but I have my daughter, so it happened for a reason. Jenny gave me the best gift of my life. I want to hate her, but I can't. No matter what, she's Andie's mother."

I lay my head on his chest in comfortable silence for a bit. He's been through more than I realized.

"It's the reason I haven't dated. How can I trust anyone's intentions after what happened? After I was completely tricked? Meeting you was so refreshing. You had no clue who I was. I loved that. When I found out about Jenny, I pledged to never let my guard down again. The night we met showed me that maybe there was a chance I could. It impacted me deeply. *You* impacted me deeply."

I have no words for all of that. He impacted me too. After meeting him, I knew on some level that my marriage wasn't going to last.

His fingers aimlessly move up and down my arm. "I've never told another person that story. The one about Jenny. No one knows."

"Your mom?"

He shakes his head. "No."

"Why? You can tell her anything. She wouldn't judge you. She unconditionally loves you."

"It's humiliating. I thought I loved Jenny. I was a fool. And I don't ever want Andie to know, so the fewer people that know the better. It will only hurt her to know negative things about her mother. I want her to think Jenny was perfect and we were in love. It's hard enough to grow up without a mother. Imagine her finding out her mother was nothing but a gold-digging whore. Like all who came before her. And before you ask, Andie is mine."

"I wasn't going to ask. I know Andie is yours. She's got so much of you in her."

"I initially didn't want to test her, and I didn't for a year, but it ate me up inside, so I finally did one. Much to my relief, it confirmed she was mine. I had decided that, regardless of the results, I'd raise her as mine, but I needed to know."

"You've done an incredible job with her, Beckett. You should be so proud."

"It's not easy. I'm not perfect. It's hard going at it alone. I feel like I fail more than I succeed."

I give a small, understanding smile. "I know. More than anyone else, I know."

He closes his eyes briefly as it hits him. "Shit, I'm sorry. Of course you know. You managed it all on your own. And you did it without any money. I'm such an asshole."

"We both have done what's best for our kids as we navigated things alone. Money or not, it's hard. A toddler doesn't give a crap if you have money."

"I don't know how you did it."

"The same way you do. One day at a time, full of love and good intentions."

"Well, you did it right. Jade is one of the most dynamic, confident women I've ever met in my life."

"She's had her share of issues, but I think she's on a good path now."

He looks like he's about to ask more but drops it. He

sweeps my hair out of my face. "Enough of the heavy stuff. We're here to have fun."

I smile. "Yes, let's have fun."

And that's what we do all day. We swim, relax, drink, talk, everything. He's so loving and romantic. I can't get enough of him. He must feel the same because his hands haven't left my body the entire day.

We don't bother to get dressed for dinner, not wanting to leave the pool area, so we eat outside. As it's getting later in the evening, the kitchen staff brings us ice cream sundaes, which I've learned are Beckett's weakness. We're in the hot tub when they arrive, so they set up the toppings right on the lip of the hot tub so we don't have to get out. There must be twenty different toppings.

I rub my fingers through his sexy beard. "Close your eyes."

He does.

I grab a sash from the robes that were left for us and tie it around his eyes.

He smiles as he nods, knowing what's coming.

I then move and straddle his big, hard body.

He pulls me down to him and thrusts his hips up. "Ooh, I like this game. Any game where you're on top of me is a good one."

"No peeking."

"I won't."

"Tell me what you taste."

I spread one of the chocolate dips on my lips and then kiss him. He kisses and licks my lips before tasting his own. "Hmm. That was the dark chocolate."

He's right. "Ooh, you're good at this."

He smiles. "I know my sweets."

I try it with a few different flavors. He guesses them

right each time, and I'm enjoying him tasting them off my lips.

I then trace a cherry all around his lips. He licks it. "Yum, you know this is my favorite. It tastes like you."

"I should stick it inside you like you did to me."

He manages to quickly grab it with his mouth and swallow it down. "Guess you can't do that."

I let out a laugh.

I see there's a cherry sauce. I want to have fun with that one. I'm sure it's his favorite of all the sauces here.

I quietly remove my top and dribble the cherry topping all over my breasts. I lift a bit and rub my nipple over his lips. He flicks his tongue over me before sucking it into his mouth.

He licks and sucks every last drop off one breast.

With his eyes still covered, he smiles and says, "That was delicious. I think I just came in my pants."

I giggle as I feel between his legs. "Nope. Still *very* hard. And I still have another body part covered in cherry sauce for you."

He opens his mouth and I feed my other breast into it. He moans as he licks and sucks every last drop off that breast too.

"I definitely came that time."

I smile as I feel again. "No, you didn't. But you will soon. Both of us will."

I reach down and pull his thick, heavy cock out of his swimsuit. He's rock hard and ready to go. He always is.

I run my fingers over his piercing while I remove his blindfold. "When did you get this?"

"When I was in my twenties."

"What made you get it?"

He runs his nose up my cheek. "For your pleasure."

I giggle. "Tell me the truth. Why did you get it?"

"Because people expect me to be a certain way. Sometimes I like to do just the opposite of what's expected. Even if most people don't know about it, I know it's there and it's my silent protest to always having to act a certain way."

I pump it a few times. "I like that answer. And my body *really* likes that you have it."

I pull my bottoms to the side, bring his tip to my entrance, and sink down onto him. He lets out a low groan. "Your pussy is always so wet and soft. I love being inside you."

My forehead is pressed to his. I'm already breathing heavily. I manage, "I love it too."

Like every time he enters me, I need a moment to get myself together. The combination of his size and the piercing make it so that I don't have full control of my body for a few minutes. Every. Single. Time. He doesn't even need to move, and I feel like I'm already heading toward my first orgasm. The first of what I know will be many with him. He's such a generous lover.

And then there are his words of praise. They're everything I never knew I needed. They set me on fire. *He* sets me on fire.

As the world comes back into focus, I grab a handful of cherries and toss them in my mouth. Wrapping my arms around his neck, my lips take his and the cherries pass freely back and forth during our messy, sexy kiss.

I begin rolling my hips over him while the kiss becomes more passionate and needy. His chocolate-and-cherry-flavored tongue works its way through my mouth. His hands are on my breasts, squeezing and tugging my nipples.

The cherries are eventually gone but we keep kissing.

He applies extra, nearly painful, pressure to my nipples. "Tell me, cherry pie, does a little pain turn you on?"

"Umm hmm." My hips are moving faster, nearing an out of control pace.

"You're so perfect. We're so perfect."

My head is now buried in his neck, but he pulls my hair. "Open your eyes."

I do, and he stares into them. "Look down. Look at where my cock is entering you. Doesn't it look so perfect?"

I look down and barely manage, "Yes. God yes. Beckett, I can't last."

"I know. I can feel you gripping me with that cherry-pie pussy of yours."

My fucking eyes legitimately roll to the back of my head. I think I partially black out from both the pleasure and his mouth. I'm losing control.

He takes over my now-erratic movements and pistons up into me. I can hear the water from the hot tub pouring over the edges onto the deck.

"Beckett, you're so deep. So damn deep."

"That's where my gorgeous girl likes it. Needs it. Now let go. Give in to what your divine body craves."

I do. And then he does. We come together. Forcefully. Powerfully. Beautifully.

When it's over and his movements stop, I'm overcome with my feelings for him. I don't know exactly when it happened, but I've completely fallen for him.

I breathe heavily. "Beckett...I think I'm in love with you."

He rubs his nose on my cheek. "I *know* I'm in love with you."

CHAPTER TWENTY-THREE

AMANDA

On our first full day on the coast, we explore around and on the island of Capri. We take out the small boat, which is still a pretty big boat, and travel through the love rocks. It's also known as the Tunnel of Love, and legend has it that if you kiss while traveling through it, you'll stay in love forever. We happily take video of ourselves kissing while traveling through.

Beckett doesn't care that the captain, crew, and Nico are there. He outwardly loves and romances me at every turn. I've never felt more cherished than I do right now. I've spent forty-four years dreaming of the way love is supposed to look, but it's never been my reality. Until now. I feel like I'm living in a storybook.

We swim in the Blue Grotto, which may be a hidden wonder of the world. I didn't know places like this existed. There is one hiccup in there. When Beckett swims back to the boat to grab me a hair tie, a young man approaches me and tries to grab my ass. Before I realize what's happening, Beckett has him by the throat, holding him under the water.

While I often chastise this type of behavior from Declan, I know on some level I'm attracted to it. There's something incredibly raw and masculine about a man feeling so protective over me that he loses all control. It's something I must need on a certain level.

Beckett's overly alpha, territorial behavior completely turns me on. Immediately after Nico pulls Beckett away from the man, I take Beckett to a hidden alcove in the cave and let him fuck me against the rocks.

Once we circle the island on the smaller boat and get back to land, Nico drives us up the crazy, winding roads to the top of the mountain-like island. After a lunch with spectacular views, Beckett takes me shopping at all the designer stores. He's so happy buying me clothes and other gifts. Every store treats me like a princess. One even closed for us to assure each salesperson was devoted to me.

I've certainly never felt so pampered in my life. I let him pick everything. I don't really care about the items. I'm just happy to see him smiling and carefree. Glinda was right. He takes genuine joy in giving me things.

I put up a little fight over the sheer volume of items but don't want to spoil our day, so he eventually gets his way.

He gives all our bags to Nico and tells him to take them to the boat, that we're going to have dinner up here and then ride the tram straight back down to the docks, as it goes from the top down to the harbor area.

After dinner, we step onto the tram. Though it looks like eight adults can likely fit on it, we get on and they don't let the people behind us enter. I see the tram operators talking to the other people in line.

I look at Beckett in question and he simply takes my hand and kisses it. "I want to be alone with you on here."

"You have something sinister in mind, don't you?"

He smiles. "I might."

I look at the bench on the tram that currently has multiple blankets folded on it. I can only shake my head. "Does public transportation in Italy often come with blankets?"

He doesn't answer. He simply winks and then spreads one of the blankets on the bench and motions for me to sit.

He sits next to me, and the tram begins to move. About two minutes into what I'm guessing is a fifteen-minute journey, the tram stops and all the power goes off, leaving us in the dark.

"You are deeply disturbed, Beckett Windsor."

He chuckles. "Look at the view now that the lights are off."

I do and am in awe. It's breathtaking. We're suspended at the top of a mountain overlooking the entire island and the water. Even though it's dark out, the lights of the town and boats illuminate everything. In my wildest dreams and fantasies, I've never imagined anything like this.

His hand starts to move up my thigh, underneath my dress.

I smile. "You know, if I'm on my back, I won't be able to appreciate the view."

His eyes flash with mischief. "Good point. I guess we'll have to get more creative. We have thirty minutes. Let's make the most of it."

"You're going to make all those people wait thirty minutes just so you can have sex with me up here?"

As he sinks down to his knees in front of me, he says, "I

arranged for transportation for them, along with a little something for their troubles."

I don't think I want to know what this *excursion* cost him.

He reaches higher up my thighs and slides my bathing suit bottoms down my legs, removing them. Spreading my legs wide, he lifts my sundress and stares at my exposed lower half.

He whispers, "So beautiful," as he bends forward and licks up my thigh and then slowly through my center. My head falls back and my eyes close as I exhale a long breath.

"If you close your eyes, you'll miss out."

I open them while he licks through me over and over, treating me to a slow, sensual souvenir. I look around, taking in my surroundings. I'm overlooking one of the most beautiful places on earth while Beckett's face is buried between my legs. How did this become my reality?

He expertly builds me up, like always, until I explode all over his face. When I do, he shifts my hips and moves his tongue to my back entrance, licking all around there.

I scrape my nails over his scalp. I breathe, "Get inside me."

"Where?"

I look down at him and our eyes meet. "Exactly where you are now."

He lifts his head. "I haven't been able to stop thinking about your ass."

I look at him in challenge. "Then do something about it."

He moves to sit next to me and quickly slides down his bathing suit. He pulls out his mammoth cock and gives it a few pumps. I can't help but lean over and circle the tip with my tongue before taking him into my mouth and then deep down my throat.

He rubs my head. "Look at you. Look how perfect you are up here with my cock down your throat. Get it nice and wet for me, cherry pie."

And I do. Long, deep, wet strokes as he works in and out of my throat.

After only a few minutes, he lifts my head by the hair. "I want to be inside you. Straddle me with your back to my front. I don't want you to miss the view."

"What about your view?"

"The only view I want is of my cock in your ass."

The way he talks during sex is an aphrodisiac to me, adding to my gratification.

I do as he asked and straddle him. While I'm still standing, he lifts my dress and slowly rubs my ass. I squirm, anxious to move this along, but he grips my cheeks hard. "Slow down. I need to drink you in. You have the most perfect ass. I can't wait to own it, but I want to savor every second of it."

He's driving me wild with this build up and his words. I continue to squirm, and he spanks me. "Relax. You'll get what you want. You have no idea what you're doing to me."

I'm about to protest prolonging the wait when I hear and feel him spit into my ass and then bring his tongue to my back entrance again. Cheez, that's hot. I'm completely filled with lust for him. I can feel it dripping down my thighs.

He rubs our joint fluids around my back entrance until he sinks two fingers in.

"Oh god. Yes. Keep going. I need more."

"You want my cock in there, dirty girl?"

I breathe, "Yes. Please."

I feel his fingers exit me. I hate the loss but know it's about to get so much better.

He gradually lowers me until I can feel his tip teasing me. Eventually, he enters me, slowly pushing me down until our bodies are completely joined. He stills, only gripping my ass with his fingers. "Oh, cherry pie, I wish you could see this. You taking my cock in that luscious ass of yours."

My eyes meet his in the reflection of the glass to the side of us. They then move down to where I can just make out our bodies joining. It's extremely erotic to see us like this. I want to commit it to memory so I never forget it.

He pulls down my top until my breasts fall free. Grabbing onto them, he begins to encourage my movements.

I move up and down on him until we establish an otherworldly rhythm. He continues with his words of praise. I take in my surroundings and what we're doing. My life has changed so much for the better since Beckett fully entered it.

I don't ever want to do this or anything else with anyone but him. I don't think I've ever truly had that feeling before in my life. As I watch his face reflected in the glass, my heart practically bursts with a fullness I've never known. I know for sure that I'm completely in love with him. It's both exciting and terrifying.

My orgasm is gradually building, but when he slides two fingers into my front entrance, my head falls back and I go off like a rocket ship.

I hear him curse as he then gives in to his own orgasm, filling me.

We slow our movements until we're still, both breathing heavily, covered in sweat.

He squeezes my breasts. "Why are you so perfect?"

I lean my head back onto his shoulder and smile. "Probably because I just gave you my ass, in the dark, suspended a thousand feet above a town, in a vehicle of public transportation."

He lets out a laugh. "Sounds perfect to me."

ON THE SECOND DAY, we explore Positano. I've seen it in a million paintings, but I've never seen the real thing. It's like art coming to life. We have lunch, lay on the beach, and buy fun souvenirs for Andie, Jade, and Glinda.

I spend the early mornings and any other free time painting. Several are of the views I'm looking at while a few are from memory. They're some of the best memories I've ever had.

I'll remember these days fondly because everything is about to change, and not in a good way.

CHAPTER TWENTY-FOUR

AMANDA

My cell phone ringing wakes me up. I turn and see that Beckett isn't in bed. That's odd. I'm usually the first one up.

I look at my phone and notice that it's super early but it's Jade, so I answer. "Hey, love."

"Hi, Mom. What are you up to?"

I stretch and yawn. "Just waking up."

"It's nearly noon. You must be *pretty* tired."

I forgot about the time difference. She's acting weird though.

"Is everything okay with you and the baby?"

"Oh, we're fine. I'm more interested in what you're up to."

She knows something.

"Same ole stuff. How's Collin?"

"Great. So, I decided not to go out for lunch today. Instead, I'm having a sandwich at my desk. I thought it was a good time to catch up on a few of the gossip sites. Imagine my surprise when I see my very own mother on all of them. *All* of them."

"What do you mean?"

"You're everywhere, Mom. Are you in Italy with Beckett Windsor?"

I guess that cat's out of the bag. "I am."

"No shit. There are pictures of you two practically dry humping at some fancy event in Rome the other night. We're going to talk about that amazing dress you wore and the million-dollar necklace around your neck in a minute. There are also a lot of pictures of you two kissing on the Amalfi Coast. And there are pictures of you on a giant mega yacht, and let's just say they're even more intimate."

"What does that mean?"

"You guys are in a hot tub and his head is in your chest. It's a little grainy, but I'm pretty sure you're topless."

"Fuck."

"It definitely looks like you were getting fucked."

"Can you see everything?"

"Not at all. Strangers wouldn't even know it's you. I saw the picture from Rome and that's how I knew. Otherwise I wouldn't have known."

"Where are these pictures?"

"Everywhere. Like every gossip website in existence. Since when are you seeing Beckett?"

"For a bit. You know I met him years ago. We saw each other again recently and there was a spark."

"Well, we can all see the spark now. What does Mr. Pierced Cock think of you spending time with Beckett?"

I'm silent.

She gasps. "Do *not* tell me that it's Beckett with a pierced cock. A fucking Jacob's Ladder?"

"Okay, I won't tell you."

"Beckett's cock is pierced? Holy shit. I would never have guessed that. He's always so damn prim and proper."

"He has to be like that publicly, but that's not who he really is. He's down-to-earth and fun. And sweet. And romantic. He's such a good dad to his daughter."

"But has a big and pierced cock?"

"You're very focused on that."

"I imagine you are too."

I can't help but laugh. "I enjoy *all* sides of Beckett."

"I bet. Have you met his daughter?"

"Yes."

"Why hasn't he met yours?"

"You work with him. You see him nearly every day."

"You know what I mean."

"Perhaps when we get home, we can all get together. Andie, his daughter, has seen pictures of you. She thinks you're a real-life Barbie."

"I *am* kind of Barbie."

"Foul-mouthed, Dirty Barbie. You need to behave in front of her. She's only five years old."

"Ha! Dirty Barbie. I'm telling Collin that one. He'll love it."

"I'm sure he will."

"Should I start calling Beckett *daddy* at the office?"

I sigh. "You wonder why I don't tell you things. We're just dating. Relax."

I'm trying not to get too excited about us, though it's hard not to. I've fallen so hard for him. I think he might be my Prince Charming.

"I'm doing a lot of things, but relaxing isn't one of them. Mom, he's so hot. Every woman in our office drools over him. Every woman in the damn country drools over him. Good for you. Does he make you happy?"

I think about everything he says and does. I can't help but smile. "Yes, baby, he makes me very happy."

"Well then, fantastic." She turns uncharacteristically serious. "Mom, stay off the gossip sites. They'll fuck with your head. It's all made up bullshit. You know what's real and what isn't. Don't forget that."

"Okay. I better go find Beckett and tell him about the photos."

"When are you coming home?"

"I'll be home tomorrow."

"Have fun."

"I will. Love you."

"Love you too."

I'm about to get up when I decide to Google Beckett's name. All the recent hits are now pictures of us this week. There are so many headlines.

Former Playboy Beckett Windsor is Finally Back Out There

Arrivederci Sad Beckett Windsor

Six Years of Hibernation After Wife's Tragic Death, Beckett Windsor Rejoins the Meat Market

Who is the Mystery Brunette Beauty That Has Beckett Windsor So Enamored?

The photo with the last one makes my heart race. It was when we were walking into the party in Rome. I'm smiling at the camera, but Beckett is looking down at me like he's about to devour me, which he sort of did that night. I love this photo. I wonder if I can get a copy.

I flick over to my texts and notice that I have several from Reggie and Victoria. Clearly they've seen all the pictures too. I can't believe how many people look at these gossip websites. I never go on them. Who cares?

I brush my teeth, throw on clothes, and head out in search of Beckett. It doesn't take long before I hear him screaming. "You're my fucking head of security. How did you let this happen to her? I want someone's head on a platter. Sue everyone if you have to. Make them bleed!"

I peek into the room. Nico is cowering while Beckett lays into him. I interrupt, "Is everything okay? Beckett, calm down. Don't yell at him."

Beckett's face immediately softens as he comes to me. He takes my face in his hands and gently kisses me before turning back to Nico. He grits, "Fix this."

Nico nods and we exit the room, heading back to ours. Once we're in there, he closes the door and pulls me into his arms. "I'm so sorry."

"For what?"

He sighs. "There are photos of us all over the place."

"I know. Jade called this morning and told me. What's the big deal?"

"It's a massive invasion of our privacy. *Your* privacy."

"Jade said you can barely make me out in the photos on the boat."

He holds my face. "Baby, someone took our pictures from above while we were making love. That's not okay. I pay a lot of money for security so these things don't happen."

"You can't control drones in the sky."

"The hell I can't. I won't have you mistreated."

"I'm not worried about it, Beckett. You can't let it rain on your parade. I don't want it to ruin the rest of our trip."

I lean into his chest, inhaling his scent. "I want to enjoy our last day here together."

BECKETT

"I want to enjoy our last day here together."

She has no clue what's about to happen, but I won't burst her bubble. If she wants a fun, happy last day, that's what she'll get.

I'm pretty sure I know what's waiting for us when we get home. What have I done?

CHAPTER TWENTY-FIVE

AMANDA

We're on our flight home from Italy. I lean my head on his chest. "Thank you for inviting me. This was the best week of my life."

He tucks my hair behind my ear. "More weeks like this to come. I promise."

"I can't wait to give Andie all her presents. Do you think she'll like them?"

"She'll love them."

Nico interrupts us by whispering in Beckett's ear. Beckett nods. "Grab us a few hats."

"Yes, sir."

He turns to me. "The press is camped out at the airport. The airport is going to give us as much security at they can spare, but with telephoto lenses, those fuckers will capture us. Thus far, they don't have your name. It's up to you how you want to handle things."

"Why would they care about me? Why would they want my name?"

He blows out a breath. "After we met at Reagan's party, you Googled me, right?"

"Yes."

"What did you find?"

"Articles about your business, the sale of your business, and *a lot* of photos of you with various women."

"Right. Before I got married, there was a fascination with my dating life. I don't understand it, but that's why I have Nico. Back then, I had a much bigger security team because they were so intrusive in my life. After Jenny passed and I stopped attending things, the interest waned. That's why it's mostly been Nico for the past five or six years. Perhaps I made a mistake taking you to the event in Rome. I was just so excited for you to have that experience. But the press will now follow us. I've beefed up security, but I think I should get you your own guard that will stay with you full time."

I let out a laugh. "What? That's crazy. I don't need a guard. Like you said in Rome, let them get a few pictures, and then they'll move on to something more interesting. I don't think we do anything so exciting it warrants being followed around. What about Andie?"

"She always has someone shadowing her. People are crazy, and I have a lot of money. I never wanted her to know, hoping she could have a normal life. Her guard stays in the shadows. Obviously, Nico also keeps an eye on her, but the other man stays at school and wherever Andie goes."

Wow. I'm in shock. I had no idea.

We land and Beckett hands me a hat before placing one on his head. "Keep your head down as we walk to the car waiting for us."

This seems like overkill, but I do as he asks. It turns out

he was right. There must be fifty men and women with huge cameras clicking away from just outside the landing strip fences. I hear them shouting questions. They're definitely asking my name.

Beckett simply intertwines his fingers with mine as we walk to and get into the car. Nico must get our luggage because I feel it being loaded into the back of the car.

He turns to me. I can see the pain written all over his face. "Things are going to be different. Just remember that I'm still me and that I love you."

I rub his worried face. "I see you, Beckett Windsor, and I love you too."

"And please don't believe everything you read. They make up whatever they want. They manipulate photos catering to whatever dialogue they please. Remember what's real. What we feel for each other is real."

Jade said the same thing to me. They're both scaring me a bit, but maybe it won't be as bad as they seem to think.

I can see he needs comfort. I kiss him just as Nico gets into the car and he smiles.

We drive through the gate of the airport and can barely make it through the sea of reporters. This is nuts.

We finally make it out to the highway. I try to give him a reassuring smile. "That wasn't so bad."

We sit in silence through the ride home as he nervously strokes my hand. When we pull up to the house, the front gate is swarmed with photographers.

I never really understood the need for his gate and security before, but I guess I do now. We slowly drive through the gate. When it closes behind us, he breathes a sigh of relief.

Fortunately, he has a long, winding, tree-lined driveway,

so the reporters at the front gate can't see the house. I'm now guessing that was likely by design.

As soon as we pull up, the front door opens and Andie comes flying out. Beckett opens the car door. Andie practically dives in and tackles him. She buries her head in his chest. "I missed you, Daddy."

He laughs as he kisses her head. "I missed you too, baby. That's the longest we've ever been apart."

She nods her head into his chest. That hadn't occurred to me.

Glinda walks out and smiles at the interaction. Beckett manages to stand and get out of the car with Andie still attached to him. She doesn't seem to want to let go.

Glinda hugs me. "Are you okay? Damn paparazzi."

I hug her back. "I'm fine. This nonsense will blow over in a day or two."

She rubs my back. "I hope you're right."

We go inside and give Andie and Glinda all their presents. Andie's clear favorite was a painting I made for her of the spot in Capri that Beckett told me is her favorite. She immediately asks to hang it in her room, which is now covered in paintings, both hers and mine. I love it so much.

When we're finished, I stand. "I'm going to head home."

Beckett looks at Glinda and then at me. "I'd like for you to stay here tonight until we figure out your security."

"I told you; I don't want security."

"I understand, but I need you to be safe."

"I have dinner plans with Jade and Collin."

"Invite them here."

Andie jumps up and down. "Yes, I want to meet Jade. Please, Amanda. Tell them to come here. What's her favorite food?"

"Rocky Road ice cream."

She thinks for a moment. "I don't think we have any. We'll order some."

"Sweetie, thank you, but I'm going to meet them for dinner."

Glinda takes my hand. "Amanda, I understand this is all new for you. Trust me when I tell you Beckett only has your best interests at heart. Let him come up with a plan. One night. Andie and I are dying to meet Jade and Collin anyway." She squeezes my hand. "Please. Consider staying. For us."

Shit. I can't say no to her. "Okay, I'll tell them to come here."

BECKETT

Amanda is upstairs showering before Jade and Collin arrive. Mom sits with me. "She doesn't understand what's about to happen."

"I know. I don't know how to protect her."

"I don't think you should be seen in public together. It's only going to fuel more interest in her background. I don't know the details, but I know she had a less-than-ideal childhood. I can't imagine she's interested in the world knowing."

I run my fingers through my hair and blow out a long breath. "I don't know if I can stop it."

"Do your best. You'll have to continue to show her what's real and what isn't. The lines may get blurry for both of you at times. You need to hold it together."

I nod as the doorbell rings. I start to head that way, but Andie sprints past me to answer it. She swings the door open to see Jade and Collin standing there.

"Wow, you *are* Barbie."

Jade lifts an eyebrow. "You must be Beckett's mother. I'm Jade. It's nice to meet you, Mrs. Windsor." She holds out her hand as Andie bursts into hysterics.

"No, I'm his daughter. I'm Andie."

"His daughter?"

"Yes, silly."

"I thought you were much older. My bad." She throws her thumb toward Collin. "This is my baby daddy, Collin."

"What's a baby daddy?"

"The daddy of my baby that's coming in a few months."

"Oh. Well then, I guess my daddy is a baby daddy too. I'm his baby."

Jade has been with my kid for thirty seconds and somehow has already taught her the term *baby daddy*.

Collin holds out his hand for Andie and she shakes it. "It's nice to meet you, Andie." He crouches down. "I need to tell you a secret. But you have to promise not to tell anyone else."

Andie's face lights up. "I promise. What is it?"

He looks around, pretending to make sure no one else is listening, before turning back to Andie. "I love getting my hair braided. Do you know how to braid hair? Because Jade isn't good at it, and I want to look nice for dinner."

Andie's eyes widen. "I *love* braiding hair. You'll really let me do it?"

"I told you; I love it. My niece braids my hair all the time. She's pretty good at it. Are you good too?"

"I think so."

"I can't wait to find out. We'll send her pictures. It will make her jealous."

"What's her name?"

"Lucy."

"How old is she?"

"Five."

"I'm five too. Almost six."

"Maybe you two can meet one day and braid my hair together."

"Really?" Andie looks back at me. "Can I meet Lucy, Daddy?"

"I don't see why not. How about you let Jade and Collin inside the house?"

"Oh. Sorry. Come in."

They walk in and look around. Jade whistles. "I didn't think I'd ever see a house bigger than Carter and Reagan's. I was wrong."

"I love Carter and Reagan's house. It's the most unique, well-thought-out home I've ever seen in my life." I much prefer theirs to mine.

Jade smiles proudly. "Collin designed and built it. It's his dreamchild. Every inch."

I look at Collin in a bit of shock. "Is that true?"

He humbly nods.

"You're very talented. If you have a business card, leave it tonight."

"I will."

Jade asks, "Where's my mother?"

"Just finishing up a shower. She'll be down in a minute."

Jade motions to Collin. "Take Andie to braid your hair. I need to have a little chat with Beckett."

Collin holds out his hand and Andie happily takes it.

As soon as they disappear, she's got her finger in my face. "This fucking sucks for my mom. You need to get your shit together and keep her out of the spotlight. She doesn't deserve it."

"I'm trying, Jade."

"Why did you take her to the party in Rome? That started this mess."

"It was at The Vatican. I wanted her to experience something special. It's been so long since the paparazzi gave a shit about me. I wasn't thinking. It was stupid."

"She's fucking clueless about all this."

"I know."

"Despite her shit life, she believes everyone is inherently good. She doesn't understand that there will be people out there chomping at the bit to tear her down."

"I know. It's one of the things I love about her."

Her eyes widen. "You love her?"

"Yes."

"Does she love you?"

"She says she does."

"Shit. Don't fuck with her, Beckett. She's had enough pain for ten lifetimes. If you hurt her, pierced dick or not, I'll kick you so hard in the balls no amount of money will bring them back."

I hear a laugh. I turn around and see Mom standing there with a huge smile. "I suppose it shouldn't surprise me that Amanda has such a strong, fantastic daughter." She holds out her hand. "I'm Glinda. It's nice to finally meet you."

She shakes Mom's hand. "The good witch of the north? Nice to meet you too."

"Your mother said the same thing to me when we met."

"The genius doesn't fall far from the tree."

We hear a voice. "There's my glowing girl."

We look up and see Amanda at the top of the stairs. I think my heart skips a beat. She's so gorgeous.

Jade mumbles, "For fuck's sake, you're already pussy-whipped."

I smile. "You bet I am."

I take Amanda's hand as she makes her way down the stairs. "You look beautiful."

"I'm in jeans and a T-shirt."

"You wear them well."

Jade moans. "Ugh. Are you guys the mushy couple? I don't think I can deal with that."

Mom laughs again. She's getting a kick out of Jade.

"Thanks for coming. Where's Collin?" Amanda asks as she hugs Jade.

"Andie's braiding his hair."

Amanda smiles as she takes Jade's hand. "I missed you. How are you feeling?"

"I'm fine. I wouldn't know I was pregnant if I didn't know. Show me around this fucking palace."

Amanda takes Jade straight to the studio. I knew she would. Jade looks around and then at me. "You did all this for her?"

I shrug. "It's a fantastic space with great lighting and views. It's perfect for her."

Jade nods toward the smaller easel. "Andie paints too?"

Amanda smiles. "Yes. She's talented. She loves learning. We have so much fun together."

"I'm glad you finally have a little one to paint with." She turns to me. "I inherited zero of her talent. She tried all the time when I was little, but I could barely paint a stick figure."

"You have talent. You have her creativity. In spades."

She shrugs. "Maybe."

We head back downstairs and sit down for dinner. Jade and Collin immediately ingratiate themselves with Mom and Andie.

Mom says, "Jade, I know your stepmother quite well. She and I served on several charitable boards together."

"She's the best. I have no clue how my dad got her."

Mom giggles. "You're refreshingly direct, aren't you?"

I mumble, "You have no idea."

Jade asks Mom, "How long are you in town?"

"I was supposed to head back to Florida last week but stayed when Beckett was asked to go to Italy. I'm leaving tomorrow."

I see Amanda's shoulders drop. She genuinely cares for my mother. I imagine most women would not be okay with the amount of time my mother spends here. I love their relationship.

Amanda turns to her. "Why so soon?"

Mom smiles affectionately at her. "I need to get

back; you two need some privacy. My next visit is only a few months away."

I look at Collin. "Tell me more about your construction and design company."

"I worked with my family for years, but they prefer smaller, more traditional homes. I prefer bigger, unique homes like Carter and Reagan's. I'm in the process of breaking off and going at it alone."

"That must be scary with the baby coming. Do you need backing?"

"Reagan and Carter are my silent partners."

"Oh right, you and Carter are childhood friends."

"Yep. He's been my best friend since we were little kids." Collin smiles. "He wouldn't be who he is today without me."

I let out a laugh. "No doubt. I meant what I said, leave your card."

Mom asks, "Are you thinking of building?"

"I wouldn't mind a house more in my style." I look at Amanda. "Our style."

Jade's eyes move between us, taking it all in. "What the hell is happening here? I just learned about you two yesterday and now you're talking about building a house. How long has this been going on?"

Andie answers, "Amanda moved in here last month."

Jade stares at Amanda. "Is that so?"

Amanda answers, "I stayed most of the last month to get to know Glinda while she was visiting, but she's leaving this week. I'll be heading home."

I see Andie about to protest.

I take her hand. "I'd like you to stay."

Amanda doesn't look happy that I'm saying this in

front of everyone. Before she can respond, Jade says, "I think you should stay here, Mom."

Jade knows that the press will hound her at her house. She's safer here.

I just hope she listens.

CHAPTER TWENTY-SIX

BECKETT

I t took the press two weeks, but they eventually found her name. Because she paints under a pseudonym, they don't know about her many paintings that have sold. They listed her as a struggling artist. She's being portrayed as a gold-digger.

A month after that, they found out about her father. Several people in her hometown were interviewed about him being a thief and a scoundrel until he died. It was twenty-five years ago and has nothing to do with Amanda, but that's not what they focus on. They're insinuating all types of things about her.

I know she's tried to stay away from the online nastiness, but I caught her crying while watching an interview about her father this week.

The press is camped out at her house. She finally

understood the need for security, and she allowed me to hire her a guard. As far as she knows, Lou is her only guard. They seem to get along well. Of course she won't let him sit outside. She feeds and coddles him. She has three others she doesn't know about whenever she leaves the house. I figured she'd freak out.

We spend all our time at my house. We haven't been out in public together since Italy.

I think she's getting stir-crazy. I suggested inviting friends over, which made her happy.

Her two closest friends and their husbands are coming over tonight. I'm looking forward to meeting them, especially Reggie. Her family obviously did a lot for Amanda growing up.

Amanda said she told them to be casual. I'm finding it's nice hosting people and not getting dressed up. It's new to me.

Andie is sleeping at her friend Dylan's house, so she's not here.

The doorbell rings at seven. I'm introduced to Reggie, Sam, Victoria, and Cliff. Amanda hugs them all in such a warm, loving, familiar way.

Reggie and Sam call her Mandy instead of Amanda. I learn that everyone who knew her before she left college always called her Mandy. It wasn't after she dropped out that she had people call her Amanda.

Amanda hates sitting anywhere in the house except the family room. She loves it, so I suggested we do appetizers and drinks in there instead of the more formal living room.

We're all sitting around with drinks, making small talk.

Reggie says, "Mandy, my mom and dad are coming in for a visit next week. They asked about seeing you."

Amanda smiles. "I'd love to see them. It's been years. I didn't realize they're able to travel."

"It's not easy, but they want to come in for SJ's graduation party."

"Has he decided on a school?"

She and Sam look at each other and then she sighs. "We want him to go to a state school. It's a lot cheaper. He got into a few Ivy League schools and wants to go, but they're triple the price. We can't afford it and I don't want him graduating with a pile of debt."

I can't help but interrupt. "What about a scholarship? I know those schools offer several for deserving kids."

She shrugs. "He applied to a few, but it doesn't look like he qualified for any."

We'll see about that. I pull out my phone and fire off a few texts, before turning back to her friends. "Where do your parents live, Reggie?"

"In California. My brother passed when we were teens."

I nod. "I heard. I'm sorry for your loss."

"Thanks. They couldn't stay in the house. They couldn't even stay in the area. The minute I graduated high school, they moved to a small town in Northern California, as far away as possible. They practically died with him. They fell apart and have never been the same since."

I turn to Amanda. "That's when you lived there, right?"

Amanda nods.

"She did more than live with us. She carried us.

My brother wouldn't have lasted as long as he did if not for her."

"Reg..."

"No, Mandy, it's true. My parents were amazing before his illness. The best parents you could ask for, but they fell apart when he got sick. They couldn't manage to do anything knowing their son was dying. Mandy was the one who held me when I cried. Mandy is the one who played nurse to my brother. She managed his medications and doctor's visits. She cared for my parents when they should have been the ones taking care of us. She's a fucking angel sent from above. There's no better human being on this planet."

Amanda shakes her head. "She's exaggerating. They were losing their child. Any parent would feel the same."

"He needed them. I needed them. They failed us both. I have five kids. I can't imagine anything worse than losing one, but I'd like to think I'd go on and live for the others."

Amanda wipes the tears trickling down her face. "Anyway, I'd love to see them. Just let me know when and where."

Reggie nods.

I can tell we need a subject change. I turn to Victoria and Cliff. "How many children do you have?"

Victoria answers, "I have one from a previous marriage, Pandora. She's Jade's childhood best friend. That's how Amanda and I met. Cliff and I have two sons in elementary school. And I agree, Amanda is an angel from above."

I smile. "I guess it's unanimous." I kiss her hand. "You're an angel."

Reggie looks between both of us. "I think I should give some kind of interview. I've known you longer than anyone. I can set the record straight on all this nonsense coming out. Tell them about the real you."

Amanda shakes her head. "Absolutely not. You don't need to be in the line of fire. Think of your kids. That's the last thing I want. This will all blow over at some point."

"At what cost, Mandy? This is so fucking wrong."

I see pain in Amanda's eyes. She's hurting and it's my fault.

AMANDA

The past two months since we returned from Italy have been difficult, but one thing has remained. My love for Beckett. I'm weathering this storm because I can't be without him anymore. I know he's the love of my life. The man I've been waiting for. My Prince Charming.

Is he perfect? No. But he's close. The only thing we ever argue about is his fighting. When something nasty comes out about me, he gets so angry. The next day I inevitably see bruises on his body and face. It's his bizarre coping mechanism. He can't go on like this, but he won't have a conversation with me about it.

I wake up and look down. Beckett's hands are where they always are in the morning. On my breasts.

Without bothering to move them, I reach for my phone. I see a text from Reggie.

> Reggie: Thanks for dinner tonight. My heart is so full for you. You finally found HIM.

I look at the time of the text. It was sent late last night when Beckett and I were otherwise engaged.

I respond immediately.

> Me: Sorry for the delay. We were… otherwise indisposed.

> Reggie: I figured. I got some action too. Sam rolled me in flour and found the wet spot.

> Me: REGGIE! Cut it out!

Reggie gained weight when Jared got sick. Even though some of her jokes are funny, I know they come from a place of hurt and therefore I can't stand them.

> Reggie: Lighten up. I meant what I said. I'll give the interview. I'll set the record straight.

> Me: I love you for offering, but no. This, too, shall pass.

> Reggie: Guess what? SJ got a call this morning about a scholarship. A full ride to any school of his choice. Interestingly enough, he never applied for this scholarship, and it doesn't exist online. Know anything about it?

> Me: I don't, but I'm pretty sure I know someone who does.

> Reggie: Yep. Give him a category-five BJ from me.

Me: LOL. Will do.

I place my phone down and turn around in his arms. He's fast asleep. I run my thumb over his gorgeous, kissable lips and think back to our first kiss. The one that basically altered the course of my life. I was already fairly certain my marriage was a mistake, but kissing Beckett confirmed it for me. He and I shared something in our brief encounter that I knew I had never come close to sharing with my husband or anyone else.

I suppose on some level, I knew then that he was the man for me. I couldn't do anything about it, but in my heart I knew.

I continue to stare at him. He's a beautifully complex man, but I know to his core he's a good man.

I reach my hand down until I get to his cock. He's fast asleep but it's a steel rod right now.

I'm about to work my way down to make good on my promise to Reggie, but before I realize what's happening, my hands are pinned above my head and he's situated between my legs. I look at his face. He's still asleep. I'm the more than willing victim of his sleepfucking at least once or twice a week.

He starts mumbling, as he always does. "I'm sorry. Don't leave me. I love you. I'm trying to protect you. I'm failing. I need you."

And then he moves his hips and sinks into me. Oh god, he feels good. I'm not sure why the level of pleasure he gives me continues to shock me, but it always does.

He slowly begins to rock in and out of me. As is often the case, he wakes in the middle of it, smiles at what I'm allowing to happen, and then really ramps things up as he pounds into my body.

After two category-five orgasms for me, he gives in to his own. When we're done, he rolls to his side and pulls me close.

I run my fingers down his body. "Are you responsible for SJ's sudden free ride?"

He looks away. "I don't know what you're talking about."

"Yes you do."

He scrunches his face. "Are you mad?"

"No, love, I'm not. Thank you."

"I know what that family did for you, getting you out of your house. It's my way of thanking them."

"I love you, Beckett. So much."

"I love you too. Unfortunately, I have to go into the office today."

"Ugh. It's a Sunday."

"I know. Hopefully just a few hours. Do you mind hanging with Andie?"

"I would love nothing more."

He gets out of bed and goes to his closet to get dressed.

I yell out, "You aren't showering?"

He pops his head out with the smile that makes my knees weak. "I want to smell you on me all day, reminding me what I'm missing at home."

Holy hell that's hot.

After he leaves, Andie and I spend most of the day painting. In the late afternoon, I hear my text tone.

> Beckett: I still have a few more things to get done. You two have dinner without me.

Me: Okay. Miss you.

Beckett: It was a mistake not to shower this morning. Smelling you on me all day has me stuck in my chair with a constant boner. It's driving me nuts.

I swear I'm dating the sexiest man ever.

Me: Hurry home for a refresher. Maybe I'll lick it clean for you.

Beckett: I think I just came in my pants.

I giggle at our ongoing joke. He never actually comes in his pants but likes to say he did.

"Andie, I know Daddy only keeps cherry ice cream in the house. What do you say we get lots of flavors and figure out your true favorite. Not his favorite."

"After dinner?"

"Let's make it our dinner. Why not?"

Her eyes light up. "Yes! Can I try Rocky Road like Jade?"

"Absolutely. Let me text Lou."

I text my bodyguard about running to the store. He usually hangs at the front gate. He said he'll pull the car around in five minutes.

Andie and I walk out front to Lou waiting in the car. Though resistant at first, I realized that Beckett was right about me needing a guard. The press doesn't just take pictures. They touch you and stand blocking doors everywhere you go. It became unbearable.

I finally relented and allowed Lou to guard me. He's very sweet and unobtrusive. He's a burly, ex-military man with dark, short hair. He looks scary, but he's kind of a pussy cat once you get to know him.

Andie and I slide into the back. Lou nods his head. "Good afternoon, Ms. Tremaine."

"Lou..."

"Sorry. Good afternoon, Amanda."

"Thank you."

"You as well, Ms. Windsor."

Andie mimics me. "Lou..."

He smiles. "Good afternoon, Andie."

Andie and I giggle as he drives us to the store. The three of us walk in and head right for the frozen dessert section. Andie and I are piling the pints of ice cream into our basket when I turn to Lou. "What's your favorite ice cream, Lou?"

He fidgets nervously. "Do you promise not to tell anyone?"

Andie and I look at each other and smile in excitement. I turn back to Lou and nod. "We promise."

"I like Pink Bubblegum. It's my favorite by far."

That may be the girliest ice cream on the planet. If you gave me a million guesses for Lou's favorite favor, I wouldn't have guessed that. He's six foot four and at least three hundred pounds of muscle.

Andie and I look at each other and then practically fall over in a fit of complete hysterics.

Lou is turning fifty shades of red. He attempts to muzzle our mouths, but we're too busy laughing.

We end up getting ten flavors, eleven if you include the rarely seen Pink Bubblegum flavor.

When we arrive home, I insist that Lou join us for our taste testing.

I taste the Pink Bubblegum. "Lou, this is so gross. I can't believe you like it."

He smiles as he takes a heaping spoonful. "You're crazy. It's the best."

Andie makes a face of disgust. "It's not very good."

She focuses her attention on the Rocky Road. "I think this one is my favorite."

I think she just wants to be like Jade, but I say nothing.

I hold up the Mint Chocolate Chip. "This is my favorite."

Now it's Lou's turn to make a look of disgust. "Ugh. It tastes like toothpaste."

I hear the front door open and close. Beckett walks into the kitchen. He's scowling. "What's going on in here?"

"Daddy, Amanda and I are having an ice cream tasting contest. Lou likes girlie ice cream, but I'm not allowed to tell you which flavor."

He looks at Lou. "I didn't realize ice cream tasting was in your job description."

Lou's eyes widen. "Sorry, sir."

I sigh. "Relax. I invited him."

"Yes, I saw the photos of you three in the grocery store. One big happy family."

Lou points toward the front door and mumbles, "I'm just going to head to the front gate."

Beckett gives him a death stare. "You can come inside when *I* invite you. That's it."

He quickly nods and walks out.

I'm furious, but I'm not getting into things in front of Andie.

He looks at Andie. "What did you have for dinner, sweetie?"

"I just told you. We're doing an ice cream tasting contest for dinner. I think I prefer Rocky Road like Jade."

He gives me a dirty look. "Not exactly a nutritious meal."

He gives her ice cream for dinner at least twice a month. He's got nerve.

I smile at Andie. "Do you want to see if your painting is dry? If it is, wrap it up to take to school tomorrow."

"Okay. I think Dylan is going to love it." She happily skips off toward the studio.

As soon as she's out of earshot I snap at Beckett. "What is your problem?"

"It's not exactly thrilling to get a Google alert with photos of you, Andie, and Lou laughing in the grocery store. He had his fucking hands on you. Touching you. You're mine. Not his."

"Are you crazy? We were laughing at him about his ice cream flavor choice. He was embarrassed and trying to quiet us."

"He shouldn't ever touch my property."

"Your property?"

He barks, "Yes!"

"What century do we live in? I'm not your property, Beckett."

"You know what else you're not? Andie's mother. You don't get to decide when she does and doesn't eat ice cream for dinner."

"Go to hell, Beckett. I don't need this. I'm leaving. I can't deal with you when you get like this."

I start heading for the front door.

"That's right. Do what you always do when things aren't a perfect fucking fairytale. Go back to *your* house."

I turn back. "What is that supposed to mean?"

"You were married for four years to a man who lives in New York, yet you never sold your house. You always have one foot out the door. You're ready to escape at a moment's notice."

"I kept it for Jade. She was in high school when I got married."

"And what about when she left for college?"

"You know what, I don't have to justify shit to you. The spoiled rich boy didn't get his way tonight so he's having a temper tantrum. Call me when you grow up."

I walk out the door and leave.

CHAPTER TWENTY-SEVEN

BECKETT

I didn't sleep all night. I know I'm an asshole. I saw the pictures online of Lou with his hands on her and all I saw was red.

I walk down to the kitchen and see Karen. "Thanks for staying over."

She nods as she examines the cut on my lip. Without saying a word, she fills a bag of ice and hands it to me.

She's otherwise silent as she goes about preparing breakfast.

My phone rings and I see that it's Mom. I accept the call. "Hey, Mom."

"Is she okay?"

"Is who okay?"

"Amanda."

"Why? What happened?" I can't imagine Amanda called her after our fight last night.

"Have you been online this morning?"

"No. Why?" What now? When will this end?

"Go to your computer. You need to see it."

I hurry to my home office and power it on. "Which website?"

"*All* of them. Everyone is running the story."

I click on one that seems to be particularly interested in us. And then I see it. Oh my god. It's an interview with a woman claiming to be Amanda's mother.

"Fuck." This is going to gut her.

"When did she last see her mother?"

"When she was three years old. She doesn't remember her. This charlatan knows nothing about Amanda. She's cashing in."

"Trust me, Beckett, this one will cut her deep. I know firsthand. Make it go away. Do whatever it takes. I hope she's upstairs still sleeping and doesn't know anything about this yet."

"Umm. I was a dick to her last night. She slept at her house."

I hear her sigh in disappointment. "When will you learn? Go take care of things."

"I will. Thanks. I think I'm going to take her away. She needs a break from all this. *We* need a break from it. The press won't let up. It's wearing on all of us."

"That's a good idea. I'll come and stay with Andie."

"I want to bring Andie. Why don't you come too? I feel like she might need some motherly time with you."

It's silent.

"Mom, are you there?"

She croaks out, "I would love nothing more."

"I'll set it up and send you the information."

I make a few necessary calls, get Andie off to school, and then head straight for Amanda's house. I tried calling Jade, but she didn't answer.

I practically jump out of the car before Nico stops and run to her front door and start banging on it.

Jade answers and looks at me with disgust. "Meeting you is the worst thing that ever happened to her."

"Where is she?"

"I'm not letting you in. You're the reason for all this."

We hear Amanda's voice. "Let him in. I need him."

With a ton of attitude, Jade reluctantly steps aside so I can enter. I practically sprint past her and run to Amanda, lifting her and taking her in my arms. "I'm so sorry, baby."

She sobs into my chest. I carry her over to the sofa and sit with her on my lap.

Jade and Collin sit on the loveseat across from us. Collin asks, "Is that really your mother?"

She shrugs. "I don't know. I guess I sort of resemble her."

Jade shakes her head. "Are you fucking nuts? That woman looks like a saddlebag with eyes. You're beautiful. She looks nothing like you."

"She knew things about where I grew up and my father. Small details that I don't think she'd otherwise know."

She turns to me with so much pain in her eyes. Pain caused by her affiliation with me. "When will it be over? When will they be done painting me as gold-digging trailer trash?"

I rub her back. "Try to ignore it."

"Like you did last night? Somehow a trip to the store to get ice cream with your daughter, with the bodyguard you forced me to have, set you off in a fit of jealousy. Is that ignoring the nonsense put online about me?"

I blow out a breath. "You're right. I'm sorry." I rub her arms. "I hated his hands on you, and I overreacted. I don't like another man's hands on your body."

Jade scoffs. "Holy shit. You have a very clear type, Mom. He's a possessive lunatic just like Dad."

I scowl at her. "I'm not possessive. I'm protective. There's a difference."

She deadpans, "That's exactly what my dad said after he pushed Collin through a glass wall for hugging me."

Amanda looks at her. "Why don't you and Collin get going. I know you both have work."

Jade shakes her head. "I'm not leaving you."

"I'm fine. I have Beckett. I need to talk to him. You two go."

Jade is about to speak when Collin grabs her hand. "Do what your mom asked. Let's get going. Let them talk. It's what she wants."

She stands. "Ugh. Fine. I hate it when you're the sensible one. I'll call you in a bit, Mom."

"Thank you for being here."

Jade and Collin both kiss Amanda's cheek and then leave.

When the front door closes, she sinks her head into my neck. "Why are they out to get me? What have I ever done to them?"

I rub her back. "Nothing. You're perfect. They

can't handle perfect, so they make up things. I was thinking that we should go away. Let's get out of the spotlight for a few weeks. A little relaxation is needed for both of us."

"Where do you want to go?"

I smile down at her. "To our happy place."

"To the boat? Back to Italy?"

I nod. She starts to protest, as I knew she would, but then I say, "We'll bring Mom and Andie this time. You and Andie can paint landscapes. We'll sightsee, swim, eat good food."

Her face lights up. "Really? I think I'd like that."

And that's what we do. For two glorious weeks, we hide from the world.

CHAPTER TWENTY-EIGHT

AMANDA

Things have been great. Going back to Italy with Glinda and Andie was a dream. Beckett practically had SWAT team surveillance above and around the boat. I didn't even put up a fight. I just wanted my time with them away from the constant spotlight, and that's exactly what I got.

Andie and I painted every morning. She's getting better with each passing day. I love that time with her. Glinda and I talked for hours in the early evenings. Beckett and I made love for hours at night. We needed that reconnection after the stressful few months we have had. All of us swam, ate, and explored. It was perfection.

I was hoping the media attention would die down when we returned, and it did for a few weeks. But another story came out about my father today. I'm finally beginning to desensitize to it all. Beckett was losing his shit about it. I told him I needed a night away from him. I can't handle it when he gets angry at the world.

I came back from Italy with a sense of peace, and I want to keep it that way.

I decide to have dinner with Jade and Collin. They told me to meet them at one of their favorite restaurants. She's already sitting but stands when she sees me. She's such a stunning pregnant woman.

I can't help but shake my head as we embrace. "You should model pregnancy clothes. You're gorgeous."

She gives me a soft smile. "Thank you. Collin said the same thing the other day, but it might have been because I was naked and on top of him."

I let out a laugh. "I think he loves you very much. You have no idea how fortunate you are to have found a man who loves you the way he does."

Collin throws his arm around me as he kisses my cheek. He's so warm. "Listen to your mom."

She smiles at him with so much affection. She's so in love with him. "I know." She briefly pauses before looking at me. "How are things going with Beckett?"

"They're fine. Italy was magical and we've had a wonderful few weeks since. I'm sure you saw the article this morning. He freaked out. He can be a spoiled child sometimes. When he gets grumpy, I know we need to take a break. I can't be around him when he plays the victim."

She scrunches her nose. "I was hoping you didn't see it. Clearly you did."

"Yes. It's about me and yet he lets it impact him more."

"Because he cares about you."

"I know, but part of being spoiled is being unable to manage when things don't go your way. That's him. As soon as things go off script, he breaks down. I think I'm just more accustomed to it. My life has always gone off script."

I suppose Jade was right when she mentioned it weeks

ago. Beckett is a lot like Declan. As much as I get annoyed by his behavior at times, admittedly, the alpha in him also turns me on. Why am I attracted to men like that? What does it say about me?

I'm deep in my thoughts when both of their phones chime at the same time. They look down at them. Jade turns a shade of white and Collin breathes, "Fuck."

I look at them both with concern. "What's wrong?"

Jade has panic written all over her face. "Carter was in a motorcycle accident. We need to get to the hospital right away."

Collin looks like he's in shock. Jade pulls his head to hers. "Stay with me. He's going to be fine. We have to go and be there for Reagan. She needs us."

Collin nods. On autopilot, he reaches into his pockets and drops a wad of cash on the table.

I grab his keys from his hand. "I'll drive. Let's go."

As we walk out, Lou stands, appearing surprised that we're already finished with dinner. "I'm driving them to the hospital in their car. Just follow in mine."

He doesn't ask questions. He simply says, "Will do."

Collin is beside himself the entire car ride to the hospital. I'm driving while he and Jade are in the back. She's consoling him. While Jade sadly had to take care of me on more than one occasion growing up, she's never had to console a man like this. She's holding him, whispering reassurances in his ear. I can't help but be proud of her for how she's handling this. She's matured so much in the past year. Their love and dependence on each other shine through. I'm so happy for her that she found this type of intimacy and commitment with Collin, and I know without a doubt that he would do the same for her.

We arrive at the hospital to see the Knight and

Lawrence families taking up the entire waiting room. Reagan is whimpering in Darian and Skylar's arms. As soon as she sees Collin, she runs into his waiting embrace and starts sobbing heavily.

"I need him to be okay. I can't live without him, Collin. He's my everything."

"He'll be fine. No one is stronger than Carter Daulton. He's not leaving you. Not ever. I promise."

Collin is holding her up, trying to be strong even though I know he's hurting inside. Jade is rubbing both of their backs as she fights back her own tears.

Darian's daughter, Harley, and her husband, Brody, are both surgeons at the hospital. I don't see them. They're the only members of the family missing. They must be helping Carter.

I whisper to Cassandra, "What exactly happened?"

"Apparently a woman in a car blew through a stop sign and straight into Carter on his motorcycle. The police said both the motorcycle and car were totaled. They haven't told us anything about his condition."

"How terrible. I hope he's okay."

We all sit around in silence for a while. Everyone is consoling each other while taking turns consoling Reagan. This family is always there for one another.

At some point, Harley and Brody walk through the doors in surgical scrubs. Reagan can barely stand as she waits for them to speak. Collin and Jade are supporting her. I can't help but worry about Jade. She's heavily pregnant. I'm not sure she can handle all this stress, but she's not letting it faze her, and I know now isn't the time for me to hover over her.

They remove their masks and have big smiles. Oh, thank god.

Brody shakes his head in what appears to be disbelief. "Only Carter could be hit by a car while on his motorcycle and have fewer injuries than the driver of the car. He's like a fucking Mack truck. That, or he's a superhero."

Reagan lets out a small laugh through her tears. "He's okay?"

Brody nods. "We found no spinal or head injuries. No internal injuries whatsoever. He has a broken leg, a lot of cuts and bruises, and some road rash, but somehow, that's it. The driver of the car will be okay, just a few more broken bones than Carter. I've never seen anything like Carter. It's kind of a miracle that he's not in worse shape."

Reagan breathes a sigh of relief. "Can we see him?"

He nods. "I'd say just you, but I know none of you will listen. He's starting to come out of sedation. He's on a lot of pain meds though, so he may be in and out of it."

I make eye contact with Jade and mouth, "Should I go?"

She shakes her head and mouths back, "Stay."

I nod.

Everyone follows Brody to the recovery room where Carter is in the bed with his eyes closed. He has a ton of scrapes and bruises, and his entire right leg is in a huge cast, but he otherwise looks okay. His face barely shows any evidence of the accident. The helmet must have helped with that.

Reagan immediately crawls into bed with him on his left side, peppering his face with kisses, tears pouring from her eyes.

His eyes blink open and she breathes a sigh of relief, rubbing his face. "Hey, baby. Thanks for coming back to me. You scared the shit out of us."

He looks at her sitting on his bed. "Who are you?"

She turns to Brody, wide eyed.

Brody says, "I'm sure it's just the pain meds. He sustained no head trauma. It's a good thing he was wearing his helmet and he's a mountain of a man." It's true. Carter is enormous. All the men in this room are big, but Carter is the biggest.

Before she can turn her head back, Carter's hands are on her breasts squeezing them. "I'm just kidding, baby, I'd know these tits anywhere. They're the bestesist tits in the whole wide world. If there was a police lineup of tits and I had to feel them all to identify you, I'd know yours. Best on the planet, right Collin?"

Collin offers a huge grin. "Second best."

Everyone starts laughing. Even Reagan laughs through her tears. Carter continues rambling on and on about Reagan's breasts and how much he loves them. It's clear the pain meds have him in a state, but she doesn't remotely attempt to stop him. I imagine she's simply happy he's well enough to be talking, despite the less-than-ideal topic.

At some point, he takes her hand and places it on his gown over his groin area. "You'd know me in a lineup too, right?"

She nods. "Of course. No one could ever be as big as you."

Collin clears his throat. "Not true. Some of us are equally blessed in that department." He winks at Jade, and she rolls her eyes.

Cassandra nods in agreement. "Yes, Trevor too."

Jackson scoffs. "Are you all kidding me right now? Carter was just in a major accident. Are we really debating lineups for breast and penis identification and sizing?"

Darian smiles as she slides her hand up Jackson's chest. "But you'd know me, right?"

He quickly nods and mumbles, "In a millisecond."

ONCE I KNOW that Carter is okay and Jade doesn't need me, I leave the hospital. Even though it's after midnight, I tell Lou to drive me to Beckett's house. The fragility of life and the amount of love in that room is running through my mind.

For the first time in my life, I'm finding that I not only want a man, I need one. And not just anyone. I need Beckett. I need to be close to him tonight, to feel his body on mine. I'm mad at myself for being angry with him earlier. He's just protective of me. He loves me. I know he does.

I quietly enter the house, but when I get to Beckett's room, his bed is empty and unmade.

I look in Andie's room. She's sound asleep. An adult must be here somewhere. He would never leave her alone. I check the guestrooms and see Karen asleep in one of them. I delicately shake her shoulder. Her eyes creep open.

I whisper, "Sorry to wake you. Where's Beckett?"

Her nose scrunches. She doesn't want to tell me.

I'm starting to freak out. Is he with another woman?

"Karen, tell me where he is."

She thinks for a moment before rolling over and pulling out a piece of paper, handing it to me. It has an address scribbled on it. "He won't have his cell on him. You can try Nico, but I doubt he'll answer. The address is only supposed to be used in case of an emergency with Andie. Don't make me regret this."

Without saying another word, I grab it and storm down the stairs. I had sent Lou home, so I manage to slip out without a guard. I drive like a madwoman to the address. It's in a really bad neighborhood in North Philly. I'm totally confused. What the hell is Beckett doing out here in the middle of the night?

I park near the rundown building and push open the big, old wooden front doors. It appears empty, but as soon as I take a few steps inside, I hear a small crowd cheering from a lower floor. It's almost like a sporting event with hooting and hollering. But what sporting event would be in the basement of an abandoned building?

And then it hits me. This is where he comes to fight. I can't believe he does it in a hellhole like this.

I walk two levels down a stairwell. It smells like sweat, blood, and urine. I'm pretty sure I see all those things on the floor and walls as well. It's disgusting. This place should be condemned.

The further down I go, the louder the yelling gets. My hands are shaking as I reach for the metallic door, not knowing exactly what I'll find.

I open it and am shocked by what I see. Beckett is shirtless in a makeshift boxing ring, fighting another man. A *huge* man. A man that must be twenty years younger and have thirty pounds of muscle on him.

They're not even wearing regular boxing gloves. They're wearing fingerless ones, simply trading punches back and forth, with sixty grown men watching them and cheering them on.

I stand there for what feels like forever, but in reality, it is probably only a few minutes. I think Beckett is actually winning. He's like an animal in there. His muscles are rippling; the sweat is glistening off his body. I'm not sure I've ever seen anything hotter in my life. And then I chastise myself for feeling that way about this barbaric event.

When the other man lands a punch on Beckett's jaw, I can't help but scream out. Beckett's head whips my way, and his eyes land on me. They're full of anger. I've never seen this side of him. I've seen him angry, but not like this.

The distraction gives the other man an opening and he lands another punch on Beckett's jaw. This time Beckett goes down.

Before I know what's happening, Nico is in my face, looking furious. "You need to get out of here. You're a distraction for him."

I yell back, "I'm not leaving without him. How could you let him do this? He's going to get himself killed. That man is half his age."

Nico gives a sly smile. "Trust me, Beckett will win. He's a fucking machine. He doesn't lose. Ever."

Just then, Beckett stands. I've never seen the rage that I see in his face right now. It's not directed at me though; it's directed at his opponent.

He wipes the blood from his brow and then charges at the other man. They start brawling, trading punches. I grab Nico's arm, partially hiding my eyes. I don't want to watch but I do. I can't seem to stop.

At some point, the only thing the other man can do is try to defend himself as Beckett hits him over and over. He punches him in the face, the ribs, the kidneys. Everywhere.

I'm in complete and total disbelief over what he's doing in the ring.

After delivering a relentless onslaught, Beckett lands a brutal punch across his jaw and the man goes down, out cold. The crowd erupts in cheers as Beckett raises his arms in triumph and growls. He looks like a gladiator.

After a brief celebration, six men quickly whisk him away. I start to follow, but Nico grabs my arm. "You should go. His adrenaline is pumping. You don't need to see him like this."

My adrenaline is pumping too. I shout, "I need to see him, Nico. I need to make sure he's okay."

"He's fine."

The crowd starts to make its way toward the door, which we're blocking. As soon as we're surrounded by bodies, I make a break for it. I run toward where Beckett and his team disappeared.

I hear Nico mumble, "Shit," as he starts to chase me. Given my size, it's easier for me to weave through the crowd. The distance between us is growing.

There are only two doors in the hallway where Beckett went. I open one door and it's empty. I open the other and it's a small locker room. Beckett is sitting on a table while one of the men is cleaning and treating the cuts on his face.

I walk past the other people. They all look like trainers of some sort, in matching jackets with an imprint of Beckett's Griffin tattoo on the backs.

The room falls silent when I walk in. I slowly make my way to him. I can practically smell the testosterone oozing off him as I approach.

The trainer treating him steps away as I move to stand between his legs. Tears sting my eyes as I carefully touch his chin. "Are you okay?"

He nods.

I run my fingertips over his sweaty, battered face. "Does it hurt?"

He shakes his head.

I hear Nico behind me at the door, out of breath. "Sorry, boss, she gave me the slip."

Neither of us acknowledges him. There's practically

steam coming off Beckett. I can feel the heat emanating from his body. It's affecting mine. Deeply.

My breathing picks up. Why is this so hot? Why am I so turned on by this side of him? I must be sick in the head.

I can feel my face flush and my nipples harden at his gaze. He tilts his head to the side in wonderment. I see a small sign of his signature smirk. He knows I'm turned on right now. No man has ever known my body like he does. He's touched, kissed, and loved every inch of me.

I'm standing close to him. He calmly says, "Why don't I get in the shower and then we can talk?"

That's not what I want. I shake my head.

"I'm covered in nasty sweat."

I lean my head forward and slowly lick a line of sweat off his chest. "I want that nasty sweat all over me."

His eyes widen before he growls, "Everyone out! Now!"

They all scurry to leave. When the door slams shut behind them, it's like a starting pistol for us. Our mouths and bodies crash together in unison.

I don't care that he's sweaty. If anything, the smell, taste, and feel are turning me on even more. I meant what I said. I want it on every inch of me. The manly scent of sweat and victory is driving me wild.

He's animalistic in the way his mouth and hands attack my body. I think I could come just from the passion between us right now. The intensity is unlike anything I've ever imagined.

He grabs my T-shirt and rips it off my body. He tears my bra off too before lifting me, turning us around, and slamming me down on the table.

Making quick work of my jeans and panties, he flips me over so my ass is in the air and I'm bent over the table.

He jams his fingers inside me and pushes them deep.

Leaning over my back, he licks his way to my ear and says, "Is this what you want? What you need?"

I breathe, "I need you to fuck me. Hard. Dirty."

Before I can say another word, his cock slams into me. There's no slow entry. No waiting a few seconds for me to acclimate to his giant size. He's pulverizing my pussy without any thought of the consequences. I love it.

He fucks me harder than I've ever been fucked in my life. I can only hold onto the table and enjoy the ride. He's completely out of control right now. I will definitely be marked all over from this.

"Do you need your words of praise? Do you need me to tell you how I'm addicted to your cunt? How I can't get enough of it? Of you?"

"Beckett!"

"Do you understand that you're mine?"

"Yes."

"Say it!"

"I'm yours!"

"Fuck yeah you are."

I'm ravenous for him right now. He pounds and pounds. I'm screaming bloody murder as my hips relentlessly crash onto the table over and over again.

He's so deep inside me. The piercing is rubbing me in all the right ways. His bruising grip is digging into me.

I'm going out of my mind. The buildup is swift. I scream out my orgasm as it smacks headfirst into me. It's like an explosion of fluids. I can physically feel my come dripping out of me. Pouring out of me.

As soon as I'm done, he pulls out and gets on his knees. His mouth sinks into my ass, licking all around and in my back entrance.

I feel him eventually pull away and stand. Spitting

down one more time into my ass, he rubs it around with his fingers and then slides them in. He pumps them deep a few times before pulling them out, lifting me, and carrying me across the room.

As he walks, he asks, "You want dirty?"

"Yes. Give it to me."

"How dirty?"

"Filthy."

He shoves my front against the lockers. Hard. With one hand, he holds both my wrists above my head. I feel his tip nuzzle its way into my ass. I take a deep breath and then feel him pushing himself all the way in. Straight to the hilt. Right away.

"Ah, Beckett."

"You like having my cock in your ass, don't you?"

I grit, "Yes."

He begins his strokes. "Your ass is taking me so deep and tight, cherry pie."

He starts slowly but quickly builds to the same pace as earlier, straddling the line of control and frenzy.

He grabs hold of my hair and pulls my head back toward his. "So. Fucking. Perfect. Can you feel it too?"

"Y...y...yes."

Continuing his punishing pace, he reaches around and grabs both of my breasts. "These fucking tits. Mine. All mine."

My hips continuously crash into the lockers as he thrusts in and out of my ass. I can feel the fullness throughout my body. That fucking piercing is blowing my mind right now. Beckett is blowing my mind.

"Say it! Say they're mine."

"They're yours!"

I'm covered in sweat too. It must be a hundred degrees

in here. The smell of sweat and sex is overwhelming. I've never had a man treat my body like this. It's everything I never knew I needed and wanted.

He licks up my neck before grabbing hold of my throat from the front. "I love the taste of your sweat. I love everything about you."

He tightens his hand and fingers. It makes my clit throb with need.

"I can feel you squeezing me. I know you love this. You love it dirty."

I moan, "Oh god, Beckett. Touch me."

As soon as his fingers meet my clit, I yell out, "I'm coming again."

"Fuck yes you are. Let go. Now."

And I do. It numbs my whole body. He shoves in deep and twitches as he fills my ass with his warm seed.

We both immediately slump forward, covered in sweat, completely out of breath.

We stay like that for a few minutes. Our breathing is loud, but it's the only sound we make. He's holding me up. I have no use of my limbs.

Eventually he lifts his weight off me and turns me around, still supporting me. His lips immediately find mine. The kiss is so tender, especially compared to the way he just fucked me.

Without breaking the kiss, he lifts me like a bride and carries me to the shower. He turns the water on, and we continue kissing while it warms.

After two minutes, he steps us inside. He places my feet on the ground, though I still need him to support my worn-down, lifeless body.

We stand under the stream. Well, he stands for us. He

holds me up and washes my entire body before washing his own.

Slow, gentle strokes everywhere. He meticulously cleans me. It's so loving and intimate.

We still haven't uttered a word to each other. When we're almost done, I look up and gently touch his scrapes. "Why do you do this to yourself?"

His jaw ticks. "Sometimes I need the pain to feel alive. To escape the prison I live in."

I finally get my footing and step back. "Does being with me feel like prison?"

"No, being without you does."

CHAPTER TWENTY-NINE

AMANDA

The holidays have come and gone. It was so full of love and family. Such a contrast to how Jade and I did it when she was a child, and it was just the two of us.

I'm awakened in the middle of the night by a noise. Beckett is wrapped around me. His hands are under my shirt, per always.

I realize it's my phone. I quickly grab it and see that it's Jade. "Hey. Is everything okay?"

"Mom, it's time. We're heading to the hospital."

Tears immediately hit my eyes. "Are you in any pain?"

"A little." She pauses. "Mom, I'm scared. What if it hurts too much? What if I'm not meant to be a mother? What if I'm no good at it?"

"I know your mind is racing right now, sweetie. It's totally normal to have those feelings. I can't promise you that it won't be painful. But in the end, you're going to hold your child and you'll forget the pain. It will be the greatest moment of your life. You'll feel an intensity of love that you didn't realize could exist. A feeling of unconditional love and protectiveness will kick in. I promise you. I love you so much."

"I love you too. Are you coming?"

"Of course I'm coming. I'll meet you there."

I hear Collin calling her name in the background.

"I need to go, Mom. I'll see you soon."

"See you soon."

I end the call and take a deep breath.

Beckett pulls me close. "You're such an amazing mother. I don't know how you can ever doubt yourself."

"Thank you. I hope she's able to manage everything."

"I've spent plenty of time with Jade at work. She can handle anything. I hope Andie grows up to be just like her."

"You do?"

"A strong-willed, smart, independent woman who takes no shit from anyone? Of course I want that for her."

For some reason that makes me happy. I turn in his arms and kiss his lips. "Thank you."

I wiggle a little, but he doesn't budge, maintaining a tight hold. "Beckett, I need to go."

"I know. I wish I could come, but there's no one here for Andie."

"She wants me in the room with them. You'd be alone in the waiting room anyway."

"As soon as she's off to school, I'll be there."

"Okay."

He finally releases me. I quickly get dressed and head to the hospital.

When I arrive, they're already in a room. I walk in and Jade breathes a sigh of relief. "Thank god." She points to Collin. "Get him out of here. He's driving me nuts."

I roll my eyes at her. "He's the father. He's staying."

"Ugh. I should have slept around more so we couldn't be sure he's the father."

The nurse looks at her like she's crazy. Not everyone understands my daughter's sense of humor.

Collin laughs though. And that's why he's perfect for her.

He grabs her face and kisses her. "Sorry, you're stuck with me. Forever. Do you need me to rub your back? That's what Reagan needed."

"No."

"Your belly? That's what Skylar needed."

"No."

The nurse narrows her eyes at him. "How many women have you impregnated?"

He points to Jade. "This is my first baby mama..." He winks. "That I know of."

EIGHT HOURS LATER

Jade is now screaming. Collin is struggling watching her in so much pain.

The machine beeps letting us know another contraction is coming. We each grab a hand.

The doctor says, "One more hard push, Jade. I see the head."

Jade pushes and screams. She manages to grit out, "I'm not going through this again. We're only doing anal from now on."

Collin smiles. "I have no problem with that."

I'm confident the two of them have permanently scarred the doctors and nurses today.

We start to hear a baby cry. The doctor pulls it out and announces, "It's a boy."

He holds him up and then places him on Jade's chest. This is surreal. Watching the exact moment your daughter becomes a mother is like nothing you can ever imagine. I feel my heart pounding deep and hard in my chest.

Collin's mouth is wide open. He's in shock.

I have a flashback to the day Jade was born. Reggie was with me holding my hand. They placed Jade on my chest. I remember being so overwhelmed with love.

I'm looking at Jade now. I can already see on her face that she feels the same.

She gingerly places her hands on the baby and looks at the doctor. "Is he okay?"

"We're going to take him in a minute, get him cleaned, and check him out, but so far so good."

Collin gently caresses her head. "You did it. You're amazing. I love you."

He bends and kisses her and then their son. It's a beautiful family moment that I'm happy she has and I get to witness.

He lifts his head and smiles at me. "Congrats to you, Grandma. You're officially like the hottest grandmother ever."

I let out a laugh. "Thanks, Collin."

Jade smiles. "That's true. You're a GILF, Mom."

I shake my head. "Let's focus on the baby."

We look down. It's slightly hard to tell right now, but it looks like he has blond hair.

The nurse says, "We're going to take him and get him cleaned and tested. We'll be back as soon as possible."

Collin asks, "Can I go with you?"

She shakes her head. "Sorry, Dad. We'll have him back to you shortly."

He nods. "Don't switch him out with some other baby. I watched a Lifetime movie last week where that happened."

The nurse indulges him. "I'll be extra careful."

The doctor is working on Jade. Collin winks at him. "There's a twenty in it for you if you give her an extra stitch or two."

Jade starts laughing and Collin smiles down at her.

This poor doctor. I imagine he'd welcome a subject change. "Do you guys have a name picked out?"

They look at each other and nod. Jade says, "Tyson. The T is for Tremaine."

I kiss Jade's cheek. "I love it. It's perfect. It's a strong name. I'll give you two a moment of privacy together. I'm going to the waiting room to tell your dad. I know he's been here the whole time, undoubtedly pacing, making everyone crazy."

I give her one more hug and whisper, "Are you okay?"

She nods. I turn to leave but she grabs my arm. I see tears in her eyes. "You were right, Mom. You always are."

I squeeze her hand. "You're going to be an amazing mother."

"Because I had the best."

I swallow hard as tears freefall from my eyes.

I walk out into the lobby. The entire Knight and Lawrence crew are there. I love how many people care about Jade and Collin.

I look at Declan, my heart filled with so much emotion. "We have a beautiful grandson."

Cheers erupt from everyone. Tears fill Declan's eyes as he pulls me into a hug. He whispers, "Is she okay?"

"She's great. She's perfect. They all are. His name is Tyson."

I notice all the smiling faces but don't see Beckett. I look down at my watch. Andie has been at school for hours. I wonder where he is. I can't help but be disappointed. I want to share this moment with him.

Eventually, we all head into Jade's room. They're holding a clean and healthy baby boy. He definitely has a full head of blond hair.

I reach out my hands. "Can I hold him?"

She nods and I take him. I can't help but start crying. It's such a crazy feeling of instant love. I turn around, willing Beckett to walk in, but nothing.

Looking back at Jade, I say, "He looks just like you as a baby."

I notice Declan wince. I know he regrets not being there for her birth. He never got to experience this moment as a parent. I want him to have it in spades as a grandparent.

I carefully place Tyson in his arms. Tears are pouring out of his eyes. I've never seen him cry like this.

Melissa wraps her arm around me. "Are you okay?"

"I'm perfect."

"I mean about the article this morning."

"What article?"

Her eyes widen. "Oh, nothing. It doesn't matter."

I sigh. "What now? Who else could they possibly find from my life? There's no one left."

She shakes her head. "Enjoy today. Deal with it later."

Tyson is passed around to all the extended family. He's going to be surrounded by so much love.

Reggie and Victoria arrive and run to hug me and offer their congratulations. Reggie scrunches her hose. "Shitty timing for a bullshit article. Are you okay?"

"I've been here since the middle of the night. I guess I need to go online. I haven't seen it yet."

I pick up my phone and Google my name. I audibly gasp at what I find. There was an alleged source this morning claiming that I engaged in prostitution for drug money in my early twenties.

I cover my mouth. "Oh my god, Reg. What the hell?"

"I'm sorry, babe. You don't deserve this."

I text Beckett a few times throughout the day but he's not answering. I have no idea why.

In the late evening, I kiss Jade, Tyson, and Collin goodbye as I head out for some much-needed sleep. I just want to crawl into Beckett's arms and sleep for an entire day.

When I exit the hospital, I hear a few cameras click. These people are vultures.

Nico is standing there. I smile at him. "Is everything okay with Beckett? I haven't heard from him all day."

Nico is stoic. "Mr. Windsor said for you to stay at your house tonight and that he'll call you in the morning."

"What's going on? Is this about that stupid article?"

"Ms. Tremaine, you should go home."

Who is Nico right now? He's acting like a stranger. Whatever. I'm too tired to care. I won't let their nonsense bring me down on such a magical day.

BECKETT

I walk into my kitchen at breakfast time. Karen immediately sets out the coffee in the chair next to mine. "Is Amanda coming down?"

"She didn't stay here last night."

"Oh."

"Her grandchild was born yesterday."

Her eyes light up. "What did Jade have?"

"Umm. I don't know. I'll find out today."

Karen looks confused. I don't blame her. I should know. She knows me well enough at this point to know I fucked up.

I try to lighten the mood. Nodding to my juice on the counter, I say, "What's in my juice today?"

For the first time ever, she answers. "Carrots, kale, celery, spinach, and regret."

Okay then.

Fortunately, Andie comes running in, ending the awkwardness. "Where's Amanda? She's not in the studio."

Does anyone care about me? The first question anyone asks in the morning is about Amanda.

"I wanted you to myself today."

"Is she in the shower?"

"She's not here."

"Why not?"

"She's with Jade. Jade and Collin had the baby."

Andie screeches. "Oh my god. I bet it's so cute. Is it a boy or a girl?"

"I don't know."

"Does it look like Jade or Collin?"

I shamefully admit, "I don't know."

"Can we go to the hospital to see it?"

"Not today. You have school."

"What about when school is over?"

"We'll see."

She pouts. "Fine, grumpy bear. Tell me my joke."

"What does one ocean say to the other ocean?"

She crosses her arms, still mad at me, like every other woman in my life. "I don't know."

"Nothing. They just waved."

She scowls. "I don't like it."

It's going to be a long day.

After I drop Andie, I head over to Amanda's. Nico opens the car door. He looks like he wants to punch me. "You should be crawling to her on your hands and knees, asshole."

"Do your fucking job and none of this would happen, Nico."

He stares at me with venom in his eyes.

I knock on the door. It takes a while, but she eventually answers looking like she just woke up. She's in that fucking tight half-shirt that drives me wild.

Her sad eyes meet mine. "What do you want? I'm exhausted."

"Can I come in?"

She thinks for a moment before opening the door wider in invitation. I walk inside.

"I'm sorry about yesterday."

"You mean one of the most special, emotional days of my life? A day when I needed you by my side? What happened?"

"Did you see the article?"

She sighs. "I don't control the bullshit that comes out about me."

"Yes, I learned this morning that it wasn't true."

She holds her hand, out stopping my forward progress. "Wait a minute. Does that mean yesterday you thought it *was* true?"

I'm silent at first. Her shoulders slump and tears fill her eyes.

I shuffle nervously. "I know it was a tough time in your life. I'm sure it was hard to make ends meet. I thought maybe..."

"You thought I resorted to prostitution? Selling my body?"

"I...umm..."

"And then you ghosted me on one of the most important days of my life. When I needed you."

My head is down in shame. I have no words.

"All this time together, and you don't know me or trust me at all. Even if you weren't sure about those horrible things, you could have asked me. I've only ever been truthful with you. I've never been dishonest. Not for a single second."

I whisper, "I'm sorry."

"You know what, that's not enough. I deserve better." She points to the door. "Get out. I can't look at you right now."

I nod as we start walking toward the door. I mumble, "Will you tell me what Jade had?"

"I have a grandson."

"Congratulations. Andie wants to see him."

She sighs. "Tell Andie's school that I'll pick her up at the end of the day."

"I can bring her."

"Let me be clear: I don't want to be around you right now. I'll take her to see the baby and give her dinner. I'll drop her home afterward."

"Will you stay over tonight?"

"No."

"Will you come in and talk to me?"

"We'll see. I need to go back to bed and then get to the hospital. Goodbye, Beckett."

She closes the door in my face.

I walk toward the car and Nico has a big smile on his face. "I told you to crawl to her."

"Stop fucking smiling. Set up a fight for tonight."

"Yes, sir."

CHAPTER THIRTY

BECKETT

It's been a week since I've seen Amanda. She's giving me the silent treatment. I'm miserable. I've had three fights this week. I don't remember a time when I've done so many in such a short period of time. I'm sinking.

I've gone to her house every day. She's either not there, or if she is, asks me to leave and give her space. How long is she going to punish me?

The only happy news is that Dominic Mazzello came back to town this week and Reagan immediately invited him to rejoin Daulton Holdings. I offered him his old office, it's the least I could do. I moved to a slightly smaller office down the hallway. I don't really care; I don't care about anything besides getting my girl back.

Dominic and I got along so well when we met a year and a half ago, and we've picked up right where we left off. It's nice to have someone in my age bracket in the office. Everyone else here is so young.

He's trying desperately to win his girlfriend back. The one he abruptly left when he moved to Cuba. He said it's not going well. I can certainly commiserate right now.

I'm sitting in my office, getting little done. I must be imagining things because I see Amanda's ponytail go by my door. I quickly stand and see her walking toward Jade's office. She turns in.

I run in after her and close the door. "Hey, cherry pie."

Her shoulders fall. "I purposefully avoided walking by your office."

"I have a new office."

"I'm not here for you. Jade said she needs a few things. I'm just here to grab them."

I can't help myself. I pull her into my arms, and she lets me. "I'm sorry I doubted you. I made a mistake. How much longer are you going to punish me?" I inhale her. "I miss you."

She rests her head on my chest. "I miss you too, but you hurt me."

"I know. I'm sorry."

"I asked you for space and you didn't give it to me."

"I just miss you. I'm used to seeing you every day."

She looks up and touches the bruises and cuts on my face. "What are you doing to yourself? It needs to stop. You need help."

I pull back. "I'm a grown man, don't tell me what I need. The only thing I need is you back in my fucking bed where you belong."

She pulls away, grabs a few things from Jade's desk, and makes her way to the door. "Call me when you're done being a spoiled brat. Not before then." She closes the door behind her.

Shit. Me and my big mouth.

YET ANOTHER WEEK has gone by. I stop by every day, and she always tells me to go away. This is torture.

It's after midnight and I'm wide awake. My mind is racing. Her scent is gone from my sheets, from her pillow. I hate it. It's like I can't breathe without her. How did I become so dependent on having Amanda in my life?

I see my bedroom door open. I assume it's going to be Andie, unable to sleep, but it's Amanda.

She stands there for a few beats. At some point, she blows out a breath in resignation and walks over to my bed. *Our* bed.

We stare at each other. Not a word is spoken for several minutes. The pull between us is magnetic. I can see in her face that she feels it too. I'm internally pleading with her to take the final step and come back to me.

I can't help but reach for her hand. I squeeze it in mine as I whisper, "I'm sorry."

"You hurt me. What you did is not okay..."

"I know."

"...but I love you. I can't seem to help myself."

I nod in agreement. I know I was wrong. "I love you too."

Without uttering another word, she removes all

her clothes, slides into the bed, and immediately crawls on top of me. Her lips are close to mine. She looks pained while whispering, "I miss you. I can't be without you anymore."

I run my hands up and down her soft body and take her in. "I feel the same. I'm so sorry I hurt you."

She runs her hands through my hair as her lips meet mine, and all is right in the world. Her feel, smell, and taste soothe me. They quiet the chaos in my head.

She immediately pulls my boxer briefs down until my cock springs free and falls heavy against my stomach. She grinds over it several times, growing wetter and wetter with each pass.

"Do you need me inside that beautiful pussy of yours?"

She breathes, "Yes. So badly. I'm aching for you. I feel empty without you."

"Take what you need. Take what's yours."

She brings my tip to her entrance and sinks down onto me. She lets out a loud moan. "Oh god, Beckett. I've missed this. I need to be close to you. As close as two people can be."

"Me too, my love."

She swivels her hips, riding me slowly and deeply. Our hands are all over each other's bodies. Our lips never break. We finally reconnect in the way we both have been craving.

Iᴛ's time for another dinner at my father's house. Amanda refuses to go as she has every month since the very first time. I don't blame her.

She usually stays at her house when I go there, but this time she promised to wait at home for me. With Andie sleeping out, we can use the alone time as we continue to try to move past the bump in the road we experienced earlier this week. We need to fully reconnect.

Nico drives Andie and me. Andie tells me all about her friends at school. I was so worried that I may have held her out of school for too long, but she's doing great and seems to have a lot of friends.

We walk in through the front door of his house, and Dad looks behind me. "You didn't bring your plaything?"

I get in his face. Through gritted teeth, I say, "Don't call her that, especially in front of Andie. If you do it again, it will be the last time you see Andie."

He shakes his head. "You're a fool. That woman is only after one thing, and it isn't your winning personality."

"You don't know her, and you don't know us."

"I know women like her. Get in and then get out. She's trash. She's using you. I hope you're using protection. Women like that know how to trap you."

Why the fuck do I keep coming here? Why do I keep trying to maintain a relationship with him?

I see him smiling at someone behind me. "Speaking of suitable women for you…"

I turn around and see Bunny Pendleton. Shit.

She kisses my cheek. "Beckett, where have you been hiding? I haven't seen you in ages."

"Hi, Bunny, you look well."

My father pats my back. "I'll leave you two to get caught up." He looks down at Andie. "Andrea, would you like a beverage?"

"Can I have a piña colada with extra cherries?"

"People like us don't drink that. We'll find you something more appropriate. Come with me."

He takes her hand, and they head off toward the bar.

I roll my eyes. I should tell her to ask for some of the Pussy Juice that Jade drinks all the time. That would really get my father going.

Bunny smiles at me and rubs my arm. "You look well."

I try to subtly step back, out of her reach. "Thank you. So do you."

She fiddles with her glass. "Are you seeing anyone?"

"I am and it's serious. She's the one."

Her eyes widen. "Anyone I know?"

"You met her years ago at Reagan Lawrence's party. I was with her that night. We got reacquainted last year and have been together since."

"The tattooed woman?"

"The beautiful, smart, talented artist? Yes."

My eyes catch Andie's across the room. I tug on my ear. We've created a mutual bat signal for these dinners.

She smiles as she walks over to me. "Daddy, I need to go to the bathroom."

I shrug. "Duty calls. Excuse us, Bunny."

She nods. "Of course."

We walk away laughing and high fiving. "Thanks for the save."

She wiggles her little, dark eyebrows. "Time to pay up."

"Okay, okay. How do you put a baby astronaut to sleep?"

She sighs. "I don't know. How?"

"You rocket."

She quietly giggles. "That's funny."

I look down at her innocent face. "Andie, if you don't want to sleep here anymore, you don't have to."

She shrugs. "It's okay. They're more fun when everyone leaves. Grandy teaches me about art. We look at all his paintings. I like that. And sometimes I watch old movies with Buffy, and she makes really good popcorn. Well, she doesn't make it, Elaine does, but it's still good." Elaine is their chef.

"Okay. If you ever change your mind, just let me know or give me the secret signal."

She smiles. "I will."

As soon as dinner is over, I kiss Andie goodnight and head back out to my car, anxious to get home to my girl. I need to get lost in her tonight.

Nico looks at me suspiciously. "Are you okay?"

"No. My father is truly an asshole. I don't know why I keep trying with him."

He looks like he's about to say something and then thinks better of it. We mostly ride home in silence until his eyes meet mine in the rearview mirror. "When we get back to the house, can I get a few minutes of your time?"

"I know Amanda is waiting for me. What's up?"

"I want to talk to you about your mom, man to man."

I nod as my jaw stiffens, knowing what's coming. I suppose I've known it was coming for a long time.

When we arrive at the house, I walk through the front door first and see Amanda sitting on the stairs completely naked, with her legs spread, holding a pie. "I've been waiting for you." She gives me a sexy smile and breathes, "Are you hungry for your dessert? I thought you might like a little pie tonight." She sticks her finger in the pie and then pulls it out and seductively sucks it into her mouth before pulling it out with a pop. "Want to taste my cherry pie?"

Fucking. Hottest. Woman. Ever.

Nico can't see her but can hear her and undoubtedly knows what's going on. I place my hand on his chest before he can move any further. "Raincheck?"

He smiles knowingly as he nods and turns around to leave.

I close the door and look at the goddess sitting on my staircase. "I'm feeling *very* hungry for my cherry pie."

She gathers more pie on her fingers and rubs them around her nipples. "Come and eat your dessert, big boy."

I practically charge at her and dive headfirst into her tits, pushing them together and then lapping up every ounce of the cherry pie on her.

I grab a heaping handful of the pie and smear it all over the front of her body.

Working my way down, I lick it all clean before

diving headfirst into her pussy. I mumble, "You taste better than the pie."

I lap her up too, practically devouring her pussy. Her fingers are in my hair, her back is arching, and she's moaning my name. Exactly how I like her.

I plunge my tongue into her, rubbing my thumb over her clit. "Oh god, Beckett. Yes. So good."

She's thrusting her hips into my face. I love how into it she always gets. Always chasing after her own pleasure.

As soon as my tongue licks up and sucks her tiny bud into my mouth, she begins shaking uncontrollably and screams out her first orgasm.

I lick my way back up her body until my lips meet hers for a deep kiss. It's a mixture of Amanda and cherry pie. It's the best dessert I've ever had.

She reaches for more pie, grabs a handful, and smears it between our lips. We both eat every last drop as we devour the pie and each other. It's dirty, sticky, and sexy as hell.

When we finish our current helping, she mumbles, "My turn," as she quickly drops to her knees, undoes my pants, and pulls out my cock. As soon as she looks down and sees it, her nipples harden into pink pebbles, and she has goosebumps all over her body. I love her reaction to me. She moves her eyes up as they meet mine. "I ache for you, Beckett. Physically ache for you."

"Trust me, I know the feeling." We both look down at my cock which is now leaking for her attention.

She smiles at it as she grabs another handful of

cherry pie and unashamedly rubs it all over my cock and balls.

Moving her head to me, she begins licking me up and down, going to town in the best way possible. I gaze at her. "Taste good?"

With a mouthful of my balls, she mumbles, "So good."

"That's what you always taste like to me, cherry pie."

She smiles as she feeds my cock into her eager mouth, flicking her tongue against my piercings on the way down.

She squeezes my heavy balls, hard, before working her way down and sucking them into her mouth again.

Once I know all the cherry pie is licked clean, I swiftly pick her up so she's straddling me. "Put my dick inside you, baby. It aches for you too. Bring it home."

She adjusts her body and does just that. I enter her wet, warm, snug pussy. I take in my surroundings. I'm standing at the bottom of my stairs with my pants around my ankles. I have a goddess among women wrapped around me. I just ate cherry pie off her, and now I'm sinking deeper and deeper into her. This is heaven.

Every time I first enter her, she flutters around me like nothing I've ever felt. She's always in another world, absorbed in the pleasure I give her. It's so fucking sexy. She's the hottest fuck I've ever had.

I whisper in her ear, "Does it feel good, cherry pie?"

She moans her answer as she gyrates her hips. "Yes. Always."

I have both hands on her ass as I begin long, hard thrusts inside her. Once I establish a rhythm, I move one hand up her soft, curvy body. Over her hips, across her stomach, and over her breasts until I reach her throat. She loves a little neck play.

She throws her head back granting me access. "Do it."

I wrap my hand around her throat and squeeze in sync with each thrust inside her.

Her mouth widens in pleasure as she scratches her nails down my chest. "Yes. Yes. So good. Harder."

I'm not sure if she means my thrusts or my chokehold, but I give her both and she definitely seems to like it. I can feel her juices sliding down my cock onto my balls. She's in another universe right now.

I watch her cheeks grow pinker by the minute. Her heels dig into my ass, forcing me to push deeper and deeper inside her with each thrust.

It's a good thing no one is home tonight, because she's screaming down the house. Watching her get like this is pushing me closer and closer to the edge.

Her nipples tighten further, and I feel her telltale pulsating. Her orgasm hits her hard and long. I'm trying to hold off mine. I'm not ready for this to end.

As soon as she's done, I sit down on the ground with my cock still inside her. "Ride me, cherry pie."

She smiles as she grabs my hands and moves them up her body, over her breasts to her neck. "Squeeze me hard, Beckett. I love it when you do that."

I've got both hands around her throat. The more I squeeze, the faster and harder she rides me.

She bounces on top of my cock like the rockstar she is. I feel her spasms. She's about to come again. She's so into this. I fucking love it.

I squeeze her neck harder than I've ever done before and she yells out as her pussy grips me and then explodes all over me. It's too much. She's too much. I feel my balls tighten. She must sense it because she reaches back and grips them. I groan, "Oh fuck," as I grunt into my own orgasm and come so damn hard, deep inside her.

When she's sure I'm done, she slows her movements until she stops and collapses lifelessly on top of me. She licks up my neck until she gets to my ear. She nibbles on it and coos, "Best cherry pie ever."

CHAPTER THIRTY-ONE

AMANDA

The week I fell back into Beckett's arms was incredible. He was doting on me like crazy trying to make up for things. We were insatiable for each other. It was some of the best sex of my life. The cherry pie scene on the stairs may have actually been the best sex I've ever had in my life.

But life with Beckett can be a bit of a rollercoaster, and at some point, the rollercoaster heads back down. This week is a mess. This week is a perfect storm.

A photograph surfaced of me and Collin smiling at each other, suggesting I was having an affair with my daughter's boyfriend. There was no acknowledgment of the reality that Jade was walking next to Collin, and the photograph was from months ago. She was cut out of the picture and a story was manufactured.

There was another picture of Declan and I leaving Jade's apartment building after visiting Tyson, suggesting we're rekindling the old flame.

There was a photo of Lou and I laughing as we

walked down the street, along with a headline that my bodyguard and I are an item and are swindling Beckett for millions. Given what happened with Jenny, that one really hit home for Beckett. He's been throwing fits left and right.

There was even a photo of me having coffee with another wealthy Philadelphia businessman. He was a buyer who was looking at photos of my paintings, but the press doesn't care about the truth or the damage their fabrications cause.

Beckett says he understands that they're not true, but I can tell it's wearing on him. He's possessive, which I usually enjoy, but all the insinuations are chipping away at his fragile psyche. He innately mistrusts people. Apparently, I'm not immune from that either. I feel a distance growing between us. Going back to him without any real conversation was probably a mistake. I was just hurting so badly without him.

The good news is that it's time for another Glinda visit. I couldn't possibly be happier about it. Andie and I decide to surprise her at the airport and are in the car when Nico picks her up. We told him not to tell her we're here. When he opens the back door and she gets in, we plan to shout surprise to her.

We can see them walking toward the car. Andie is about to explode, she's so excited. Admittedly, I am too.

When he opens the door, I hear her say, "Come to my room tonight after everyone goes to bed."

Oh my god.

"Why would Uncle Nico go to your room, Gigi?"

Glinda bends to look in the car and her eyes widen. I can't help but let out a laugh. Good for them. It's about time.

I say, "He just needs to carry Gigi's bags to her room, sweetie."

"Oh." She mercifully then remembers our initial mission and shouts, "Surprise!"

Glinda smiles. "I'm most definitely surprised, but I'm happy to see my two favorite girls in the world."

She slides in and hugs us both. "We're going to have so much fun this month."

"Gigi, you need to see baby Tyson. He's so cute. He's got light blond hair like Jade. Amanda sits and smells him all day long."

She pokes Andie's nose. "I remember when you smelled like a baby. It was so yummy."

Andie pouts. "I'm not still yummy?"

Glinda nibbles on her cheek. "You're still yummy."

Andie giggles.

The three of us chat like old friends the entire ride to Beckett's house. I've missed having Glinda around. It's like she gives me a sense of peace and comfort I've never known. I think she also centers Beckett at times, being the voice of reason in his often-unreasonable head. I know her presence will be good for him and me.

The three of us have lunch together at the house. Karen prepared a huge spread. She's just as happy as us when Glinda comes to town.

I tell them I'll be back around dinnertime. I've got a few of my annual doctor's appointments this afternoon, and then I'm going to run home and switch out my clothes. I really do need to start keeping more things at Beckett's. I didn't bring much back when we reconciled. If I'm being honest with myself, I think I'm always waiting for the other shoe to drop with him.

I have my annual mammogram, which hurts like a

motherfucker. I can't imagine what it would look like if men had to go through this nightmare.

I then head down a floor for my annual OBGYN visit. My longtime physician, Dr. Crest walks into the room.

He smiles. "How are you, Amanda?"

"I'm well. How are you?"

"Just fine. I see you in the newspapers all the time."

"Ugh. Pay no attention to that nonsense. It's all lies."

"Of course. Tell me how you're feeling."

"I'm great."

He runs through the normal list of questions until he gets to the date of my last period. I try to remember, but I can't think of it. I pick up my phone and scroll through my calendar. It hits me. It's been about two months.

I look up at him, wide eyed. "It's been two months."

"Are you ever irregular?"

"No. Never."

"It's possible that you're entering menopause. Irregular periods are usually the first indication."

"Oh. Right. I'm sure that's it." I can't help but feel a pang of disappointment.

"Why don't we run a quick blood test though? It's best to be sure."

"We can't do a simple urine test?"

"We can, but at your age, I'd like to be as thorough as possible. It will take just a little longer."

"Okay. That's fine."

They draw my blood and I sit in the waiting room. My head is all over the place. I don't want to let myself get too excited. He's probably right. It's menopause. I know I'm a few years early for that, but it's the likely cause. I'm on the pill. It would be pretty hard for me to get pregnant. Though Jade got pregnant while on the pill.

About an hour later, Dr. Crest calls me into his office. He smiles at me. "Brace yourself, you're about to become a mother again."

"I...I'm pregnant?"

"Yes. Your numbers are quite high, which indicates a more than healthy pregnancy. That's why I wanted to do the blood test over the urine test. If we didn't know your last period was two months ago, I'd say your numbers show you're ten or eleven weeks along."

It's not computing. "I'm pregnant? But I'm a grandmother."

He lets out a laugh. "Even grandmothers can get pregnant."

He gives me a bunch of prenatal vitamins and some pamphlets on prenatal testing I should consider given my age.

I'm barely listening. I'm just processing.

I leave on autopilot, though I do notice a few cameras snapping shots of me.

I drive around for a bit, finding myself at a park. For at least an hour, I watch mothers and fathers chase around their little ones. That will be me again in a few years.

I eventually walk into my house with my mind still racing. I'm a mixed bag of emotions. I thought this door was closed for me, but now it's open. And it will be so different this time around. I'm in love with the father. I rub my belly, which obviously shows no evidence of the pregnancy, but I can't help already feeling overcome with emotion and love. This baby will have the stable family life Jade never had. I'm getting my do-over.

"Was it always your plan?"

I shriek at the surprise of hearing Beckett's deep voice.

I can barely make him out sitting in the darkness of my kitchen.

"Oh my god. You scared the crap out of me. What are you doing here?"

He looks down at my hands which are splayed across my stomach. "It's true, isn't it? You're pregnant."

I look down and at my hands, which are already protective. I look back up at him and smile. "Yes. How did you know?"

"You were seen at the doctor's office today and someone inside leaked it."

"Well, that's a gross violation of my privacy, but I suppose I'm getting used to that. I don't want to let the press bring us down during this beautiful, miraculous moment."

I start to walk to him but then I see the anger in his face and stop short.

"Like I asked when you walked in, was it always your plan to get pregnant?"

"What? I'm forty-five. I'm a grandmother. Was this my plan? Of course not. But I couldn't be happier. Aren't you happy? This baby was conceived in love. This baby will have something Jade and Andie didn't have. Two present, loving, devoted parents from the second he or she is born."

"Was anything we shared real or was this always your endgame? Hook the rich guy for life."

If he physically punched me in the stomach right now, I'd be less shocked. "What's going on? I'm really confused right now. Where is this coming from?" How can he say these things to me after everything we've shared together?

He stands with a look of both pain and disgust on his face. My sweet, loving, romantic Beckett isn't here. Pained, damaged, spiteful Beckett is in the house.

"You're obviously in shock. Why don't you take a little time to process this? Then you'll see it for the incredible gift it is."

He scoffs. "All this time. All this time, and it turns out you're just like the rest of them. A gold-digging..."

At least he had the dignity to stop himself before finishing that sentence. He thinks I've been faking my feelings, plotting this to do what Jenny was planning to do to him. I know he's damaged, but I'm not sure I realized how much until this very moment.

"I think it's time for you to go. Come back when you've calmed down and gained a little perspective."

He nods. "I couldn't agree more. It's time for me to go." There's more to the statement, but it's not until his next comment that he officially sticks a dagger in my heart. "I want a paternity test."

Tears spill from my eyes. I have no words. Everything I thought we shared is gone in an instant. I thought we were special. I thought he was the one I was waiting for. Once again, I was wrong.

"Let me be clear, Amanda. You're not getting a dime without a paternity test."

I'm speechless for several long beats as his words continue to sink in. Eventually I wipe my eyes and steel myself, like I've done so many times before in my life. "I would rather raise my child in the trailer park I grew up in than take a dime of your precious fucking money you hold so near and dear. In fact, I don't ever want to see you or your fucking money again." I point to the door. "Get out of my house, and this time, don't bother coming back."

He gives one slow, emotionless nod. I don't even recognize the person standing before me. Did I ever know him at all? I thought he was my Prince Charming. There's nothing princely or charming about this heartless person. Just another broken man I thought I could fix. I'm such a fool.

He walks toward the front door, opens it, and walks through. Before he closes it, he says, "You'll hear from my lawyers."

I KNOCK on Jade's door. Collin opens it without a shirt, with Tyson sleeping soundly on his chest. He whispers, "Sorry, he sleeps better on my bare chest."

I smile through my own personal pain because of what my daughter has. A man like Collin who is there for their child.

"Don't worry about it. I think it's sweet. Cherish this time with him."

He nods. "I will. Jade is sleeping. She's still pretty beat up from the delivery. I'm trying to keep this guy quiet and fed so she can heal and catch up on some sleep."

"Thank you, Collin. Thank you for looking after her."

"Always." He pinches his eyebrows together. "You seem upset. Do you need her? I can wake her up."

"No. Let her sleep. She needs it. I'm taking a little trip. I wanted to kiss Tyson before I left."

"Oh, where are you guys going this time?"

"It's just me. I'm not sure where I'm going. I need a little alone time to think. I'm going to text you from a new cell number. I'm turning my regular cell phone off when I go. You and Jade are the only people that will have the new number. I'd like it to stay that way."

He nods in understanding of who can't get in touch with me. I don't need to spell it out for him. "Why don't you stay here tonight? You two can talk in the morning. You shouldn't drive while you're upset."

"I'm okay. I need to go." I lean forward and gently kiss Tyson's head so as not to wake him. "Take care of my babies, Collin."

He nods. "Take care of yourself and hurry home. Jade needs her mom and Tyson needs his grandmother."

I barely whisper, "I will."

CHAPTER THIRTY-TWO

BECKETT

I drove around for hours unable to bring myself to go home. It's nearly midnight before I finally walk in. Mom is sitting there waiting. "What did you do?"

"What do you mean?"

"Well, it's the first time you've ever not been here to put Andie to bed without explanation or a call to say goodnight. You look like you've aged ten years since this morning. I saw the photos of Amanda leaving the doctor's office, an OB's office. She didn't return for dinner as promised. When I called her, I received a message that her phone has been disconnected. So like I said, what did you do? What self-sabotage have you engaged in this time?"

Why does she fucking know me so well? "I accused her of planning this pregnancy all along to get my money and then demanded a paternity test."

Before I can even process what's happening, my

mother's hand strikes me so fucking hard across the face that I think she might have dislocated my jaw.

I stand there holding my burning face in shock. In my fifty years, my mother has never once lifted a hand to me or anyone else.

"How dare you. How dare you treat her that way. I did everything in my power to raise you to be the opposite man of your father, so imagine my disappointment when it turns out you're just like him."

"I'm nothing like him."

"You're right. You're worse. He doesn't even pretend to be a sheep. He's a wolf in wolf's clothing. You're a wolf in sheep's clothing."

"Mom..."

She points her finger. "No. There's nothing you can say to explain what you've done. Life has blessed you, Beckett."

"Money isn't a blessing."

Her eyes widen in bloody murder. "Not money, you moron. Life has blessed you with love. You have a wonderful daughter who thinks the sun rises and sets with you. It took fifty years, but you finally have the love of a good woman. A pure-hearted woman. The right woman. And then you get blessed again by her becoming pregnant. You get a chance to give Andie a sibling. To have the family life you've always craved. To raise a baby with a partner full of love, and you throw it away? Why? Because of your ego? Because of your insecurities? Because of a few photos and stories this week you know full well are manufactured nonsense?"

"Because people always want the same thing from me."

"Tell me, Beckett. Deep down, do you believe that? Do you believe Amanda is interested in you for your money? I've seen the way you two are together. I know how she feels about you. What she's endured this past year to be with you. You can't possibly be that stupid." She turns her head. "I can't look at you right now. I've never been more ashamed of you. I'm going to bed. We'll finish this tomorrow."

I mumble, "I can't believe you hit me."

She turns back with pure venom in her eyes. "That was for Amanda. Frankly, you deserve much worse."

She's right. I do deserve worse, and I know exactly where I can get that.

"DADDY, wake up. Why are you so sleepy?"

My face is buried in the pillow as Andie continues to shake me. I mumble, "I need sleep."

"Daddyyyyyyy, come onnnnnn. I need my morning joke before school."

I sigh. "Fine."

I turn over and Andie screams out. Tears immediately run down her face. "Daddy, what happened to you?"

Mom walks into my bedroom and her eyes widen. She covers her mouth in horror and whispers, "Oh my god, Beckett. What have you done to yourself?"

I feel my face. It's swollen and it hurts. Shit. It must look bad.

Mom quickly composes herself. "Andie, Karen

needs help. Why don't you run downstairs. Maybe you can make a bag of ice for your daddy."

Andie stares at me in shock. I rub her arm. "Baby, I'm fine. It looks worse than it feels."

She slowly nods as her shocked little face leaves the room.

As soon as it's clear she's out of earshot, Mom steels herself. "Time to grow up, Beckett."

"You don't understand."

"Oh, bullshit. Your woe-is-me crap is growing quite tiresome. You know what's *actually* hard, Beckett? Growing up the way Amanda and I did. We had *zero* parental love and support. Zero. Yet here we are, thriving in our own ways. We don't mistreat other people or ourselves. We don't find ways to sabotage our lives. We are appreciative of what we have and make the most of what we're given. You had the love of two parents. Your father might be an asshole, and he might be misguided at times, but he loves you and always took care of your needs. You didn't scrounge for lunch money or rides to school. You had a closet full of clothes and toy chests of toys. You didn't worry about Santa coming for Christmas."

"I'm sick of feeling used." I yell out, "My own fucking wife used me. I was nothing but a meal ticket to her."

Mom quickly closes the door. "Quiet your voice. Andie doesn't need to hear what a lowlife Jenny was."

I stare at her in disbelief. "You knew? All this time, you knew?"

"I always suspected."

"Why didn't you say anything?"

"You were happy. She got pregnant quickly after you got married. I didn't want to upset the applecart."

I rub my face. "I didn't see it. Not at all. I can't trust anyone, even myself. What does that say about me?"

She sits on the side of my bed and takes my hand. "That you have a pure heart. That you want to believe the good in people. That before Jenny, you gave people the benefit of the doubt, despite a few of the other women using you for publicity." She swallows. "Did you have actual confirmation that Jenny wasn't as you thought?"

I nod.

"Shortly after she passed?"

I nod again. "How do you know?"

"I remember a shift in you. You went from sad to angry. I thought it was perhaps the stages of grief, but the anger and darkness were stronger than I had ever seen from you. That's when you started showing up with bruises here and there. What is it that you do?"

"I fight."

"Like a bar fight?"

"No. Underground boxing ring fighting."

"You may legitimately be the dumbest smart person I know."

I can't help but smile. "Amanda said the same thing when she found out."

"Because she's legitimately smart." She pauses. "And perfect for you. And in love with you, the real you. And she's about to be the mother of your child. The exact kind of woman you want to be the mother of your child. Of *both* your children."

I run my fingers through my hair. "I don't know if

I can fix it. I fucked up really bad. I said some terrible things to her. We were already on edge. I was shitty to her a few weeks ago too."

She sighs and shakes her head in frustration. Frustration with me. "You'll never know unless you try. Get your ass up and go start begging for forgiveness."

"Okay."

"You need to fix yourself too. You can't go on like this."

I put my head down. "I know."

"Time to clean up your mess. First, go downstairs and tell your daughter one of your ridiculous jokes."

AFTER BANGING on her door for fifteen minutes, I realize her car isn't in the driveway. I decide to head over to Jade's and knock on her door.

Jade opens it holding Tyson in her arms. She looks at me with pure venom. "What the fuck did you do to my mother?"

"Where is she?"

"She took off."

"What do you mean? Where did she go?"

"I don't know. I was asleep when she came to say goodbye. Collin said she was upset and told him she needed time to herself. If my vagina didn't feel like it was full of razor blades right now, I'd dropkick your sorry ass. Hasn't she suffered enough in her life? She let her dignity be questioned in the public eye because she loves you. You're a fucking idiot."

"I know. Just tell me where she is."

"I told you; I don't know. I wouldn't tell you if I did, but I genuinely don't know."

"Her cell was turned off. There's no way she wouldn't have left you a phone number."

"Maybe I have one of those, but I'd sooner give birth again next week before giving it to you."

I blow out a breath. I know Jade enough to know I won't get her to crack. "Tell her...tell her that I'm sorry. Tell her I made a mistake. Tell her...tell her I love her."

"You don't deserve her." She gives me the finger and slams the door in my face.

CHAPTER THIRTY-THREE

TWO MONTHS LATER

AMANDA

"He's rolling now, Mom. Look."

I smile into the camera. "I can see. He's all over the place. He looks just like you did as a baby. More so every day. I can't get over it."

"He's a little devil."

"Well then he's *exactly* like you as a baby."

She laughs. "Come see for yourself. I miss you."

"I miss you too. I'm sorry. I needed this time to myself, to live in anonymity and think about what I want to do with my life. I have one stop to make this morning and then I'm coming home."

Her eyes widen. "You are?"

"I am. I'll be home later today."

She blows out a breath. "Thank god. Have you, umm..."

"No, I haven't spoken with him."

"I don't know what happened, and obviously I'm team Amanda, but he's so fucking depressing to be around. He's like a lost puppy without you. He mopes around the office all day. He stops by my office every morning to ask how you are and to remind me to tell you that he's sorry and that he loves you."

"I'll deal with him when I get home. How is it being back at work?"

"It's good. Reagan is flexible. My work is computer based so I can run back and forth. I go in for a few hours in the morning and Collin stays home. Then we switch in the afternoon. We know we can't do that forever, but we're not ready to leave him with a stranger just yet. Collin's mom offered. I'm not sure how much Tyson should hang with Collin's crazy-ass family though. I don't want Tyson growing up thinking women belong in the kitchen with aprons on. Maybe one day a week with her. Hopefully that won't damage him too much."

"I'll be back and will help. She and I can alternate days. We'll come up with something that will help you guys."

"That would be great. Dad has been really helpful. He's over here all the time. He and Melissa both."

"He didn't have that time with you as a baby. I'm happy he's getting it now."

"Me too. Oh, and we broke ground on the new house this week."

"Honey, that's wonderful. You must be so excited."

Collin and Jade designed a house together for them to eventually live in. Collin's company is building it.

"Very excited. And Collin proposed again. It's getting annoying."

I let out of laugh. "Yes, it must be tough having an

attractive, kind, loving man beg you to marry him every day. The struggle is real."

She smiles. "I'll let him know when I'm ready." She briefly pauses. "Maybe soon."

I look at her and she bites her lip. That's about as close to marriage talk as she's ever gotten.

"Jade, I'm so proud of you. I love you."

"I love you too. I can't wait to see you."

"Me too. I'll come by after work hours."

"See you then."

We hang up and I look around at the empty small house I've called home for two months. I've been in the Outer Banks, the beaches on the North Carolina shoreline. It's quiet and peaceful here in the offseason. It's just what I needed to clear my head. After the whirlwind of the past year of my life, I needed the serenity.

I get into my car, which is packed to the brim with canvases. I learned that the emotions of heartbreak and the hormones of a pregnancy are fantastic for creativity. This was the most artistically productive nine weeks of my life.

I look down at my stomach, which has already popped a bit, way earlier than it did with Jade. I rub it. "On to our next adventure, Baby L." I started calling it Baby L for love. Because whatever mixed emotions I have now, I know this baby, unlike Jade, was conceived in love, and that means something to me.

I call into the Zoom meeting with Dr. Pearl we had scheduled for this morning.

She appears on the screen. "Oh, Amanda, are you driving right now?"

"Yes, so excuse my lack of eye contact. I needed to hit the road."

"No problem. Are you ready to go home?"

"I think so. I knew this date was coming. I have my first ultrasound tomorrow. And I miss Jade. Leaving her with a newborn isn't the most motherly thing I've ever done."

"You needed this time. Jade understands. Collin is very hands-on. She's fine."

"I know. She hasn't complained. She just misses me, and I miss her. I've never gone this long without seeing her."

"I know you video-called her and Tyson every day. I'm proud of you for taking this time for yourself. You needed it."

"I did."

"Are you ready to see Beckett?"

"I'm not sure. I loved Beckett. I still love Beckett. In his own fucked-up way, I believe he loves me too. He just doesn't trust me or anyone, and that's not acceptable."

"Good. It took us a while to get here, but I think you're right. Just know he's dealing with things too. While he may have grown up with privilege, he battles demons just like you do."

"I know. I keep telling myself that it's the reason for his actions, not because he doesn't love me. I needed to take a breath to decide what I want. I do want him, but I deserve to be treated a certain way. I don't know if he's up for it."

"There's nothing wrong with taking things slowly to make sure your emotional needs are being met."

"I'm not sure what he wants. Honestly, I expected him to break down the door to my rental house every single day, but he didn't. Jade said he misses me, and Glinda mentioned his regret, but I haven't heard from him directly."

I called Glinda once a few weeks ago. I missed her. She's

become like a mother to me. She told me that Beckett is dying to talk to me. That he realized his mistake. I just can't continue to play this game with him. He's an insecure, spoiled little boy in the body of a grown man. But I can't deny that he's a wonderful father. I hope my child will have him in its life, but if it's not what he wants, I'll manage.

"As you know, every road is paved with bumps and storms. You'll have to decide if you want to keep traveling on this particular road, despite them."

"Dr. Pearl, why do I always choose broken men? Why do I always think I can fix them? It's not like I've ever been successful at it."

"In my opinion, you have a bit of regret and shame over leaving your father just as he was slipping into alcoholism. You were fourteen. It wasn't your job to care for him, but you're a caregiver by nature. I think we both know you've done more than your fair share of caring for others."

Perhaps she's right. "If I stayed with him, maybe it wouldn't have gotten so bad."

"It would have gotten worse for you. We both know that. You did the right thing. That's why I'm proud of you for taking these two months. You didn't allow yourself to get pulled down. You're a survivor."

"I suppose."

"Are you still planning to make a stop?"

"Yes."

"Are you ready for this next big step?"

"Not really, but I agree it needs to be done. I'm almost there."

"Wonderful. I look forward to hearing what happens. Take care of you."

"I'm trying."

We hang up. I drive the last few miles to my last stop and think about what it's going to be like when I get home. Obviously, Beckett will have to be in my life to some extent. He's the father of my child. Like I've done with Declan for so many years, I'm hopeful that we can at least peacefully co-parent. I certainly want Andie and Glinda in Baby L's life. I'm just so uncertain what's in store for us.

I pull into the address I had researched at Dr. Pearl's urging. The road is gravely and uneven. I look around. This trailer park is even shittier than the one I grew up in.

I knock on the door. The woman who answers makes my stomach turn. I suppose I look like her, though it's clear life hasn't been kind. She appears forty years older than me, even though she's only seventeen years older. Her skin is leathery, and her teeth are decaying, likely from decades of drug abuse. This so easily could have been me if Jade didn't save me.

She scowls. "I was wondering if you'd ever show up here. Hurry inside before anyone sees you."

"Good to see you too, *Mom*."

She scoffs. "Mom? I'm no mother."

"I suppose we can agree on that."

She opens the door wider and then quickly closes it when I'm inside. I walk in and nearly puke at what I see. It's a disgusting, smelly mess. Expired food, dirty dishes, and soiled clothing are all over. There's drug paraphernalia everywhere. I need to make this quick.

"Elphie, I just came by to meet you and to thank you for staying out of my life."

She practically spits out, "Yeah, well, I wasn't good for anyone. You're very welcome."

"I want to tell you that I'm nothing like you."

She picks her tooth and then fiddles with whatever came out with her tongue. "Is that so? I happened to see something on the television about you being an addict. I guess the apple didn't fall too far from the tree after all."

"I haven't touched drugs since the day I found out I was pregnant with my daughter twenty-four years ago. That's what you do for your child. You do whatever it takes to make them safe and happy. Maybe my daughter didn't have a picture-perfect childhood, but she never once doubted that she was loved. She never doubted that I would always be there for her in her times of need. I *know* I was and am a good mother."

"Listen, I don't need this bullshit. Are you here with my monthly allowance or not? I'm not supposed to be around you. Tell Daddy Warbucks that I didn't come to you. You came to me."

"What are you talking about?"

"Your rich boyfriend."

"What about him?"

"His henchman showed up here months ago, right after I gave that interview."

"Henchman?"

"Some big, bald, scary guy in a black suit." Nico. "He said if I promised to never speak of you or contact you, an envelope of cash would show up here each month. And it has. It's the gift that keeps giving. Thank you for spreading your legs for a rich guy."

What? Why would Beckett do that?

I don't want to be here anymore. I make my way to the door. "I said what I came to say. Have a good life."

AFTER A STOP at the gallery to drop my work off to an exceedingly happy Norma, I'm finally on my way home.

I pull down my street and notice a familiar black Suburban in front of my house. As I pull into my driveway, I see Beckett sitting on my front step in his blue suit pants, shirt, and tie. The sleeves are rolled up. I don't need the vision of his forearms with my pregnancy hormones working on overdrive right now.

He stands as I pull in. I see tears welling in his eyes.

I walk to the back of my car to open the truck for my bags, but Nico is there. "I've got them. Go talk to him."

"Thanks, Nico."

He nods before whispering, "No need to beat him up. He's already done it to himself."

I give him a small smile before making my way to the front door. Beckett flashes me his crooked smile. He holds out flowers and chocolate-covered cherries. The flowers are kaleidoscope roses. I once mentioned how much I like them. He remembered.

"Thank you."

I step to take them from him, and he sinks his nose into my hair and inhales deeply. "I missed you. So much. It was like losing a part of me, a part that I need to survive."

I know the feeling, I felt the same, but I say nothing in return.

I let him linger a second longer than I should just because I need it too.

I eventually pull away. "Let's go inside. We should talk."

We walk in and I look around. Clearly someone has been here cleaning and bringing in my mail. I walk into my kitchen to see it full of groceries. All my favorite foods.

I remove my jacket and he sucks in an audible breath. "You're showing already. You look beautiful."

I stare down at my small belly. "I popped much earlier this time around. You couldn't even tell I was pregnant with Jade for six months."

"Do you know if we're having a boy or girl yet?"

"I guess now you believe it's yours?"

He lowers his head. "I deserved that. I'm sorry for what I said to you. I've regretted it every minute since. I didn't mean it."

"Then why did you say it?"

"I have no explanation. Whether I have a right to be or not, I'm damaged. Weak and damaged. I've been working on it though. I'm trying to be a better man for you. The kind you deserve."

"I'm happy for you, Beckett. And no, I don't know what we're having. My first ultrasound is tomorrow."

"Can I come?"

"Of course."

"Can I hold you for a minute? Please."

Tears well in my eyes because I need it too, but I know I can't give in. "Beckett, I'm happy that you're working on yourself. I want you to be the best version of you. But I'm not falling back into your arms or your bed. Not this time. You hurt me. You broke us. I don't trust you with my heart right now."

He nods. "I know. Trust is earned. Everything you said and did in our time together warranted my trusting you, but I threw it in your face and messed it up. Now you don't trust me. Rightfully so. But I'm going to earn it back. I'll do whatever it takes, for however long it takes. The simple fact is, I love you, I want to be with you, I want to raise our child together, and none of that will *ever* change."

I'm in town for two minutes and he comes over and says everything I needed to hear. And then it hits me. I've been back in town for two minutes. How did he know? Jade wouldn't have told him.

"How did you know I was back?"

"I'm a resourceful man."

I lift an eyebrow in question.

"I knew your lease was up in the Outer Banks today."

"You knew where I was?"

"Of course. I wouldn't be able to sleep at night without knowing you and our child were safe. You had a full security detail down there."

"Why didn't you come to me?"

"Because I knew you needed the time away from me. Away from the spotlight you've been under. I needed it too. I needed to spend time working on me so that I can be everything for you and our child."

"Thank you for staying away. Thank you for the space. I *did* need it."

He gives a small nod.

"I saw my mother today."

His eyes widen, knowing he's busted. "How did it go?"

"Why do you give her money?"

"I didn't want her bothering you. Hurting you. I did it to protect you."

"I know, and I appreciate it, but I don't care what lies she spreads. You're feeding her drug habit. I want you to stop."

"Okay. No more payments."

"Thank you."

"Have you seen Tyson?"

"Not yet. I'm headed over there in a bit."

He smiles. "She brought him in the other day. He's a rascal. That kid is going to be trouble."

"Well then, he's just like his mother was. For our baby's sake, and our sanity, let's hope that comes from Declan's side of the family."

He laughs. It's deep and so uniquely him. I can't believe how much I missed hearing it.

"How's Andie?"

"She's good. She misses you. I told her you went on a painting retreat where they don't allow phones. I didn't know what else to say, and I didn't make her any promises about your return."

"I missed her. I'll come by this weekend to see her. I'll be at Darian and Jackson's. I have a painting for them I need to deliver, and she invited me to their pool party and barbecue. I'll stop over after that."

"Thank you. She'll be very excited."

"How's your mom?"

"She didn't talk to me for a month after you left. She lived with us for the entire month and legitimately didn't say a single word to me."

I smile.

"She beat the crap out of me, both figuratively and literally. It turns out I get my right hook from her."

I can't help but giggle. "I love her."

"She loves you. We all do."

I think I need him to go. I wasn't expecting to see him so quickly. I wasn't expecting him to say everything I needed to hear. My head is a mess.

"My appointment is at eleven tomorrow. I'll see you then?"

He nods. "Your mail is on the counter. I've...umm... sorted it for you."

"Are any of my bills in there?"

He has a guilty look on his face. "They may have been misplaced," he mumbles, "and paid."

I shake my head and sigh. I don't have the will to fight him on this right now. "Thank you."

He hesitates for a moment. I know he wants to touch me, but I'm not letting that happen. Not yet.

He seems to understand without me having to say it. Giving me a small smile, he says, "Goodbye, cherry pie."

When he leaves, I begin looking through my mail. I eventually get to a pile of letters. Long letters. There are dozens of them. All from Beckett to me. They're dated. It looks like he wrote one every single day I was gone.

I sit and start reading them. They're quite possibly the most loving, romantic things I've ever read in my entire life. Every single one expresses how sorry he is and how much he loves me. And not only that. They're his journey of self-reflection. How he is learning to trust again after what happened with Jenny. How he knows that fighting for the sake of pain is wrong. As the days go on, I can see in his words how he's healing from his struggles and how much he wants and needs me in his life.

One of his first letters hits me particularly hard.

My mother told me that you confided in her what my father said to you the night you met him. I asked you a million times to tell me and am realizing you were trying to protect me by keeping silent, but I want to protect you too. If someone hurts you, they hurt me. What he said to you is unforgivable. He's toxic. I've cut him out of my life. I realized that I tried so hard for so many years to have a relationship with him, but he's not the kind of person I want in our life. Yours, mine, Andie's, and our baby's. Our family.

Cherry pie, I acknowledge that what I said to you cut even deeper because it came from someone you love. Someone to whom you've given your unconditional love. You were owed the same. I'm ashamed of how I treated you. Thank you for loving me. I promise to always do the same for you every minute of every day moving forward.

The letters get more and more remorseful and reflective as the days go on.

I know that I've been more fortunate than most in my life, but being used by people has taken its toll on me. My wife never loving me cut me deeper than I ever realized. I've allowed the damage to continue to chip away at me for over six years until it's left me as a shell of the man I once was. But he's still in there. Please don't give up on him. He's full of love for you. Please know that.

I love every single thing about you, but it's your pure heart that I love most. I'm in awe of you. You've been knocked down so many times, but you still stand tall, and you give people the benefit of the doubt. I want to be like you. I'm a work in progress, but I know with certainty there's one person I will NEVER again doubt. That's you, my love.

Our child will be so incredibly blessed to have you as his or her mother. If I could cook up the most perfect mother ever, it would be you. I couldn't ask for anyone better.

My own mother thinks we were always fated to be together. I believe that too. She considers you the daughter she never had.

I admittedly never gave much thought to fate, but I suppose that was before we met. You burst into that room at Reagan's party all those years ago and my heart just about exploded. I think when you reached for my hand that night, I knew. That's why I had to kiss you even though I shouldn't have. It's because we're two halves of the same heart, always meant to find our way to the other. I closed my eyes and felt your lips on mine every single day until I felt them again for real during our first intimate night together. The night that you took the leap of faith. Thank you for doing that.

Making love to you is everything. A connection that it's hard to believe is real, but it's

*real between us. Nothing has ever felt more
right. I know you feel it too.*

Every single letter ends with something he can't wait for us to do with our baby. Things neither of us were able to do for our other children. Things he wants to do as a full family.

Each letter is signed:

*Forever Enchanted,
Beckett*

By the time I finish, I'm in a puddle of snot and tears. What am I going to do with him?

I'M SITTING on Jade and Collin's couch, inhaling every bit of Tyson. I love this baby smell. "Oh, Jade, he's perfect."

Just then, Tyson grabs my nipple and squeezes it. I wince in pain.

Collin quickly grabs him. "Buddy, I told you that you're only allowed to touch the nipples of non-family members. And be gentle." He loudly whispers, "Unless they like it harder. Some of them do." He winks at Jade, and she blows him a kiss. I love their playfulness.

Without me thinking about it, my sweater falls open, leaving me in a now too-tight T-shirt. Jade just about chokes on her water. "What. The. Fuck."

I look down. Shit. I was planning to tell her after

tomorrow's ultrasound. That's why I wore an oversized sweater. I guess this conversation is happening right now.

Her eyes are wide open. "When there was a photo online two months ago of you coming out of the OB's office, I said, *every woman goes to an OB, and my beloved mother would definitely tell me if there was something else to report*."

"I was planning to wait until after my ultrasound tomorrow, but I guess that ship has sailed. I'm pregnant."

Collin says, "Did you hear that, Tyson? You're getting a playmate. Is it a cousin?"

Jade shakes her head. "No, it will be Tyson's aunt or uncle, because it's totally normal to have an aunt or uncle younger than you."

Collin starts laughing. "Holy shit. That's amazing." He kisses my cheek. "Congratulations. That's one fucking rich baby." He talks into my stomach. "Did you hear that? You're not even born yet and you legit never need to work a day in your life. Party it up, brother."

I can't help but laugh at him.

Jade smacks his ass. "Don't encourage him, Mom."

He smiles at her. "You love me."

"I love your piercing, that's it. I'm using you for that."

He chuckles as he sits down.

She takes my hand. "Are you okay? How do you feel about it?"

"Honestly, it was one of the happiest moments in my life when I first found out two months ago."

"Two months? Interesting timing."

I nod. "I was so happy thinking this wouldn't be the struggle it was when I had you. I was thinking how different it was going to be this time around. I wouldn't have a lot of the same worries. My relationship with the father, having a co-parent, the love between us. But then Beckett went off the deep end."

"And that's why you left?"

"He said some truly hurtful things to me. In retrospect, I don't think he meant them, I know he didn't, but they were said. It was a crazy year. I needed a minute alone to breathe. I needed to take a minute just for me."

"Good for you. Fuck him. When will you see him? I guess now you have to."

"He was waiting at my house when I got home."

"Stalker."

"Pretty much. He apologized. Said he's working on some things. He wants to earn my trust back. I appreciate that he knew it wasn't happening in a single moment. That's progress for him. He said just about everything I needed to hear. I just don't know if I can trust him with my heart again. To be honest, I'm a little afraid."

She gives me a knowing look. "It's always a risk. Sometimes the risk is worth the reward."

I can't help but smile at her echoing the words I said to her when she was struggling with trusting Collin with her heart.

"He's coming to the ultrasound tomorrow."

"Wow. I guess I knew you always wanted a bigger family."

I smile. "I was certainly sad that I couldn't have any more little Jades running around."

Collin mumbles, "God help us all."

She narrows her eyes at him before turning back to me. "If you're happy, I'm happy. I can't wait until our kids are in school together and get to fuck with everyone about their relationship."

"I see you're thinking big picture."

She grins. "Totally."

WHEN I GET HOME, I decide to pick up the phone and call the one person who truly understands both me and this situation.

She answers right away. "I'm so happy you're home. I almost got on a plane today."

My voice cracks. "Glinda, I'm so confused. He was here saying everything I needed to hear. But I'm afraid of getting hurt again. I couldn't bear it."

"I understand. He needs to earn back your trust. Make him work for it, but be open to it. Amanda, he does love you. Deeply. He's just overcoming his own demons. His hurtful words were not about you. They're about him and his internal struggles that he never dealt with until now."

"I know you're right, but I feel like it would be weak of me to just take him back right away. My heart wants him, but my head tells me that I need to protect myself."

"Weak? That's the last thing in the world you are. Let me tell you something, Amanda Tremaine. You have a strength I never had. I grew up poorer than poor, with absentee parents, praying every day for a better life. I latched on to the first stable man willing to take care of me. I pretended not to notice how incompatible we were. I looked the other way for years when I knew he wasn't faithful to me. You, on the other hand, decided you'd take care of yourself without someone else doing it for you. What makes it more incredible is that you also had a daughter to care for. I admire you and your strength. You're the strongest woman I know. And look how strong your daughter is. That's not a coincidence. It's because you're her mother and paved the path."

"Thanks, Glinda. That means a lot to me coming from you."

"I was a dreamer like you. I still believe in fate. Fate brought you and Beckett together at that party. Fate brought you to his house that day I was there. Imagine how many things had to line up for those two events to happen. It's because you're meant to be together. I believe that with every ounce of my soul."

I wipe my tears that are practically pouring from my eyes. "You're making me cry."

"Don't shed another tear over him. I want you to relax. Let nature take its course with Beckett. Time will heal your wounds and you'll find your way back to each other. You just worry about taking care of my grandbaby."

"I will. I wish you lived here."

"I'm considering moving back to the area. Next time I'm in, I'm going to house hunt."

My tears quickly are quickly replaced by a big smile. "I can't tell you how happy that would make me. Jade didn't have any grandparents. I'm so thrilled our baby will have you."

"So am I."

"Can I ask you something, Glinda?"

"Of course. Anything."

"It was obvious at the airport that things have progressed with Nico. When did that happen?"

"As you know, there's always been some flirting. But Italy was when we took things to the next level. We sat down with Beckett recently. Though he was in no position to resist, he gave us his blessing. He said he wanted me to be happy."

I squeal with excitement. "I'm thrilled for you. This has been a long time coming." And I'm relieved that Beckett offered no resistance.

"It has."

"Is that why you want to move back?"

"In some part, but I also want to be close to my growing family."

"I'm so excited about all of it. And he's hot."

"Oh, dear, you have no idea just how hot he is."

CHAPTER THIRTY-FOUR

BECKETT

I'm pacing a hole in the floor. "Is it normal for it to take this long? Where are they?"

Amanda shakes her head and smiles. It immediately soothes me. She always calms the crazy bouncing around in my head. "It's been three minutes. Relax."

"I donated a wing to this damn hospital. I want you to have VIP service. I'm going to the front desk."

In a stern voice, she says, "Beckett, sit down and be quiet."

Because I'm totally whipped, I stop dead in my tracks, find a chair, and sit.

A few seconds later the doctor finally walks in, and I mumble, "It's about time."

"Ignore grumpy, Dr. Crest."

He gives a cocky smile. I dislike him immediately. "How are you feeling, Amanda?"

Why does he know her first name? How familiar is he?

In her normal, cheery demeanor, she replies, "Totally fine. No morning sickness at all."

No morning sickness? "Isn't it healthy to have morning sickness? Maybe something is wrong."

Dr. Fuckface shakes his head. "Not necessarily. Some women don't have any. Did you have it with Jade?"

Amanda shakes her head. "No. None."

"There's your answer. Why don't we have a look at Baby Tremaine?"

I feel my throat close but say nothing. I need to be on my best behavior for her. No slip-ups.

"Windsor," Amanda says. "It's Baby Windsor."

Fuck, I love her.

I take her hand and kiss it in appreciation as they prepare her belly with the jelly.

Dr. Fuckface starts moving the wand over her adorable little belly. "Let's see if we can find Baby Windsor."

A small form starts to take shape on the screen. "There's Baby Windsor. Looking good. Everything seems in order." We hear a whooshing sound. "And there's the heartbeat."

I panic. "It's so fast. Is that normal?"

"It's very healthy, Mr. Windsor. I promise. Everything looks perfect. It's a drop early, but do you want me to try to see what you're having? The baby is in a good position for it."

Amanda shrugs. "I don't care either way. Beckett?"

My eyes widen. "Me? You're letting *me* decide whether we find out what we're having?"

She lets out a laugh. "Yes. You made this baby too. It's half yours. The crazy half."

"I don't care what it is, but I wouldn't mind knowing. It might be fun to prepare things. Is that okay?"

Amanda turns to the doctor. "We want to know. Tell us."

Dr. Crest moves the wand a bit and says, "Yep. Clear as day. You're having a boy."

I clutch my chest, suddenly finding it hard to breathe. A son. I'm having a son. About a million different images flash through my mind of things I want to do with him.

I look at Amanda's smiling face. I hope he looks just like her.

Because I'm a puddle of emotions and can't help myself, I grab her face and kiss her. Hard. Long. Deep.

She doesn't stop me. In fact, she grabs my hair and kisses me right back. Our tongues meet for the first time in two months. It's perfect. She's perfect.

Oh my god, I've missed her. I can never be without her again. I'm a moron for treating her like I did. I swear, if she takes me back, I'll spend every single day of my life making it up to her. I'll never take her for granted again.

I don't know how long we kiss. It feels like both two seconds and two hours. When we eventually breathlessly break free, the doctor is nowhere to be found.

I keep my forehead pressed to hers. "I love you. Marry me."

She runs her fingertips over my scruff in her special way that always makes my dick hard. "Beckett, we just had a conversation yesterday about taking it slow. Earning trust back. Proposing less than twenty-four hours later isn't exactly taking it slow."

"Right. Hmm. Move in with us."

She holds my face. "Take a breath."

I do. A deep one.

"Slow. We're taking things slowly. We're building back the trust. We may or may not get there. Regardless, we're bringing an innocent child into the world. *He's* our priority."

He. My son.

I swallow and nod. "You get dressed. I'm going to have a chat with the doctor."

"Beckett, behave."

I smile and lie. "Absolutely."

I find Dr. Fuckface in the hallway and grab him by the shirt. He nearly pees himself when I shove him against a wall. "Amanda and my son will be your top priority for the next five months of your life. You will be available at all hours and make sure everything is happy and perfect for her. She will *never* wait for you. *Nothing* will go wrong in her labor, or I will bring holy hell down on you and everyone you care about." I let go of his shirt and smooth it out. "And don't fucking call her by her first name. It's disrespectful. Do we have an understanding?"

"Y...yes, sir, Mr. Windsor."

"Thank you."

He walks away and I can't help but smile. Fucking coward.

I turn and see Amanda standing there with a look I can't quite read, though her face is flushed. She bites her lip. Is she turned on right now? She may say she doesn't like when I'm aggressive and confrontational, but I think she does.

I walk over to her and pull her lip out from between her teeth. "You know what that does to me."

She visibly swallows as she nods.

I take her hand in mine, and we make our way to the elevator. We stand there quietly and calmly as the doors open and then close. As soon as they close, she pushes me until I'm pinned to the wall, grabs my face, and smashes her lips to mine. I squeeze her ass and grind my quickly forming erection into her. She practically mewls. Her hands frantically move all over me. She's so worked up. Hell yes.

As soon as the elevator pings our arrival, she pulls away. Taking deep breaths, she whispers, "I'm sorry. I shouldn't have done that. It's hard to have all these pregnancy hormones and not be having sex. And then you do what you did with the doctor..." She bites her lip again.

I love that she gets turned on by that side of me. She's so fucking sexy. I pull her lip out again. "Whatever you need, cherry pie."

I quickly lead her to the car. As we're getting in, I discreetly mumble to Nico, "Drive around the block a few times before heading to her house."

He chuckles as he closes the door. "Yes, sir."

Once we're in, I pull her to sit between my legs and run my hands up and down her body. "Beckett, I'm not having sex with you right now."

"I know. Let me help you. Let me give you some relief. I know you need it."

She thinks for a moment before leaning back into me, giving me the permission I'm seeking. I inhale her cherry scent. The one I've missed. It's so nice to have her close again.

I unbutton and unzip her jeans before sliding my fingers into her panties. She's wet. Very wet. I kiss up her neck as my fingers move through her. "You feel so soft and warm. I love it when you soak your panties for me, cherry pie."

She grips my pants. "Ah, Beckett, that feels amazing. It's been so long."

I slip my fingers into her opening. "One day soon, my cock will be back in here making you feel good."

She's moaning and writhing, grinding her ass onto my cock. I might legitimately come in my pants this time.

With my other hand, I wrap it in her hair and pull it hard until her face is tilted back to mine. I stick out my tongue and she happily sucks it into her mouth.

My fingers glide in and out of her while my thumb moves over her clit. I talk into her mouth. "I can hear how needy you are." She's like a waterfall right now. My fingers are practically making a splashing noise as they move in and out of her. I'm not sure I've ever felt her this wet. I would give anything to stick my dick in her, but I know that's off the table. This is all about her.

Her lips are sealed over mine while her fingers are threaded through my hair. She fucks my fingers with her hip movements until she eventually yells her orgasm into my mouth, soaking my hand.

I don't stop my fingers until I'm sure she's done. When she is, I pull them out and move them between our kissing lips. We both lick them and continue to kiss through them, tasting her sweet come. Oh god, I've missed her taste.

As the car comes to a stop, we breathlessly pull apart. I zip and button her jeans. "Feel better?"

She breathes, "Yes. Thank you." She turns to me. "What are you doing now?"

"First, I'm going to jerk off with my Amanda-soaked fingers in my mouth, then I'll go back to the office."

She giggles. "That sounds fun." She swallows. "Thanks for being there today. It's the first time I've ever had the father at an ultrasound." And then my heart breaks a little thinking about everything she's been through in her life. "I'll see you this weekend."

My shoulders drop. "Not before? That's, like, four days from now." I know I'm whining, but I have no shame anymore. I just want my girl back.

"Slow, Beckett. Slow. I want to trust you again. I need to be sure. I won't live on edge, fearing one of your moments. I won't accept you unnecessarily lashing out at me ever again. I don't deserve to be a victim of your insecurity."

I open the door and jokingly shove her toward it. "Go, before I lose my boner from all this insecurity talk."

She laughs before she turns back and seductively licks across my lips one more time.

"Boner here to stay."

I hear her giggling as she closes the door to walk inside.

One step closer.

AFTER GIVING myself some much-needed relief with her taste on my tongue, I make my way back to my office. I see Dominic as I walk in.

He looks at me suspiciously. "I don't think I've ever seen you smile like this before. What's going on?"

I feel my face. I guess I am smiling. "Can you keep a secret?"

"Of course."

"My girlfriend is pregnant. I'm having a son."

He has a huge grin as holds out his hand. "Congratulations."

I shake it. "Thank you."

"Is this the same girlfriend that wasn't talking to you for the past two months?"

"Yes. I was an idiot. I'm working on winning her back and definitely making progress. It's only a matter of time."

He lets out a laugh. "I'm doing the same with my girlfriend. Let's hope we're both successful and we both stop being boneheads."

I smile. "You'd think we'd be better at this by now."

He nods. "At our age? Yes." He looks around like he's making sure we're alone. "Can I ask you a question?"

"Sure."

"Why are there cans of something called Pussy Juice in the refrigerator?"

I let out a laugh. "Apparently it's an energy drink that Jade likes."

"Ah, Jade. I should have known. Where there's smoke...I'm sure she drinks it to get a reaction out of people."

I nod in agreement. "No doubt."

"Have you ever tried it?"

I look down in embarrassment. "Once. I just kind of wanted to know what it tasted like. It claims to be one hundred percent natural ingredients."

He looks intrigued. "And?"

I twist my mouth searching for the right words. "It's...pungent. It tastes like an oyster you know is going bad tomorrow."

He bursts into laughter. "Wow. That is shockingly descriptive. I think I'll stay away from it."

I smile as I nod. "That would be wise. I need to get to work. I'll stop by later."

I walk down the hallway and step into my office. Jade immediately follows me in and closes the door behind her. She appeared out of nowhere. She's like a ninja.

"How was the ultrasound?"

"The baby is healthy."

"Good." She crosses her arms. "What are your intentions with my mother?"

"To love the fuck out of her every single day for the rest of my life."

"You know, Beckett, my mother believes in fairy tales. She believes in Prince Charming. All she's ever wanted is to find him and have a bigger family. This is her last chance for it. You can't fuck with her head anymore."

"I'm not." I look her square in the eyes. "Believe me when I tell you that I love her, and I know we're meant to be. She's the air I breathe. She's *my* fairytale come true."

"If you're in, you better be all fucking in."

"I'm all fucking in. I'm working on earning her trust back. Once I do, she'll get everything she wants and more. I'll never treat her as anything but the queen she is. She'll get her happily ever after. I promise. I know what I'm doing."

She narrows her eyes at me. "You have a plan, don't you?"

I smile. "I might."

CHAPTER THIRTY-FIVE

AMANDA

I'm on my way to Darian and Jackson's house to deliver a painting I created for them. I told Jade I would text when I was close so she could help me carry it in. I'm wearing an oversized sweatshirt. I'm not ready for this whole crew to know about my pregnancy. I'm not sure what the status of my relationship is with Beckett, and I don't want to answer any questions.

When I pull into the driveway, I shoot her a text. She immediately opens the front door.

"Hey, baby."

"Hey, Mom. Everyone is out back. Aunt Darian said to join them when we're done."

"Sounds good."

We maneuver the painting into Jackson's office and then walk toward their massive backyard. The back of their house has a big glass wall. I suppose it's new considering Declan and Collin crashed through it last year. As we get closer, I notice that all the adults are eating at the table and the kids are in the pool.

Jade walks out first, with me behind her. As soon as I step outside, I hear, "Mandy?"

I look up and, for the first time in twenty-five years, I see Dominic Mazzello. My first love whose life I ruined that day in college. The impetus for my life spinning out of control for the next two years. He's older, but unmistakably the same handsome man I dated and loved all those years ago.

I throw my hand over my mouth as tears immediately form in my eyes.

Dominic looks at me in complete and total shock. I'm sure he hates me. Seeing me likely brings back so many painful memories for him.

Jade touches my shoulder, undoubtedly confused. "Mom, how do you know Dominic?"

"He...he...he was a friend from college." I give her a knowing look. "Just before I dropped out."

She nods, knowing exactly who I mean.

Dominic looks at her in disbelief. "Jade, your mother is Amanda Tremaine? But your last name is McGinley."

"My parents were never married. I use Tremaine as my middle name and McGinley as my last."

Wait, they know each other's names. I ask, "How do *you* know Dominic?"

"I work with him."

Oh my god. She works with him? Holy shit. That means Beckett does too.

Dominic keeps staring at Jade. "How old are you?"

She answers, "Twenty-three."

I can see Dominic running the math in his head.

I know what he's thinking right now. "She's not yours, Dom. She was born nearly two years later."

Jade attempts to lighten things for me by saying, "Wow. I've always had a crush on him. We could have had a major Greek tragedy on our hands. Are you sure I'm not his?"

I roll my eyes. "Look at you and look at Dom and me. Does it look like the two of us would have produced you?" Dominic is Cuban, with darker skin, eyes, and hair. "I haven't seen Dominic in over twenty-five years."

Cassandra asks what I'm sure everyone is wondering. "What the fuck is going on here? I feel like I'm in the Twilight Zone."

Her sister, Beth, answers, "Dominic and Amanda dated when they were in college."

How does she know? I just then notice Dominic and Beth's close proximity. Is that who she's dating? Is Beth with Dominic?

Darian clears her throat. "Dominic, if you and Amanda would like some privacy to talk, feel free to use Jackson's study."

He looks at me and I nod. We obviously need to talk. It's way late, but at the very least, I owe him an apology.

He walks over to me. I wouldn't blame him if he slapped me across the face right now. But that's not what he does. He simply holds out his arms and I fall into them as if no time has passed.

He breathes, "Cariño." That was his term of endearment for me in college.

He smells and feels the same. Even though it's been such a long time, it's still so comforting. He exudes warmth. I can't believe I'm hugging the first man I ever loved. I know he loved me too.

He whispers, "You smell the same. It's oddly comforting."

I let out a small laugh. "I know exactly how you feel."

"Let's go talk."

I nod and we walk inside to Jackson's study. After I close the door, he pulls me into his arms again.

I let out a sob into his chest. "I'm so sorry, Dominic."

"What are you sorry for?"

"I know I ruined your life."

He caresses me in that loving way he always did. "You didn't ruin my life. I'm responsible for what happened to me. I lost my temper. I caused it. Regardless, I've had a good life. I have no regrets. My only regret was never getting to say goodbye to you."

How can he be so forgiving after what I did to him?

He lowers his arm and points to the sofa. "Why don't you have a seat so we can talk. I think we both have questions. I know I do."

After handing me tissues, he sits across from me. "Mandy, tell me why you left."

"Because of the guilt."

"What did you do? Where did you go? I know you had no family."

"Honestly, I was pretty fucked up for the next year or so. I floated around. The drug use became extreme. I was out of control. I became addicted." I can barely look at him, so I don't. "A lot of sex and a lot of drugs. It was bad."

"Why did you run and turn to all that?"

"I couldn't handle what I did to you. I numbed the pain. The next year, I met Jade's father, Declan. I assume you know him?"

"I just met him today."

"He's ten years older than me. He was a user too. Even

worse than me. Together, we were toxic. We were on and off for a few months when I found out I was pregnant with Jade. That's the last day I ever used. He wasn't so lucky. It took him another eight years to shake it. Jade and I were very much on our own the first seven years of her life, struggling to make ends meet."

He looks pained. "I'm sorry for what you went through."

"It was tough, but we made it work for us. When Declan got clean, he began to help financially."

He smiles. "That explains Jade's toughness. She's tough like you."

That's the last thing I am. "I'm weak."

"You're strong. I can't imagine it was easy to go cold turkey when you found out you were pregnant, but you did. I can't imagine it was easy being alone with a baby, but you did it. You raised a superstar. Look at all that Jade's accomplished at such a young age. She's the toughest young woman I know. It's clear where she got it from. You should be very proud of her."

He has no idea how much I needed to hear this right now. He and Glinda both telling me how strong I am means so much to me. It almost makes me believe it. "Thank you. I am."

He points to the painting I just brought inside. "It appears you're still a very talented artist."

"I never stopped painting, even at my worst. Though I had limited success until about five years ago. Things have sort of taken off since then." Because of Beckett. Besides Jade, Collin, and Tyson, everything good in my life right now is because of Beckett. I miss him. I swore to myself I would take things slowly with him, but I'm only hurting myself. I just want to be back in his arms. His big, comforting arms. I wish he was here with me right now. Holding me. Loving me.

Dominic breaks me out of my Beckett reverie. "I've seen your work in Jade's office. I didn't know it was yours, but I do now. The paintings are beautiful."

I smile. "Thank you. What about you? What have you been up to?"

"I suppose you now know that I work at Daulton Holdings. I have two children. Valentina is eight and Matteo is four. They're in the pool if you want to meet them."

Little kids. How sweet. "I'd like that."

"I'm divorced, and I've been seeing Beth for a while."

"I adore Beth. She's so sweet." I've only met her a handful of times, but she's always been kind and welcoming to me.

He smiles. I know that smile. He's in love with her. I'm happy for both of them.

"She is. It's funny, I've thought about you some in the past year. I considered reaching out to you. Just to get a little closure. We never really had that."

"I suppose we didn't."

"Sebastian thought I should call you."

Oh god. Sebastian. The man who told me I was no good for Dom. Who told me to end things with him. "You're still friends with him?"

"I am. Kevin too." Kevin was their other best friend in college. "Can you tell me what happened at the end? I know you were on drugs, but I thought we were in love. Finding you in bed with two men impacted me on a deep level. I'd like to try to understand it. I've always just assumed you didn't love me the same way I loved you."

Oh no. Of course he'd think that. It was the furthest

thing from the truth. "I did love you, Dominic." I pause. "I'm not sure I should tell you."

"It's been twenty-five years. I'd like to know and then move on. Please. Whatever it is, I can handle it."

I guess he needs to hear it. I have no reason not to tell him the truth. "After your arrest and team suspension, Sebastian came to me. He told me I was pulling you down. That I was ruining your shot at making it to the big leagues. He said you were madly in love with me, and that if I loved you, I should do something drastic to change your mind and set you free. I staged the whole thing. Being in bed with those guys. I knew you were coming over to tell me about the suspension being lifted. I made it look like I was being intimate with them, so you'd break up with me. I never expected the fight, and I certainly never expected you to get injured." The tears come again. "I'm...I'm so sorry, Dominic."

He squeezes my hand. "I don't think you have anything to apologize for, but to the extent it helps you, I forgive you."

"Thank you. It *does* help."

"Did you ever get married? Do you have other children?"

The second question is a loaded one right now. I look down at my covered belly. I'm not ready to tell him about my pregnancy. That's mine and Beckett's news to share with other people when we're ready.

"Unfortunately, I never had any more kids. I wish I had, but the right opportunity never came along." Until now. "Jade was my sole focus for a very long time. I was briefly married a few years ago, but it wasn't right. I'm dating someone now. We're *very* different, but I like him and I'm seeing where it goes."

Actually, I love him. Deeply.

He gives me a warm smile. "He's a lucky man. Speaking of lucky men, I need to go find Beth. I was a little shocked to see you and didn't consider how it would impact her."

We both stand. I smile at him. "It was good to see you. You look great."

"And you haven't aged a day."

"Always a sweet talker."

As we walk back toward the pool area he says, "I still can't believe you're Jade's mom. I've worked with her for five years. I never connected the dots."

"We don't look anything alike. Why would you?"

As soon as we step outside, Jade runs over to me and wraps me in her arms. "Are you okay, Mom?" Worry is written all over her face.

"Yes, baby, I'm fine."

Her eyes sparkle. She's about to say something ridiculous. "Did we settle my paternity? I've always wanted to call you daddy, Dom."

I have to hide my smile. Such a Jade thing to say.

Dominic simply shakes his head. "I can only imagine what a handful she was as a kid."

I let out the laugh I was holding in. "You have no idea."

He looks around and asks about Beth. Apparently, she was upset about my presence. I'll have to talk to her. She certainly has no reason to be concerned.

He grabs Beth's son, Luke, and two kids I assume are his, and disappears around the corner in search of her.

I squeeze Jade's arm. "I think I might head out. I really need to go see Beckett."

She motions toward the door where Beckett and Andie are walking out. "I thought you might need him right now. I called him when you went inside with Dom."

I hug her. "What did I ever do to deserve such an amazing daughter like you?"

"Obviously something very good."

As soon as Andie sees me, she comes running for me and straight into my arms. I lift her up and hold her tight. "I missed you so much, sweetness."

Her little arms are around my neck. "I missed you too. I'm so glad your painting retreat is over. I can't believe they didn't let you have a phone. Can I see all the paintings? Are you coming home? Gigi missed you. Daddy *really* missed you. He looks at your pictures all the time. I even saw him cry twice while looking at them. And once..."

Beckett places his hand over her mouth and kisses my head. "Are you okay? Jade called and said something happened and you needed me." Then he mouths, "Is the baby okay?"

I nod. "We're fine. I'll explain in a minute. Let's talk more about you crying and missing me."

Andie giggles.

Jade covers Andie's ears and looks at Beckett. "You're so pussy-whipped. It's pathetic."

Andie pinches her eyebrows together. "What does pussy-whipped mean?"

Jade tries to contain her laughter. "Umm. When a man loves a woman *a lot*."

"Oh, then yes, Daddy is definitely pussy-whipped."

As I set Andie back on the ground, Jackson and Darian walk over, mercifully ending this conversation. Darian crouches down. "You must be Andie. It's nice to meet you. I'm Darian."

Andie holds out her hand. "That's a pretty name. It's nice to meet you too. This is my daddy, Beckett. He's pussy-whipped."

Jade bursts out laughing. Darian and Jackson are trying not to laugh but failing.

Beckett sighs, whispering in my ear, "Does Jade have to be around our baby?"

I giggle.

Cassandra's daughter, Dylan, comes running over and hugs Andie. I forgot that they go to school together. "I didn't know you were coming. Want to go swimming with my brother and cousins?"

Andie looks up at Beckett and he nods. "Have fun. Be careful." They run off to the pool.

I intertwine my fingers with Beckett's, needing to feel him right now. He smiles down at it and squeezes me tight.

Dominic, Beth, and their kids reappear from around the corner with huge smiles. What a relief. I'm glad everything is okay.

Luke yells out, "Mommy and Dominic just got engaged. They're getting married. We're going to be a family."

Everyone flies over to see her ring and congratulate them.

Beckett is smiling. "I didn't know Dominic would be here. He's a good friend of mine from work. I want to introduce you to him."

BECKETT

Amanda tries to say something but before she does, Dominic walks over. He looks at our joined hands and then lifts his eyes to Amanda's. "Beckett is the man you're seeing?"

She nods.

I toggle my head between the two of them. "How do you two know each other?"

Dominic looks at Amanda to answer. She moves her eyes to mine, looking a bit nervous. "Dominic was my college boyfriend. I've mentioned him to you before."

I can feel my heart racing. Sweat is now covering my brow. All of a sudden, I want to fucking strangle Dominic, but this is my first test since she's back. I need to try to stay calm.

Through gritted teeth, I say, "I didn't realize you two kept in touch."

She shakes her head. "We don't. Today is the first time I've seen him since college."

Oh my god. He was the one she loved. Does she still love him? Does she want him back? I'm now finding it hard to breathe.

Amanda releases my hand and hugs the woman standing with Dominic. She says, "Congratulations."

Oh right, they just got engaged.

Amanda then whispers something in her ear. The woman smiles as she returns Amanda's hug.

I hold out my hand for Dominic. "It sounds like congratulations are in order."

"Thank you. I...umm...didn't realize it was Mandy you're seeing." He blows out a breath. "I didn't even know she was Jade's mother until today. What a crazy coincidence."

This must have been quite a reunion.

He pulls the other woman close as I get my first good look at her. I immediately recognize her from Reagan's party all those years ago. She has a unique shade of blue eyes that you don't easily forget. I saw them together that night. Interesting. There must be quite the story there.

"This is my fiancée, Beth O'Connell." They both smile at the term fiancée. It's likely their first time using it.

I hold out my hand. "It's a pleasure to meet you. Congratulations."

She shakes it in return. "It's a pleasure to meet you too."

Dominic looks down at Amanda's sweatshirt-covered stomach, wide eyed. Shit. I told him about my girlfriend being pregnant.

Amanda notices where he's looking and then she turns her head to me.

I scrunch my nose. "I may have told him about our news in the office this week. I was over-the-top excited, and he noticed."

Beth picks up on what's happening. "You're pregnant, Amanda?"

She immediately covers her mouth, realizing she practically yelled it. It's like a record scratch. Everything, and everyone, goes quiet.

Declan walks over to her. "You're pregnant?"

She nods.

He's still for a moment before holding out his arms. "I'm so happy for you. I know you always wanted more kids."

She hugs him in return. "Thank you."

I look over at the kids in the pool. I don't want Andie to learn about it like this, but they're yelling and screaming, not paying attention to the adults. They didn't hear anything.

Jackson pops a few bottles of champagne. There's a toast to Beth and Dominic's engagement and our pregnancy.

Jade looks around and happily announces, "Wow, Mom, you've slept with, like, a third of the guys at this big table."

I feel like my throat is about to close, but the table breaks out into hysterics and Amanda joins in. While I don't share their excitement over it, I manage to remain calm.

We sit around all afternoon and into the evening with the big family. They're all so close. I'm learning that risqué humor is their norm.

Amanda hasn't stopped touching me all night. I don't know what happened with her and Dominic before I got here, but my girl is needing constant contact with *me*, and I'm loving it. And I'm proud of myself for remaining calm and not saying or doing something stupid in the heat of jealous, insecure moments.

I whisper in her ear, "Come home with me. I need to hold you."

She turns to me with so much love and affection written on her face. How did I ever doubt her?

"I need it too, Beckett, but I'm not ready to be physical with you yet. I'm a little scared to let myself go with you. I get so lost in you."

"I don't need sex. Well, I do, but I understand. I just want you in my space again. Let me breathe you in all night."

She hesitates for a moment before eventually nodding. I feel the most relief I've felt in over two months.

When we're about to leave, Reagan pulls me aside. "Have you heard anything about the Cougars?"

"As in the Philadelphia professional baseball team?"

"Yes."

"No. I know Harold Greene is getting old, but I haven't heard anything specific. What's going on?"

"I went to college with his grandson. He called me this morning. He said the Greene family is considering selling the team and asked me if I want to put a group together to put in a bid. This isn't public information yet."

A blow out a breath. "Wow. The Greene family has owned the Cougars for over half a century. It must be close to a billion dollars to buy."

She nods. "I was thinking the same. I might put a small group together and make a legitimate play for it. Any interest in joining forces?"

"I'm pretty sure it's the dream of every Philly kid to one day play for or own the Cougars. I'm in. Who else are you thinking of asking?"

"I'm meeting with Auburn Bouvier this week."

I let out a laugh. "That grumpy fucker? I hear he's finally getting married."

"He is. My mom and Jackson met her at a party a few months ago. They love her."

"He's a good guy. He'd be great for this. I'll be there."

We say goodbye to everyone, and Andie and I start our journey home. Like an impatient child, I keep checking my rearview mirror to ensure that Amanda is following us.

When we get to the house, we put Andie to bed.

She's so happy that Amanda is back. Amanda has to promise to paint with her in the morning just to get her to go to sleep.

We lay in bed and talk for hours, like we did the first month she was here. I get to hear about all the paintings she's created in the past two months. I can't wait to see them.

There's a lot of touching and kissing, but nothing more. I can't remember a more intimate, perfect night without sex in my life.

CHAPTER THIRTY-SIX

BECKETT

I wake in the very early morning to an empty bed. I didn't dream it, right? She slept here.

I inhale her pillow and am immediately at ease. Yum. Cherries. My girl was here. I wasn't dreaming.

I bet I know exactly where she is.

I throw on shorts over my boxer briefs and head to the studio, immediately seeing her there in her favorite room. She doesn't notice me, so I just watch her do her thing. I love seeing her like this in her natural element. It looks like she's sketched something on a canvas and is just starting to paint over it.

I think this is the right time. I quietly go to my office and grab the paperwork I've been dying to share with her.

I reenter the studio and tiptoe until my front touches her back. She doesn't even flinch. It's like she was expecting it.

Sitting on the stool behind her, I wrap my arms

around her and kiss up her neck. "I've missed seeing you in here."

She leans back into me. "It's nice to be back. I've missed this time with Andie."

I run my fingertips along her arms. "She won't be up for another hour. I wonder how we can occupy ourselves."

Her breathing picks up. "Beckett, you're making this so hard."

I thrust my hips a bit so she can feel what she does to me. "You're making *this* so hard."

She giggles. "You know what I mean."

"Then give in."

She turns her head and nuzzles her nose into my neck. "Paint with me."

"I can't paint."

"Put your hand over mine."

I do and she turns her focus toward the painting again.

She moves our joint hands until I see a cherry start to take form. I marvel. "Wow, I'm a good artist."

She laughs. "This is like that scene from the movie *Ghost* when he sits behind her on the ceramics wheel."

"I hope it ends like that scene does." They have sex.

"You're incorrigible."

"That's why you love me."

"I do love you. And I'm finding it hard to resist you. I want to trust in us again."

I continue kissing her arms, neck, and shoulders. "Have you ever noticed the editing mistake in that scene?"

"In *Ghost*?"

"Yes."

"No. What is it?"

"Their hands are all gooey in the clay, but as soon as they start kissing, their hands are clean all of a sudden."

She stops and thinks for a brief moment. "Huh. I never noticed."

"Movies are clean. They have the benefit of reshooting scenes when they mess up. And editing. They can edit things. Real life is messy. I'm messy."

"I've noticed."

I continue kissing her all over.

She whines, "Beckett, I'm trying to be strong. We can't just sweep what happened under the rug."

"I know we can't, but I want to show you that I trust you and that you can trust me."

"I know you do, but you can't snap your fingers and make that happen. It takes time."

"I don't want to wait."

She sighs in frustration.

I remove the paintbrush from her hand and turn her around, pulling her close to me.

"Beckett, I..."

I cover her mouth with my hand. "Let me speak."

She nods and I remove my hand from her mouth.

"I fucked up. I did exactly what I told you not to do. I let the press get in my head. I lost sight of what was real and what wasn't. I hate myself for it. I know we're real. I know our love is real. I've never been more sure of anything in my life." I touch her stomach. "Our son was conceived out of so much love that my heart feels like it might burst. I thought Andie was conceived out of love, but now that I have you, I know she wasn't. I know Jade wasn't either. But our son was. No matter how I've fucked things up, our son has something that our other children don't have."

"I know. That exact beautiful thought was running through my mind two months ago when you sat in my kitchen and ruined it."

"I'm going to fix that. Every single day for the rest of our lives I'm going to show you love and trust."

I reach down and pick up the file. "I know trust is earned. I'm going to trust you with the most important thing in the world to me."

I hand it to her. She opens it and begins reading. I see it in her eyes the moment she realizes what it is. They immediately fill with tears as she looks back up at me.

"You want me to adopt Andie?"

I take her hand and run it over my tattoo. "Yes. I trust you with my biggest treasure. We'll protect her together. I want you to be her mother."

Her tears begin spilling over, running down her face. "I...I don't know what to say."

"Do you want to be her mother?"

She sniffles. "More than anything."

"Then it's settled. Everything is filed. It just needs your signature to be finalized."

"It's already filed? When did you do this?"

I wipe her tears with my thumbs and stare into her beautiful face. "The day after you left."

She wraps her arms around my neck and brings her forehead to mine. Her tears are streaming down her face. "Thank you for trusting me. I love you."

"What kind of love are we talking about? I love

you and I want to cuddle? Or I love you and I want you to stick your dick into me?"

She giggles as she kisses me, but before she can answer, Andie walks in.

"Amanda, why are you crying?"

"They're happy tears, baby." Amanda reaches out her hand. "Come here."

Andie walks over and I pick her up and place her on my leg. I look at Amanda and she nods. I look down at Andie. "Sweetie, we have a lot of good news to share with you."

"Like what?"

I smile as I rub Amanda's stomach. "First, you're going to be a big sister. Amanda and I are having a baby. A baby boy."

Her eyes widen and she looks at Amanda. "A baby? A baby brother?"

Amanda nods.

"Can I touch your belly?"

"Of course."

Amanda lifts her shirt and Andie touches her belly. "Wow, there's a baby in there? A whole baby? My brother?"

"Yep."

"So Daddy is now your baby daddy?"

Amanda laughs. "Yes, he is."

"What's the other good news?"

Amanda takes her hand and kisses it. "Your daddy asked me something special this morning, but before I answer, I want to make sure it's okay with you. He asked if I want to be your mommy."

She pinches her eyebrows in confusion. "What about my mommy who's in heaven?"

"We can both be your mommies. She'll be your mommy from heaven, and I'll be your mommy here."

"Will I call you mommy?"

"You can call me whatever you want."

"Do you have to go on anymore painting retreats? I didn't like that."

She shakes her head. "No more of those."

She thinks for a moment. "I think I'd like to call you mommy."

Amanda fights back the tears. "I'd like that too."

CHAPTER THIRTY-SEVEN

FIVE MONTHS LATER

BECKETT

"Amanda, these readouts are concerning. Stop pushing."

I'm holding her hand getting flashbacks of Jenny when she was in labor. The same look of concern is on the doctor's face.

Despite being the one in labor, Amanda squeezes my hand. "Relax. Breathe. I'm going to be fine."

After she signed the paperwork to adopt Andie, Amanda finally sold her house and officially moved in with us, but it's only temporary. We've been designing a new house with Collin that he's building for us. We want it to be cozy and perfect. My only stipulation was that Amanda's studio be the greatest one ever built.

I'm obsessively twisting her engagement ring. She

won't marry me until after the baby comes, but she finally agreed to get engaged. It took me a while to fully win her back, but I did.

Once we got engaged and the pregnancy news broke, the press lost interest in us. Apparently happy families aren't interesting. It was the greatest gift we could have asked for.

I try to calmly nod at Amanda even though I've spent the past month hiding my nightmares about this day from her. I'm so scared. I need her to make it through.

Dr. Crest looks at the nurse with alarmed eyes. "Prep the OR."

I stand. "What's happening?"

"There's something off on these readouts. I don't want to hold off. I want to get the baby out. Mr. Windsor, I'm sorry, we're going to need you to wait outside. We don't have time for you to get dressed and properly prepared for the OR."

Oh my god. I point my finger at him. "Everything. You do *fucking* everything for her."

"We've got this. Please, you're holding us up. Let us do our job."

A nurse escorts me to the waiting area where I find Jade, Collin, Declan, and Melissa. I had told Mom to keep Andie at home until we know everything is okay.

They all look up. Tears hit my eyes. "Something is wrong. They took her to the OR. They won't let me come."

Jade stands to sprint toward the OR, but Collin grabs her around the waist. "Babe, let them do their thing."

Tears are streaming down her cheeks. I walk over

to her and hug her. For the next thirty minutes, the longest of my life, she and I sit together crying. I'm not sure who's comforting who.

The doctor eventually walks out and removes his mask. His face is stoic. I'm fucking terrified.

"Well, this has never happened before. I've read about it happening, but I've never personally seen it."

My jaw is stiff as I ask, "Is she okay? Please tell me she's okay."

"She's fine. She's in a little bit of shock and asking for you, but she's fine."

I breathe out a sigh of relief.

Jade asks, "What about the baby?"

The doctor makes a weird face. "That's the thing. There's a technical term for it, but the everyday term is hidden twin. Sometimes one baby is sneaky and simply hiding behind the other in ultrasounds. Like I said, I've heard of it, but I've never seen it." He mumbles to himself, "That explains the higher numbers in her original blood test."

I pinch my eyebrows. "What exactly are you saying?"

"There were two babies in there. You have twin sons, Mr. Windsor."

I hear Jade breathe, "Holy shit."

I need to see Amanda. I need to make sure she's really okay. "Can...can we see her? Them? All of them?"

He smiles. "Of course. Follow me, Mr. Windsor."

I grab Jade's hand. "She's coming with me."

The doctor nods and we make our way to Amanda. I walk in and see her holding one baby while a nurse holds the other. Amanda is covered by some big curtain from the waist down.

She turns and smiles when she sees me. Relief fills every ounce of me.

She shakes her head. "Can you believe this?"

I lean down and kiss her. I haven't even processed the twins yet. I'm just relieved Amanda made it through.

"No, I can't."

"Why don't you hold our son?" She smiles again. "One of them."

I take the one from the nurse into my arms. He has a blue hat and is bundled in what looks like an ugly white dishrag. It's surreal. It's so different this time around. The last time was marred by so much tragedy. Now we're experiencing a real-life miracle.

I look down at her. "I love you."

"I love you too."

Jade peeks below the curtain. "Don't look at that mess, Beckett. You'll never have sex with her again."

I roll my eyes. "I promise that will never happen."

She laughs. "Let me see my brothers. My baby's uncles."

I hand her the baby I'm holding, and she takes him into her arms. She gazes down at him. "I'm your sister, Jade. I will always shoot straight with you. Come to me for booze and condoms. Your nephew, Tyson, is a fucking nightmare. You're going to have to be a good uncle and start babysitting him soon."

I can't help but laugh. Jade is certainly one of a kind, but I wouldn't mind one just like her. Only one though. I don't think I could take two of her.

The nurse asks, "Do you have names picked out?"

Amanda answers, "We were thinking of Forrest for one. We didn't know about the second until a few minutes ago."

I look at her. "How about Beckett Junior?"

Jade scoffs. "You're not fucking naming my brother BJ. That's social suicide."

"Hmm. Fair point."

She asks, "Why Forrest?"

"Your mom named you a color. Forrest was the closest to a color we could agree on."

She thinks for a moment. "What about Blaze for whichever one was hiding? It's kind of a devilish name for the twin we know will be my mini-me."

I smile. "I like it."

Amanda nods. "Me too."

AMANDA

An hour later, we're sitting in my hospital room. Andie and Glinda come running in. Glinda toggles her eyes between the two babies. "Oh my god, it's true. Two of them?"

Beckett and I both laugh. I shake my head in disbelief. "It's true. It's hard to believe, but it's true."

Glinda holds out her arms and walks right by Beckett to me. She grabs my face and kisses my cheek. "You are such a blessing. Thank you so much. I love you."

We both have tears in our eyes. "I love you too."

Beckett mumbles, "What about me?"

Glinda and I giggle before she turns and hugs him. I hear her whisper, "I love you. Can you believe this?"

I see Beckett's body release a few sobs. She rubs his back

and says, "She's okay. Everyone is okay. It's a good day. A great day."

He nods. Andie tugs his leg. "Can I meet my brothers?"

Declan walks over and kisses my cheek. "Melissa and I are going to head out. It looks like you've finally got your full room. Congratulations."

He's right. I do. "Thank you."

Andie and Glinda happily trade the boys back and forth. We get lots of pictures of every possible combination. I can't believe I have four children now. Five if you count Collin, which I refuse to do considering he's only six years younger than me.

Andie looks at Beckett. "Daddy, I'm thirsty. Do you have anything to drink?"

Jade reaches into her bag. "If you want an energy drink, I have a can of..."

Beckett snaps his head to Jade. Before she can get out another word, Beckett grits out, "Don't even think about finishing that sentence."

Jade smiles at him. It's her special Jade mischievous smile. One I have no doubt *hidden twin* Blaze will share. I have no idea what their silent communication is about, and I'm confident I don't want to know.

He looks down at Andie. "You can grab some water from the bathroom." Which she does.

It's time to feed them so Beckett and I each take a baby and give them a bottle.

As I'm feeding Blaze, I look around the room and take in the surreal scene. I'm holding one baby and Beckett is holding the other. Glinda is sitting next to me, aimlessly playing with my hair. Jade is sitting in a chair with Andie on her lap. Collin is sitting on the floor in front of them holding Tyson. Andie is braiding his hair.

I can't get over how different this is from when Jade was born. I felt so alone and afraid then. I feel the exact opposite now.

Andie looks up at Beckett. "Daddy, you didn't tell me a joke yet today. I need it."

Jade looks at me in question. "Beckett tells Andie a corny dad joke every morning. It's their tradition."

Jade looks at him. "Let's hear it, Beckett."

He smiles. "I guess this will be Forrest and Blaze's first official dad joke. The pressure. Let me think. Hmm. If you have twin daughters and name the first Kate, what's the name of the second?"

Andie thinks for a moment. "I don't know. What?"

"Duplikate."

Jade makes a gagging noise. "That's horrible."

Glinda nods. "They're all horrible. Every single day."

Beckett smiles. "I have another. What's the preferred fruit of twins?"

Andie thinks and then her face lights up. "Pears!"

"Good. One more?"

Andie nods.

"This one is for Mommy." He turns to me. "Knock, knock."

"Who's there?"

"Eyesore."

"Eyesore who?"

"Eyesore do love you a lot."

If I didn't know better, I'd swear he was looking at me with hearts in his eyes.

EPILOGUE

THREE MONTHS LATER

AMANDA

Melissa is busy adjusting every last inch of my dress. I sigh. "I think it's fine."

Her head pops up and she gives me an appalled look. "This dress isn't *fine*. It's a work of art. Would you release a painting into the world if it wasn't perfect?"

"I suppose not."

"Let me paint my canvas. I'll let you know when it's ready." She goes about manipulating both my body and the dress, moving everything into perfect position.

I look down, though she's buried under the layers. "I feel like my husband is the only one that should be under my dress tonight."

She shouts, "It's totally normal for the woman married to the father of your child to be under your dress on your wedding day."

Glinda and I both laugh as she hands me a piña colada. "Have a drink and relax. Let Melissa work her magic. No cherries though. We can't afford an accident with that dress."

I take a sip of my cold drink and try to relax. I don't need all this craziness, but Beckett was dead set on making this day special. He said I deserved the full fairytale, and that's what he's giving me.

Jade and Andie emerge from the dressing room in matching hot pink dresses, hairstyles, and grins. I gasp. "You two look gorgeous."

Jade holds out her hand for a fist bump. "We're fucking rock stars, right, sis?"

Andie nods as she returns the fist bump. "Yes, sis. Total fucking rock stars."

I shake my head and sigh. "Jade, watch your mouth around her."

Jade has her mischievous look. "Just wait until you hear Andie's speech."

"Oh god, what did you do?"

She points to herself. "Me? I'm innocent. It was all Andie." She winks at Andie. "Right?"

Andie giggles. "Yep. I wrote it *all* by myself." She tries to wink back at Jade but fails adorably.

God help us.

Melissa stands. "There. Now it's perfect. You look magnificent."

I look at myself in the mirror. Admittedly, I look good. I let Melissa pick out the dress and she did an amazing job. I've never seen anything like it. It's *very* fitted on the top with what I hope are rhinestones but am pretty sure are diamonds. I know Beckett will enjoy how it shows my assets. I prefer the more traditional and whimsical bottom with layers of organza and silk.

I touch the ridiculous necklace around my neck. The one I wore on our first night in Italy. Beckett said it's his wedding gift to me. I'm terrified of knowing what it cost him, but I can admit that it's beautiful and brings back a lot of good memories. It's also looking very purple right now.

I take in my entire appearance. I truly feel like a princess today.

Glinda starts to tear as she squeezes my hand. "You are beautiful, inside and out. Perfection."

"Thank you." I take a deep breath. "Let's do this."

The music starts, and though I can't see anything yet, I hear oohs and ahhs. Collin and Tyson must be walking down the aisle. Then I hear it again. Beckett must now be walking down the aisle with the boys in their mini tuxedos.

Andie and Jade walk down together next. I can't help but take a peek. They each have flowers in their outside hands but are holding hands on the inside. I love their budding relationship. Andie practically worships the ground Jade walks on.

We decided to limit the bridal party to family. We're a bit old for a long list of bridesmaids and groomsmen, but I do catch Reggie sitting up front already bawling her eyes out. I know how happy she is for me that this day finally came.

I look around the room. It's completely covered in lights and flowers. It truly is right out of a fairytale. I look up at Glinda. "It's so beautiful."

She smiles down at me. "You deserve nothing less."

She offers me her arm. "Shall we?"

Glinda is the closest thing I've ever had to a parent in

my life. I now call her *Mom*. I wanted her to give me away. After only twenty minutes of crying, she agreed to it.

We make our way down the aisle. I see Darian and Melissa cradling the boys. They hold up the babies' little hands and wave them at us.

My eyes then find Beckett's. They're full of tears and love. I study my soon-to-be husband standing there in his tuxedo. He's so handsome. He really is my Prince Charming, though with an occasional dash of grumpy and possessive. I wouldn't have him any other way.

He's changed since our separation. He's lived up to every promise he made to me, both with his spoken words and his words in those letters. It's like a cloak of darkness has been lifted. That feeling of waiting for the other shoe to drop is gone. Even when things aren't perfect, Beckett no longer has kneejerk reactions. He no longer lashes out at me. We've become a true team.

And watching him be a father to our babies is possibly the most rewarding thing I've ever experienced. He's nothing but loving and patient. The stress and worries I had when Jade was an infant are nonexistent this time around. I know he feels the same. He struggled when Andie was a baby, and he was on his own. Now we can both truly savor and appreciate what we have.

When we reach Beckett, Glinda kisses us both on the cheek. She then sits down next to Nico. He takes her hand in his and kisses it. They now live together in a house near ours.

Beckett whispers, "You are beautiful."

I whisper back, "So are you."

The officiant begins, "Normally I would welcome everyone, but it's my understanding that Andie is going to do so today." He points to her. "Go ahead, little lady."

Andie stands between us and nervously unfolds a sheet of paper. "Welcome, everyone, to my mommy and daddy's wedding. I'm so happy that my daddy became pussy-whipped last year."

Everyone starts laughing as we both snap our heads to Jade. She just smiles proudly at Andie. I can't believe Jade let her use the word *pussy* in her speech.

Andie looks around, having no clue why everyone is laughing. I think it scares her.

I place my hand on her shoulder. "Go ahead, sweetie. You're doing great."

She nods and looks back down at her piece of paper. "I love that my daddy is not only a baby daddy to me, but also to my new baby brothers. I love that my mommy and I paint every morning. I want to be an artist just like her. I also love that my daddy tells me a joke every morning at breakfast. I think as a wedding gift, I want to end my speech with a joke."

She looks up at us. "Do you know why the King of Hearts married the Queen of Hearts?"

We both shake our heads.

"They were perfectly suited to each other."

A collective *aww* rings out from the crowd and we both bend to kiss her cheeks in unison. She giggles in pure glee.

The officiant runs through a few lines before it's Beckett's turn. He takes my hands in his. "Amanda, you are the breath of fresh air I needed in my life. I knew it the first second I laid eyes on you. You've brought me joy I never imagined possible. You're kind and loving. Sweet and considerate. Smart and talented. Pure-hearted and so damn beautiful that sometimes it's hard for me to breathe. I'm in awe of you every single day. You bring color to the canvas of our life. Andie and I are incredibly blessed to have found you. Jade, Andie, Forrest, and Blaze are so lucky to have you as their mother. You consistently shower them with love, affection, understanding, and unwavering loyalty."

He swallows, getting a bit choked up before continuing. "You've changed me for the better. Our love story is like a real-life fairytale. It's not always perfect, real life isn't, but it's always magical. I've learned that every fairytale is different. Each couple takes their own bumpy path to happily ever after. And at the end of some fairytales, the best ones, it's the princess who saves the prince."

THE END

FOR A GLIMPSE into Amanda and Beckett's future, subscribe to my newsletter for a bonus scene.

Scan Here For Bonus Scene

ACKNOWLEDGMENTS

To Amanda and Beckett: You allowed me to return to my roots and write about an older couple. It gave me so much joy to give you your later-in-life story. It's never too late for an HEA. It was brought to my attention that Beckett is the most flawed MMC I've ever written. Declan might argue with that, but it could be true. I still love you, Beckett, flaws and all.

To the Queen, TL Swan: This amazing journey would never have begun if not for you and your selfless decision to help hundreds of women. You are a shining example of the girl power quotes I place in each dedication. This crazy and unexpected new path in my life has brought me so much happiness. I owe it all to you. Please know that I try every single day to pay it forward.

To Lakshmi and Thorunn: You're my daily sounding boards. Like Amanda does for Beckett, you calm the crazy in my head. This entire series wouldn't be what it is without my Queen Bitches. You're so damn appreciated.

To Jade Dollston, Carolina Jax, and L.A. Ferro: You are my bookish besties. Our daily texts are my lifeline. I love the support we have for each other. **L.A.:** You challenge me, you push me, you support me, you tolerate my immature sense of humor. I can't tell you how much I value our friendship. **Jade**: Don't make me cry. Every book I write is made better because of you. This entire journey is better because of you. **Carolina**: I adore you and your support. Your taste in football teams still sucks.

To Brittany Mckeel: The damn dedication was to you. That's enough.

To Mindy Menotti: Thank for the insight into the... umm...piercings.

To My OG Beta Readers Stacey and Fun Sherry: Thank you for being there for me since day one. You've been my biggest and hottest cheerleaders every single step of the way. Dr. Pearl is for you, Fun Sherry.

To My Amazing ARC and Street Teams: Watching this group grow and support each other has been an honor. I think back to the beginning when there were so few of you. Now we are big and mighty (and the street chat is a little out of control - in the best way possible). I appreciate every single ounce of support you throw my way.

To Chrisandra and K.B. Designs: **Chrisandra**: Thank you for making me feel illiterate. That's what makes you such a great editor. **Kristin**: Thank you for helping this artistically challenged woman. You have breathed life into all of my books. I'm so proud of them thanks to you. This cover may be my favorite (don't tell the others).

To My Family: I truly feel bad for you. An immature mother and wife can't be easy. To my daughters, thank you for tolerating me (ish). Thank you for telling everyone you know that your mom writes sex books. I appreciate that by the time you were each six, you were more mature than me. To my handsome husband, thank you for your blind support. You never question my sanity, which can't be easy. But let's face it, you do reap the benefits of the fact that I write sex scenes all day long.

ABOUT THE AUTHOR

AK Landow lives in the USA with her husband, three daughters, one dog, and one cat (who was chosen because his name is Trevor). She enjoys reading, now writing, drinking copious amounts of vodka, and laughing. She's thrilled to have this new avenue to channel her perverted sense of humor. She is also of the belief that Beth Dutton is the greatest fictional character ever created.

AKLandowAuthor.com

ALSO BY AK LANDOW

Signed Books: www.aklandowauthor.com

Printed in Great Britain
by Amazon